DEATH'S HEAD

A Soldier With Richard the Lionheart, 1190-1191

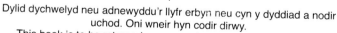
ROBERT BROOMALL

Books by Robert Broomall

California Kingdoms
Texas Kingdoms
The Lawmen
The Bank Robber
Dead Man's Crossing (Jake Moran 1)
Dead Man's Town (Jake Moran 2)
Dead Man's Canyon (Jake Moran 3)
K Company (K Company 1)
Conroy's First Command (K Company 2)
The Dispatch Rider (K Company 3)
Scalp Hunters
Wild Bill and the Dinosaur Hunters
Murder in the Seventh Cavalry

Thanks to Alan Amrhine, Amy Bock, Jodie Clemen, Keith Hoskins, Lisa Miller, Paul Sekulich, and Dave Stelzig for their help and comments.

TABLE OF CONTENTS

Prologue   1

Part I: THE GREAT ADVENTURE   9

Part II: THE SIEGE   79

Part III: A GATHERING OF KINGS   293

Part IV: TO THE DEATH   497

Epilogue   597

Historical Note   599

PROLOGUE

The Horns of Hattin
July 4, 1187 A.D.
The Feast of St. Martin of Tours

There was no formal surrender. The Christians, those who were still alive, simply collapsed on the field of battle, overcome by heat and thirst and exhaustion, and offered their weapons to the victorious Saracens.

The war had boiled up like a summer storm, during a time of truce, while the Christian nobles of Outremer squabbled over who should be their king. When a Christian lord named Reginald of Kerak broke the truce by raiding a caravan, the sultan of Damascus responded by crossing the Jordan with a large army. Putting aside their enmities at this time of danger, the Christians offered the kingship to Guy of Lusignan—a French adventurer whose only claim to the crown lay through the bed of the lawful queen, Sybelle—and they mustered the kingdom's entire military force at Sephoria to counter the sultan's possible attack.

Things might have remained that way, in check, as they had many times before, until the storm blew over and both sides disbanded and returned home. Then Sultan Yusef— whom the Christians called Saladin—lay siege to Tiberias, on the Sea of Galilee.

The native Christians saw the trap; this sort of trick had been tried before. It was an attempt to lure the Christian host away from its base and into the waterless plain between Sephoria and Tiberias. Most of the nobles—including the lord of Tiberias, whose lands were the ones under siege—advised Guy to remain at Sephoria. But Guy, who was a newcomer to Outremer and anxious to make a name for himself, listened to a few rash voices, including Reginald of Kerak's, and ordered an advance.

Encumbered by heavy armor, tormented by searing heat and lack of water, the Christians struggled across the barren plain, fighting a running battle with mounted Saracen archers as they did. Near the Horns of Hattin, twin hilltops that guarded the descent into Galilee, the Christians came upon Saladin's main army, drawn up to block their advance. Too exhausted to push on, the Christians made camp. The Saracens surrounded them, setting fire to the dry grass, beating drums and chanting through the night to keep their enemies awake.

At dawn, the battle resumed. What had begun as an effort by the Christians to relieve the siege of Tiberias ended as a desperate attempt to reach water. But the advance was halted. Order broke down. Infantry and cavalry separated and occupied separate hills. Without infantry protection, the knights' horses were vulnerable to Saracen arrows. If the horses were killed, the knights would be rendered immobile and, thereby, helpless. So the knights attempted to fight their way through alone. Charge after charge they hurled at Saladin's banner. A small party of men, under Raymond of Antioch and one-eyed Henry of Deraa, broke through the Saracen line and escaped. The rest were driven back to the hill, where they made a last stand. From behind the Saracen center, Saladin watched—a tall, slender, sad-eyed man. When the Christian king's tent fell, signifying victory, Saladin did not join in the general rejoicing but knelt, touched his forehead to the earth in the direction of Mecca, and offered a prayer of thanksgiving.

❖ ❖ ❖

Now, the hills and plain were littered with the bodies of men and animals, obscured by drifting smoke from the dry-grass fires. The air was pierced by the cries of the injured and the ululating shouts of the Muslim tribesmen.

Never had the Christians suffered such a defeat. The entire chivalry of Outremer—not only the kingdom of Jerusalem, but the principality of Antioch and the county of Tripoli, as well—lay dead on the field or captive. The True Cross, guarantor of victory, had been captured; and its bearer, the bishop of Acre, had been killed. Of the Templars and Hospitallers—the militant religious orders that formed the backbone of the kingdom's army—two or three hundred survived. These armed monks were Islam's most implacable enemies, and Saladin ransomed each of them from his captor for fifty dinars. He then gave the captives the choice of converting to Islam or death. A few converted; most preferred martyrdom. Saladin delivered these men to the *sufis*—religious fanatics—who followed his army. The Templars and Hospitallers were beheaded with swords—one *sufi* to one prisoner. Some of the *sufis* performed well, dispatching their victims with a single stroke. Others hacked away clumsily at their captives until the job was done. Still others were unequal to the task and gave their places to those with steelier nerves. Contemptuous of their enemies, the men of the Temple and Hospital died well.

❖ ❖ ❖

Afterward, King Guy and his leading nobles were brought to the sultan's tent. Guy and Reginald of Kerak were led into the tent's inner chamber. The two Christians were weary, hair and beards matted with dust, hauberks and surcoats covered with congealing blood. Guy was lean and, in better times, vain of his good looks. Reginald, dubbed "the Wolf," was burly and grizzled. Guy entered the inner tent with trepidation, his usual arrogance mollified by fear. Reginald swaggered into the tent

3

as though he were entering his own quarters.

Saladin awaited them. The sultan had removed his armor and now wore a purple tunic and loose-fitting trousers tucked into soft leather boots. The tent was dim and cool after the harsh sunlight outside. Smells of cinnamon and saffron tinted the air. Saladin gestured to cushions on the floor. "Please, sit."

Guy and Raymond sank gratefully to the cushions. Saladin made another gesture, and a serving boy came forth with a chased silver goblet. Saladin took the goblet and handed it to Guy. "Rose water," Saladin said, smiling. "Cooled with snow from Mount Hermon."

Guy held the goblet in trembling hands and drank for the first time in two days. The water spilled from his mouth and formed muddy rivulets in his dust-caked beard. He took the goblet from his lips and passed it to Reginald.

As Reginald reached for the goblet there was a rasping sound, and a curved sword blade interposed itself between the goblet and Reginald's outstretched hand.

Reginald looked up and stared at Saladin—for it was he who held the sword—with undisguised contempt.

To Guy, Saladin said, "Tell that man it is you who gives him drink, not I. By Muslim custom, to give drink to a prisoner means that his life will be spared."

Guy mumbled something to Reginald, who interrupted with a growl. "I heard him." Reginald kept his eyes on the Saracen leader.

Saladin pulled back the sword. Reginald took the goblet and drank, spilling not a drop. When he was done, he admired the goblet wistfully. Then he tossed it aside and stood. To the Muslims, Reginald the Wolf was the most hated Christian in Outremer. From his remote desert fortress of Kerak, he had raided far and wide, leaving a path of death and destruction. He was under no illusions about his fate.

Saladin stepped closer to Reginald, looking the older man up and down. "I have waited many years for this day," he said. He indicated Guy, who still sat on the cushions. "That man is a noble, a king. But you are worse than a dog, worse than a pig. You have killed innocent Muslim men, women, and children; you have destroyed their possessions, laid waste to their lands, defiled their houses of worship. You are not fit to live."

Reginald drew himself to his full height and stared Saladin in the eye. "I have done nothing to Muslims that you have not done to them yourself, Lord Sultan. The only difference is that I am honest about my crimes. I do not cloak myself in piety and false humility. I am not a hypocrite like you."

Saladin's eyes blazed. With a strength belying his slight stature, he raised his sword and swung it. Reginald made no effort to defend himself. The sword's fine Damascene blade sliced through Reginald's neck and took off his head with a spray of blood. The head landed at Guy's feet. Reginald's body spurted blood from its neck while its hands and legs jerked spasmodically, as though it might start running. Then it sagged and collapsed, blood flowing across the rich carpets that covered the tent floor.

Wide eyed, Guy stared at the severed head. Reginald had been his friend and closest advisor. A moment ago, Guy had been talking to him. Guy trembled and looked up at Saladin.

With an effort, the Saracen leader brought his temper under control. He cleaned his sword blade on a piece of cloth and returned the weapon to its plain scabbard. "There could be no other fate for that man," he told Guy. "His perfidy had gone beyond all bounds."

Calmer now, Saladin pulled at his graying beard as though trying to straighten it. As his bodyguards carried the headless corpse from the tent, he said, "Two of your Frankish lords I have sworn to kill with my own hands. The first, Reginald the Wolf, lies at my feet. The second, the one-eyed man called Henry the Falcon, has escaped me this day, but Allah willing, I shall soon serve him a similar fate."

Guy swallowed. "And—and me, lord?"

With the toe of his cordovan leather boot, Saladin maneuvered Reginald's head so that its sightless eyes were looking up at him. He smiled, then kicked the head out of the way. It rolled across the tent with another spray of blood, while Guy watched in unabashed horror.

"And you?" Saladin spoke as though he were conversing with an old friend. "First, I am going to reclaim all your lands for Islam, starting with al Quds, which you Infidels call Jerusalem."

Guy went on, panicked. "I can pay ransom, a lot of it. I can—"

Saladin held up a hand for silence. "After that," he continued, "I intend to let you and your chief nobles go free. There need be no ransom. You will be free to travel wherever you wish, and no harm shall come to you."

Guy shut his eyes and his shoulders sagged with relief. "Thank you, Lord Sultan. That is—that is most generous."

"In the meantime," Saladin said brightly, "you shall be my guest." He clapped his hands, and one of his courtiers came forward. "Show the king and his chief retainers to their tent," Saladin ordered. "Get them fresh clothes. Let them bathe and have food."

The courtier bowed. "And the rest of the prisoners?"

Saladin's tone hardened. "You know what to do with them."

Guy said not a word in protest about this. He was going to be spared; that was all that mattered to him.

When Guy had been led off, Al-Adil, the sultan's younger brother and chief confidante, approached. "Is it a good idea to set the Feringhee king free? We should keep him prisoner, hold him for ransom. The Christians would pay a fortune for him."

"Guy is an arrogant fool," Saladin said. His tired eyes twinkled, and he gave his brother a conspiratorial smile. "Trust me, he will be far more valuable to us as a free man than he would be as a prisoner."

Guy and his nobles went into temporary captivity. For the poorer knights and common soldiers, however, the future was more forbidding. In the coming days, the slave markets of Damascus would be so glutted that the price of an able-bodied man would fall to three dinars. A gentleman of that city would trade a Christian slave for a pair of sandals.

But that was for the future. On this day, all men—Christian and Muslim alike—knew one thing. The cities and strongholds of Outremer were now defenseless. There was no one to stop the Saracens from rolling them up, one by one, until all of Outremer lay under the green banner of Islam. If the Holy Land was to be restored to Christianity, it would require a great new crusade from the west.

Robert Broomall

Part I

THE GREAT ADVENTURE

Robert Broomall

England, 1190 A.D.

Chapter 1

"Here they come!" someone shouted.

In the distance could be heard the wild skirling of bagpipes and flutes, driven by the heavy rhythmic thump of a bass drum. They were playing the jaunty marching song "Girls of Falaise."

Roger stood at the edge of the forest with a crowd of men, women, and children. The paths from several manors debouched here, and the crowd had gathered to watch the earl of Trent and his men depart for the crusade.

Roger was twenty, tall and broad shouldered, conspicuous in this throng of villagers by his tonsure and monk's black robe and hooded scapula. He was equally conspicuous by his well-fed look. Most of the folk around him rarely got a good meal, and on some days they might have nothing to eat at all.

Roger had sneaked away from the abbey to come here. Brothers were not allowed outside the abbey precinct without the permission of the abbot or the prior, but this was a sight that might not be repeated in Roger's lifetime, and Roger was determined not to miss it. It had been three years since the True Cross had been lost at Hattin. Three long years for the chief rulers of Christendom—the emperor of the Germans and the kings of England and France—to raise money and armies and set out for the Holy Land. The earl of Trent was taking forty knights and five hundred footmen, the largest force that he, or any of his predecessors in that title, had ever put into the field. The earl had pawned his jewels, sold some of his lands and mortgaged the rest to raise this force, supply it, and keep it paid. He stood to lose everything he owned, but the risk was worth it for the everlasting glory of God.

The music grew louder, some of the children dancing to it at the edge of the trees, older men and women swaying and tapping their feet. Then a cheer erupted as, around a bend, came the band, playing for all they were worth and basking in the attention, the drummer pounding his drum and twirling his sticks between beats, one of the pipers skipping back and forth as he marched. They were followed by mounted heralds and a snooty-looking page carrying the earl's red dragon banner. The heralds were supposed to act stoic but they couldn't help smiling as they passed the cheering crowd, even though it was far from the first crowd they had passed this day. People had turned out all the way from the earl's castle near Badford to see the crusaders off.

The cheering rose in volume. A furlong behind the heralds, Geoffrey of Trent himself appeared, mounted on a white palfrey. Years ago, before he had first witnessed knights setting off to war, Roger had imagined them riding in shining coats of mail, with burnished helms and gonfalons flying from lance heads. Reality had proven more prosaic. Armor was heavy and cumbersome, and men only donned it when battle was near. Instead, knights traveled in sturdy riding clothes, with their arms carried in carts or on pack animals. Roger had seen Earl Geoffrey before, but never this close. Tall and wiry, with a long face and short, reddish beard, a large red cross sewn on his shoulder, the earl radiated power and authority. He acknowledged the crowd's cheers with a languid, almost sad, wave of his hand. He was accompanied by his saturnine brother Hugo, as well as his steward, marshal, chaplain, and other members of his household, all wearing the red cross. Mounted squires led the group's huge war horses, while servants prodded the oxen that pulled carts filled with weapons and armor, which were protected by oilcloth covers.

Behind the earl's immediate party came his chief tenants, then his knights and men-at-arms. They rode in small groups, in order of rank, talking and laughing among themselves, sometimes waving to the crowd, young girls squealing and throwing flowers at them, while more squires and pages followed with spare horses and wagonloads of equipment.

Roger watched them pass, leaning forward, soaking in every detail. The man beside Roger sized him up knowingly. "Wish you was with 'em, don'cher?" The man, a gnarled ploughman of indeterminate age, spoke in English, which Roger understood. Latin was the everyday language of the Church, and French the language of the nobility, but most members of these groups knew at least some English.

"I do," Roger acknowledged, speaking loud, almost shouting, above the music and crowd noise. "What greater cause can there be than liberating Jerusalem from the Saracens?"

"Why not join up, then?" said the ploughman. His garments were not as patched and mended as most, so he must be relatively prosperous. "You look more like a blacksmith than a monk. I'm sure King Richard could use a lad like you."

"Our son is with them," the ploughman's doughy-faced wife interjected proudly, as if that might be an extra incentive for Roger to join.

Roger shook his head. "I cannot leave the abbey. I have taken vows of poverty and chastity, and I must obey them all my days."

"People breaks their vows all the time," the ploughman observed with a squinted though not unfriendly eye.

Roger frowned. "Not me. A vow is a sacred oath to God. To break it would mean my eternal damnation."

The crowd's cheers roared to a crescendo, because following the knights came the spearmen, the earl's dragon badge on their thick leather jerkins, red crosses on their shoulders, helmets and rolled mail tied to their packs. These were the local men, the men the crowd had come to see. Grizzled oldsters who had fought in a score of battles marched alongside youngsters flush faced with enthusiasm, the younger men happily roaring the ribald lyrics to "Girls of Falaise," lyrics which made Roger blush.

"Look—there's Will!" squealed a pregnant woman. She and the ploughman's family stood on tiptoe and waved frantically. "Will! Willie!"

A pleasant-faced young spearman waved back, a bit self-conscious because his mates were laughing and nudging his ribs good naturedly. The spearman had a shock of sandy hair and a wide, infectious grin. Others in the crowd were waving and calling to friends and relatives among the soldiers.

"Good luck, Will!" cried the pregnant woman. She brushed tears from her cheek. "Please come back safe!"

"We'll be praying for you, Will!" added Will's mother.

"Godspeed, son!" echoed his father.

"Keep your head on!" shouted a mischievous younger brother.

A little girl standing next to them yelled, "Bring me back something from the Holy Land, Willie! A Saracen princess for my slave!"

"A sword for me!" called yet another younger brother.

"I'll try!" Will shouted. He looked back over his shoulder, waving to his family for as long as they remained in sight.

After the spearman came a smaller company of axe men, then a unit of archers. Following the infantry were artillerists, cooks, and laborers, then the wives and whores and children who always accompanied the common soldiers, the nobles having been forbidden to bring their families.

Last came the supply train—wagons and carts, horses and oxen and pack animals, bearing food and tents, spare clothes and weapons, bedding, horseshoes, a portable altar, a forge, a mill for grain, rope, and hardware for constructing mangonels. The train was close on a mile long.

And the earl's formidable force was but a rivulet, a tiny fraction of the whole. All across England—all across Europe—there were similar columns, bound for Dover and Southampton, for Marseilles and Genoa, for Bruges and Venice and a hundred other ports, coalescing into a mighty flood of soldiery that, when it reached the Holy Land, would wash away all in its path.

The last stragglers passed. The music and singing and tramp of marching feet faded into the distance like ghosts. Or dreams.

The crowd broke up, the laborers returning to their fields. The ploughman and his wife bade Roger farewell. "It's never too late, lad!" the ploughman reminded Roger.

Roger started back along the ill-defined path that led to Huntley Abbey, the only person in the crowed to do so. He should be in the scriptorium right now, inking his copy of *De Trinitate*. Maybe he would be able to slip back in with no one the wiser. Ancient Brother Paulinus, his mentor in the scriptorium, had been asleep when Roger had left. Maybe he had not awakened yet, though hours had gone by. Maybe no one had passed their carrel and noticed Roger's absence.

And maybe Roger would be the next king of England.

Like as not, they would take the cane to him for this. Brother Gregorius, the monastery's circuitor, loved to apply the cane to a miscreant's bare back and buttocks, especially to Roger's, who had no highly placed family members to complain about any ill treatment he might receive. Gregorius, as always, would do his best to make Roger cry out. Gregorius took great pleasure in that, just as Roger took pride in biting back his cries no matter how great the pain.

Roger was in the deepest part of the wood now, his sandals slapping the faint dirt track. Shafts of bright June sunlight filtered through tall beeches and oaks. Birds sang, insects buzzed. Though it seemed idyllic, it was dangerous to be out here alone. The forest was the haunt of outlaws like Brock the Badger, men who would slit your throat for the sheer enjoyment of it.

Roger stopped. He heard distant sounds—a struggle.

He strained his ears. Could it be outlaws? Poachers? There was always the chance of running into poachers in the forest, always the danger they would kill you so that you could not identify them later in manor court. The penalty for poaching was blinding or castration—or, if you were lucky, loss of a hand or foot. There was no shortage of men in Trentshire who had already suffered one or more of these punishments, no shortage of men who would do anything to avoid becoming the next victim.

This didn't sound like poachers, though, or outlaws. Roger thought he heard a woman's voice. She seemed to be in distress. There was a masculine growl, followed by twigs snapping and scuffling feet. Whatever was happening, it was off the path to the right, in the opposite direction that Roger was headed. It was none of his affair. He should keep going.

He crossed himself and started toward the noise.

He jogged through the trees, quiet as possible, till he came to the edge of a small clearing. A man and a woman wrestled there, kicking up dirt. The woman was young and blonde; and to Roger's surprise the man wore a Benedictine's black robes. The woman wrenched free. She got up and tried to run away, but the monk tackled her. He rolled her on her back and straddled her while she bit and clawed and spit at him. With a shock, Roger recognized the monk—it was Auberie of Vouzin, Gregorius's protégé and Roger's most dangerous enemy at Huntley Abbey.

Chapter 2

Auberie was four years older than Roger. He had bullied Roger since Roger had been old enough to walk. They had fought more than once, and Auberie had always beaten Roger badly and had fun doing it. Roger had grown since their last fight, though, and hours of chopping wood as punishment for infractions of discipline had added pounds of muscle to his frame.

As Roger watched, Auberie punched the girl in the face, stunning her. Auberie hit her again, the thud of his fist against her flesh loud in the clearing. This time her head hit the grass and she lay still. Auberie yanked up the girl's coarse dress. He raised the hem of his black robe, pushed aside the girl's long, pale legs, and knelt between them.

Roger stepped into the clearing. "Stop."

Auberie whirled in surprise. The surprise intensified when he saw who it was. Then he relaxed, and his handsome face assumed its usual air of smug superiority. He was athletic and well built, and his dark, wavy tonsure was longer than it should have been. "Well, well," he said, rising and brushing his robe, "look who it is. The Foundling."

Roger felt his face go red. Auberie and his friends had called him by that name all his life.

Auberie smiled at Roger's discomfiture. "What are you doing here, Foundling?"

"I might ask you the same question," Roger said, nodding toward the girl.

"You might, but it's none of your business," Auberie replied in his aristocratic drawl. Behind him, the girl groaned and moved a bit. "Now get away from this place and forget you saw me."

17

Roger didn't move.

"I'm your superior," Auberie said. "That's an order."

At twenty-four, Auberie was already the abbey's sub-prior, and that made Roger subject to his commands. "Let the girl go," Roger told him.

"Leave while you can, Foundling. You're in enough trouble as it is. I rather doubt you have the prior's permission to be outside the abbey walls."

"And I rather doubt that rape falls within the purview of your vows," Roger said.

"Vows?" Auberie sneered. "What do you know of vows, you English whoreson."

"I'm as well born as you are," Roger swore.

Auberie barked a laugh. "Oh, please. My father is one of the most powerful men in Acquitaine, a confidant of King Richard. You don't even know who your father is—or your mother, for that matter."

Roger clenched his fists, and Auberie smiled again, knowing he'd struck a nerve. "Last chance, Foundling. Will you leave?"

"No."

"That's it, then. Frankly, I'm glad. I'm going to teach you a lesson." He smiled, as though he'd just had a wonderful idea. "In fact, I think I'll rid Huntley of your verminous presence once and for all. It's not like anyone's going to miss you. They'll probably think you ran away. I'll hide your body in the forest for the animals to feast upon, and it will be as if you had never existed, which is the way it should have been."

With a lithe motion, Auberie stooped and picked up a stout tree limb. He'd probably had his eye on it all the while he'd been talking. While Roger had been stewing in anger, Auberie had been looking for a weapon.

Auberie tapped the heavy limb in the palm of his hand. "In a way, I'll be doing you a favor, Foundling. When I am abbot— and I will be—there will be no place at Huntley for curs like you. I intend for our members to come from only the finest families. So, you see, you would have to go eventually. I'm just speeding up the process."

"What about the girl?" Roger said. "Are you going to kill her, too?"

The girl still lay on her back, moving her head from side to side and moaning softly. Auberie smiled. "That depends on how much she pleases me. And if she's willing to keep her mouth shut."

Auberie advanced. The two men circled in the clearing—Roger crouched, Auberie holding the heavy branch with two hands. With a cat-like movement, Auberie stepped forward and aimed a blow at Roger's head. Roger raised an arm in self-defense and, even as he did, realized that he had made a mistake. The blow was a feint. Before Roger could recover, Auberie lowered his arms and smashed the thick branch into Roger's ankle. Pain shot through Roger's left leg; his ankle and foot went numb. He tried to move, but couldn't, as Auberie aimed a second blow at his head. Roger ducked away awkwardly, and the force of the blow hit his shoulder, the branch glancing off the back of his head, making him see stars. Another blow caught him in the back of the ribs. He cried out and straightened with pain, and when he did, Auberie moved left and rammed the end of the branch into Roger's gut, taking away his breath, doubling him over, and leaving him defenseless.

Auberie raised the branch over his head for the killing blow to Roger's skull. As he stepped into the blow, putting all his weight behind it, the girl slid forward on her rear and swept a foot between Auberie's, tripping him. The momentum of Auberie's swing knocked him off balance. He stumbled across the clearing and fell, but quickly regained his feet. He glared at the girl, who had staggered upright and was running away, then he turned back to Roger, who, ignoring his pain, had summoned all his strength, lowered his head and charged.

Roger hit Auberie square in the stomach with his shoulder, lifting him off the ground and slamming him onto his back, making him drop the branch and taking the wind out of him. Roger straddled Auberie and smashed his fist into Auberie's nose, breaking it. As the blood spurted from Auberie's nose, Roger hit him flush on the eye. He hit him in the eye again, and again, and again, crying with rage. The skin over Auberie's eye split and blood spilled out, Roger's fist getting slippery with it. Roger's fist and wrist hurt. He was aware of strange noises around him, but he paid them no mind as he pounded his enemy. Auberie was defenseless. Roger raised his fist once more, intending to drive it clear through Auberie's face if he could. As he readied the blow, his wrist was grabbed in a vice-like grip.

"Enough!" cried a voice.

Roger turned and looked up. The hand holding his wrist was that of Turold, the abbey's burly chief huntsman. The voice belonged to Raymond of Montmorain, seventeenth Abbot of Huntley.

Chapter 3

"Stop this brawling!" the abbot commanded. "I won't have members of my community thrashing about like drunken stable hands."

The abbot, tall and stately, sat his horse in the clearing, gloved fist on his hip. Beside him was Huntley's prior, Amalric. Turold hauled Roger to his feet. Seething with rage, Roger wanted to go after Auberie again, but Turold held him fast.

"What is the meaning of this?" Abbot Raymond demanded. In the abbey all communication between the brothers was done in Latin, but out here Raymond used his native language, French. Raymond was the kind of man whose lordly authority made him seem even taller than he actually was. His black robe and scapula were cut from the finest cloth, and a jeweled crucifix hung from his neck. His grey beard and tonsure were carefully trimmed, though a healthy appetite and lack of exercise in later years had given him a bit of a paunch. Amalric, the prior, was shorter and darker than the abbot, with close-set, suspicious eyes. A green-clad huntsman held the girl—he must have caught her as she tried to run away—and Amalric dismounted to look her over.

Roger's blood-splashed hand throbbed, so did his ankle. Wincing with the effort—it hurt his ribs to draw breath—he bowed to the abbot, as custom demanded, and began. "Auberie—"

"*Domnus* Auberie," the abbot corrected. The abbot was a stickler for punctilio, and brothers were to be addressed by that title.

"*Domnus* Auberie," Roger went on, "was trying to rape that girl. I stopped him."

The abbot and prior stared at him as they might have

stared at someone who had just fallen from the sky.

"It's true!" the girl added. "I swear it!"

This was the first chance Roger had gotten to look at the girl. Though her cheek was bruised and swelling where Auberie had struck her, Roger could see that she was attractive, with a lively, intelligent face. Her dress was dirty and torn. Her blonde hair was braided in the English style, with dirt and twigs and blades of grass in it from her struggle.

Another huntsman—the abbot must be leading a hunting party—assisted Auberie to his feet. Auberie stood unsteadily, blood dripping from his broken nose and staining the front of his robe. More blood flowed from the cut above his eye, and blood was smeared over his face from where Roger had hit him. He glared at Roger as he straightened, then he bowed to the abbot. "I wasn't raping the girl, Lord Raymond," he said in a voice thick with blood. "An it please God, I could never be party to such an horrific sin. I was protecting myself from her."

The abbot arched a brow. His cultured voice brimmed with irony. "*Protecting* yourself?"

"Yes, my lord. The girl is a witch."

The clearing went silent. Roger started after Auberie again. "You lying—!"

"*Domnus* Roger!" the abbot thundered as Turold and the second huntsman held Roger back. "I will not remind you again. Maintain the dignity of your order, or I will have you bound and gagged."

The girl was outraged. "I'm not a witch!"

With difficulty Roger held himself still, as Auberie went on, gathering self-assurance. "She's a witch, my lord, and she cast a spell on me. She tried to make me break my vow of chastity and lead me into Mortal Sin. I was in a fair way of overcoming her when *Domnus* Roger—" Auberie hesitated. His arrogance was gone now; he was meek and attentive toward his superior. "Well, that's when *Domnus* Roger attacked me. I don't know why he did it. Mayhap the witch saw that her spell would not be powerful enough to ensnare me, so she put Roger under a spell, as well, using him to get her revenge on me."

"I put no one under a spell!" the girl protested.

Abbot Raymond shifted in his high-backed saddle, clearly preferring to be anywhere but here. Roger heard the hunting party in the distance. The abbot addressed Auberie with reluctance. "Are you making a formal accusation of witchcraft against this girl?"

Using his wide sleeve, Auberie wiped blood from his face and nose, spit more blood from his mouth, and stood tall. "I am, my lord. I must."

Roger said, "My lord, you can't possibly believe this—"

Abbot Raymond held up a gloved hand, stopping Roger. As he did, the girl wrenched free from the grip of the huntsman who was holding her. "He's telling the truth, my lord—I'm no witch!"

The abbot looked down at her, studying her. His voice was not unkindly. "What is your name, child?"

"Ailith," the girl said.

"How old are you, Ailith?"

"Seventeen."

"And where is your husband?"

"Don't have a husband," the girl said, looking away.

"You're a widow?"

The girl hesitated. "I never been married."

Raymond and Prior Amalric shared a glance. For a girl this age—an attractive one, at that—never to have been married was highly unusual. There must be a reason for it, and the unspoken thought passed between the two men that the reason might be that she was a witch.

Amalric's close-set eyes narrowed so that he looked like a ferret. "Why have you never married?"

The girl shrugged. "Dunno, my lord."

"What is your manor?"

Ailith pointed back over her shoulder. "Longleigh, my lord." She hesitated before going on. "I was looking for a missing—a missing goat. It run away from our house. I run

23

into Brother Auberie here, and he offered to help me find it. He brought me here, said strays often end up here for some reason. Then he—he tried to have his way with me. Would have done it, too, if the other one hadn't saved me."

Auberie shook his head in amazement, a pitying smile on his lips, his hands spread wide. "You see how deftly the witch spins her lies? The truth is, she enchanted me with a song. I heard the song and followed it, and it led me here. I never saw her before I reached this clearing."

"I've heard her sing before," the big huntsman Turold added helpfully. "She's known for her skill."

The girl glared at Turold. Amalric frowned and nodded his head at that last bit of news, as though it had sealed the girl's fate. Abbot Raymond stroked his short beard. He had suspicions about what had really happened here—Auberie was rumored to have been with women before, though he'd never been caught at it. Raymond noted a wineskin by the trees, as well. But Auberie's father, the count of Vouzin, was King Richard's close friend. Abbot Raymond had supported the late King Henry during Richard's rebellion against him, and he needed to tread warily now because Richard was said to have a long memory. Punishing the son of Richard's best friend was not likely to endear Raymond to the king. Auberie was already being spoken of as a future abbot; Raymond didn't want that future to arrive too soon, and at his expense.

"She'll need to be questioned officially," Amalric said.

"Questioned!" Roger was incensed. "Tortured, you mean. I can't believe this. This girl is no more a witch than I am, my lord, and you know it. Auberie's father may be rich and powerful, but that doesn't give Auberie license to go around raping village girls. Our vows—"

"I don't recall you being so squeamish about breaking your vows before," Amalric told him. "I can't remember a member of our order who has spent so much time in punishment."

"This is different. I never—"

Abbot Raymond held up his hand once more, silencing

Roger. Raymond felt more and more like a man caught in a trap. A formal accusation of witchcraft, brought by the scion of a powerful family, could not be ignored.

"Why were you outside the abbey, *Domnus* Auberie?" Raymond asked.

"I was gathering groundsel for the almoner's gout," Auberie said. "Prior Amalric sent me."

"That is true," Amalric acknowledged.

Raymond turned to Roger. "And you, *Domnus* Roger? You are supposed to be in the scriptorium, if memory serves. What are you doing in the forest?"

There was no use lying about it. "I—I came to watch the earl of Trent leave for the crusade."

The abbot sighed. "I might have guessed."

To Raymond, Amalric said, "All these years, and he still dreams of becoming a knight." He turned back to Roger. "You've taken a solemn oath, boy. You'll be at Huntley until the day you die—scrubbing latrines, too, at the rate you're going."

Roger bit back the kind of retort that had gotten him in trouble before. He heard horses, dogs—the hunting party was close. He continued his story. "I was returning to the abbey when I heard a struggle. I investigated, and I found Auberie beating this girl—"

"Witch," Auberie corrected.

"—and trying to rape her. I made him—"

"Enough!" Amalric snapped. Amalric had risen from a parish school in La Roquelle. He was reputed to be a bastard son of the baron of Coutances. Roger wondered how Amalric would fare in Auberie's new order. To the abbot, Amalric said, "Shall we question her ourselves or send for the bishop's man?"

Raymond didn't want to involve the bishop. This was a mess he was well clear of, and the sooner the better. "We'll do it ourselves. Gregorius can handle it."

"Gregorius will kill her!" Roger protested.

"God's will be done," Amalric said. "We must arrive at the truth of this matter. If she is a witch, Gregorius will discover it.

25

If not—"

"If not, she'll be dead," Roger said.

"Then her soul will proceed immediately to Heaven." Amalric replied innocently, as if that outcome would make everything all right.

Ailith didn't seem to realize how much trouble she was in. She seemed to think that Roger was exaggerating, that all she needed was a chance to tell her side of the story. "Let them ask what they will," she said confidently. "I'm no witch." She pointed to Auberie. "What are you going to do to this one, that's what I want to know. He needs to be punished for what he done to me."

There was an awkward silence; no one answered her. Behind them, members of the hunting party, as well as huntsmen and grooms—some mounted, some on foot—pushed into the clearing, along with a score of dogs. Some of the dogs milled around Roger, sniffing him and nosing his hands so he would pet them.

The abbot straightened in the saddle, "This business has spoiled a good day's hunting," he told his party, which included wealthy travelers and important landowners from the neighborhood, men it was the abbot's duty to entertain. "Leave us return to the chase. Perhaps something may yet be saved of the day." He ticked off a pair of huntsmen. "Take the girl to the abbey and place her in confinement."

"Yes, my lord," said one of the huntsmen, a fellow with a scarred cheek.

"Don't let her trick you," Amalric added. "Mind she doesn't turn into a bird and fly away."

The scarred huntsman looked at his younger partner and they grinned conspiratorially. "Oh, she won't, my lord, we'll see to that."

"And keep your hands off her!" Amalric warned them. "She's not been found guilty of anything yet."

The grins faded. "Yes, my lord."

To Auberie, the abbot said, "Return to the abbey and have

your wounds tended. Await my pleasure there."

Auberie bowed low. "My lord."

"Are you going to whip him?" the girl asked. "Is that what you do to his kind?"

Once again, she was ignored. To Roger, the abbot said, "You will confine yourself to your cell until we can determine whether you were under a spell or whether you assaulted *Domnus* Auberie for other reasons."

"I assaulted him because—"

The abbot silenced him. "If there *are* other reasons, I will pronounce sentence upon you at the next chapter meeting. Brother Gregorius can deal with you at that time."

Roger stiffened. "Yes, my lord."

From the corner of his eye, he saw Auberie smile.

Chapter 4

Roger knelt in the darkness of his cell, praying. The chapter had just returned from nocturns, night services, in the church. Soon they would go back for the dawn service, matins. Roger knelt on a small bench covered with leather, but with no padding. Padding would have represented too much worldly comfort. In addition to the bench, the cell's furnishings consisted of a straw mattress on a wooden frame, a small chest, a table, and a crucifix on the wall above the bed. There was a nub of a candle on the table, but it was not lit. Candles were expensive and to be used only in emergencies. Besides, Roger didn't want anyone to know he was awake.

Roger was shaken. If Abbot Raymond had not shown up when he had, Roger would have killed Auberie. Roger's soul would have been condemned to the flames of Hell. Roger had never dreamed he had it in him to kill a man. Not only would he have killed Auberie, he was afraid he would have enjoyed it, and that was what had him so upset. He closed his eyes and clasped his hands firmly, entreating God's forgiveness, ignoring the pain in his swollen right hand.

When he and Auberie had attended vespers that evening, the entire chapter had stared at them. There had been wild rumors about a fight between the two, and now there were nudges and a buzz of whispers, the Rule of Silence notwithstanding. Both men had cleaned themselves and gotten the blood off their robes as best they could, but Auberie's once-handsome face had been a mess—his eye swollen grotesquely with stitches over it, his nose splinted, his skin purpling—and he had glowered at Roger through the entire service and in the refectory after that. Later, in the cloister, when the brothers were enjoying the soft evening air, Auberie had passed close to

Roger and whispered, "I'll kill you, Foundling. I swear it."
When Auberie had gone, Roger had found Gregorius, Auberie's
patron, watching him with anticipatory grimness.

Roger could accept punishment for himself. He had been
punished before and he would no doubt be punished again. He
could accept Auberie's threat, as well; he was no longer afraid
of Auberie. There was one thing he could not accept, however,
and that was injustice.

He finished praying, crossed himself, and rose, wincing
from the pain in his ribs and ankle. Cautiously, he opened his
door and peered out. Wooden partitions had been erected
down the sides of the long dormitory to give each brother his
own cell, leaving a wide corridor in the middle. Horn lanterns
at either end of the room provided light when the brothers
filed downstairs for night services or if they needed to use the
latrines. There was no one about.

Roger stepped into the high-ceilinged room, quietly
shutting the door behind him. He moved down the corridor,
placing his feet with care to avoid creaky floorboards. The stale
air was filled with snores and the restless shuffling of bodies.
Roger passed Auberie's cell, and for a second he was possessed
with a wild desire to go in and finish what he had started that
afternoon. But he continued on.

He reached the back stairs, not the night stairs that led into
the church but the ones that led past the latrines to the parlor.
He started down the winding stone steps, feeling his way into
the deep gloom. He heard a sound and he stopped, his heart
pounding. It was a scrabbling sound—a rat. Roger let out his
breath and kept going. He didn't have much time. He wished it
was winter, when there was a longer period between nocturns
and matins. This close to midsummer, with the nights so short,
the two services came almost atop one another.

He reached the bottom of the stairs and went through the
parlor into the southeast corner of the cloister. A light rain was
falling. Past the cloister was the warming room, where the
brothers revived themselves after winter services in the

unheated church. Roger passed through that and came outside again, to the storehouse, where the girl Ailith was being held.

The abbey had no prison. Anyone who needed to be locked up or restrained was placed in an empty storeroom. There was no need for a guard. With stout walls on all sides, the abbey was a fortress of God. No one could break in. Anyway, who would want to free a village girl like Ailith? Her family? It was likely the family knew she was being held as a witch by now—rumors spread with amazing speed through the countryside—but there was precious little they could do about it.

Cold rain pattered on Roger's shaven tonsure; he smelled grass and the rich, loamy earth of the fields beyond the walls. It was easy to find the girl's room—it was the only one with a barred door. Roger lifted the heavy bar from its rest and set it down. From within, he heard the girl's anxious voice. "Who is it? What's going on?"

"It's Roger." He stepped inside.

Ailith sat in some straw with her back to the wall. She struggled to her feet. Dark circles beneath her eyes showed that she had not gotten any sleep. They had given her a candle, presumably to frighten away vermin. "What do you want?" she said. The left side of her face was bruised and so puffed that she looked like the victim of a bad toothache.

"I'm getting you out of here," Roger told her.

"In the middle of the night? That makes it sound like I'm escaping."

"You are."

"No." Ailith backed away. "I don't know what your game is, but I'm staying here."

"You've been accused of witchcraft," Roger told her.

"What of it? I'm innocent."

"That doesn't matter."

"Of course it does. They won't—"

"Let me tell you what will happen to you." Roger said. "First, they'll strip you naked. They'll look for the Devil's Marks—a third nipple, for instance."

Ailith couldn't help but laugh at that. "A third nipple? That's the most—"

"Next, they'll search you for birth marks. They'll examine every inch of your body, and I mean *every* inch. Every orifice, as well. Examine them thoroughly—with sharp objects, if need be." He paused, so that she understood what he meant.

Ailith's smile faded, and she stiffened.

Roger went on. "A witch doesn't bleed, so next they'll cut you in various places. Like as not, they'll slice off one of your breasts, that's always a good test. But if you bleed, that's not ironclad proof you're not a witch; so then perhaps they'll have you lick a red-hot iron. If your tongue doesn't burn, you're a witch. If it does burn, well, maybe you're human, after all. Maybe. But to be completely certain, they'll tie you up, weight you down, and toss you in the river. A witch will float, you see, rejected by the water, but a human will sink."

Ailith said, "But—how will I get back to the surface?"

"They'll wait a while, to be on the safe side, to see if the water tosses you back up, then they'll send someone down to get you."

"A while? How long?"

"Longer than you can hold your breath, I'll wager. Auberie has no interest in you spreading tales about him."

Even by the weak light of the candle, Ailith had grown pale. "How do you know all this?"

"We had a witch scare here about five years ago. A girl not much older than you. I was on punishment at the time. I had to clean up after Gregorius and his assistant, who happened to be Auberie, got finished with her. Very thorough, Gregorius is, doesn't miss a thing. The Devil won't sneak past him."

Ailith stood rigidly.

"Now you see why you must leave," Roger told her.

In a subdued voice she said, "Where will I go? Home?"

Roger shook his head. "That's the first place they'll look. You can't remain in Trentshire. They'll take your escape as an admission of guilt and comb the shire for you. Have you family somewhere else?"

Ailith shrugged. "I don't know. I don't think so. What will I do? I'll starve."

"That's better than what Gregorius has planned for you. Go to a town—Leicester, maybe, or Coventry. Perhaps you can find a position as serving girl to a wealthy merchant." More likely, the poor creature would end up as a prostitute if she wasn't murdered on the road, but it did no good telling her that.

"What about you?" she said. "Are you coming?"

"No. I swore a vow not to leave Huntley, and I can't break it. I'll take you to the postern gate at the south wall. After that, you're on your own."

"But they'll know you helped me escape. They'll—"

"I'll be all right. Now, let's get out of here, we don't have much time. The chapter will be rising for—"

There were footsteps outside and an exclamation of surprise. Then the storeroom door banged open, revealing Auberie. The swelling around Auberie's eye and nose hadn't gone down; the skin around them was blackish purple. Blood seeped through the bandage over his eye. Behind Auberie loomed a tall, sallow man with an upturned chin and an arrogant, hooked nose, his hands stuffed in the full sleeves of his robe.

"Gregorius," Roger breathed.

Auberie's lower lip dropped in surprise, then his battered mouth widened in smile. "My God, the Foundling really *is* under her spell. Here's proof for you, Gregorius."

Auberie moved aside and the circuitor stepped forward. "I've come for a look at the witch," he intoned in a smooth voice. "It's been a while since I've seen one." He stared at Ailith, looking up and down her lithe body, his dark eyes shining with anticipation, his breath quickening. "A fetching creature she is, too, the kind of vessel Satan loves to employ in order to trap the unwary." He turned to Roger. "Consorting with witches now, are we, Roger? That's not good. Perhaps you're a witch yourself—who knows? I'll enjoy finding out, though."

Roger whirled and blew out the candle. In the sudden darkness, he swung a fist at Auberie, hitting Auberie's pulped face, hearing Auberie squeal. Roger lowered his shoulder and slammed it into Gregorius, knocking the saturnine circuitor to the ground. He grabbed for Ailith's hand. "Come on!" She stumbled after him and they ran from the storehouse. Behind them Auberie yelled, "Help! Help! The witch is escaping!"

Roger thanked God for lack of a moon. He didn't head toward the postern gate—that's where he and Ailith would be expected to go. A portion of the north wall had cracked during last winter's frosts. It had been torn down and workers were in the process of rebuilding. Part of the gap had not yet been filled, and that's where Roger was headed. He led Ailith past the lavatories, through a small gate in the wall there, then around the infirmary with its kitchen and protruding chapel. His sandals beat on the rain-slick grass. Ailith was a good runner. Roger let go her hand and she was able to keep up with him. Behind them were yelling and confusion.

Another wall, another gate, and they were into the gardens, with the rounded apse of the abbey church looming high on their left. Roger took Ailith's hand again, guiding her between rows of pear and apple trees, between cabbages and peas, between lungwort and samphire and chive. The deeper darkness to their right was the fish pond.

They reached the north wall. The abbey had served as a real fortress in the days of the Norse raids and during the civil war between Stephen and Matilda. The last half-century had been relatively peaceful, however, and the walls had fallen into disrepair, which had led to the north wall's crumbling. Behind Roger and Ailith, voices were getting nearer. "They went this way!" someone yelled. It sounded like Turold the huntsman.

In the darkness, Roger picked his way through scaffolding, ladders, tools, and buckets, knocking things down and causing a racket, but he didn't care. He found the break in the wall and climbed over the rubble-filled trough. He turned and handed

Ailith through as well. Behind them, he saw torches, their bobbing lights coming through the rain like giant fireflies. He took Ailith's elbow and the two of them started running again, heading for the safety of Dunham Forest.

Chapter 5

Roger and Ailith reached the forest. It was raining harder. It was cold and nearly impossible to see anything in the darkness. They blundered about, following the path of least resistance deeper into the trees and bracken and thorns, tearing their clothes and exposed flesh. Behind them, the shouts gradually died away.

"Do you have any idea where we are?" Ailith said.

Roger's face smacked into a wet pine branch as he walked. He held the branch aside so that Ailith could pass. "Somewhere in England," he said. "Anything beyond that is a guess."

"Wonderful," Ailith muttered, and they kept going.

At last they discovered—or rather, stumbled upon—a rocky overhang that would afford them a bit of protection from the rain. They crammed into the space, which was not large, and huddled together, wet and shivering. Ailith's dress was of thinner material than Roger's stout robe and scapula, so she felt the cold more.

"I never thanked you for what you did this afternoon," Roger told her. "If you hadn't tripped Auberie, he would have killed me."

Ailith waved him off. "It's me what should be thanking you," she said. "Just wish I'd got away before that abbot of yours showed up. I'd have been all right then. I'd be home now, all nice and snug."

They shifted around awkwardly, trying to get comfortable in the cramped space. "Put your arms around me," Ailith said. She swiveled so that her back was to him and she edged closer, sitting between his legs.

Roger hesitated.

"Go on," she said, "what are you waiting for? You act like I really *am* a witch."

Tentatively, Roger circled his arms around her waist, careful not to let his hands or arms come anywhere near her breasts, contorting himself to keep the insides of his legs from touching her thighs.

"My God," Ailith let out an exasperated sigh. "Like *this*." She pulled Roger's arms tightly around her waist, wedging herself snugly against him. "Ain't you never touched a woman before?"

Roger was shocked. "No!"

Ailith twisted her head round in surprise. "What—you've no sisters?"

"I'm an orphan. I was raised at the abbey."

"Well, if that don't beat all. In my house, the whole family cuddles together at night, like puppies. Brothers, sisters, grandparents. Got to, if you want to stay warm. Course it gets uncomfortable if Dad and Mum decide they want to . . . but I guess you wouldn't know nothing about that, neither?"

"No." Roger was glad it was dark, so she couldn't see him blush.

She sighed and pushed still closer against him, her warmth diffusing through his body. The bottom of the little rock niche was wet, and the damp seeped through the seat of Roger's robe, but that couldn't be helped. Ailith's head was against his chest. He smelled her wet, plaited hair, and it smelled good. He realized he was leaning his cheek against the side of her head, and he knew that must be a sin, but before he could pull himself away from her, he fell asleep.

Chapter 6

A strong hand clamped itself across Roger's mouth.

"S-h-h-h," a man whispered.

Roger shot from the depths of sleep, like a drowning man breaking the surface of the water just before he expires. For a moment he forgot where he was. Then he remembered—the forest, the overhang, the rain.

In front of Roger, Ailith jumped, but the newcomer held her down. "S-h-h-h. Quiet." He spoke in English. "There's men out there looking for you."

Roger and Ailith struggled upright. There was distant crashing in the brush. A dog barked.

The newcomer relaxed his grip on Roger's mouth. "Come with me," he said. "Quickly."

Roger helped Ailith to her feet. "Who are you?" he asked the man. "Why are you—"

"My name is Fauston. Now, hurry."

They followed him. Roger was tired; his body ached from yesterday's fight with Auberie. He could tell that Ailith, who went before him, was exhausted, as well. Leading the way, Fauston moved easily through the rainy darkness, several times stopping to let Roger and Ailith catch up.

"You know the forest well," Roger huffed.

"I was born not far from here," Fauston explained.

They went up and down mud-slicked hills; Roger had no idea what direction they followed. The distant noise of their pursuers faded until finally it could be heard no more. They splashed across a stream, the water stabbing cold on Roger's sandaled feet, then up a rocky incline. "This way," Fauston said.

There was a path among the rocks. They rounded a bend guarded by an ancient oak tree, and Roger made out a dim light from the mouth of a cave. "In here," said Fauston.

Roger bent and followed Fauston and Ailith into the cave, the top of whose entrance had been painstakingly rounded into a decorated arch. Inside, the narrow cave opened, giving them room to stand upright. The cave was smoky; it was musty and damp; but at least they were out of the rain. On the right as they entered, a four-foot high crucifix had been carved out of the rock. The dying fire burned in a pit in the cave's center. The smoke burned Roger's eyes and made him choke. Ailith was coughing from it, waving it away with her hand. Fauston added wood to the fire, and as the light flared, Roger saw that the cave had been hollowed out, its ceiling rounded, columns carved into the rock along its walls and decorated with diamond-shaped patterns. Shelves had been carved into the walls between the columns, along with a platform that must have been used for a bed. Another platform at the cave's far end had a familiar shape, and Roger realized it was a crude altar. The cave had been turned into a church.

"When I was a child, we used to visit the eremite who lived here," Fauston explained, "a wonderful old fellow named Oswold. Oswold had been a soldier in his early life. He had followed Duke Robert on the great crusade to liberate Jerusalem, and he was full of tales about the East. He was a learned man, too, could recite the lives of the saints as though they were his own. He used to preach under that great tree outside. People came from miles around to hear him and to ask him for spiritual advice." Fauston paused. "I helped bury him after he died."

Gradually the smoke dissipated; there must have been another opening somewhere to draw it out. This was the first chance Roger had to get a good look at their new companion. Fauston looked to be a few years older than Roger, stocky, with thick curly hair and beard. His dress was conspicuous only by its ordinariness—a long brown shirt and hose of murrey—the sort of clothes any ploughman might wear. His green cloak had once been of good quality, but now it was patched and worn. His eyes were a luminous blue, the kind of eyes that looked as though they usually radiated a humorous twinkle, though right now that humor seemed to have been replaced by wistfulness, or maybe it was sadness.

Fauston went on. "You should be safe here. The firelight can't be seen unless someone stands directly in front of the cell's opening. The rain will cover your tracks, so will the stream and the rocks." He took a half-loaf of old bread from his heavy leather scrip, which lay near the fire. With some effort, he sawed the bread with his knife and handed a piece each to Roger and Ailith.

Ailith gnawed at the hard bread as best she could. "Why are you helping us?"

Fauston stared into the fire for a long moment, then a bit of the humor returned to his eyes and he smiled. "Maybe I have a soft spot for runaway lovers."

"Lovers!" Roger said.

Ailith almost choked on what little bread she had been able to work loose. "We're not lovers!"

"I'm a brother of St. Benedict!" Roger protested, indicating his muddy robe and scapula. "I've taken a vow of chastity."

"I know many monks who have taken that vow," Fauston said, "and it's been of little impediment to them. But that's by the bye. If you're not lovers, why in the name of all that's holy are you out here, at night, in the rain, with men chasing you?"

"Because I'm a witch," Ailith said pertly. She jerked her head toward the cave entrance. "Leastways, that lot out there thinks I am. Roger here's helping me escape."

Fauston cocked his head in disbelief. "What could a comely lass like you have done to make anyone think you're a witch?"

She told him how Roger had saved her from being raped by Auberie and Auberie's excuse for the incident.

Fauston nodded sourly, as though it was the kind of story he had heard before. "Let me guess. This Auberie comes from a rich and powerful family, and no one dares dispute his word."

"Good guess," Roger said.

Fauston shook his head in disgust. "Such is the way of our world, I fear." He cut slices from what was left of a brick of yellow cheese and handed them to Ailith and Roger. "You have my sympathy, lass. 'Tis is a terrible fate to be cast as a witch. I pray that all works out for you."

Roger took a bite of the cheese. The cheese was hard with age and it had a sharp, almost metallic, taste, not the kind of rich, smooth cheese served in Huntley's refectory. "What about you?" he asked Fauston. "Why are you here?"

Fauston made a graceful flourish with his hand. "I am a wandering scholar. A gyrovage, if you will, a seeker of truth and knowledge."

Roger frowned. "If you're a scholar, why have you no tonsure?"

"It's hard to keep your pate shaved when you're on the road," Fauston explained. "Expensive, too, for a poor man like me." He cleared his throat apologetically and ran a hand across his curly locks. "Besides, I like my hair this way. I'll get it cut in Chartres. That's where I'm headed—to the cathedral school. After that to Paris, to study Canon law." To Roger, he said, "You must be from Huntley?"

"I am," Roger said.

"I understand you have a large library there."

"The fourth largest in England," Roger said proudly. "A hundred and seven volumes."

"I had planned to spend the night at Huntley, but the road was clogged with soldiers and transport heading for the East; and that, along with the rain, impeded my progress. I realized I would never get to the abbey before the gates were barred, then I remembered this hermitage. 'Tis unwise to be abroad in the forest after dark."

Ailith said, "Then why were you out in the storm when you found us?"

"I had journeyed a number of miles with a—with a pedlar from Coventry. The stubborn old coot was determined to go on, though I warned him not to. I was hoping to find him and bring him to shelter, but I got turned around myself in the dark and the rain. I'd only just got my bearings again when I ran into you." He looked off into the unseen distance. "God knows what happened to the pedlar."

Fauston cut another hunk of cheese for himself and set the rest atop his scrip. "Help yourselves to the food. After that, get some sleep—you two look done in. I'll stand watch in case your friends show up." He rose and put more wood on the fire, then headed to the front of the cave.

Ailith needed no urging. She edged toward Roger, no doubt thinking they could huddle again, but Roger moved away. Ailith shrugged, curled in a ball by the fire, heedless of the smoke, and fell asleep. Ailith's dress was made of blanchett—cheap, undyed wool—that over time had turned a mottled brown from ground-in dirt and wear. Roger removed his scapula and laid it over her, to provide her extra warmth. He wrapped his wet wool robe around himself and lay down, far enough away from Ailith that he wouldn't accidentally touch her if he shifted while sleeping. He heard the rain drumming outside, and he stared through the smoke into the dancing flames.

What would become of him?

He had helped a witch escape. The fact that she wasn't really a witch made no difference. Her flight would be taken as evidence of her guilt—and of his. In aiding her escape, he had assaulted Gregorius and Auberie, officers of the abbey. Gregorius would want to interrogate Roger to ascertain whether he was a witch, as well, Roger was certain of that. Amalric the prior probably wouldn't object to such a proceeding, but Roger doubted that Abbot Raymond would go along with it.

Raymond was a good man, put in an awkward position. He must know, or at least strongly suspect, that Ailith wasn't a witch; but he had to investigate her because Auberie's father was powerful and close to the king. Roger was confident that Raymond would draw the line at torturing a member of his own abbey chapter, especially since he must know that Roger's version of the incident was true.

Roger *would* be punished, though; there was no doubt about that. Maybe they would flog him bloody, then cover his exposed back with honey to attract bees and flies. Or maybe they would rub salt in his wounds. Whatever it was, it would be the most severe punishment he had faced in his twenty years at the abbey. He clasped his hands and prayed to God for strength to face the coming ordeal.

Chapter 7

Grey light filtered through the cave entrance, throwing the decorated columns and the altar into hazy relief. Roger rose, stiff and chilled and heavy lidded, his robe still damp from the rain. He coughed—the fire had died out but smoke lingered in the air. Ailith still lay sleeping, Roger's black scapula clutched tightly around her. Roger took stock of his surroundings. The amount of ash in the fire pit along with a stale, onion-like scent inside the cave, and the general tramped-about look of the floor suggested that people stayed here on a fairly regular basis, and that wasn't a good sign for him or Ailith.

Roger made his way past the carved crucifix to the cave entrance. He found Fauston just inside the rounded arch, wrapped in his worn green cloak and watching the surrounding forest intently. Roger listened. There was no sound of men, no dogs. Just birds singing.

Roger started to say something, but Fauston held a finger to his lips. He rose and motioned Roger forward. Cautiously, the two men left the cave. The first glimmers of sunlight appeared low through the trees. The forest smelled fresh from the rain. Fauston led Roger past the towering oak where the hermit used to preach, down the rocks to the stream. Alert, they knelt and took cold water into their mouths with cupped hands.

"We can't stay here," Roger said. "A lot of people must know about this cave, judging by the looks of the place. That means Turold, the abbey's huntsman, must know about it, too. They're certain to search for us here. They may be on their way even now."

Fauston thought that over. "You're right." He winked. "We'd better wake the witch."

43

"Told you, I'm no witch," Ailith said from behind them. She had pulled Roger's scapula over her head, and she clutched it around her. "If I was, I'd have conjured up a feather bed to sleep on last night, 'stead of flipping rock. Maybe a nice pile of blankets, as well."

She came down to the stream to join them. In the crisp dawn air, her left cheek was puffed and discolored.

Fauston winced. "Did this Auberie fellow you told me about do that to you?"

Ailith nodded and knelt to drink. "He'd of done a lot worse, wasn't for Roger."

Roger stood. "We need to be on our way. Ailith, you head for Leicester; I'm going back to the abbey."

Ailith scooped water into her mouth. "Sure that's a good idea—you going back to the abbey, that is?"

"There's nowhere else I can go. I've taken my vows."

"What'll they do to you for helping me?"

"Nothing I can't handle. The important thing is getting you to safety. You're dead for certain if they catch you now. Have you ever been to Leicester?"

"Before yesterday, I never been nowhere but Leighton Manor. That glen where you saved me was the farthest I ever been from home. After that, the abbey was the farthest, now this hermitage. Getting to be a world traveler, I am. So where is Leicester and how do I get there?"

Roger scratched his tonsure. He had no idea how to get to Leicester from here. He'd been to Badford twice—to the cathedral on feast days with the rest of the chapter—but aside from that, he'd never been away from Huntley.

"I'll see you there," Fauston told Ailith. "It's on my way." He frowned in warning. "Mind you, there won't be much to eat, and we'll have to sleep rough. They'll be searching for you at manor houses, churches—any place travelers stay for the night." To Roger he said, "I know a little used path that will take us part way through this forest. We can stay together until the path splits."

Roger knelt and took one last drink from the stream. "Let's get going, then."

"Wait," Fauston said.

Fauston hurried back to the cave. Roger fidgeted, expecting at any moment to see Turold and his men crashing through the brush.

At last Fauston returned, a heavy canvas sack over his shoulder.

"What the Devil is that?" Roger said.

"My books. The few I haven't been forced to sell for food and lodging, anyway." He gestured across the stream. "This way."

Ailith pulled off Roger's scapula and handed it back. "Thanks."

"I hope it was of some help," Roger said.

She smiled at him. "It was."

He put the scapula on, and they followed Fauston across the stream.

Chapter 8

The path was so faint that, at times, Roger couldn't tell how Fauston followed it. They picked their way through trees and bracken, stopping every few minutes to listen, but there was no sign of pursuit. Ailith went in front of Roger. She didn't have the large, spade-like feet typical of peasants; and she walked with an erect, self-assured gait, more like a noblewoman than the ragged village girl she was.

It was chilly; the sun hadn't risen high enough to burn off the morning damp and dry their wet clothing. Roger had missed prime, and he was likely to miss terce—and with it, Mass—as well. With the exception of a few days spent in the infirmary, he had heard Mass every day of his life since he was five. At the rate they were going, there was a good chance he would also miss sext, maybe even nones. Roger felt as though his soul was being deprived of its daily nourishment, as essential to his spiritual well-being as food was to his body. He crossed himself and prayed for forgiveness.

The worst part was, he didn't have to be here. Had he arrived at the glen a few minutes later, it would have been the abbot who discovered Auberie trying to rape Ailith, not Roger. Any other time, Roger would have heard a large hunting party like that miles away; but he'd learned later that the party had stopped for lunch and that Abbot Raymond, the prior, and Turold had gone ahead to scout the land. No doubt Auberie would still have accused Ailith of witchcraft, but Roger would have been well out of it.

And who would then have helped the girl escape? Roger thought.

This was God's plan, and Roger must accept it.

After a difficult uphill stretch, Fauston said, "Let's stop for a bit."

They were all breathing heavily and sweating. Ailith and Fauston half-collapsed onto a fallen tree, Fauston dropping the books beside him, while Roger sat nearby, watching their back trail. Around them were the chirping of birds, the hum of insects, the thousand and one noises of the forest. The sun broke through the trees and heated Roger's sweaty face.

Fauston pulled the remaining bits of bread and cheese from his scrip and cut them into three equal pieces. Ailith took her rock-hard bread and ground it between her teeth with relish, like it was some kind of treat instead of the dregs of a leather sack. Roger wondered if she'd ever had a proper meal in her life.

Fauston offered bread to Roger, but Roger held up his hand. "I'll eat when I get back to the abbey. You two share."

Fauston seemed happy with that arrangement—as a student, he probably didn't get much to eat, either. He split the remaining piece of bread between himself and Ailith, giving the girl the larger share without appearing to. He split the cheese, and he and Ailith ate that, as well. Ailith was sitting close to Roger. She studied his left hand, then pointed at it. "Nice ring," she observed between bites of cheese. "Ain't seen work like that before."

Roger stared at the ring, as he had stared at it most every day of his life. He took it off and handed it to her. "My father left it for me."

Ailith turned the ring over in her hand. Fauston peered at it, as well. The ring was old, very old. It was made of silver inlaid with blackening niello. Inside the circular bezel was an ornate, cruciform decoration surrounding the depiction of a four-legged animal of some kind, possibly a lion. It was hard to tell because it was so worn.

"Old English design," Fauston remarked favorably.

Ailith squinted at something inscribed inside the band. "What's this?"

"The letter 'A'," Roger said.

Ailith gave an uncomprehending shrug.

"It has to do with reading," Roger explained.

Ailith shrugged again, as if that meant nothing to her.

"You say your father left it for you?" Fauston asked Roger.

"He left it at the abbey, along with a bag of gold to pay for my upbringing. I was an infant."

"Then you never knew your father?"

"Or my mother." There were many men who did not know their father, but few who didn't know their mother. "I don't even know their names. My father wouldn't reveal his identity to the abbot. After he left me, he set off for the Holy Land to atone for his sins." Roger looked away. "For all I know, he's still out there."

Ailith said, "So that's why Auberie calls you Foundling."

Roger nodded. Then Fauston hoisted his books. "We'd better be going."

Ailith sucked nonexistent food off her fingers, and the three of them set off once more.

❖ ❖ ❖

The sun rose higher. Roger was sweating profusely in his heavy black robe. He pulled his hooded scapula over his head and carried it. There was no telling how many miles they had come. "Still no sign of pursuit," he said, looking around.

"We must be safe by now," Ailith said.

"*You* won't be safe till you're out of Trentshire," Roger told her. "Until then, you're in mortal danger."

Fauston wiped sweat from his brow. To Roger he said, "She's got a point. Perhaps your friend Gregorius has given up the chase."

"You don't know Gregorius," Roger replied. Then he thought about what Fauston had said. If there *was* pursuit, they should have seen or heard sign of it by now. He rubbed his chin. "Gregorius wouldn't give up, but Abbot Raymond may have called him off the search. I'm sure the abbot would be happy to see Ailith go free instead of being punished for something she didn't do. He knows I'm coming back to Huntley, so there's no need to look for me."

"Does that mean we can slow down?" Ailith asked hopefully.

Fauston and Roger shared a glance, Fauston letting Roger make the decision, "I suppose," Roger said at last. He spoke to Ailith sternly, "But you still need to be careful on your way to Leicester."

"Thank the saints," Ailith said, letting out her breath. "If I'd wanted to spend me life running through the woods, I'd have been a poacher like me brother John was, before they hung him for stealing the bailiff's horse."

With the threat of pursuit seemingly gone, the forest, which had been menacing until now, suddenly seemed to be transformed into an earthly paradise—rich smells of greenery and earth, sounds of birds and rustling leaves, shafts of sunlight through the trees forming a golden mist about them.

"So why *aren't* you married?" Roger asked Ailith as they continued on, walking at a more leisurely pace.

"It's not like me dad ain't tried," Ailith snorted. "When I was fourteen, he wanted to hitch me to a geezer of thirty-five, a widower with five grown kids and a big carbuncle on his nose." She lowered her voice, mimicking her father. "'E's got three cows and two-and-a-half strips in the common—a rare catch for a girl like you, with no dowry.'" She resumed in her own voice. "Well, la-di-flipping-da, two-and-a-half strips. Regular king of Persia, weren't he?"

Fauston cast an amused look over his shoulder. "So what did you do?"

"I said no, wha'cher think? Cleaning and cooking and wearing meself to the bone for that old goat and his five kids— some of 'em with brats of their own? Told him they could drag me to the church and I still wouldn't say yes. Dad threw a fit and beat me, but I didn't care. Twice more he tried to marry me off, but I wasn't having none of it."

Roger frowned. "Why?"

"Why should I marry somebody Dad picks? Why can't I marry somebody *I* like? Where's the sin in that?"

"If everyone did that, the social order would be destroyed," Fauston pointed out.

"Maybe it needs to be destroyed," Ailith said. "Don't see it doing nobody much good, leastways not where I live, 'cept maybe for old Lord Simon up at the manor house. Why should I be unhappy just so's he can have a good life? I'm sick of sleeping with the pigs. I want something better out of life, and I'm going to get it."

"No wonder your father beat you," Fauston said.

"Oh, he beats me regular, he does, and me mum, she tears out her hair, crying woe is me, what kind of she-devil have I give birth to? Meanwhile all me old friends are long married—one of 'em dead already from childbirth. And me—I'm an old maid. Finally, Dad says I got to marry this boy from Swinfield. Fifteen, this boy is. I seen him once—brain like a turnip. But his father has land. Dad says it's him, or he's turning me out of the house. That's when Auberie comes along."

Roger and Fauston stopped and stared at her. This was not the tale she had told them earlier.

"All right, I sort of knew Auberie before," Ailith admitted sheepishly. "He comes round the village from time to time, gathering herbs. Real friendly, he is. I told him my problem—well, he's a man of God, ain't he? He should be able to help. I met with him a couple times, prayed with him. Each time we went a bit farther from the village. Then yesterday he takes me to that glen, brings a skin of wine with him. Never had wine before. And the rest—well, you know."

"So you weren't looking for a runaway goat?" Roger said.

Ailith snorted again. "Like we ever owned a goat."

"Why didn't you tell the truth when the abbot asked you?"

"'Cause there's women in the village saying maybe I'm a witch cause I ain't married. Didn't want the abbot to get wind of that, did I? 'Course now everybody thinks I'm a witch anyway, so what's it matter?"

Roger and Fauston looked at each other again and kept going.

After some distance, the track crossed a broader, well-worn path. Fauston held up his hand and stopped. Around them, the forest seemed unusually quiet. Fauston looked left and right, and he listened. He stayed that way a long time, frowning.

"What is it?" Roger whispered.

"S-h-h-h."

Fauston watched and listened. He looked behind them, as though trying to gauge whether they should turn about and retrace their steps.

Ailith said, "Why are you—?"

Fauston put a finger to his lips. He waited and listened some more, then at last he gave up. "Must be me," he said, and he motioned the others forward, into the path. He pointed to the right. "That way takes you back to Huntley, Roger. Ailith and I will go left and pick up the Leicester Road later in the day."

There was a crude wooden shrine at the little crossroads. Roger knelt beside it and crossed himself. Still looking around, eyes narrowed, Fauston said, "This used to be a shrine to good St. Edburga of Bicester, but the French changed it to Our Lady of the Highway."

Roger crossed himself again and rose. "You don't like the French?"

Fauston harrumphed. "Were it in my power, every French speaker in England would be gone tomorrow."

"I speak French," Roger pointed out.

Fauston grinned with a cockiness Roger had not seen before. "But you also know English, and you rescue fair witches from the clutches of those who would harm them, so in your case we'll make an exception. Now, let's away from here."

At that moment, there was a noise in the brush and a voice cried, "Take them!"

Chapter 9

Ailith was the quickest. She turned and ran—straight into the arms of Turold, who had emerged as if by magic from the nearby brush. Two more green-liveried huntsmen blocked escape to the left and right. Behind Roger, Auberie and Gregorius rose from positions in the trees. Even on this warm day, Gregorius's hood was up, casting his face in shadow. Auberie's nose was bandaged and both his eyes were black, with the left one swollen shut and a line of stitches above it. Roger would have laughed at him had the situation not been so desperate.

"So much for the pursuit being called off," Roger muttered to Fauston.

Turold held the struggling Ailith easily. He was big and grizzled, and his long hair was tied behind his neck. He came from an estate near Caen. He had been brought to Huntley by the previous abbot, another Norman, and he made no secret of his disdain for England and everything English. The abbey's other huntsmen, most of whom were local men, were said to despise him. "Don't wear yourself out, little witch," he cooed to Ailith in heavily accented English. To the clerics he boasted, "I told you they would come this way, my lords."

"Indeed you did, Turold," Gregorius replied. "Very prescient of you." He tossed Turold a coin. Turold caught the coin and touched his forehead in thanks. Gregorius distastefully brushed mud and woodland debris from the front of his black robe. "Though I'd have preferred not to have lain in the dirt all morning waiting for them."

Gregorius was cold and pale from lack of sun. He was a man who liked dark places. Because he was so feared as a circuitor, Huntley, unlike some abbies, kept good discipline. Of course, Gregorius could sometimes be persuaded to overlook transgressions—for a price, or for the favor of well-born brothers such as Auberie, whose battered face was now flushed with excitement.

Turold said, "Should I summon the others?"

Gregorius nodded. Turold raised his hunting horn to his lips and blew three blasts—two long and one short. The sound reverberated through the forest, to be answered a moment later by a far-off blast in reply.

Hands stuffed in his sleeves, Gregorius picked his way through the bracken. He stared at Ailith and she stared back in defiance. "Well," he told her, "now we know you really are a witch. Your flight is an admission of guilt. You'll be burnt, of course."

Ailith went rigid in Turold's grip. The blood drained from her face.

Auberie gazed at Ailith with undisguised lust. "We should still question her thoroughly, Gregorius. She may know of other witches in the area. There may be an entire coven of the creatures for us to apprehend."

"I was thinking the same thing," Gregorius said with a smile, if such a frightening expression could be called a smile.

"She's no more a witch than you are," Roger told Gregorius. "Questioning her is an excuse for you to vent your sick hatred of women. That, and to cover up what your friend Auberie tried to do to her."

Gregorius regarded Roger without visible emotion. "You would do well to think before you speak, *Domnus* Roger. You're already in serious trouble for helping the witch escape. Unfortunately, I doubt we'll be allowed to fully interrogate you on this matter. For some reason, Abbot Raymond seems to have a fondness for you."

"He has a fondness for all of society's castoffs," Auberie sneered.

"True," Gregorius agreed. Then he brightened. "Perhaps he'll at least allow us to cure Roger of the spell the witch has put upon him." He smiled again. "That could prove to be enjoyable."

"Most enjoyable," Auberie agreed. "By the by, I trust you'll allow me some time alone with the witch before we begin the official interrogation? Perhaps I may persuade her to confess her sins."

"If you wish," Gregorius said. He knew how to curry favor with those of high birth. His lust for blood could wait a bit. Waiting made it stronger.

Auberie smiled at Ailith, the way a cat might smile at a trapped bird. Then he looked at Fauston, as though seeing him for the first time. "Who, or what, is this?"

Fauston raised his hands defensively. "Hold on, my lord, I've no part in this. I don't know anything about witches. I thought—"

"Your name?" Gregorius snapped.

"Fauston, your worship. I'm a scholar, on my way to Chartres." Fauston spoke in French but deliberately misplaced the accents on the words, as many Englishmen did. He seemed to shrink in size, his shoulders hunched. "I met these two just after dawn. They asked me to show them the way to Leicester. Told me they were running away to be married."

Auberie gasped with surprise, then he laughed. "Married? Our Foundling?"

"That's what they said, my lord."

Gregorius eyed Fauston coldly. "Surely a *scholar*—" the word dripped from his lips, as though an Englishman could not possibly be learned—"knows that aiding a runaway monk is a serious offence."

"I know that, your worship," Fauston said, "but what was I to do? This fellow is bigger than I am. He threatened me. Please, I don't want any trouble. Just let me be on my way."

Roger couldn't blame Fauston for lying. Fauston just wanted to get away from this place alive. Still, Roger felt betrayed. He'd come to regard Fauston as a friend. In the distance, a horn sounded, revealing that the other searchers

55

were getting closer.

Gregorius considered Fauston, his dark eyes boring into Fauston's, as though trying to read his soul, then he nodded reluctantly. "I'm not certain you're as innocent in this matter as you profess, but I've no authority to hold you. I'm not an officer of the king."

Fauston sagged; he closed his eyes and let out his breath with relief. Auberie pointed to Fauston's heavy canvas sack. "What is that?"

"My books," Fauston said.

Auberie yanked the sack open and glanced inside. He nodded to Gregorius, to confirm Fauston's claim.

Gregorius dismissed Fauston with a curt wave of the hand. "Go on, *scholar*, be on your way. In the future, have more care whom you befriend."

"I will, your worship" Fauston promised. "Of a surety." He crossed himself, refusing to look at Roger and Ailith, too ashamed to meet their eyes. "Thank you."

Fauston closed the sack and picked it up. As he started to hoist it over his back, he shifted his weight and in one motion stepped forward, whirled the sack and swung it with all his strength, hitting Turold in the side of the head with a loud *thunk*. The burly huntsman let go of Ailith and dropped to the ground like a felled ox.

"Run!" Fauston shouted.

Ailith needed no urging. She was off like a startled hare. Gregorius reached for her arm but Roger grabbed the older man by the waist, turned him, and pitched him head first into the bushes.

Auberie snatched a dagger from one of the bemused huntsmen and lunged at Roger with it. Roger barely sidestepped the blow; the blade tore his robe. Auberie lunged again; again Roger jumped back, drawing his own knife from his belt as he did. Auberie followed with a backhanded slash that ripped open the front of Roger's robe. "Ha!" Auberie shouted and lunged again, aiming for Roger's heart. Without thinking, Roger stepped forward, parrying Auberie's lunge with his left forearm, at the same time driving his own knife into Auberie's chest, just below the breastbone.

The two men remained like that for a moment, Auberie staring into Roger's eyes in surprise. Then Roger stepped back, drawing his knife from Auberie's chest, aghast at what he had done.

Auberie dropped the dagger. Stunned, he watched blood spreading over the front of his black robe and scapula. He dropped slowly to his knees, remained that way for a moment, then toppled onto his face.

Chapter 10

Auberie lay in the dirt, his blood a widening red pool beneath him. Roger had never realized that a man's body held so much blood. It seemed as though it would never stop pouring out of him. Crazed by anger and desperation, Roger waved the dagger at the two remaining huntsmen. "Keep back!" he shouted.

The huntsmen—one of whom was young and just married; the other who was middle aged and missing part of an ear— had no intention of interfering. They weren't about to risk their lives on something that was none of their affair, especially since their chief, Turold, still lay unconscious from the blow he'd taken to the head from Fauston's books. Behind him, Roger heard Ailith and Fauston running away.

"Come on!" Ailith yelled to him. The second party of searchers was close now, the noise of their approach loud in the forest.

Gregorius was tangled in the bushes where Roger had thrown him. His hood had come off, revealing his long, sharp nose and thin lips. He disentangled himself and tried to get up, but Roger put his foot on his chest and pushed him back down, hard. "Stay where you are! Don't try to follow!"

Gregorius struggled to control his anger. He hated having his dignity compromised, but above all things he hated being touched. "Follow you? Why should I follow you? All I need do is wait for your return to the abbey. It's not as though a base-born cur like you has anywhere else to go." He stared up at Roger, and his dark eyes gleamed with anticipation. "Not even Abbot Raymond can save you this time, Roger."

"Roger!" Ailith called again.

Roger flourished the dagger once more at Gregorius and

the two huntsmen, then he turned and ran. Behind him, Gregorius rose and waved the two huntsmen toward Auberie. "See to him, you fools."

Roger joined the other two, and they plunged deep into the forest. They pelted along, Fauston in the lead, the sack of books bumping his back as he ran. Roger thought Fauston might get rid of the books, but Fauston was sturdy and the heavy load didn't seem to bother him.

"Do you know a safe place to hide?" Roger called to Fauston.

"Not after what you just did," Fauston shot back.

They ran until they could run no more. They stopped, bent over, chests heaving, sweat pouring out of them, their skin lacerated by branches and thorns; their clothes, already in bad shape, were torn even more. Ailith's face was beet red; Fauston winced as he eased his sack of books to the ground.

"What's in there, anyway?" Roger asked him between breaths.

"My *Doctrinale*, Donatus, Ovid, and my Missal," Fauston said, rotating his shoulder and stretching his back. "You should have seen how heavy it was before I sold the others."

They were near a hill. They caught their breath, then a short climb brought them to a vantage point from which they could look out upon the surrounding country. Gregorius and his men might have vanished into the very air for all there was sign of them. In the far distance, just visible above the trees, Roger made out the tower of the abbey church, the Caen stone white in the sunlight. He heard the tower bell ring nones, its sound faint. Reflexively, he dropped to his knees, crossed himself, and began to pray. If he were with his fellows, he would be trooping into the Chapter Hall right now, to sing a hymn and hear Psalms. Then it would be back to work in the cloister, copying Augustine on a drowsy summer afternoon.

A shiver ran through him and he hung his head.

What had he done? What had he been thinking? His life, the entirety of which had seemed preordained just two days ago, was forever altered.

Altered? It was destroyed.

And yet . . .

God had intended this to happen to him. Why? To punish him for his lax ways, for his failure to fully commit to the life of a cleric? Or was there another reason, a reason Roger was unable to perceive?

He crossed himself again and stood. "I'm not going back to the abbey," he announced.

He hadn't thought about the decision; it was as though the words tumbled from his mouth of their own volition. He went on. "I can't go back. I just killed a man. I committed Mortal Sin and condemned my soul to Hell."

Fauston stood beside him, gazing at the distant abbey. "You killed him in self-defense. It was no sin."

"Wasn't it?" Roger said. "Did I have to kill him? Could I have found another way out of the situation, or was I acting selfishly, out of my dislike for the man?" He shook his head. "It makes no difference. Gregorius was right. The abbot can't save me now. No one can."

"Would they hang you?" Fauston said.

"Worse than that. The man I killed was my superior at the abbey. His father is one of the most powerful men in France, a friend of King Richard. The Church will hunt me to the far ends of the kingdom for this. Gregorius and Turold will be in charge of my capture, and if I'm lucky, I'll be killed outright. Otherwise I'll be tortured to death for being a witch or maybe for being possessed by the Devil, which is even worse. I need to get as far away from here as possible."

Roger gazed at the church tower, peaceful in the late afternoon sun. Glumly he added, "Of course, if I don't go back to the abbey, I will have broken my vow to God. Another Mortal Sin."

Ailith had taken a seat on a rock. She wiped sweat from her brow. "So what will you do?"

Roger didn't know. And then the answer came to him,

again unbidden, as if by inspiration, and he straightened. "I'll go on the crusade."

Ailith frowned. "The crusade? What will you do on the crusade?"

"Die," Roger said. "Anyone who perishes in the Holy Land, in the service of God, receives a plenary indulgence for his sins and is admitted straightaway into the Kingdom of Heaven.

"Not everyone on the crusade will die," Fauston pointed out.

"Then I'll remain in the Holy Land until I do," Roger said. "It's the only way to save my soul. Besides, it's a chance to take part in the great adventure. It's what I've dreamed of doing. Now there's no reason not to. Who knows, I may even learn what became of my father."

Ailith was skeptical. "The Holy Land is far away. How will you get there?"

Roger smiled broadly, as if the thing were simplicity itself. "Why, I'll turn to the east and start walking."

Fauston and Ailith shared a glance, then Fauston scratched his thick beard. "Is this where we part ways then?"

Roger looked at the forest, at the abbey and the villages and fields beyond, stretching to the horizon. A view he would never see again. Gregorius would begin searching for him in earnest tomorrow, when it became apparent that he wasn't returning to the abbey. Roger needed to put miles between himself and Huntley. But he needed something else, as well. A distant figure caught his eye, a man riding a donkey.

He turned to his companions, feeling more alive than he had in all his twenty years. "There is one more thing we can do together. Something that may prove of benefit to us all."

Chapter 11

Otho of Malcherce took a switch to the little donkey he was riding, beating its rear. "Faster, curse you. I don't want to be out here come nightfall."

The donkey did his best, but he was, after all, only a donkey and not bred for speed. Otho sighed. Otho was in his mid-thirties. The handsome face that had once elicited flutters in the hearts of serving girls and tavern wenches by the score had now assumed a cherubic look, brought on by overeating and a receding hairline. Otho came from a prominent family in Poitou, and as a second son, he, like most second sons, had been tasked for a career in the Church. First came education. As a young man, Otho had traveled the "Student Road"—Paris, Pavia, Aachen (he hated Aachen—hadn't been warm a single day there). He had enjoyed the roistering student life. He had enjoyed learning, as well, and he might happily have become a teacher, but his family connections were too important to permit him to assume such a lowly office. For his family's sake, he must have power and benefices. He had found his way to England in the service of the late king Henry, who had made him a member of the cathedral chapter at Winchester, where he presently served as aide to the bishop. In the future he could look forward to becoming a bishop himself, maybe even an archbishop, maybe even king's councillar or justiciar of England, all the while accruing ever more benefices that would contribute to his lavish lifestyle.

It was these benefices that concerned him now. He was making a grand tour of the parishes where he was listed as rector, both to introduce himself to the vicars of those parishes and, more importantly, to make sure those vicars were not holding back any of the tithes due to him. The trip, which had been planned as a triumphal procession, had quickly become a nightmare. Otho had planned to travel in state, but guards, servants, animals, and supplies were impossible to come by, because nearly all the available men and materiel were headed to the Holy Land, and what was to be had came at rates that would make a Jew blush. Otho had been forced to employ a greatly reduced establishment from the one he had envisioned, but even then fortune had not been kind to him. The little rounsey he had bought to ride had been stolen near Litchfield, and he had to use this wretched donkey instead. His clerk had gotten drunk, fallen down some steps and broken a leg; and he had been left in Abingdon. His servant had been stricken with dysentery, and *he* had been left in Oxford. Then the guide Otho had hired for the journey had taken the cross in a fit of religious frenzy near Southam and left Otho by himself. All Otho wanted to do now was get back to Winchester. Next time he would send a clerk and a squad of strong-arm types on a mission like this one. What was it to him if he ever saw any of his parishes?

At the moment, he was on his way from Huntley Abbey to Keslow Priory. That was where he had planned to spend the night, but he had gotten lost on these cursed English roads—if "roads" was what you chose to call them. He was on a winding lane that led, as far as he could tell, nowhere. To one side of him was a thick hedgerow—hawthorn and blackthorn and crab apple, alive with flowers and fruits and birds; to the other side, forest.

As he rounded a bend, he saw a girl in the lane, coming his way. The girl was ragged and dirty, but she was attractive for all that—tall and blonde, with a bold carriage. There was something in the way she swayed her hips that Otho found provocative. She had neither basket nor farm implements, which was odd for a peasant girl—or perhaps not. English peasants were notoriously lazy. There was a saying at the bishop's palace in Winchester -— "It takes two Frenchman to make one Englishman work." It was a wonder anything got done in this country.

The girl drew closer to Otho. She did not stop and bow to her obvious superior, as might have been expected, and that both irritated and intrigued Otho. He halted the grateful donkey, blocking the girl's progress. He smiled down at the girl—flattering himself that he was still attractive to women. "Good morrow, *mademoiselle*." This was a chance for him to practice his English. He had learned the language out of curiosity; no one of any importance spoke it.

The girl's blue eyes looked squarely into his. "Good morrow yourself." The minx gave him no title of respect.

Otho cleared his throat and touched the silver crucifix that hung prominently round his neck and rested against his garnet robe. "Call me, 'Father,' child. I am a priest."

The girl seemed unfazed. "Don't look like no priest I ever seen. Not with them fancy clothes. And that ain't much of a tonsure now, is it? Just a snip round the back of the head."

Otho straightened and cleared his throat again, unused to such impudence. A French peasant speaking to him like that would have had the hide flayed off his—or her—back. Still, there was something about this wench that piqued Otho's interest. "I come from the bishop of Winchester's court, where we are expected to maintain a certain style," he explained.

"Winchester's a long ways off," the girl said. "Wha'cher doing out here?"

"Visiting my parishes. Meeting my vicars and inspiring them to do God's work. Tell me, is this the way to Keslow Priory?"

"It is."

"Will it get me there by nightfall?"

The girl pouted her very kissable lips in thought. "You'd have to hurry. Even then, 'tis not certain."

Otho made a face. "I was afraid of that."

"There *is* a shortcut," the girl said. "Through the woods." She pointed to Otho's right.

Otho looked apprehensively toward the forbidding mass of

trees. "Could I find this shortcut by myself?"

The girl shook her head, and of a sudden there was a sparkle in her eye. "I expect someone would have to show you."

"Could *you* show me?" Otho asked.

The girl stared.

"I'd be willing to pay," Otho said.

"How much?"

"As much as would make it worth my while. How much time will I save?"

The girl smiled slyly. "Why, sir, that depends on how far you want to go."

Otho's heart skipped a beat. Was he hearing right? He lowered his voice a note. "Let's say I wanted to go all the way."

The girl idly ran her fingertips down the donkey's neck, letting them brush Otho's thigh as if by accident. "If you go quick, you'll save a great deal of time. But if you go *slow*—" she stared at him boldly— "well, you'll not save much time, but I can assure you the ride will be pleasant."

Otho's heart pounded. "How pleasant?"

The girl cocked her head. "How much did you say you would pay?"

"Two pence." The sparkle in the girl's eyes faded. "No—three pence. Four."

"Five would be better."

"That's a lot."

"It'll be worth it." The girl raised the hem of her dress, as though studying her ankle, which, Otho noticed, was exceptionally well formed. "Might be, I'd have to guide you into a dense thicket."

Otho's heart thumped so hard against the inside of his chest he was afraid it might burst through. "Very well—five. You drive a hard bargain."

The girl let her dress down and blinked her eyes innocently. "*Very* hard, I hope?"

Otho moaned. Despite himself, his voice went up an octave. "What if it—the ride, that is—goes, ah, *faster* than I had hoped?"

The girl smiled. "That's a problem that can be licked, Father. I'll make certain you don't come to where you're going too soon."

"Excellent," Otho croaked, "excellent. Let's be on our way then, shall we?"

The girl took the donkey's bridle and led Otho off the road and into the woods. Otho watched her hips—her rear tight beneath her ragged dress. He thought of her breasts, firm and ripe, like melons waiting to be plucked. And he knew that he had been blessed by God this day. "What is your name, child?"

"Mary," she said.

"Mary." He repeated the word to himself, "Mary. What are you doing out here alone, Mary?"

"Helping travelers such as yourself. Got no choice, have I? The bailiffs took our cow for the new lord's accession. Then they took our goat for King Richard's accession. After that, they took our chickens for the Saladin Tax. They've took everything we own. I'm doing what I need to survive."

Praise God for taxes, Otho thought.

As they entered the trees, Otho leaned down, took one of the girl's blond plaits and caressed it. He ran his fingers over the bare skin beneath the plait and she arched her neck at his touch. He hadn't lost his way with women, after all. "Perhaps we should stop?" he suggested. He didn't think he could control himself a moment longer.

"Almost there," the girl said.

She led the donkey off the path, through some trees, and into a little bower with the sun streaming into it. Otho almost fell from his saddle in his haste to be at the girl. He reached for her and drew her to him. She let him run a hand under her dress and up her smooth thigh, then she pushed him back and held out her hand, palm up. "Pay first," she said.

Otho fumbled in his purse with fingers made thick by urgency. He thought he heard movement in the bower, but it was probably the donkey grazing. He counted out the coins, nearly dropping them, and he turned to the girl again—to find a dagger at his throat.

Robert Broomall

Chapter 12

The knife was wielded by a strapping young man with a
tonsured head and the black robe of a Benedictine monk. The
monk's hooded scapula was missing; his robe was slashed open
across the front and splotched with blood. The knife was plain,
with smears of dried blood on its blade and crossguard.

Otho was stunned. He was still consumed by his near
explosion of lust, blood pounding in his ears and chest, his
breath coming so hard it was difficult to accommodate himself
to this sudden change of events.

The monk gave a little bow of his head, smiled and spoke
in perfect French. "Good day to you, Father."

Otho stumbled backward and tried to run, but his path was
blocked by a second man—stocky and curly haired, blue eyes
twinkling, knife in his hand, as well. The girl evinced no
surprise at what had taken place; her once saucy face had gone
cold and she regarded Otho with dead eyes.

Otho turned back to the monk, still finding it difficult to
believe what had happened, his loins still throbbing for a
release that was not going to come. "What do you want with
me?" he said, voice cracking.

The monk pressed the point of his knife under Otho's
fleshy jaw, forcing Otho's head back. "Why, that's easy, Father.
We want your purse."

Otho raised his hands in supplication. "Please, don't kill
me. I have perhaps three marks in my purse, a goodly sum.
Take it and welcome, but for the love of God don't kill me."

The monk lowered the knife a fraction. "Three marks?
Faith, this is our lucky day." He held out his free hand and
beckoned with his fingers impatiently.

With shaking fingers, Otho untied the purse from his

68

belt—difficult to do with a blood-specked knife at his throat—
and gave it to the monk. The monk peered into the purse.
"Thank you, Father. Your charity is appreciated. This will fill
our bellies for a while."

The monk lowered the blade, and Otho let out a sigh of
relief. Sweat poured from Otho's thinning hair; his legs were
shaking. He turned to leave. Damn that wench, he should have
taken her right there in the road. He should never have let her
lead him —

"Wait." The stocky robber stepped in front of Otho,
blocking his path. "Lift your arms, Father."

Otho didn't understand. "Why—?"

"Do as I say," the stocky robber ordered, flourishing his
knife. The monk and the girl looked puzzled but didn't say
anything.

Otho complied. The stocky fellow patted Otho expertly
about the waist, as though feeling for something under his
finely tailored robe. Otho protested, "Really, I don't see what—
"

"Quiet," the monk told him.

The stocky robber found what he was searching for. He
looked Otho in the eye and smiled. Using the tip of his dagger,
he cut a slit in the back of Otho's garnet robe, which was made
of the finest Bruges cloth. "Hey!" cried Otho indignantly. He
tried to turn around, but the monk stopped him.

"Quiet," the monk repeated.

The stocky robber cut through Otho's robe and his shirt
beneath it. Otho tried to say something but the monk stopped
him yet again. "Quiet."

The stocky robber wriggled his hands into the slit, sliced
through something strapped to Otho's back, and withdrew a
leather pouch.

It was a second purse, much larger than the first. Jingly and
heavy.

"Well, well, well," said the monk in surprise.

"Mary, save us," gasped the girl.

"I thought you had only three marks?" the stocky robber said to Otho.

Otho made no reply. His face was red, his chest heaved.

The stocky robber tisked reprovingly. "For a servant of God, you don't trust your fellow man very much."

He tossed this new purse to the monk, who caught it to the sound of clinking metal. As the girl crowded close to watch, the monk opened the purse's drawstring and poured out a small avalanche of coins and halves and quarters and eighths of coins. There were pennies and deniers and florins; there were so many coins that they dribbled out of the monk's hand and onto the ground. He gathered them up, and it took him some time to sort and count them all. When he was finished, he looked up in amazement. "It's difficult to say for certain, but I make this to be just over twenty-three marks." He figured in his head. "That's a bit more than fifteen pounds. By Heaven, we're rich!"

The stocky fellow whistled. The girl's eyes opened about as wide as it was possible for eyes to go. Likely the scabrous wench had never imagined such a sum was even possible. Her entire manor could likely have been purchased for fifteen pounds, with money left over.

The monk fingered through the treasure. He counted out a small number of coins and handed them to Otho with a grin. "Here you are, Father. You told us you had three marks, and now you do. If nothing else, we've made an honest man of you."

"You don't understand," Otho protested. "That money's not mine. It belongs to our Lord, Jesus Christ."

"Who was always happy to share with those less fortunate than Himself," the monk observed with a raised forefinger. "But I'm curious. How does a holy man like yourself come by such a princely sum?"

"I have been visiting my parishes," Otho explained, straightening and trying to recover his dignity. "This is tithe money, the Lord's share, given by hard-working souls for—"

"For fat swine like you," interrupted the stocky robber, and his blue eyes flashed with anger. "Men who sit on their arses and complain about the tithes being in arrears, while their poor vicars labor from dawn to dusk in the service of Our Lord and are reduced to begging because you don't furnish them enough to live on. Tell me, is Newton-on-Eal one of your parishes?"

Otho knew his parishes by heart, unlike some rectors who had to struggle to remember theirs, or others who had so many they never even bothered to learn their names. "It is," he replied with a trembling heart. "Why do you ask?"

"I passed through there a few days ago. Spent time with the vicar. A good fellow, but dirt poor. Has to hire out to the villagers to get money for food, because all his income goes to the rector."

Otho was shaking. "I don't make the rules."

"No, and you don't have any qualms about enforcing them, either. God help some poor fellow if he's late with his share. Family starving? That's his lookout, the Church needs its tenth. Can't pay, and we'll take your property. Still can't pay, and we'll take your land."

The stocky robber looked like he was going to tear Otho apart. The monk and the girl seemed surprised by his intensity. In a small voice, Otho said, "Are you going to kill me?"

The stocky fellow's chest rose and fell beneath his patched green cloak, as though he were considering it, then he relaxed and shook his head. "Ah, what good would it do? Some other thief would just take your place."

Otho almost emptied his bladder in relief.

The monk added, "The Lord will decide your fate, Father, but you won't meet Him today, not at our hands anyway."

Otho swallowed. "You mean I can go?"

"Yes," the monk said. "But before you do, I would exchange clothes with you."

Exchange clothes? Otho viewed the monk's torn, blood-stained habit with revulsion. "Why?"

"That's none of your affair," the monk growled. He flourished the knife again. "Take off your garments and be quick about it."

"Wait," said the stocky fellow, "I have a better idea. Why not send our rotund rector here on his way without any clothes at all?"

"What!" said Otho.

The girl laughed and clapped her hands. "I like it."

Otho fulminated. "You dare not—"

"By robbing you, we broke the law, and we're prepared to accept the consequences," the stocky fellow pointed out. "You, on the other hand, do your thieving legally, so call this your Penance."

Otho crossed his arms. "I refuse. And there's nothing you can do that will—"

"Don't be so sure about that," said the stocky fellow. He flipped his dagger by the blade, caught it, then flipped it again.

Otho swallowed. He glared at the girl from the corner of his eye. How could he have been so stupid? He should have known she was up to no good. He tried to keep his last shred of dignity. "You'll at least—you'll at least let me keep my braies?"

"I think not," the stocky fellow said, smirking. "Let the brothers at Kenslow appreciate the full glory of your manhood."

"Quickly now," the monk said. "You may keep your three marks and that crucifix about your neck."

Otho took a deep breath. He started to pull the garnet robe over his head, then stopped and nodded toward the girl. "Must she watch?" A few minutes earlier, he'd have liked nothing better.

"Nothing I ain't seen before," the girl remarked. "'Cept maybe not so small."

Muttering deep in his throat, Otho removed his clothes, placing his hands over his private parts for modesty's sake when he was done. Otho seethed inside, he boiled. Not only was he being robbed, he was being made a fool of by these peasant rogues.

The monk donned Otho's long linen shirt along with his robe and hose of Flemish cloth, and he surveyed himself in wonder, like a child seeing his first snow, or a man released from prison after many years. "A bit small," he said of the clothes, "but they will suffice."

The stocky fellow held up his knife and ran a finger thoughtfully along the blade. "Maybe I should shave the holy Father a new tonsure, so's folks can tell he's really a priest. That patch he's got up there now's so little you can barely see it. Folks might suspect he's not as devoted to the Faith as we know him to be."

The monk shook his head. "Good idea, but we don't have time."

Otho would never live this down. What would the cathedral chapter say when they learned of this? What would the bishop say? "Now may I leave?" he asked through teeth that were gritted so tightly he thought they might break.

The monk bowed pleasantly to him, making an exaggerated flourish with his hand. "By all means, Father. Enjoy your journey."

Holding the purse with the three marks over his private parts, Otho turned and reached for the donkey's reins, but the monk's voice stopped him. "The donkey stays with us."

Otho looked back, and the monk went on. "I see welts on the creature's flanks where you've been beating him. You'll not do that anymore."

This nightmare kept getting worse and worse. "You mean I must walk?" Otho said.

"Yes, and I'd get a move on were I you. It will be dark ere long, and you don't want to be caught in the woods at night. I hear there's robbers about."

The girl and the stocky fellow laughed.

Otho drew himself up as best he could. "I suppose you think yourself witty. Well, you won't find it so funny when you're dangling from the end of a rope." He turned to the girl, the cause of all his troubles. "And you, you Devil's spawn. I'll see you—"

"I'd think twice before you called me a name," the girl said.

"Why?"

She leaned forward. "Because I'm a witch, and I'll turn you into a frog."

Otho went pale.

"Now get out of here," the girl ordered.

Otho needed no further urging. He turned and ran off through the trees, uttering little yelps of pain as his bare flesh was scratched by thorns and brambles. At one point he tripped and fell forward into a bush, but he got up and kept going as fast as his heavy legs would allow.

Chapter 13

When the priest was out of sight, Fauston turned to Ailith with a whoop of delight. "I believe he thought you were really going to turn him into a frog."

Ailith said, "I wish I *was* a witch—I would have done it."

Roger wrinkled his brow. "I think he was more afraid of *you* killing him," he told Fauston. "To be honest, so was I."

"Maybe I did get carried away," Fauston admitted, "but I couldn't help it. Men like him give the Church a bad name. Makes it hard for the rest of us."

Roger divided the priest's money equally between Fauston, Ailith, and himself. Ailith ran her fingers through her ratty pouch, which, having been empty for most of her life, was now bulging with coins. "Five whole pounds," she breathed, gazing at her haul. "I never dreamed I'd have five pounds. I never dreamed this much money even existed. I can go to Leicester now and be a proper lady."

Fauston scooped his share of the booty into his purse. "Stealing from the Church is a considerable sin," he told Roger.

"I'm already going to Hell," Roger pointed out. "What's God going to do, send me there twice? If you feel guilty, I'll be happy to take your share."

"We don't feel guilty," Ailith said hastily, punching Fauston's arm. "Not a bit of it."

Roger couldn't stop admiring his new clothes, luxuriating in the feel of fine linen against his skin. He had worn nothing but coarse wool all his life. He no longer felt like himself, or who he had always imagined himself to be. He fingered the garnet robe, the silver embroidery around its neck. The cloth was so soft and smooth that it felt like . . . Roger wasn't sure exactly *what* it felt like. It was too fine for rough travel, though;

it was also too conspicuous. He had needed to get rid of his monk's robe because the men who would come hunting him would be looking for someone in religious habit. But he also needed to blend in with the mass of the people, so he would sell these garments and buy something plainer the first chance he got. He'd let his tonsure grow out, as well. He ran his hand across the shaven top of his head. He'd been tonsured since age seven, and he wondered what it would be like to have hair up there.

"We'd better be going," he told his companions. "That fat fool of a priest will raise the hue and cry as soon as he reaches Keslow—assuming he doesn't turn into a frog first—plus, Gregorius's men will be after us." He smiled ruefully. "I guess *this* is where we part ways."

"Are you really off to the Holy Land?" Fauston asked.

"I really am," Roger said. "I'll try to catch up with the earl of Trent's forces and join them. If I can't do that, I'll go to Tyre. They say that's where the armies will gather for the advance on Jerusalem."

After the disaster at Hattin and the subsequent fall of Jerusalem, Saladin and his forces had spread across the Holy Land like a vast wave, taking out every city and castle in their path. They had finally been repulsed at Tyre, the last Christian stronghold on the coast. The Christians had held on by an eyelash, but they had held, led by an Italian count named Conrad of Montferrat. Now, Conrad and what remained of the chivalry of Outremer waited at Tyre for the armies of England, France, and the German Emperor to arrive. Roger had learned this from his mentor in the scriptorium, Paulinus. Old Paulinus had been a knight in the Holy Land long ago, and he liked to keep abreast of developments there, pestering travelers for news.

"Why go to Tyre?" Fauston said. "Why not Acre? From what I hear, our forces have laid siege to that city."

Over a year ago, Guy of Lusignan—the man who had lost the kingdom at Hattin—had been refused entry to Tyre by

Conrad and the surviving barons of Outremer. In a fit of pique, Guy had led a small band of followers south and laid siege to Acre, wealthiest city on the coast.

"I heard that, as well," Roger said, "but the siege must be over by now. Most likely, Guy and the few men he had with him are long dead. No, Tyre is where I'll go."

Fauston frowned. "Do you even know where Tyre is?"

Roger laughed. "I'm not even sure where the *Holy Land* is. I've never been farther than Badford. I'll find it, though. I only pray I'm in time. Once King Richard gets there, things will happen quickly."

"You place a lot of faith in our new king," Fauston observed.

"Everyone does," Roger said. "Richard is the greatest warrior of the age—maybe of all time, if what men say about him is true."

"Men *said* that God would never permit us to lose Jerusalem," Fauston pointed out, "but we did." Then he smiled and held out his hand, "Good luck to you, Roger. God keep you safe."

Roger took the hand and clapped Fauston's sturdy shoulder. "Good luck to you, as well, my friend. Still bound for the scholar's life at Chartres?"

Fauston jingled his sack of coins. "I'll take Ailith to Leicester first and see her settled, then I'm going back to Newton-on-Eal and give this money to the vicar there. I'll give him the donkey, as well." He saw the shocked looks on his companions' faces and he shrugged. "You can't be a real scholar unless you're poor."

Ailith muttered, "Glad I'm no scholar then, if that's what learning does to you."

Roger turned to Ailith. He started to hold out his hand, then stopped, uncertain what the custom was. "I—I've never taken leave of a woman before," he confessed. "I'm not sure how you . . ."

"God's love, but you're a goose," Ailith said. She put her

hands on his arms and kissed his lips. The kiss lingered; her lips were soft and sweet but at the same time salty; Roger's own lips tingled with an unwonted crackling of energy.

Ailith drew back and they stared at each other, and then something happened that neither of them had expected. Something snapped, something changed, and suddenly they were no longer in control of themselves. They stepped into each other's arms and kissed again, Roger pressing his lips to Ailith's, feeling her warm body mold itself against his, smelling the richness of her hair, wanting to be one with her, awakening sensations he had never known before as he felt both of their hearts pound faster and faster and a hot tear from her eye fell on his cheek.

They drew apart, breathing hard, Roger's eyes lost in the depths of Ailith's blue ones. He wanted to pull her to him and kiss her again; he wanted to do it as much as he had ever wanted anything in his life. But he knew that if he kissed her again, he would never leave her, and he knew he would have been happy never leaving her, but if that happened, his sins would go unatoned.

Slowly, reluctantly, he let his hands fall. He could barely speak, so choked with emotion was he. "Goodbye," he told Ailith. "I'll—I'll never forget you."

"I won't forget you, either," Ailith said in a breathless voice. "Good luck. I'll pray for you."

Roger raised a hand in farewell to his two friends. Then, with a heavy weight in his heart, he turned to the east and began walking.

Part II
THE SIEGE

Robert Broomall

Chapter 14

What they noticed first was the smell.

It was the smell of shit, human shit and animal shit, borne far out to sea on the land breeze. Overlaying that was another smell, a sickly sweet smell that Roger could not place but one that curdled his stomach even at this distance.

Soon a reddish glow illumined the nighttime sky to the south. "Is that Acre?" asked one of the *Quail*'s passengers.

"Has to be," replied a sailor who, along with Roger and the *Quail*'s other passengers and crew, had crowded the ship's raised forecastle for a better look.

The unworldly glow spread across the horizon. "It looks like we're sailing into Hell," said a second passenger in awed tones.

"Maybe we are," murmured a third.

The *Quail* was a cog out of Marseilles. She had been bound for Tyre when she had encountered a Christian convoy sailing north. The convoy had come from delivering supplies to Acre, where, against all odds, the siege still continued, and where, according to the convoy's captains, the full effort of the crusade was now being concentrated. On hearing that news, Ernoul, the *Quail*'s owner and captain, had altered course and headed south down the coast.

Roger jostled with the other men against the tiny forecastle's crenellated bulwark, gazing at the distant red glow. Roger no longer had that well-fed look; he had lost weight, and the planes of his tanned face were sharp and hard. Sandy hair sprouted where once there had been a tonsure, and he wore a short beard. The fine garments he had taken from the priest had long since been replaced by a coarse, knee-length shirt and breeches, along with a jack and a hood that he carried in his pack. Save for a boat ride across the Channel, he had walked from Huntley to Marseilles. He had slept rough and he had eaten rough. He had gotten drunk and he had liked that. He had slept with a woman and he had liked that, too; and because he had liked it so much, he had slept with more women, until inevitably he had slept with the wrong one, and she and her accomplices had beaten him and robbed him of all his money. After that, he had begged for food and stolen food and run out of food and nearly starved to death. When all had seemed lost, he had been taken in by a group of pilgrims, who had saved his life. He had been penniless when he reached Marseilles, but Ernoul had needed crewmen, and he had allowed Roger to work his passage east.

As the cog drew closer to the coast, the smell worsened. The reddish glow resolved itself into thousands of fires, great and small, and now there was noise to go with it—the clamor of men and animals and machines of war. Gradually the eastern sky lightened and the city of Acre resolved itself against the dawn.

Acre was situated on a headland that jutted into a bay, and it was defended by two sets of walls. The outer circuit of walls was at least a mile long, studded with ten great towers. From the largest tower, in the center angle of the circuit, a huge green flag flew defiantly. A separate tower sat on a rock in the harbor, guarding the entrance to the port. To the north of the city, the sea was filled with Christian ships of all sizes and descriptions, masts and sails stretching to the horizon as vessels came and departed.

Beyond the city walls lay the Christian camp. Roger had passed through the great cities of Europe—London, Paris, Lyon—but this camp was larger than all of them put together. Tents and banners stretched as far as the eye could see. The distant hills were flowered with myriad dots of color that Roger guessed were the tents of Saladin's men. One of the passengers remarked that the dim headland to the south was

Mount Carmel, where Elijah had challenged 450 prophets of Baal to see whose was the real god.

He had done it, Roger thought. He was really here.

The Holy Land.

"Take down the sail!" cried the *Quail's* captain. "Unship the oars!"

As other men hastily lowered and furled the sail, Roger took his place on one of the rowing benches, next to a huge Moor from Algiers named Patricio. The tide was coming in. Ernoul grasped the steering oar. Ernoul was short and swarthy, with dark curly hair and beard. He had broad shoulders and bandy legs, and he wore a gold ring in his right ear. He judged his moment, then shouted orders. The men bent to the oars, and the *Quail* began its run in to the shore.

The passengers gathered on the forecastle to watch as Ernoul bent over the steering oar, peering intently forward, weaving the *Quail* through the mass of shipping till he had a clear path to the beach. "Now, boys!" he shouted. "Row! Row for all you're worth! Faster! Steady, steady." Then, "Ship oars!" The men stopped rowing and, with practiced precision, brought in the oars. The ship's momentum slowed. The incoming tide flung the vessel forward one last time, and she grounded with a gentle thump on an open patch of beach. On the forecastle, the passengers applauded.

As Roger helped secure the ship, the gangplank was lowered and the passengers began disembarking. A few of these were pilgrims, come to see what they could of the Holy Land and maybe buy relics or souvenirs to take home with them; others were men like Roger, eager to take part in the crusade; others were merchants or stragglers from military units. Some had served in the East before or were returning from leave, and these settled in with the ease of old hands, commandeering animals and emaciated native boys who were only too glad to earn a few coins by carrying the newcomers' gear.

Roger said his farewells to Patricio and the other members

of the ship's crew. Last was Ernoul. "Goodbye," Roger said, shaking the captain's hand.

"Goodbye, Roger," Ernoul replied, white teeth bright against his nut-brown face. He dug in his purse and handed Roger some coins. "I only promised you passage, but here's extra for doing a good job. God grant we meet again. Until then, kill a few of the bastards for me."

Roger promised that he would, then he swung his small sack of belongings over his shoulder and walked down the gangplank. The solid ground felt strange after a month on the rolling sea. He found himself on a broad, litter-strewn beach that ended abruptly at a low bank, atop which stood warehouses and the sailors' camp. He made his way past sweating seamen and laborers, who were rolling barrels across the pebbly sand and leading horses and mules to the camp. The stench was even more overwhelming here. To the original stink it was now possible to discern the additional reeks of urine and decomposing garbage, joined by the odor of thousands upon thousands of unwashed men. Mingled in were the smells of animals, cooking food, and pungent spices. And still that strange, sickly-sweet smell overlay everything, burrowing into the fiber of Roger's body until he wanted to gag from it.

Roger climbed the bank, made his way past the warehouses—most of which were little more than open-sided tents—and entered the camp proper. Seen up close, it was not one camp but a series of them. Streets ran through the camp, as they would through any city. Most of the structures were tents, but there were a few semi-permanent buildings of wood and canvas. Roger was looking for the English army, but he had no idea where it might be, so he pushed his way along what appeared to be a main street, surrounded by a Babel of languages and nationalities. There were tall blond men of the North, carrying long axes. There were Normans and Irish kerns and wild tribesmen from Scotland. There were dour Flemings and suspicious Walloons. There were arrogant

Champenois, cheerful Gascons, and Provencaux with their red caps. There were Venetians and Pisans and Genoese. There were native Franks, dressed in turbans and flowing robes; there were Armenian and Syrian Christians, white-robed Templars and black-robed Hospitallers, Arab and Nubian laborers and servants. There were crosses—red crosses and white crosses, green crosses and yellow. Crosses sewn on shoulders and breasts and caps, crosses painted on shields, crosses burned into the flesh of animals.

There were soldiers and sailors and merchants, along with clerics of every order and rank, from purple-robed bishops to humble deacons. There were few women, though, and even fewer children. There were horses and oxen and mules, scavenging dogs and strange humped beasts that somebody called camels. Cries of donkey drivers mingled with the banging of hammers, with music from sackbutts and nakers, with shouts and singing from columns of armed men, and with the never-ending rumble of the catapults.

Roger seemed to encounter every nationality but English. He ducked into a wine vendor's tent, both to quench his thirst and to inquire after the whereabouts of King Richard's army. The tent was open on all sides in the hot morning. A plank placed across two barrels served as a drinking platform. The tent was about half full, and even at this hour some of its occupants were drunk, one of them passed out on the dirt floor.

Using the money Ernoul had given him, Roger bought wine. The wooden cup, which was tied to the plank by a cord to keep people from stealing it, was layered with grime. There were teeth marks around its softened edges. Roger took a long drink and almost choked. The wine was sour and mealy tasting. A year ago, at the abbey, he would have thrown it away in disgust. Now, he braced himself and took another drink. He'd had worse in his travels.

"Where can I find King Richard and his men?" he asked the wine vendor.

The vendor, a gimpy fellow, snorted derisively. "That's what everybody wants to know."

Roger stopped the cup halfway to his mouth. "What do you mean?"

"I mean they haven't got here yet, and no one knows where they are or when they'll arrive. It's like they fell off the face of the earth."

Roger had not expected this. "Are there *any* English units here?" he asked.

The vendor stroked his sweaty chin; he had a thick accent that Roger couldn't place. "Well, there's the Londoners who come out last spring—not many of them left now, of course. Then there's the archbishop of Canterbury and the earl of somebody or other."

"The earl of Trent?" Roger said, hope rising in his chest.

"Trent, that's it," the vendor said, snapping his fingers and pointing at Roger. "Got here a few weeks ago, they did."

"Where would I find their tents?" Roger asked.

The wine vendor jerked a thumb toward the street outside. "Go past the Toron—"

"The Toron?" Roger said.

"The hill where the quality are camped—you can't miss it. Keep going, as I said, and after a bit you'll see the black tents of the Bugars."

Roger was totally confused. "Who are the Bugars?"

"How the hell do I know? Don't want to mess with 'em, though, I'll tell you that. Anyway, turn east up Resurrection Road when you see them black tents. Go maybe a mile, and the English will be to your right."

"Thank you," Roger said. He bought another cup of the vile wine. "What about the other kings—Philip and Frederick? Are they here?"

The vendor grunted. "No, Philip ain't here, neither. Affairs of state delaying him, he says. And Frederick's dead."

"Dead!" Roger was stunned.

"Hard to believe, ain't it?"

It was hard to believe. Frederick was old, over 70, but he had been emperor for what seemed like forever and people thought he would never die.

"Drowned crossing a stream in someplace called Anatolia," said a huge, black-bearded fellow nearby.

The man on Roger's left, a glum redhead with sunburned cheeks and nose, stared into his cup. "They say Frederick set out with seventy thousand men—women and children, too. Know how many of 'em got here?" He paused for effect. "Two thousand. The rest is dead."

While that sank in, the redhead went on. "This place'll be the graveyard of us all. There was a hundred and twenty men in my company when we got here last autumn. There's thirty left, and we're no closer to taking the city than we ever were."

"Stop bellyaching," said another fellow, a foot soldier wearing a quilted jack embroidered with the black cross of the Hospitallers. "We'll take the city soon enough. That new belfry they're building will do the trick."

"We've built belfries before," the redhead said.

"Not like this one, we ain't. We'll be inside the city by Advent Sunday, you'll see."

"Hope they got women in there," said the black-bearded giant, drinking deep. "Been so long since I got my wick dipped, some of them sheep the lords keep for their meals are starting to look good." He slapped the redhead's back with a hearty grin. "Hell, boy, *you're* starting to look good."

Roger downed the rest of his wine and wiped the liquid's oily film from his lips. "On that note, gentlemen, I'll take my leave." He thanked the men for their assistance and left the tent.

It was a long walk. Each camp had space for footmen and horsemen, for wagon parks, for horses and oxen and pigs, for supply tents, parade grounds, latrines, and areas for servants and washerwomen. Some of the camps were laid out in strict order, with precisely aligned streets; others were thrown together any old way. Here and there, straggling vegetable and herb gardens lent a touch of green to the brown earth. Refuse and excrement—animal and human—were everywhere. Roger saw men urinating next to their tents. He saw men pale faced and emaciated from fever or dysentery. Venetian sailors carted off a dead mule, its legs stiff, the sailors bragging about how many meals they would get from it. Roger saw a man sitting on the ground with his head bent over. Like everyone else in the crowded street, Roger ignored the man, assuming he was a beggar or a drunk who had fallen asleep, but as he drew closer, he noticed ants crawling over the fellow. Buzzing flies clustered on him. Roger caught a whiff of something, too, and suddenly he knew what that strange odor was.

It was death.

"Dear God," he murmured. How many bodies must be here to produce an odor that could be smelled miles out to sea?

Roger's stomach knotted; there was a hitch in his stride. What had he gotten himself into? It was one thing to sit safe at home and dream of doing great deeds. It was another to be faced with the reality of death on such a massive scale. But he had come here to die, hadn't he? He nerved himself and continued on.

Whatever happened was God's plan.

Chapter 15

Roger passed tents nestled among ordered rows of tree stumps where some kind of grove had once flourished. All the trees for as far as the eye could see had long since been cut down for firewood. Roger tried to picture pleasant, shady trees, wafting with the scent of some exotic fruit, where now lay this stinking, baking plain full of men and animals and transport, but he could not do it.

A low hill, covered with brightly colored pavilions, came into view. That must be what the wine vendor had called the Toron. The hill stood roughly opposite the large city tower with the green flag. There was a ditch around the hill, and guards at its bridge kept the common people away. As Roger drew closer, traffic in the street backed up, until, like everyone around him, he found it impossible to move.

From the Toron he heard mournful chanting in Latin. It was hard to see through the crowd, but a procession was winding its way down the main path from the hill. The procession was led by chanting priests, swinging silver censers from which drifted the sweet-smelling smoke of burning incense. Behind the priests Roger had intermittent glimpses of a wagon bearing a plain casket made of rich-looking wood. Behind this was another wagon with two smaller caskets laid side by side. The mourners were led by a smug fellow with a gold circlet around his brow. He looked around him as though expecting people to applaud his presence, but no one did. Behind him was a long line of richly dressed men and clerics, along with a few women. Some of the men and clerics talked among themselves, others walked solemnly, with their heads down, some praying with clasped hands. Around Roger, people craned their necks and stood on tiptoe to get a better look.

"What's going on?" Roger asked the man next to him.

The man, who reeked of rotting teeth, looked at him. "Ain't you heard? The queen of Jerusalem died—Sybelle. Her and both her kids. Fever took 'em just like that." He snapped dirt-grimed fingers. "Now we can be rid of that donkey's pizzle Guy. He's no claim to the crown with Sybelle gone."

Around him were growls of agreement, though Roger noticed that all the men didn't seem to share his companion's thoughts.

At last the funeral procession passed, and traffic began to move again. Roger eventually reached the black tents of the Bugars, short, swarthy men from Heaven only knew where, with hair as dark as their tents. As he had been instructed, he turned east at that point, away from the sea.

He trudged along for about half a mile, and another camp came into view on his right. A working party issued from the camp, picks and shovels over their shoulders, and Roger perked up because the men were speaking English. Roger peered into the camp and there, flapping in the sea breeze, was a banner bearing the red dragon of Trent.

Roger entered the camp, whose tents were laid out in orderly rows. This section of the camp must belong to the knights—the tents were of good quality, many with scalloped edges where the conical tops met the sides, some with designs painted on them. Banners were planted in the ground before most of the tents, identifying their owners. Roger saw a few men whom he assumed to be knights lazing about while squires and pages cleaned weapons or repaired gear. He stopped beside a boy oiling a leather gambeson that was almost as big as the boy was. "I want to join up," he told the boy. "Where do I go?"

The child gave him a superior look, then pointed. "Go past the break to the foot soldiers' camp. The foot captain's tent is at the head, with our banner outside. He'll take care of you."

As Roger started off, the boy called after him, "And don't come back to this side of the camp unless you're told to."

Roger passed a wide cross street, at the far side of which were five long lines of tents, neatly arranged. A single tent, obviously belonging to the captain, sat at the head of these lines, with a smaller version of the earl's dragon banner in front of it. As Roger approached this tent, a man came out, looking hot and uncomfortable in a wine-colored velvet surcoat. "Are you the foot captain?" Roger asked him.

The man was solid and rugged, with scars on his square-jawed face and a nose that had been broken more than once. "Why do you want to know?" he asked.

"I want to join," Roger told him.

The man eyed Roger up and down. "Well, you've got the build for it, I'll say that, and God knows, we need men. We've lost four to fever since we got here, with a couple more killed on the way. There's at least twice that many in the sick tent. Done any soldiering before?"

"No," Roger admitted.

If the man was disappointed, he didn't show it. "Neither had most of these fellows before this year. You from England?"

"That's right."

"How did you get here?"

Roger shrugged. "Walked most of the way. Worked the rest of the way on a ship."

"A hell of a journey," the man observed. "Why didn't you just join up back home, like everybody else?"

"I—I couldn't," Roger said, and he cleared his throat. "Legal problems."

The man nodded knowingly. "On the run?"

Roger made a noncommittal gesture, which the man took for affirmation. "Know how to use an axe?" the man said.

Roger smiled inwardly; he must have cut down the equivalent of a small forest while on punishment at the abbey. "I'm comfortable with one."

The man's eyes met Roger's. "Ever killed a man?"

Roger lowered his voice and hoped he sounded tough. "Not with an axe."

The man nodded again. "All right, you'll do. Pay's a shilling a month and whatever loot you can get your hands on, which so far has been nothing. Come in, and we'll put you on the books. I'm James of Claire. I'm a man at arms. That means you address me as 'Captain' and not 'my lord.'"

"Yes, Captain. I know the name Claire. Are you related to Baron Shortwood?"

"He's my uncle, once removed. If it wasn't for the 'once removed' part, I'd be a knight, with the horsemen—not on foot, leading a bunch of farm boys and criminals, but that's by the bye."

Roger followed James of Claire into the tent. The captain kicked a black-robed man who lay snoring on a cot. "Wake up, Father. You've a new victim to enroll."

The priest, a slender young man who looked like he'd rather be any place than where he was, sat up on the cot, rubbing his eyes. "New man, eh?" He tried to moisten alcohol-dried lips with an equally dry tongue, gave up, and drank from a bucket of water beside the cot. He rose and sat at a crudely made table, pulling another bucket filled with parchment rolls toward him.

"Put him with the axe men," James said. He thought for a moment and added, "Dirk's section."

The priest raised an eyebrow at that, but he fumbled in the bucket till he found the right parchment. He unrolled it and spread it on the table. He opened an ink bottle and tried unsuccessfully to stir the ink with a quill pen. "Ink dries up quick in this heat," he explained. He added a few drops of water to the ink, stirred, then repeated the process. When he was satisfied with the ink's consistency, he looked at Roger. "Name?"

"Roger."

"Roger." The priest wrote it down, forming the letters slowly, as though he wasn't used to writing. "Are you from Trentshire, Roger?"

"Yes, Father."

"Where?"

Roger hadn't expected that question. "Huntley," he said without thinking.

The priest looked up. "Really? I've been to Huntley. You don't look familiar."

"I worked at the abbey."

"Did you, now? Inside, I'm guessing, by the way you speak."

"That's right."

"All the times I've been to Huntley Abbey—funny I don't recognize you. Why'd you give up a cushy job like that to come here?"

Roger glanced at James, then said, "Same as everybody—to liberate Jerusalem."

The priest finished writing. "Amen, my son. Amen."

James took Roger to a supply tent. There he outfitted Roger with a heavy leather jack, sewn all over with small metal plates. Roger tried the jack on for fit, donning it awkwardly because it was stiff. It occurred to him that the jack had probably belonged to a man who was now dead, but he forced that thought from his mind. After the jack came an iron helmet with a round top and a flared rim. Spots on the helmet were starting to rust.

"You'll want to polish that," James told him.

James tossed Roger a battle axe from a neat stack of weapons in one part of the tent. Roger caught the axe and hefted it. It was a two-handed axe, not much different from the ones he'd used at the abbey save that the head was longer and there was a stabbing spike at the top of the haft. Roger was issued a circular wooden shield with a metal boss, along with a belt, a water bottle and mess kit, and two blankets. "There'll be bedding in the tent," James told him.

James led Roger down one of the camp streets to a large, plain circular tent, made of linen canvas with a conical top. "The rest of the company is filling in the ditch surrounding the city. That's a job we draw about once a week. There's another ditch surrounding the camp, and we work on that once a week, too—digging it out. The men will be back later. Dirk, the vintenar, will show you what you need to know. He's a bit rough, but do what he says and you'll be all right. Good luck."

James departed, leaving Roger alone in the large tent. The rotten-onion smell of unwashed men was heavy in the tent, even with the sides rolled up. Gear was stacked everywhere. The bedding consisted of straw-filled sacks placed on makeshift cots. Roger counted twenty of the cots; he found one that looked unused and lay his gear beside it. He drank putrid water from a bucket, then he rested his head on his pack and, wondering what would happen next, he dozed off in the heat.

Chapter 16

The sound of the company returning awoke him. It must have been well past nones, judging by the sun. Roger rose as the men filed into the tent, sweat-glistened skin streaked with dirt, cursing, wearing only their braies, most of them. "God's bunions, but I hate that ditch," said a straw-hatted fellow with a salt-and-pepper beard. The backs of his hands were covered with burn scars. "We fill it in by day, and the Goat Fuckers dig it out again by night. What's the point?"

"We have to get it filled in for the attack," explained a black-bearded giant. "The attackers can't do anything if the ditch ain't—"

Somebody noticed Roger. "Here—what's this?"

They all stopped and stared at him. A sparsely bearded youth who couldn't have been more than fifteen stuck out his hand and looked like he was about to step forward and welcome Roger to the unit, then a last figure darkened the tent's entrance and entered.

This fellow was huge, with narrow-set eyes, an unusually heavy jaw, and blond hair cropped so short that Roger could see the flea bites on his skull. He studied Roger for a moment. "Who are you?" he said. His thick accent marked him as a Brabanter, a mercenary most likely.

"I'm called Roger,"

"Roger, eh?" said the Brabanter. "Well, *Roger*, what are you doing in our tent—looking for something to steal?" He laughed without humor.

Roger curbed his irritation. How could he be looking for something to steal if he was taking a nap? "I joined the company. I'm assigned to this section."

"Are you now?" said the Brabanter. "Well, lucky us."

One of the men—a square-headed fellow who seemed to lack eyebrows—laughed. The Brabanter went on. "You talk like a sissy, Roger. Where did you get that accent?"

Roger knew his speech was far more refined than that of the common soldiers. The men had all stopped what they were doing and were looking at him. He shrugged. "I worked at a monastery."

"A monastery!" The word seemed to set the Brabanter off. His visage darkened; his eyes narrowed. "A monastery?" He peered at Roger closely, his blue eyes radiating contempt now, where before there had only been a general hostility. "If you worked at a monastery, you must be queer. Are you a queer, Roger?"

Again, Roger contained himself. He was the new man, and he knew he'd be subjected to some harassment before he was accepted. Patiently, he said, "No, I'm not—"

"I bet you like it in the ass, don't you, Roger?"

Roger grit his teeth. "I said, I'm not a—"

Dirk pushed Roger. "Huh? Queer?"

"Come on, Dirk," said the older fellow, taking off his straw hat and throwing himself on his cot. "It's too hot for this."

"Shut up," Dirk told the man. Dirk glared at Roger. "We don't want queers in this section. Get out."

Roger thought Dirk was joking, so he said nothing.

Dirk picked up Roger's gear and threw it across the tent, toward the entrance. "I said, get out."

This was no joke. There was total silence in the tent. Roger saw the looks on the other men's faces, and he guessed that a lot of them had been subjected to similar treatment at one time or other. He sensed that most of the men felt for him, just as he also sensed that none of them was going to go against Dirk. He also knew that he couldn't leave. What was he going to do, run and cry to James of Claire? He'd never be accepted as a soldier then. "I can't do that," he said quietly.

"That wasn't a question, *Roger*," Dirk pronounced the word "Roger" in a mock-lisping voice. "It was an order."

"All right, then, *Dirk*. I *won't* do it."

Dirk's eyes widened and he moved closer. Roger was big, but Dirk loomed over him. Then Dirk grinned, as though he'd just had a great idea, and his voice turned friendly. "You want to stay? Oh, all right, then, you can stay. I have a job for you."

Roger relaxed a bit. Maybe the worst was over. *That wasn't so bad.* Dirk went on. "I'm going to make you my whore and stick my prick up your ass every night. We don't have any women here, so you can be mine."

Dirk looked around the tent. The square-headed fellow was grinning. The other men looked worried, or resigned. To Roger, Dirk said, "If you want to be in this section, that's what it's going to take. Otherwise, get out."

Roger was tempted to go. He was tempted to skulk out of the tent. It was a big army; there were plenty of other units he could join. But some perverse pride, some stubbornness, made him decide to stay here. "I'm not leaving."

"Good!" Dirk exclaimed. "We'll start now." He held up his index finger. "But first, first you better suck me, you know, and make me hard. It's been a long day."

The other men edged away. A red-haired fellow with a plaited beard said, "Dirk—" but Dirk glared so hard at him, the man stepped back. Dirk's square-headed friend punched the man's shoulder with the flat of his hand.

Dirk unlaced the top of his breeches. "On your knees, *Roger*. On your knees and suck me. When it's hard, turn around and bend over."

Roger couldn't believe this was happening. "You're kidding," he said.

"Do I look like I'm kidding!" Dirk shouted. "Get on your knees!"

Men from the other sections heard the shouting and gathered outside, peering in the tent's rolled-up sides. Everyone waited to see what Roger would do. At last, Roger's shoulders slumped and he lowered his head in shame. He positioned his feet as though he was getting ready to kneel and do Dirk's bidding, then he straightened and punched Dirk in the face as hard as he could, once with each hand.

To Roger's amazement, Dirk staggered backwards but did not go down. Before Roger could hit him again, Dirk slammed a big fist into Roger's eye, knocking him onto his back. Roger was afraid the bone around his eye had been broken. Dirk aimed a kick at Roger's head, but Roger dodged it. He scrambled to his feet and charged the big man, burying his shoulder in Dirk's gut and wrapping his arms around him. He couldn't get him down, though. The two of them wrestled around the tent, knocking things over. The other men were yelling, so were men from the other tents, more of whom were running over to watch. Dirk locked his fists behind Roger's back and squeezed. Roger felt his ribs constrict; he couldn't breathe. Dirk squeezed harder, grunting with the effort, his fetid breath in Roger's face. A few more seconds of this, and Roger's spine would crack like a piece of dry wood. Roger tried to gouge Dirk's eye, but Dirk avoided him. With his last breath, Roger smashed the heel of his hand into Dirk's nose, breaking it. Roaring, Dirk picked Roger off the ground and slammed him onto his back, knocking the air from him.

Roger saw stars. He tried to get his breath but couldn't. Dirk straddled him, blood gushing from his nose. Dirk raised a huge fist and poised it, aiming, preparing to drive the fist into Roger's face. That half-second saved Roger's life. Roger felt, rather than saw, a helmet on the ground nearby. As Dirk drove his fist down with all his might, Roger grabbed the helmet and raised it with both hands to block the blow. The force of the blow drove the heavy helmet hard into Roger's face. As it did, Roger felt the bones in Dirk's hand shatter. Dirk howled with pain. He fell off Roger, holding his wrist. Roger got up and shoved Dirk onto his back. He drew his dagger, knelt, and held the point to the big man's throat.

Dirk's square-headed friend moved forward with a knife, but the bearded giant gripped his arm. "No," he said.

Beneath Roger, Dirk gurgled with pain; blood from his

broken nose covered the lower part of his face.

"Enjoy Hell," Roger told him.

Roger gripped the knife hilt and breathed deep, ready to plunge the knife into Dirk's throat. He felt himself overcome by that same rage, that same willingness to kill—the *wanting* to kill—that he had felt with Auberie.

He held that pose a second, then relaxed, disgusted with himself—and a bit frightened. His years of religious training had vanished as though they had never existed. Abbot Raymond would have been disappointed in him. Maybe Auberie had been right, maybe Roger had never deserved to be at Huntley in the first place.

Roger removed the knife from Dirk's throat and rose. Dirk lay on the ground, moaning and sobbing with pain. The tent and its surroundings had gone quiet. Roger's eye throbbed; he could barely see out of it. Blood ran over his face from a gouge in his forehead where the helmet had struck it. He turned to find James of Claire standing in the tent entrance, tapping the fingers of one hand against his leg.

All eyes were on James, who stepped forward. To Roger he said, "I put you in this section because I thought you would be able to handle Dirk's 'leadership.' I didn't anticipate you costing me one of my best soldiers."

From the floor Dirk said, "He struck me first, Cap'n. I have witnesses. You know the rules."

"Shut up," James told him. "I've warned you about bullying the men. No doubt you got what you deserved."

Roger was still breathing heavily. "Rules? What's he talking about?"

James said, "In accordance with rules laid down for this army by King Richard, I am to have your right hand cut off for striking another soldier."

Roger stiffened and went cold. He saw Dirk grinning through his pain and the blood on his face.

"But I'm not going to do that," James told Roger. He paused, then looked around, raising his voice so the men outside the tent could hear. "I'm not going to do it because I'm going to need every man I can get." He paused dramatically. "You people like to fight? Good. Get yourselves ready, then, because I've got a real fight for you. The council of barons has given Earl Geoffrey the honor of leading the coming attack on the city."

Chapter 17

Geoffrey of Badford, earl of Trent, bade his mistress goodbye and set off to attend the council of barons.

Tonight's council had been called to discuss the coming attack on the city. Geoffrey had asked to lead the attack, not because he wanted to, but because he was fearful of what his wife, Bonjute, would say if she found out—and she *would* find out—that he hadn't. Tonight the barons were going to finalize the plans, if indeed this group could finalize anything. They argued like Badford fishwives on market day.

Geoffrey emerged from his pavilion on the Toron and wrapped his cloak about him. It was well past Lammas, the days were still hot but the nights were growing cold. Geoffrey set off for Balian of Ibelin's pavilion, where the council would be held. He heard the soothing crash of waves on the beach, underlying the raucous noise of the camp. He saw the long breakers curling silver in the moonlight, smelled the salty tang of the sea. Below him on all sides stretched the lights of the camp, and in the hills, Saladin's campfires sparkled, so that the land seemed to be covered with fireflies. There were lights in the city, as well, making it glow behind its walls. It was beautiful, until you remembered the grim reality of it.

As Geoffrey watched, a ball of fire flared upward in the darkness, poised above the city, then descended. Another followed. Then another. The mangonels were shooting bundles of flaming rushes into the city, hoping to start fires. Even if the city didn't burn, the fires would keep the defenders awake and sap their strength.

Geoffrey gazed down the walls, past a large tower—the Accursed Tower, it was called—to St. Martin's Gate. In a few days, he would be fighting on the walls above that gate. If he was successful, his reputation would shine throughout Christendom. If he failed—well, it did no good thinking about that.

❖ ❖ ❖

Geoffrey did not want to be here. He had been prepared to send his brother Hugo instead—Hugo thirsted for renown and lands of his own—but Bonjute had opposed that idea.

"You have to go yourself," she had railed at Geoffrey, "can't you see that? You're thirty-nine, and you've never performed a single deed of note. If you're to be justiciar of England, you need to make a name for yourself on this crusade."

Geoffrey protested. "I don't want to be justiciar, you know that. I—"

"I don't care what you want! I want it and that's what you'll be. You want to laze about like the lowest country knight, hunting and fishing and taking care of your estates. Well, that's not going to happen."

They had been in the privacy of the constable's chambers at Wilton Castle, where they had been staying at the time. Chill autumn rain pattered through the small, narrow windows. The servants had been sent away.

Geoffrey grit his teeth while Bonjute refilled her wine goblet. Bonjute was tall and slender. Her face was not beautiful, but it was interesting—all planes and angles, framed by blonde hair. She had strong, intelligent eyes and thin lips.

Patiently, Geoffrey said, "I enjoy life in the country, it's true. I enjoy managing my estates. And it's not lazing about, it's hard work—God knows there's enough of them."

"And most of those estates you got through me," Bonjute shot back. "Don't forget that."

"How could I forget? You remind me of it every day." Geoffrey's family came from Normandy, near Thaon, where they had once held extensive lands. Ironically, his great-grandfather Henry, the first earl of Trent, had lost most of those lands because he had been too busy in Wales and England, helping the king, to defend them.

Bonjute took a deep drink of wine. "You may think it's fun playing a jumped-up villein, but I'm tired of being stuck in an endless series of English mud holes in the middle of God knows where, listening to these savages jabber in what they seem to think is a language. I want to be at Court. I want to be part of real life, especially now that we have a new king. Henry turned into a stick-in-the-mud after he got rid of Queen Eleanor. No wonder Richard rebelled against him."

"I supported Henry," Geoffrey reminded her stiffly.

"Of course you did, you imbecile, when anyone with two eyes could have seen that Richard was going to win. You've heard how vengeful Richard is, why did you have to get on his bad side?"

"I was one of the king's chief barons. It was my duty to—"

She threw her cup at him. He dodged it. "Your duty is to me! To your family! It's what *we* want that counts, not some doddering old king who couldn't keep from soiling his underclothes."

Geoffrey glared at her.

She wagged a finger at him. "You'll go on that crusade and you'll be the hero of it, and if you're not, don't bother coming back."

Before Geoffrey could say anything, she went on. "Hire a chronicler to record your deeds, too, so that everyone knows the glorious things you did. Call it *The Song of Geoffrey of Trent and Saladin*—something important sounding like that."

Geoffrey struggled to keep his temper. "And if I don't do any glorious deeds?"

"Make them up! That's what the chronicler is for. Nobody remembers what really happened. It's what you tell them that happened that counts. If it's on parchment, people believe it."

"Where do I find a chronicler?"

"Must I do everything for you? You figure it out." She threw another goblet at him and left the chamber.

❖ ❖ ❖

As it happened, the chronicler had almost literally fallen into Geoffrey's lap, as had his current mistress, of whom he was becoming inordinately fond. Geoffrey had hoped the crusade would be short, but King Richard wasn't here yet, nor was Philip of France. Meanwhile, this siege was in its second year, men died by the hundreds from disease, and winter was coming on.

Geoffrey knew that Bonjute longed for the glamor, the wealth, and the great names of Court. She had been raised in that world. She liked the intrigue and backbiting; she didn't care about breeding cattle or getting the hay in on time, or finding better ways to grow wheat and barley. She liked minstrels and troubadors, not rustics playing homemade instruments for their betters. But she couldn't have any of what she wanted unless Geoffrey was at Court, which was why she had been badgering him for years about becoming part of the king's inner circle. As earl of Trent, he was the king's hereditary cup bearer, but that office required him to be present only on special occasions. The rest of the time he did as he pleased, which was what he liked.

Justiciar was the most powerful office in the king's employ, and powerful men, both lay and cleric, angled for it. Bonjute didn't think about it from Geoffrey's point of view, though— probably because she didn't care. Being justiciar meant trailing the king from place to place, like a lapdog. It meant endless diddling with numbers, which Geoffrey hated, and placating barons stuffed with their own self-importance, which he hated even more. And if things in the kingdom went bad, which they frequently did, like as not the justiciar took the blame and there was the chance of having his head lopped off. Geoffrey suspected, though he did not know for certain, that Bonjute was not above lifting her skirts to provide him advancement. Well, good luck to the fellow, whoever he might be. Bonjute was a cold fish in bed—for Geoffrey, anyway. For all he knew, she cavorted like a Westminster whore for other men, and he could not help but smile at that unlikely image.

He reached Balian's green-and gold-striped pavilion, the largest and most richly furnished in the camp. Inside, the pavilion glittered as the jewels of the assembled nobles and clergy reflected the light of the torches. There were over a hundred men packed into the pavilion, sweating in furs and velvet robes, most of them, though the native barons wore loose garments of cotton and silk. Servants moved back and forth with wine and food.

A deeply tanned fellow, dressed like a Turk, with oiled dark hair, approached Geoffrey, hand extended. White teeth flashed in the man's dark face; a gold ring hung from his left earlobe. "Geoffrey."

Geoffrey took the man's hand. "Lord Balian." This was Balian of Ibelin, greatest knight of Outremer. It was Balian who had led the rearguard at Hattin, Balian who had held Jerusalem against Saladin's army for a fortnight with a only handful of footmen and two men at arms. Why hadn't the barons of Outremer made Balian king when they'd had the chance and been done with it, Geoffrey thought. Then this damned crusade would never have happened. But if they'd done that, they wouldn't have anything to argue about.

With Balian was James of Avesnes, the tall, strapping Flemish magnate, with long curly hair and a slightly bulbous nose. James slapped Geoffrey's back heartily. "Ready for the big day, Geoffrey?"

"Ready enough," Geoffrey said. He'd fought in a hundred

actions, large and small, but he'd never done anything like this coming attack. Part of him was nervous about the challenge, while another part viewed it with detachment, like it was an experiment to be carried out.

James of Avesnes went on. "Please God you'll be successful. I'm sick of this siege."

"As am I," Geoffrey agreed, "and I've only been here a few weeks."

Balian and James, both of whom had been here for over a year, laughed at that, and Balian said, "Have you inspected the belfry?"

"Yes," Geoffrey replied. "It should serve. Those hides have been soaking long enough to repel any Greek Fire the Turbans throw at us—at least until we get control of the gate."

Rubbing his hands together in anticipation, James said, "And once you open the gate, the city is ours."

Geoffrey nodded. "With any luck, Richard and Philip will get here soon after that. Then it's a quick march down the coast, take Jerusalem, and we can be on our way home by Easter."

"Amen," James added earnestly.

Balian looked doubtful, but before he could say anything, a flourish of trumpets announced the arrival of the Papal legate, Ubaldo. As Balian excused himself and moved off to greet Ubaldo, Geoffrey and James of Avesnes took goblets of wine. James pawed two meat pies from a servant, as well, and crammed them into his mouth.

At that moment Count Henry of Champagne stepped into the great circle of nobles, motioning for silence. As the highest-ranking lord in camp so far, 25-year-old Henry had been elected commander-in-chief by the barons.

Gradually the throng quieted, though there was a laugh when a last voice called for more wine. Henry was a good-looking fellow, a proven soldier who seemed nervous at having been tasked to lead such a large and fractious group in the place of Kings Richard and Philip. He gazed around the tight-packed circle and cleared his throat. "This council has been called so that we may discuss plans for the upcoming attack on the city," he began. Then he added, "Because of the untimely death of Queen Sybelle, the Pope's representative—" he inclined his head toward the portly Ubaldo—"believes we should take this opportunity to clarify the succession to the throne of Jerusalem, as well."

James of Avesnes moaned. "God's drawers, did he have to bring that up?"

"There's nothing to clarify," Guy of Lusignan told Count Henry smugly. "I am king of Jerusalem. The barons of this land swore an oath to me."

"We swore our oath to Queen Sybelle," Balian of Ibelin corrected, "not to you. Sybelle is dead—her daughter Isabelle is queen now."

Guy glared at Balian. Guy was good-looking in the way that ladies liked and men despised. He was never seen without the gold circlet on his head. Geoffrey wondered if he slept with it. Guy said, "You are wrong. By French law, I retain the crown."

"In case you hadn't noticed, we're not *in* France," a deep voice replied. The speaker, Conrad of Montferrat, was big, built like a butcher's block. His square head was shaven clean of all hair save for his thick, dark brows. He wore a biretta of black silk and a tunic of bright yellow sendal. His deep-set eyes regarded Guy contemptuously. "This country has different laws. How dare you stand there and pretend a right to the crown? You lost the kingdom *and* the True Cross. Had you any honor, you would have skulked away from this land long since."

"I am king, and I shall remain king," Guy said haughtily, "and there is nothing you or anyone else can do about it."

"Of course we can," Conrad said. Even when his voice was modulated, he sounded threatening. "I shall marry Queen Isabelle, and I shall become king. I can beat Saladin—every man in this room knows that. Saladin knows it, as well. I've done it once, and I'll do it again."

There were shouts of approval, loudest from the Syrian barons, most of whom had lost all their possessions because of Guy's fecklessness.

"Queen Isabelle is already married," Guy pointed out, as though he were talking to a child.

Conrad was unfazed. "I propose to have that marriage annulled."

The pavilion fell silent for a moment, then erupted in more shouting. "I'm sick of this damned arguing," Geoffrey told James of Avesnes. "I'm going back to my tent." In truth, he longed for the arms of his mistress.

James was eating yet another meat pie—God only knew what the meat was. Shoving crumbs into his mouth, he said, "What about the plans for the attack?"

Geoffrey spoke above the noise. "It will be dawn before they get around to that. I know my part of the plan and I'll carry it out. Let the rest of these fools do as they please." Bonjute would chide him for this attitude, but he didn't care.

He turned away, but before he could take a step, something was tossed into the circle of barons.

The object bounced once, rolled, and came to a stop. There were gasps all around, and men drew back, the horror on their faces highlighted by the light cast from the torches.

The object was a human head.

Chapter 18

The head lay there, drained of blood, its sightless eyes framed by black hair and a beard streaked with gray.

A tall, rangy man with a patch over his left eye swaggered into the circle. Unlike the finely dressed lords around him, this man wore dust-covered mail with the coif pushed back, revealing a thinning hair and a grizzled beard. His old, mended surcoat had no design upon it. Both mail and surcoat were spotted with dried blood.

Geoffrey glanced questioningly at James of Avesnes. In a low voice, James said, "That's Henry, lord of Deraa—Henry the Falcon, they call him. Has a castle in the desert where he raids Saracen caravans and supply trains. He was one of the few to escape from Hattin. Saladin's put a price of ten thousand dinars on his head."

"Good evening," the newcomer said, beaming at the council and looking hugely pleased with himself. "I trust you all are well." He indicated the head. "Allow me to introduce my good friend Mahmoud ibn al-Athir, emir of Al Qarya."

"The emir of Al Qarya?" said Stephen of Sancerre, a gruff French lord of middle age. "I've heard of him. He was worth a fortune. You should have ransomed him."

"Funny, he said the same thing when he tried to surrender. Just before I took his head."

"Surrender?" cried the archbishop of Canterbury in his stentorian voice. The purple-clad archbishop was a stumpy old coot who seemed to have more hair in his nose than he did on his head. In King Richard's absence he was in charge of the English forces. "You're a Christian, sir. You should have—"

Henry the Falcon fixed Baldwin with his good eye. "You're not from this country, your grace. If you were, you'd know that

109

a few years back, Mahmoud here raided a Christian village in Galilee. He killed the men. The women and children gathered in the church for safety. Mahmoud burned them alive. Had I the time, I would have returned the favor and roasted the bastard over an open pit, but more Saracens were coming, so I had to be satisfied with taking his head."

Baldwin harrumphed weakly, but said no more.

The one-eyed man kicked the head, which rolled across the tent floor and ended up at Guy of Lusignan's feet.

Guy looked at the head with disgust. "I thought we'd seen the last of you," he told Henry. "What brings you out of your rat hole?"

"I hear you're attacking the city in four days' time and I came to join the fun. Not that I care a fig about your siege, but I have a particular—shall we say, *acquaintance*—who commands the city garrison. Qaymaz—you may remember him. I've come to do to him what I did to Mahmoud. Only I intend to take my time with Qaymaz."

"How did you get here?" Balian asked him. Balian and Henry were friends, and Balian was glad to see him.

"Through the southern end of the Saracen lines, near the Belus. Had to fight our way through at the end—that's where we ran into Mahmoud."

Young Henry of Champagne gave a concerned frown. "How do you know the day of the attack? It's supposed to be a secret."

The one-eyed man smiled. "My dear count, the entire Saracen army knows the day of the attack. The lowliest camel driver in Beersheba knows it. Mahmoud here knew it, as well."

Guy of Lusignan said, "That's preposterous. How—"

"How do you think?" Henry said.

Smoothly, Conrad of Montferrat said, "What the noble lord of Deraa means is that we have a spy in our midst."

A murmur ran through the assembly. The count of Champagne was stunned. "A spy? But that's not possible."

"Anything's possible if you spread enough money around,"

Henry said. Then his mien turned grim. "Saladin's bringing up reinforcements, lots of them. He'll attack this camp at the same time as we attack the city. If he doesn't overrun us, he'll at least keep us from using our entire strength against the city walls."

Men looked at each other. There were mutters and oaths. "Not again," growled Stephen of Sancerre, and men nodded in agreement with him.

Then Henry brightened. "But all is not lost. Saladin may know the day of the attack, but he doesn't know the exact place along the wall where we shall strike, so we may yet surprise him."

Guy of Lusignan curled his upper lip. "It's nice of you and your band of cutthroats to show up now that there's going to be some actual fighting. You leave us here to do all the hard work of the siege while you sit out in the desert free as you please."

The one-eyed knight stared at Guy. "Siege? You dunderhead, you've been here a year and a half, and what have you accomplished? Besides all the men who have been killed in battle, you've lost the equivalent of two entire armies to disease, and for what? The object of this war is to recapture Jerusalem. My remaining eye may be getting old, but I'm pretty sure that's not Jerusalem over there."

"We need Acre," Guy of Lusignan told him.

"*You* may need it," Henry replied, "the rest of us don't. Capture Jerusalem, and Acre will fall soon enough. If you think I'm going to camp in front of this miserable city and watch my men die from disease to bolster your pitiful reputation, you're insane. Anyone who follows a buffoon like you deserves what he gets."

Geoffrey's hand went to his dagger.

"Try it," Henry told him, his voice suddenly cold.

Geoffrey did not remove his hand from the dagger, but he did not draw it, either.

"Enough!" said Balian of Ibelin, stepping between the two. "No violence here, gentlemen, upon my word."

111

Guy relaxed his grip on the dagger. "You'll rue your words one day, Lord Henry."

Henry ignored him and turned to the count of Champagne. "Who leads the attack?"

Before the count could speak, Geoffrey said, "I do." He inclined his head to the one-eyed knight. "Geoffrey of Badford, earl of Trent."

The Falcon bowed in return. "Henry, lord of Deraa. My pleasure, Lord Geoffrey. I realize this is an imposition, especially as we've just met, but might I beg a great indulgence of you? Let me and my men join you in the attack."

Geoffrey hesitated. He liked the cut of this one-eyed fellow, but being chosen to lead the attack was a great honor. By sharing that honor with another, Geoffrey might seem a lesser man, even a coward. Geoffrey pictured Bonjute rolling her eyes and throwing another cup at him.

Henry the Falcon must have sensed what Geoffrey was thinking because he added, "You will be in full command. I assure you I seek none of your glory. I only wish to get into the city and make sure that no one finds Qaymaz before I do."

Geoffrey glanced at Balian of Ibelin, who gave a slight nod of the head, as though confirming Geoffrey's opinion of the one-eyed knight.

"Very well," Geoffrey told Henry. He held out a hand, and the two men shook. Geoffrey went on. "We begin training tomorrow."

"Training?" Henry said in surprise.

Geoffrey had been afraid of this. Firmly, he said, "Yes. I want the men to practice what they're going to be doing."

To Geoffrey's relief, Henry's lips widened in smile. "Lord Geoffrey, I think we shall get along well together."

"This attack must be successful, Geoffrey," said the archbishop of Canterbury pompously, as though to remind Geoffrey who was in command of the English army—and to absolve himself of any responsibility if the attack failed.

The count of Champagne glanced with distaste at the

archbishop, then added, "Lord Geoffrey knows what's at stake. We can't abandon the siege. The land route to Tyre is blocked by Saladin, and it would be impossible to withdraw so many men by sea before the winter rains come. We need to be inside the city before that. We won't be able to move a belfry afterward, because of the mud. Mining operations will cease, as well. We'll be forced to spend another winter on this dismal plain until we starve the Saracens out."

"Succeed?" said Henry the Falcon. "Why, of course we'll succeed, young fellow." He took off his gauntlets and used them to beat dust from his surcoat. "Wine!" he bellowed. "Wine here! God's stones, but I've thirst enough for five men."

Goblets were brought on a tray. Henry took one and drained it at a gulp, wine spilling down his chin and dusty beard. He took another and did the same thing. Geoffrey and Balian shared an amused glance and took cups for themselves, while James of Avesnes looked around for more meat pies. Behind them, the nobles were arguing about whose men should defend the camp and whose should attack the city after Geoffrey's.

One of Balian's servants came up. "That head, my lord. What should we do with it?"

"Give it to the dogs," Henry the Falcon told him.

So they did.

Chapter 19

Egwulf scratched his thick beard. "Big, ain't it?"

Roger angled his good eye sideways to look up at the belfry. His left eye was still swollen shut, but he no longer thought the bone was broken. There was a huge bruise on his forehead from where the helmet hit him, and it hurt like the very Devil, but the cut hadn't been bad enough to require stitches, so he had a bandage wrapped around his head.

Grizzled Offa crossed himself. "And me afraid o' heights." Offa, whom everyone called Grandad, was in his mid-thirties. He was a charcoal burner from Dunham Forest—which accounted for the scars on his hands and arms—who had joined the crusade to get away from his nagging wife. His straw hat had been replaced by a rounded helmet like Roger's. All the men wore full equipment.

The earl's footmen had been ordered to assemble at the belfry, along with the men belonging to a native baron named Henry of Deraa. They hadn't marched over in any kind of order, but had drifted in twos and threes.

Dirk was there, his shattered hand heavily wrapped, but he was only an observer. Unferth, a herdsman from Silverhill, had been named vintenar in his place. The men were glad to get away from Dirk's discipline, though they were circumspect about saying it, lest Dirk return to duty. Almost all of them had suffered at his hands, even the giant Egwulf. "First day I was in camp, he just walked up to me and punched me in the face," Egwulf had told Roger. "'Fore I had my wits about me, he'd beat me half senseless. Said that was just the beginning if I didn't do what I was told." Plaintively, he added, "It ain't like I meant to cause him no trouble."

Of the section, Offa and Egwulf, along with a youngster

named Cole—the one with the sparse beard—had accepted Roger the most readily. The other men were more stand-offish. They might have liked what Roger had done to Dirk, but Roger had not shared the long journey here from Trentshire with them. He wasn't truly one of them yet.

The belfry around which they were gathered was a tower on wheels. Access to its top platform was by three levels of ladders, with two ladders on each level. The belfry was roofed with copper, and there was a ramp, secured by chains, which would be let down on the city walls. The belfry had taken months to build. The engineers had to guess the height of the city walls, then added a few extra feet for good measure. Better the ramp be too high than too short. The ramp was lowered now, and a half-dozen ropes dangled from its edge to the ground. The area around the belfry was littered with scraps of wood, broken tools, old cook fires of workmen and engineers. The smell of new-sawn wood filled the warm air.

Three other belfries had been sent against Acre during the course of the siege. The city's defenders had burned all of them with Greek Fire before they had reached the city walls. This one would be covered by ox hides which were presently soaking in pits filled with vinegar and urine. The hides would be attached to the belfry at the last moment, and were supposed to resist the Greek Fire long enough for the army to get a foothold on the city walls.

Black John, or Blackie, a raffish fellow with bushy eyebrows, said, "Why'd they drag us out here? It's three days to the attack yet."

"Maybe they just want us to have a look at it," replied his friend, a tall, lean fellow whom everyone called Slowfoot. The letter "B" was branded prominently on Slowfoot's left cheek.

"You great lump, they wouldn't have made us wear full equipment just to look at it," Deaf Martin told him. Martin wasn't really deaf; they called him that because he'd lost most of his right ear when he'd been kicked by a mule. Before joining the crusade, he'd been a tanner's apprentice in Badford.

While they waited, Roger tested the feel of his axe. Just before they left camp, he had gotten a saw and taken several inches off the weapon's haft. He had oiled the axe's handle so that the wood wouldn't dry out and split in this heat, then wrapped cord around the lower part of the handle to improve the grip. The axe's weight and balance felt better now, and Roger hung the weapon through a loop in his belt. In the arms tent, he had found a pair of gloves with mail rings sewn on the backs of the fingers and palm, to ward off glancing blows. The gloves were in his belt, as well.

Deaf Martin pointed toward the distant beach. "More ships leaving."

Two vessels, a cog and a galley, were standing out from the beach. The lead ship, the cog, had already pointed its bows north. "Been putting out like that for a week or more now," Offa said. "Not many new ones coming in, neither."

Indeed, where only days earlier ships had stretched as far as the eye could see, open water was becoming more prevalent. The beach, which had been jammed with stores, was giving way to stretches of litter-strewn sand.

Unferth, the new vintenar, added, "They say the sailors are worried about the weather."

"Why?" said Egwulf. "You couldn't ask for better weather. There's hardly a cloud in the sky."

"Who knows why sailors do things?" Offa said. "They have to be daft just to be sailors."

"Hey—*I* was a sailor," Roger reminded him.

"Proves my point," Offa said.

While the crusaders besieged Acre, Saladin besieged the crusaders, whose only means of reinforcement and supply was by sea. On both sides, the crusader camp was protected by a ditch and a palisade. The burned and broken hulks of the three belfries, along with smashed mangonels, rams, and other instruments of war lay before the city walls like dead beetles. The plain between the crusader camp and Saladin's camp in the hills glistened white from the bones of the men and animals that had been killed there in the last year and a half. Buzzards swooped overhead. There was always employment for buzzards at Acre.

Long Tom, a good-natured beekeeper from the southern part of the shire, slapped his cheek. "Ow! Bloody flies!" He showed the smashed remains to his comrades, then flicked them away. "Big as a sparrow, that one. I come here 'cause I was tired of being stung by bees. Now I'm being stung by flies. Damn if I don't think the bees was better."

"Might be eatin' them flies soon," Offa said, "if we don't get more supplies."

"Might be?" Slowfoot said. "What do you think Matthew's been putting in the stew the last month?"

The big, biting flies were everywhere—in the food, in the tents, swarming over the kitchens and merchants' stalls. They clogged men's mouths, ears, noses. There were mosquitoes, too; every man's skin was lumpy from their bites. They were not as bad around the English camp as they were toward the Belus marshes, where the Frisians and Pisans, who held that part of the line, were said to be dying by the hundreds.

"Here comes the earl!" cried James of Claire. James wore a mail hauberk and a white surcoat with a red cross on the shoulder. "Line up!"

"Line up!" cried the vintenars.

"Move! Move!" said Unferth, shoving the men into order.

The footmen lined up—spearmen, axe men, archers. The knights and men at arms formed a loose group, out of sorts because they had been forced to don armor but had been told to leave their horses in camp. They didn't like being on foot. Henry of Deraa's men—who looked more like bandits than they did like soldiers—formed in a well-ordered group by themselves. Most of the knights wore surcoats over their armor to shield the mail's iron rings from the fiery Eastern sun. Henry's knights wore the Eastern headdress, the *keffiyah*, over their helms or mail coifs, as well, though the English knights had so far eschewed that as being too foreign. The footmen sweated under heavy jacks, and a lot of them—who didn't care about looking foreign—had devised cloth covers for their helmets, which otherwise would have turned into small ovens in the sun, cooking their brains.

The earl of Trent rode toward the men, along with his hulking brother Hugo, their squires, flag bearers, and heralds. Beside the earl was a rugged-looking knight with a patch over his left eye. Over his hauberk the earl wore a surcoat with the red dragon; the one-eyed knight's dirty surcoat had no design. The earl wore a polished flat helm over his mail coif. The one-eyed knight had an old-fashioned conical helm with a broad nosepiece riveted to it; the long tail of his keffiyah flapped as it caught the breeze.

"Who's the one-eyed cove?" said Deaf Martin.

"Dunno," Offa said. "Looks mean, though."

"Must be that Henry of Deraa we been hearing about," said Ralph the Red. Ralph was a swaggering fellow with a big red beard brushed into a fork and tied at the ends with strips of faded green ribbon given to him by a whore in England.

The earl and his party reined in. The earl's grey destrier pranced and pawed restlessly. The earl curbed him and addressed his men. "Today we're going to practice going up in the tower."

There was a lot of complaining, mostly from the knights, who thought this sort of exercise beneath them. "Why?" they said. "What for?"

"Because I said so!" the earl snapped. "God willing, I intend to take this city. Success may well depend on how quickly we get onto the walls, and I don't intend to fail because some fool couldn't get up the ladder properly."

The earl pointed toward the city. "We're going to capture St. Martin's Gate, between St James's Tower and the Green Tower."

The men looked. St. Martin's Gate was on the city's northwest side. St. James's Tower, to its left, was so named because the Apostle James had once been imprisoned there.

The Green Tower, on the gate's right, got its name because the copper on its roof had tarnished and turned green.

The earl went on. "There are two sets of ladders in the tower. There will be two columns. The left-hand column will be led by my me and my brother Hugo." The heavy-faced Hugo glowered, and the earl went on. "We will turn left on the wall and capture St. James's Tower. The right-hand column will be led by the lord of Deraa." He nodded toward the one-eyed knight. "They will turn right and capture the Green Tower. Access to the bottom is through the towers. We will fight our way down the towers, then converge at the bottom and open the gate. When we open the gate, the rest of the army will pass through and the city will be ours."

Some of the men cheered. The earl went on. "The archbishop of Canterbury's men will follow us. If help is needed to defend the two towers from counterattacks along the wall, a portion of the archbishop's men will be diverted there. The rest will follow us to hold the gate. Speed will be the key, men. We need to open that gate and hold it before the Turks can organize a counterattack. That's why we're having this practice."

The men were formed up. The knights would go first, followed by the men at arms. The earl personally placed the knights, lining them in order of rank. Captains and vintenars placed the footmen. The axe men would go after the men at arms. The spearmen would go after the axe men; their spears would be hard to use in the cramped confines of the walls but they would form a good line of defense around the gate. The archers were split between the right and left columns; they would go last, to help defend the towers and to rain arrows on any counterattack at the gate.

A few of the spearmen were seconded to the axe company to take the place of dead, sick, or injured men, like Dirk. Dirk had begged James of Claire to let him go, but James said no. Now Dirk watched from the side, glowering at Roger.

"Made yourself a friend for life there," Deaf Martin told

119

Roger. He lowered his voice. "By the bye, you ain't really queer, are you?"

"No!" Roger said.

The earl went on. "This is the order in which you ascend the ladders. ("What's 'ascend' mean?" said Deaf Martin. "S-h-h," said Roger.) You will not pass the man in front of you unless he is dead. You will not change ladders. Look at the man in front of you and the man behind you." There was a lot of head turning. "From now on, this is how you will line up every time we do this exercise."

"Every time?" complained one of the knights. "How many times do we have to do it?"

"Until you get it right," the earl's brother Hugo snapped.

Egwulf was in front of Roger, Offa and Deaf Martin in front of Egwulf. "You'll have to stare at Egwulf's giant ass all the way to the top," Offa told Roger.

"If he farts, he might blow you off the ladder," Martin added.

Roger looked at the man behind him, one of the replacement spearmen who had been assigned to his section. He was a well-built fellow with a cheerful face and fair hair. Something about him looked familiar. "You're Will!" Roger said.

The man frowned. "How did you know?"

"I was with your family when you left Trentshire."

The frown deepened. "My family?"

"It's a long story—"

"Silence!" cried James of Claire. "Eyes front, and pay attention."

Before the practice began, long rolls of painted canvas were hung down the side of the belfry to simulate the interior darkness the men would experience when the ox hides were in place.

"Thinks of everything, don't he?" said the vintenar Unferth, adjusting his shield behind his back. Unferth had been a soldier some years previous to the crusade. He hadn't taken to the quiet life of a herdsman, so when the crusade was preached, he had immediately joined up. "Eight years of soldiering, and I never heard of practicing for a battle," he said.

"Bad luck, that's what it is," Dirk growled from the side.

"Aye," muttered his friend Uwen, the Welshman, crossing himself.

The earl said, "On the day of the attack, Lord Henry and I will ride in the tower and let down the ramp. Four archers will provide us protection. The rest of you will follow behind. Begin climbing the ladders as soon as the tower is against the city walls. The first of you should reach the top as the ramp comes to rest."

The men put weapons in scabbards or in their belts. Shields and spears were slung across their backs—they would need both hands for climbing. The one-eyed knight dismounted, went into the belfry and started up the ladder. The earl gave him time to get to the top, then said, "Does every man understand what he is to do?"

There was mumbled assent. "When you hear the horn, begin climbing. When you reach the end of the ramp, slide down those ropes, so the men coming up behind you will have room."

The earl's squire raised a horn to his lips. The earl nodded, and the squire blew three blasts.

The men surged forward. "Take your time!" the earl yelled. "No one out of place."

There was an orderly, if slow, procession up the ladders, men waiting their turns. Big Egwulf went into the belfry, Roger behind him. Despite the back of the tower being open, Roger experienced momentary disorientation at the sudden loss of light. He made it up the first ladder, following Egwulf, climbing hand over hand in his heavy gear, Will behind him. "This ain't as easy as it looks," Egwulf grunted.

Roger got to the first platform and turned. Egwulf had paused to catch his breath, and Roger waited for him rather than trying to push ahead. By the time he was halfway up the third ladder, Roger was breathing hard, as well, sweat streaming out of him in the sweltering, cramped confines of the tower. He reached the top of the third ladder, hauled himself through the opening onto the platform, and stopped.

The view from this height was spectacular. Roger could see over the city to the harbor and the sea, sparkling in the sunlight. The one-eyed knight grabbed him by the collar and propelled him forward. "Stop gawking, you idiot! Move!"

Roger headed for the ramp. Offa stood by one of the ropes, ahead of Egwulf, paralyzed by his fear of heights and holding up the line. Men were pouring onto the ramp with nowhere to go. If they crammed forward, some of them would get pitched off the edge. "Get down that rope, or I'll throw you off," the one-eyed knight shouted at Offa. Offa stared, and the one-eyed knight started forward, as though to carry out his threat. Offa crossed himself. He sat on the edge of the ramp, took the rope, and slithered awkwardly down, afraid to look at the bottom. Egwulf followed, then Roger.

Offa and Egwulf, as did most of the men, slid down the ropes, and those who weren't wearing gloves had the skin on their hands torn off. Roger went down hand over hand, bracing with his feet, as he had learned to do on the *Quail*. He reached the bottom with a feeling of exhilaration.

Will landed beside Roger with a thump of feet. "That was fun!" Will said.

"Get back in line!" cried the earl. "We need to be faster. Do it again!"

Chapter 20

The next two days they practiced climbing the belfry. At first there was grumbling, especially from the knights, as they performed the exercise over and over, but as they got better at it, the grumbling stopped. The men, even the knights, started to take pride in the alacrity with which they could now mount the ladders and stream out onto the ramp. They began to realize that the exercise was going to help them in their mission, and seeing that, they strove to become even better at it. If they could put a sizeable force over the walls and into the city quickly, before the defenders could react, they had a chance of ending the siege.

In Roger's section, only Cole, the youngster, had problems. He was nervous, being the youngest man in the unit—if a gangly lad of fifteen could be called a man. On the first run through, he lost his footing on one of the ladder rungs, slipped, and fell into the men behind him, knocking them into a heap and drawing curses from John of Claire and Warin, the axe company's commander. Uwen, who was one of the men knocked off the ladder, threatened to kill him if he did it again. Not having gloves, Cole burned the skin off his hand sliding down the rope afterward. Because his hands hurt so badly, he had trouble climbing in the following practices, slowing the men down and earning more abuse from the commanders. From his vantage point outside the tower, Dirk saw all of this and his beefy face reddened with anger. Unferth, however, calmly bandaged the boy's hands during a break and found him a pair of gloves.

As they practiced, they were watched by some of the archbishop of Canterbury's men—who would be following them into the belfry. While the earl's men sweated in the hot sun, Canterbury's troops relaxed and hurled catcalls at them.

"Why are we the only ones practicing?" said Egwulf, removing his rimmed helmet and wiping sweat from his brow. His head was so big that his helmet left a red dent around the skin of his forehead.

Unferth shrugged. "I hear the earl mentioned it to the archbishop, but old Baldwin didn't think it was something his men needed to do."

"More glory for us," boasted Ralph the Red. "We'll take the gate ourselves, before those sods even get up the ladders."

"Canterbury's got four times the men we do," Unferth reminded him. "We'll need them to hold that gate. Me, I'd feel a lot better were they practicing, too."

In between practices the men sharpened their weapons— swords, axes, spears, daggers. The grinding stones rasped continuously, honing blades to a razor's edge. Squires oiled the knights' hauberks and polished helmets. Footmen mended jacks and breeches and shoes. Archers inspected arrow fletchings and waxed bowstrings.

On the afternoon before the attack, there was one last run through, then the men were told to get some rest. Roger's section lay on their cots in the hot tent, but few slept. They were awakened after dark and fed black bread and barley soup with some kind of meat in it. "Probably camel," grumbled Offa, sniffing at it.

"Camel and flies," Slowfoot corrected.

"Better than no meat at all," said a doughy fellow named Arcil. "At home we go months at a time without meat."

"Poor Arsehole," mocked the square-faced Welshman Uwen. "Don't have no meat. How'd you get so fat then, Arsehole?"

"Enough," Unferth told Uwen. "You know he don't like to be called that."

Uwen said, "Dirk always let us—"

"And I want it stopped," Unferth said. Unferth reflected on the difference between levies like this and mercenary units he had been in. In a mercenary company, giving a man a nickname like "Arsehole" was likely to get you a knife in the guts. These men just sort of went along with it.

"Yeah," Deaf Martin told Uwen, "how does him not having meat at home make him any different from the rest of us?" He turned. "Right, Roger?"

Roger, who had eaten meat regularly at the monastery— one rule that Abbot Raymond had not enforced—gave a noncommittal shrug.

The men heard Mass and took communion, then they armed themselves and marched in little groups to the belfry. Many of the knights elected not to wear surcoats over their mail, worried lest the long surcoats hamper them when climbing the ladders.

Workmen with masks over their noses and mouths were nailing the ox hides to the belfry's side. The hides dripped liquid in steady streams. Other men attached heavy cables to the belfry's front struts.

As the soldiers approached, the smell from the oxhides overwhelmed them. "God's balls, what a stink!" cried Black John. "Vinegar and piss."

"Smells like my wife," Offa said.

The earl's men were lined up in order of battle and told to wait. Around them the camp was in motion, as the army prepared for battle on the morrow. There were sounds of invisible men and horses. Roger and most of the axe men sat, covering their noses with whatever was available to mitigate the stink from the ox hides.

Cole went off to pee. As he was coming back, Dirk emerged from the darkness, grabbed the yoke of Cole's jack with his good hand and drew him close. "If you fuck this up, boy, I'll have your hide. You hear me?" Then he pushed him away.

Unferth, who was helping one of the men with his shield sling, missed this exchange. Roger saw it, though, and when Cole returned to the group, Roger put a reassuring hand on his shoulder. "You'll do fine."

That seemed to settle Cole down. Roger, who had achieved a somewhat mythic status in the company of axe men because of his defeat of Dirk—no matter how fortunate that defeat had been—was, if not yet accepted by some, looked up to by all.

Roger sounded a lot more confident than he felt. How would he behave in battle? Would he be brave or would he run away? He closed his eyes and prayed to the Lord Christ, to Holy Mary, and to Saint Cuthbert, patron of Huntley Abbey, for courage.

"On your feet!" The word went down the line.

With a clanking of arms and equipment, the men rose. They waited some more. The temperature was falling, but Roger was too charged with excitement to feel the cold. The laborers and volunteers from other units who would pull the belfry were passed forward. Unferth walked down the line. "Put your right hand on the shoulder of the man in front of you and extend your arm. Maintain that interval all the way to the wall."

Roger put his hand on Egwulf's big shoulder. Will did the same to Roger. "See you at the gate," Will told Roger with a grin.

Roger made no reply. His throat was dry. He wondered if he had time to pull his water bottle and take a drink.

A sudden grinding squeal split the night and the belfry lurched forward.

"Advance!" cried James le Claire.

"Advance!" cried the vintenars.

Roger started forward, eyes fixed on Egwulf's back, trying to keep the proper distance. They only went a few steps before they had to stop. Men staggered into each other, cursing. "Why are we stopping?"

Ahead of them, the belfry inched forward in fits and starts until the long line of men on the ropes got used to what they were doing, and then the giant tower moved forward with a heavy rumble. The assault troops followed behind. The pace was slow but steady now. Roger touched the axe in his belt, in sudden panic that he might have forgotten it.

They crossed the bridge over the camp ditch and came onto the plain before the city. Sappers went ahead to examine the ground and direct the belfry around any rough spots, marking the path with small flags. The sappers had been out at night for the last two weeks, reducing small hills and filling in ravines that lay in the belfry's path, but they wanted to make doubly sure the way was clear.

Roger moved forward, following Egwulf, trying not to think because thinking made him scared. He pictured the chaos inside the city walls as Saracen officers directed reinforcements to the point of attack.

From the Green Tower, a trail of flame shot into the night.

"Greek Fire," Unferth said.

The flame arced toward the belfry with a roar, and it landed in a smear of fire a good furlong away. The flames set some dried grass ablaze. There were jeers and catcalls from the approaching troops.

Closer they came to the city. Closer, but so slowly. Sibilant whispers filled the air all around them. After a second, Roger realized they were arrows. The archers were firing blindly toward the sound of the approaching belfry. Somewhere up front a man screamed.

More Greek Fire, from St. James' Tower. Another roar, another miss, but closer this time, the fire illuminating the approaching soldiers in stark relief against the blackness of the night. That would give the archers an aiming point. Roger put his head down, watched the ground, and prayed.

Our Father, that art in Heaven —

Another roar, and a ball of Greek Fire crashed behind them. There were screams, and Egwulf turned. "Christ," he said.

Roger followed his gaze. The Greek Fire had struck a group of archers, setting them ablaze.

Egwulf's steps faltered and Roger bumped into him. They

watched the human torches roll around in the dirt, trying to put out the fires that were consuming them. Roger smelled burning flesh. Some of the archers' friends tried to help them, but their vintenars pushed them back into line.

"Go around them," ordered James le Claire. "Don't stop."

— hallowed be Thy —

Arrows rained down. "Shields over your heads," James cried.

Roger raised his shield. Something thunked into it, and he felt the vibration go up his arm. He could tell from the cries of the wounded that the archers were firing into the unarmed men dragging the belfry, trying to slow its progress. He passed a shadowy figure flopping on the ground. From up ahead came a gut-wrenching scream as the belfry rolled over a wounded man who couldn't get out of the way.

"Keep moving!"

Another roar and Greek Fire crashed into the belfry's side. The flames fizzled harmlessly on the soaked hides. The men cheered.

Behind them, the sky was lightening. Rows of pavises had been set up before the city wals, and from behind their protection, crossbowmen fired bolts at the defenders. Mangonels hurled stones into the city itself, hoping to break up concentrations of enemy troops forming for a counterattack. More arrows stuck in Roger's shield or skidded off. The attackers crossed the city ditch. The belfry wobbled going over the ditch, which had been filled in with God only knew what, but it didn't fall. Greek Fire hit the belfry's copper roof. Roger thought about the earl and the one-eyed knight up there.

Thy Kingdom come —

More Greek Fire hit the belfry, to no effect. Arrows poured down. Roger passed dead and wounded laborers, screaming in pain. Stones hurled from mangonels on the towers crashed into other laborers, turning them to pulp, but the rest kept pulling, praying, singing hymns. A drum thumped and a flute started playing "Girls of Falaise." The men cheered. The sun was rising; Roger saw the city walls ahead of him. They had timed it perfectly.

At the front, the long line of laborers fanned out as they reached the walls, some dropping from arrows or stones, some running to the rear of the belfry, to push. There was a heavy thud, and the belfry stopped. The laborers stormed past, running for safety. Roger hung his shield behind his back; he put on his reinforced gloves. Above him, he heard the rasping of chains.

There were three long blasts from the earl's horn.

"Christ and the True Cross!" shouted someone up front.

The rest of the men took up the cry. "Christ and the True Cross!" And they started into the belfry.

Chapter 21

The line moved swiftly. Roger heard cheering from the belfry's top. He got on the first ladder, following Egwulf, Offa, and Deaf Martin, and he started climbing, trying to pretend this was another rehearsal. At the bottom of the belfry, the flute and drum were still playing "Girls of Falaise."

Greek Fire exploded again and again on the belfry, to no effect, though Roger felt a blast of heat each time a ball struck. The structure shuddered as it was pounded by rocks from the two towers.

The belfry had to remain intact long enough for the crusaders to capture the two towers. Once that was accomplished, the belfry would be protected by the towers and invulnerable to attack. The Christians would fight their way down the towers and capture the gate. Once the gate was open, thousands of men would pour through it. Acre's defenders were outnumbered by more than twenty to one. If the Christians got enough men in the city, they were bound to win. Everything depended on how long the belfry lasted.

Roger reached the first landing in what seemed like no time at all. There was shouting above him, the clash of metal, screams. He made his turn on the landing the way he had practiced it a dozen times before, and got onto the second ladder. Ahead of him men climbed quickly and efficiently. He wished they would go slower; this was all happening too fast.

As he reached the third ladder, he panicked. He didn't belong here. He wasn't a soldier. Egwulf and the others had at least practiced with their weapons; all Roger had done so far was get in a fight and help to dig a latrine. He wanted to throw himself from the ladder and run away. Then resolve steadied him, and he kept going.

He reached the top. There was a sudden glare of sunlight through the open ramp. Roger drew the axe from his belt, shifted his shield onto his arm, and started forward, passing two bodies on the ramp floor, trying not to look at them. Below him more Greek Fire exploded on the belfry's side.

He followed Egwulf to the edge of the ramp, which was about four feet above the wall's walkway. He jumped down, slipped in a pool of blood, and fell. He regained his feet but his gloved hands were wet with blood. He moved left, as he had been told to do.

The wall walk was surprisingly wide, with room enough for four men abreast. On one side was the stone parapet; on the other, a wooden balustrade. Ahead of him was a mass of struggling men. There was yelling, shouting, the ring of metal on metal. Smells of blood and shit as injured and dying men voided themselves. Roger pushed in behind. The Christians were gaining ground, clearing the battlements, but every foot cost them men. Roger clambered over dead and wounded, Christian and Saracen. Some of the footmen stopped to kill the Saracen wounded, driving daggers into their throats or eyes. Arrows flew down from the Saracens on St. James' Tower ahead and up from Saracens in the courtyard. The Saracens were so desperate they did not care whether they hit their own men. They knew they had to stop the crusaders from taking the towers or the city was lost.

As more men fell, Roger was carried closer to the front of the line. Everything was happening so fast. Ahead, he saw a surcoat with a red dragon—the earl. The earl's bloody sword rose and fell. The packed men behind Roger pushed him forward, kept him from slipping on the blood-slick stone walkway. He had lost sight of Egwulf and the others. Something whipped past his face, just missing him, and he realized it was an arrow.

The crusaders advanced steadily. More men dropped. A Christian and a Saracen wrestled and fell through one of the parapet openings to the ditch below. Somehow Roger ended up right behind the earl. The earl's squire, a boy of about fourteen, went down with a spear thrust in his throat. A young Saracen swung a mace and hit the earl atop his flat metal cap. The earl sank to his knees, stunned. With wild eyes and snarling teeth, the trim-bearded Saracen lifted the mace again. Without thinking, Roger rushed forward. As the Saracen brought the mace down, Roger swung his axe and the young Saracen's face disappeared in an explosion of blood and bone and teeth. Another Saracen thrust his spear at Roger. Roger knocked the spear aside with his shield and, using two hands, he drove the pointed end of his axe into the man's face, catching him just above the bridge of the nose, feeling the man's skull implode as the heavy axe point drove into it.

Roger swung the axe again, catching another man at the base of the neck, cleaving through the collarbone deep into his chest. He pulled the axe free, ducked behind his shield as a curved scimitar drove at him. He swung under the shield and caught the sword bearer across the ankle, nearly severing it from the man's leg. The man screamed and went down.

The earl had fallen onto his side. Roger stood over him, guarding him. The earl's dented cap had been pushed down over his forehead, gashing his nose; he lay against a pile of bodies, dazed, blood trickling down his face.

"Forward!" It was James of Claire, waving his sword, his hauberk red with blood, his face splashed with it. "Forward—take the tower!"

The crusaders surged ahead. Roger left the earl and joined them. Struggling men from both sides were intermingled—Saracens of all kinds, Christian knights and footmen. It was like a tavern brawl but with deadlier weapons. Roger didn't have room to swing the axe; he let the shield dangle from its neck strap and punched with the axe's pointed head or chopped down at legs and feet. A Saracen hunkered behind his shield; Roger couldn't get at him in the press. He hooked his axe over the shield and pulled it down, uncovering the Saracen's startled face. Roger released the axe from the shield and drove the point of the axe into the Saracen's face. An enormous Nubian with bells in his beard swung a flail at Roger. Roger caught the flail's chains on the haft of his axe, watching as the iron-studded steel balls wrapped themselves around the axe handle. One of the balls caught his glove and sliced it open. Roger pulled the Nubian forward, kneed him in the face. That move left Roger open. He saw a spear coming from his right and knew he wouldn't be able to stop it, but a shield knocked the spear aside and a man fell on the Saracen with a dagger. It was Will.

Roger got the flail off his axe—he didn't know what had happened to the Nubian—and he covered Will as Will got to his feet.

"Come on!" cried James of Claire. "We've got them on the run!"

The Saracens were falling back, but there weren't many Christians left. Roger glanced back at the belfry, which was still being pounded by rocks and Greek Fire from the two towers, neither of which had yet fallen. A trickle of reinforcements issued from the belfry's ramp where there should have been a flood. What had happened to the archbishop of Canterbury's men?

"Forward!" James cried. "The day is ours!"

They had cleared the wall almost to the tower entrance. They redoubled their efforts. Saracens fell before them. Roger had more room now; he punched with his shield, swinging his axe with both hands, yelling. He realized how thirsty he was. It seemed as though every few seconds hot liquid splashed his face and clothing and dripped from the rim of his helmet.

Saracen reinforcements pounded through the tower's passageway. Where were the archbishop's men? Just a few more men and they could take the tower, but they had to hurry. James of Claire staggered back, howling, clutching at an arrow in his eye. A Saracen threw him over the balustrade to the ground below. Roger drove the point of his axe under the Saracen's jaw, shattering it. Roger put his shoulder into the

Saracen and sent him over the balustrade. "Come on!" Roger yelled, moving forward.

But there were too many Saracens now. It was all Roger and the others could do to hold their ground. "Come on!" Roger yelled again. "One more push!" But he sensed the men behind him giving way. "Hold on—the archbishop's men will be here any minute!"

There were arrows stuck in Roger's jack. The top of his shield was split. Something banged on his helmet and he missed a step. A Saracen whose silver inlaid helmet and finely crafted mail marked him as a man of importance swung a scimitar at him. In the open, the man's skills with weapons would have been too much for Roger, but in these cramped quarters, they made little difference. Roger ducked and stopped the sword with his shield. He shoved forward and the man tripped over a body and went down. Roger drove the metal-banded edge of his shield into the man's face and tried to move forward, tried to hold his ground till Canterbury's men could get here.

"The belfry's on fire!" someone cried.

Roger sensed the men around him wavering. The Saracens redoubled their efforts.

Two short blasts from a horn. Again. Again.

The signal for retreat.

The crusaders fell back, pressed by their enemies. Roger carved breathing room with wide swings of his axe, holding the Saracens back while he looked for a place to make a stand. "Hold fast!" he cried. "Hold!"

But the line was crumbling. Roger was all the way back by the earl again. The earl sat with his back against the stacked bodies. Roger and Will and another man—it was Egwulf—made a wedge around the earl, protecting him. The Saracens must have known the earl was important because they tried hard to get at him. Roger was at the tip of the wedge, swinging his axe with two hands while Will and Egwulf protected his flanks. Roger brought the axe down again and again, like he was chopping wood at Huntley Abbey, cleaving metal and leather and bone and flesh. He smelled smoke from the burning belfry. Heard cries of panic. Sensed men behind him carrying the earl away.

Somebody grabbed his arm. "Let's go, boy." It was the one-eyed knight, Henry the Falcon. He was covered with blood as though he had bathed in it.

Roger stared at him, wide eyed. "Go!" Henry shouted, pulling him. "The belfry's going to collapse."

Will and Egwulf fell back. Roger joined them. Henry went last, covering the others with his sword. His mail and what was left of his shield bristled with so many arrows that he looked like a giant red hedgehog.

Flames and smoke poured from the belfry. It teetered to one side, its foundations cracked by the heavy stones that continued to pound it. There were yells of triumph from the towers, where arrows were shot at the fleeing men on the parapets. More Greek Fire struck the belfry.

Roger moved along the parapet as quickly as he could, following Egwulf and Will, with Henry the Falcon behind him. Roger had to be careful not to trip over bodies or slip in blood and other gore. If he went down, it meant death. He passed the vintenar Unferth lying on his back, crying for his mother, his guts spilling out of him onto the stone.

Egwulf and Will climbed the four feet into the belfry. Roger and Henry the Lion were the last Christians on the parapet. They hoisted themselves into the belfry's smoke-filled ramp steps ahead of the pursuing Saracens. Roger coughed as smoke filled his lungs. He smelled burning flesh, heard terrible screams. "Hurry!" cried Henry.

The Saracens didn't follow them—it was too dangerous. The belfry canted to one side; only one ladder was still upright. Roger stuck his axe in his belt, shifted his shield onto his back. Arrows passed Roger's head, a spear thudded into wood, then he was on the ladder. He made his way down as fast as he could, fire roaring about him. At the first landing, he passed a

135

wounded man dragging himself along. Roger shielded his face from the flames and stopped. The belfry was going to collapse at any moment. No matter—Roger couldn't abandon the wounded man. He grabbed the man—an axe man like himself—beneath the arms. "Will!" he shouted into the murk.

Will raised his head from the ladder. "Help me," Roger told him. "I'll lower him down to you."

Will nodded, started climbing down. Henry the Falcon helped Roger drag the wounded man to the platform opening. They pushed the man over, legs first, and held his arms till Will got a grasp on his legs. The man cried with pain; there was so much blood on him that Roger couldn't tell where he was wounded. Holding the wounded man's arm with one hand and the ladder with the other, Roger started down, while Henry stood guard behind.

"Quickly!" Henry urged.

The roaring grew louder. The heat was intense. Smoke made Roger's eyes burn. He heard wood cracking, splintering asunder. The belfry shifted. The metal scales on Roger's jack were hot to the touch. Arrows stuck in his jack got caught in the ladder's rungs and broke off.

Roger and Will maneuvered the wounded man to the next level, with Henry helping. Flaming pieces of the belfry were falling around them. Roger got the man through the last platform. He swung onto the ladder, Henry behind him. There was a grinding noise and the ladder lurched to one side. Roger nearly lost his grasp on the wounded man's wrist but held on. The wounded man screamed in pain. They got the wounded man to the bottom. Will and Egwulf took him beneath the arms and dragged him outside. More pieces of wood rained down, trailing fire. Roger jumped the last few feet. So did Henry. Roger hit the ground hard, dazed from the fall. There was a loud roar above him, around him. He couldn't move. He was going to die.

Henry lifted him and hauled him from the belfry. "Run!"

Roger tried to get his legs moving, but they didn't respond.

Henry pulled Roger from the collapsing belfry, stumbling into the fresher air, moving away as rapidly as he could. The two men felt a terrific blast of heat and wind at their backs. Then they could go no further and they dropped to the ground as the belfry collapsed in an inferno of flame and smoke behind them.

Chapter 22

Smoke and debris billowed from the collapsed belfry. The smoke got into Roger's lungs and he coughed violently. He and Henry the Falcon rose to their feet and stumbled away from the city wall to escape the pall of dust and smoke. They crossed the ditch, which Roger now saw had been filled in with rocks and timber and the decaying bodies of men and animals. On the other side of the ditch they dropped to the ground, exhausted, heedless of the fact that they made perfect targets for Saracen archers on the walls. For their part, the Saracens— who were just as tired—were content to jeer at the beaten crusaders instead of shooting arrows at them.

Around Roger, crossbowmen were drawing back the pavises that they had used for cover, taking their dead and wounded with them. There were distant sounds of fighting from the far side of the camp, where Saladin must be attacking. Roger was too tired to care. His throat burned with thirst. As he reached for his water bottle, he was surprised to discover that he was covered with blood. Drenched with it, as though it had rained from the sky. The blood was thicker in some places than in others, but there was scarcely a square inch of him that was not red with it. His right-hand glove was so thick with congealing blood that the water bottle stuck to his palm. Henry the Falcon looked much the same as Roger, save that his mail hauberk was stuck all over with arrows, as well.

Roger gulped down the water, then pried the bottle from his gloved hand and offered it to Henry. "Thank you, my lord. Had you not picked me up, I would have been trapped inside the belfry when it collapsed."

Henry waved him off, as though the act had been nothing. He took the water bottle, drank sparingly, then handed it back, nodding thanks. Roger saw Egwulf and Will not far away, looking done in. They sat beside the man that Roger and Will had dragged from the burning belfry. Will had a piece of cloth that he had gotten from somewhere and he was stuffing it into one of the man's wounds, to staunch the bleeding.

"Quite an act of bravery, saving that fellow," Henry said. "He's a friend of yours?"

"I don't know him," Roger replied.

Beneath his blood-streaked conical helmet, Henry raised the brow of his good eye. "You risked your life to save a man you don't know?"

Roger shrugged.

"By God, there's not many would have done that."

Around them, dazed soldiers, many of them wounded, wandered out of the smoke of the collapsed belfry. Roger squinted at the sun, across which tendrils of cloud were moving. He made it to be just past prime. So early. It seemed like it should be much later. "If only the archbishop's men had come, we would have taken the city," he said. "Do you know what happened to them, my lord?"

Henry took another drink from Roger's water bottle. "The fools got jammed up in the belfry. If they had practiced like we did, we'd be sitting in Acre right now. Baldwin's men poured into that belfry like drunken whores coming to market day. They started pushing and shoving one another and got stuck on the ladders and landings. I went down from the Green Tower, which my men had finally taken, and tried to restore order, but by then the belfry was on fire. Even then, with a bit of discipline we might have prevailed, but Baldwin's men panicked and ran away." He paused. " 'Twas I who sounded the retreat."

Roger stared dejectedly at the ground. "Is the earl alive?"

Henry didn't know. "He was unconscious when they carried him from the walls, but he was still breathing."

There was a commotion on the battlements. They looked up.

A group of Saracens, led by an ebullient fellow with a blue sash around his helmet, were yelling at the crusaders. Henry rose as though pulled upright by some unseen wire. "Qaymaz," he breathed.

Other men were standing now, because the Saracens had brought up a prisoner. "It's Martin!" cried Ralph the Red.

It was indeed Deaf Martin. He had lost his helmet; blood streaked his face where one of his eyes had been gouged out.

The Saracen with the blue sash spotted Henry in the crowd below and waved jauntily from the parapet, crying, "My lord Henry! What a pity to see you still alive!"

Henry glared at the man.

Meanwhile, Martin looked at the men below and recognized his comrades. "Help me!" he cried in a pitiful voice. "Please, God, help me! Egwulf! Roger!"

Still laughing, Qaymaz gestured, and his men forced Martin's head onto one of the wall's stone merlons.

"God help me! God help me!" cried Martin, his voice distorted from the acute angle at which his head lay.

Someone handed Qaymaz a sledgehammer. He flourished it at the crusaders on the ground, then raised it.

"No!" cried Roger. Beside him, Henry stood still.

Martin cried, "Tell my mother that—"

Qaymaz brought the sledgehammer down. Roger looked away. He heard a sickening sound, like a giant nut being cracked.

Qaymaz shouted down to Henry. "Your own death will be much longer, my friend. I will have you skinned alive and present the skin to the sultan, who shall reward me greatly."

Henry still glared at him.

Qaymaz cried, "What—nothing to say?"

While Qaymaz had been executing Martin, Henry had retrieved a loaded crossbow from a dead archer. Now he raised the crossbow and pulled the trigger. Qaymaz saw what was happening and ducked as the metal crossbow bolt sailed harmlessly between the merlons and over the wall.

"Until we meet again!" Qaymaz shouted and disappeared behind the parapet.

Henry glowered up at the wall, his chest heaving. "I"ll have that man's head if it's the last thing I ever do."

Martin's body was heaved over the wall, landing with a thud at the bottom. More Christian bodies followed, a lot of them—some dead, some wounded but dead when they hit the ground. The Saracens would bury their own dead; the Infidel enemy was not worthy of that effort.

Henry tossed the crossbow aside. "I must rejoin my men," he told Roger. "Today's failure means another winter spent before these walls, and I'll not endure that. As soon as we bury our dead, we're leaving." He clapped Roger's back. "Good luck, boy. I'll look for you in the spring, if you're still alive."

"I'll do my best, my lord," Roger said.

Henry turned and strode away, pulling arrows from his hauberk and calling for his men.

Roger went over to Will and Egwulf, who stood over the wounded man they had pulled from the belfry. Roger saw some of the other men from his section—Ralph the Red, Uwen, a quiet fellow called Hedde—nearby. The wounded man—it was hard to tell the color of his greasy hair, there was so much blood in it—moaned, semi-conscious. He had a long face with pointed chin and ears. There was a cut across the top of his head, the more serious wound in his side plugged with Will's strip of cloth.

"Let's get him to the surgeons," Roger said.

Chapter 23

The sick tent had been crowded before the assault on the city, now it was overflowing. The earl's two surgeons—or barbers, for that was their true profession—were overwhelmed. The archbishop of Canterbury had lent them his surgeons, but it scarcely sufficed. None of them had ever treated patients in such numbers. They hardly knew where to begin. A fortunate few of the wounded had gotten beds inside, the rest were forced to lie outside in the burning sun and wait there until they could be seen. Some lay crying for their mothers or thrashing in pain; others whimpered or were quiet, waiting stoically, some with the ashen pall of death already creeping over them. There were men with hideous gashes, men with arrow wounds, men missing parts of arms or legs. Pools of blood were everywhere. The area reeked of blood and shit and rancid sweat. From inside the tent came screams and the rasp of a saw on bone as a mangled arm was taken off.

Laundresses and camp followers moved among the wounded, giving water, using palm leaves to ward the clouds of flies off open wounds, rendering what other comforts they could. The young priest who had entered Roger's name in the company rolls was doing his part, as well. He examined the injured, sorting out those who were seriously hurt but could be saved for first treatment, placing strips of white cloth on their chests as markers for the surgeons, leaving the more lightly wounded for later, making the sign of the Cross over those who were likely to die.

Roger, Egwulf, and Will each had a dozen minor wounds and as many bruises, but they were expected to treat these themselves. The sick tent was only for the seriously injured. They set the wounded man down in one of the few open spaces remaining beside the tent. The cloth that Will had used to plug the wound in the man's side was now completely wet with blood. Roger grabbed the young priest as he came by. "Look at this fellow, would you, Father?"

The harried priest bent over the wounded man. Suddenly he straightened, and his face hardened. "Better you had left this one to his fate. This is Tatwine. He is a killer for hire and a thief, probably the worst man in our army. A man we'd be well rid of." He shook his head. "I suppose it doesn't matter—there's nothing we can do for him. He's too badly wounded. I'll come back and give him Extreme Unction when I can, though little good it will do the likes of him."

He started to move on, but Roger took his arm. "Please, Father. My friends and I nearly died bringing this man out of the city." Maybe this Tatwine was evil, but it somehow seemed important to save him, if only to justify the risks they had taken to get him away from the burning belfry. *This is God's plan.*

Something in Roger's voice made the priest hesitate. He looked at the three men more closely, then peered at Roger's blood-covered face. "You're that fellow from Huntley Abbey, aren't you?"

Roger nodded, and the cleric said, "Very well. Against my better judgment, we'll do what we can. Though I warn you, it's like to prove hopeless." He lay a strip of dirty white cloth on Tatwine's chest.

Roger and his companions made ready to leave when someone shouted to them. It was Offa, lying on a litter nearby.

The three men hurried over to him. "Grandad!" Egwulf shouted. "We thought you was dead."

Offa barked a laugh. "Me wife's been trying to kill me for twenty years with her cooking. If she can't do it, those damned heathens won't be able to."

Offa had broken his leg jumping from the ramp when he first left the belfry. "Bone sticking clean trough the leg, it was," he told his friends. "Nearly passed out climbing back down that ladder. Couple Italian crossbowmen carried me here. That pissant of a barber over there wanted to take the leg off, but I told him I'd take his dick off if he tried. Splint it and bind it up, says I. Hurt so bad it knocked me out." He winced as a spasm of pain sliced through him.

They told Offa about Deaf Martin. Offa shook his grizzled head. "Poor lad. He was hoping to get himself a bit of land and stay out here, did he tell you that? Well, he's in Paradise now. Not like us."

On their way out of the sick tent, they saw Dirk, his injured hand heavily wrapped, hanging around and pretending to look useful. "Probably stealing valuables off dead men," Egwulf muttered.

They started back to the company area. Will was hesitant. "I guess this is where I leave you."

"Nonsense," Roger said. "Come back with us. You fought with us, you should join us permanently."

Egwulf slapped Will's back, almost knocking him over. "I agree. With Dirk gone, you'll find us a likely group of lads." He tapped the axe at Will's belt. "Anyway, you're one of us now, ain't you?"

Will grinned. "I guess I am at that."

Back at the tent, Bald Matthew, the cook, had food waiting for the returning men—stale bread, porridge, and watered wine. He balked at giving Will food till Roger and Egwulf persuaded him that it was all right.

From nearby, Uwen said, "You two decide who's in the section now?"

"Pay him no mind," Egwulf told Will. "He's Welsh."

The famished men drank until their thirsts were quenched, stuffed the bread and porridge into their mouths, and repaired inside the tent.

Black John was sewing a gash on Ralph the Red's forearm. "Wonder who'll be vintenar now Unferth's gone?" Blackie said.

"Uwen?" said Ralph.

"I hope not," Egwulf muttered. Uwen was still outside.

Roger and Egwulf told the others that Will was joining their section, and they welcomed him. "Glad to have you," said Slowfoot. "You did good work today."

They showed Will to a vacant cot. "Fancy a turn of hazard?" Black John asked him.

"Sorry," said Will. "I don't gamble."

Blackie sighed and went back to sewing Ralph's arm.

Roger peeled off his blood-thickened gloves. He undid his helmet's chin strap and dropped his helmet and shield. He took the axe from his belt and let it fall to the ground beside his cot. Then he sank to the ground, as well, weary beyond all imagining. He was sticky all over with drying blood, upon which buzzing flies were making merry. He noticed something lodged in the gore that covered the metal scales of his jack. He picked it out, thinking it was a rock. It was a tooth. He tossed it aside.

He realized that his hands were shaking and he balled his fists to make them stop. He kept seeing the face of that first man he'd killed. The young man had been handsome and intelligent looking—almost scholarly—with a trim dark beard. A man Roger might have befriended in another life. And with one swing of his axe, Roger had ended his existence. Who had that man been? Did he have a family? Were they anxiously waiting news of him?

Roger had come to the Holy Land to do glorious deeds in the name of Our Lord Jesus Christ. If this was glory, what was sin? Could God agree with what Roger had done today, with what any of them had done? But He must agree, or they would not be here. He thought about Deaf Martin, heard the sickening sound the sledgehammer had made as it cracked his skull.

"We'll never take this city," the quiet man named Hedde said gloomily as he examined a slice on his knee.

Will held out his arms, which were almost as blood-covered as Roger's. "On a more practical side, how do we clean up?".

Roger hadn't thought about that. In the romances he had read at the abbey—they were forbidden but the younger brothers read them avidly, if covertly—heroes never cleaned up after battle; they never got dirty.

By now, Uwen, who had soldiered before, had come in. He showed them how to get the blood and gore off their equipment with sand. He said, "Usually we wash off in a stream or pond, but there ain't none here."

"Sea water?" Roger ventured.

The others seemed to think that was worth a try, so wearing only their long shirts the men trooped down to the beach. Around them were hundreds of other men who had gotten the same idea.

Roger and Will found themselves walking alongside the boy Cole. Cole's face was drawn, his eyes focused in some far distance. "You all right?" Roger asked him.

Cole didn't look at him. His voice had changed from yesterday, aged somehow. "It wasn't what I expected."

"It wasn't what any of us expected," Will said.

"Think it gets any better?" Cole said. "Do you ever get used to it?"

"I don't know," Roger said. "I expect we'll find out."

Will said, "You're a bit young for all this, aren't you?"

Cole shrugged. "I wanted to get away, make something of myself. My dad's the gongfermer at Badford Castle."

The gongfermer cleaned out the latrine pits. "A shitty job," Will observed. "But I guess you've heard that before."

"Every day of my life," Cole replied. "But—the job is hereditary. That means it can't be taken away from your family. It means that when there's famine outside the castle, you and your family always have something to eat. It means you always have a stout roof above your head and a place near the fire. It means security, and that's something few men can claim. Security isn't everything, though, and I couldn't see myself shoveling shit for the rest of my life, so when they called for volunteers for the crusade, I joined."

Will said, "What did your parents say?"

"Mum was dead against it, of course. She thought I was mad. But I think Dad understood, even if he didn't say it out loud."

Behind them, the attack on the crusader camp seemed to be ending, judging from the noise. No doubt Saladin was withdrawing now that the city was safe. In truth, the camp was so large that a major battle could be fought on one side of it while life went on completely undisturbed on the other.

On the shore, Roger and his companions stepped into the waves, tentatively at first, then plunging into the water when they found how warm it was, howling as the salt penetrated their wounds, then getting used to it and washing the blood from their hair and shirts. The beach gradually thickened with other survivors of the battle—footmen, squires, knights and men at arms. For many of the lower classes it was the first bath they'd had in years; for some, the first bath ever. Roger had bathed three or four times a year at the abbey, though he had washed his hands before every meal and washed his feet once a week. Some of the men—Ralph the Red, Blackie, Slowfoot— splashed water on each other playfully, wrestled and dunked one another in the waves, laughing the forced laugh of men trying to forget what they had just gone through.

Later, banks of clouds rolled in from the west. The wind picked up, whipping spume from the waves across the men's naked bodies. "God's blood, it's cold of a sudden," Egwulf shouted, flapping his big hairy arms to warm himself. "Where's the bloody sun when you need it?" The men splashed back to shore, shivering while they dried.

Then it was back to the tent for oiling and polishing their equipment. That took the rest of the day. The following day, Roger's section was detailed to help gather the dead from the foot of the city walls. There was an unspoken truce. The Saracens watched the crusaders from the battlements, but they didn't laugh or jeer or shoot arrows at them. Roger looked for Qaymaz on the walls, but he wasn't there. Roger and Egwulf found Deaf Martin's body, with its smashed skull. They loaded it onto a cart along with the bodies of Unferth and James of Claire, and all the others—Warin, the axe company's commander, among them—stacking them like they were collecting kindling for the Yule feast. Back at camp, the bodies were stripped of arms and valuables, then deposited in common graves on the plain, knights and footmen together—only the highest-ranking lords got their own graves—while the earl's chaplain Stephen commended their souls to God. The earl couldn't attend the burial; he was still unconscious. His brother Hugh wasn't there, either; he was in grave condition from wounds and not expected to live. All around them, similar funeral processions snaked over the plain. Saladin's assault on the camp had been repulsed, but casualties had been heavy.

After Mass, the surviving axe men took their dead comrade's effects—weapons, armor, clothes, bedding—and divvyed them up. Roger got a warm cloak and a good dagger that would come in handy in the kind of fighting he had experienced on the walls of the city.

The dead men's money was pooled, and the survivors went to a wine tent on the north end of the Concourse—the main shopping street of the camp. Only one man didn't go—a prematurely balding, gap-toothed fellow called Mayn. Mayn wanted to be a priest, and he didn't think priests should drink, so they left him to guard the tent.

In the wine tent they bought cheap arrack by the bucket. Roger had been drunk before, on his journey across Europe, but nothing like this. Once started, he couldn't stop. Drink blotted out memories of battle, drink put his mind and body at ease. Drink was good. Men who had been in peril of their lives—men who had taken lives—laughed uproariously at the slightest jokes. They acted as though they hadn't a care in the world, and for the moment they hadn't. Roger's head swam. He was dimly aware of events around him—the boy Cole throwing up while his friends laughed and pounded his back;

Arcil standing by himself, crying; Ralph the Red fighting with an Italian sailor.

Suddenly Egwulf said, "Did you hear that?"

They listened. There was a crash outside.

"Thunder!" someone cried.

"It's raining!" cried someone else from the tent entrance.

They all stumbled into the street. Rain was pouring down. Cool rain, clear rain. They turned their faces to it, letting it wash away the salt, the dirt, the sin. They waded in the puddles, splashing in them, laughing like children.

When they left the wine tent that night it was still raining. They wrapped their arms around each other and staggered up the muddy Concourse singing "Girls of Falaise," laughing at each raunchy verse, making up verses of their own, Long Tom, the beekeeper, bellowing off key.

As they passed the Toron High Road, which was what the men called the street that led from the Concourse to the Toron, they stepped aside for a mounted party. One of the riders was a woman, tall and regal, on a white horse. A hood protected the woman's blonde hair from the rain, but there was something familiar about the set of her shoulders. Roger stared at her as she went by, then his jaw fell, and he said, "Ailith?"

The woman turned. Her eyes swept the crowded street. They passed over Roger then came back to him with a shock of recognition. Then the momentum of the party forced her ahead, and she was gone.

Chapter 24

The rain slanted down in cold, wind-blown gusts. Welcomed at first, the rain now seemed as though it would never end. Day after day of it. At first, the sun-baked camp streets had turned to rivers as the rain beat on the hardened ground. Tents had overturned in swirling torrents and more than one man had drowned. Canvas, wood, bits of gear, and dead animals littered the camp's open areas in high-water lines from those days, like the aftermath of a giant shipwreck.

Now the saturated ground had turned to mud. Clinging, sucking mud. It stuck to everything; it got into clothes and food and water. Tents and carts and mangonels sank into it. Animals became mired. Equipment disappeared beneath it.

And still it rained. What food there was, rotted. Clothing fell apart. Men sickened and died. The losses were great among the common soldiers, and the native servants who hadn't run away were dying in droves. The only good thing about the rain was that it had driven off the flies and washed away the stench of death and latrines that overhung the camp.

The rain got so bad that Archbishop Ubaldo, the Papal legate, led a procession through the camp, imploring God to make it stop. Relics were shown—32 hairs of the Virgin, an arm of St. Denis, and the jaw of St. Andrew. But it did no good. The rain continued to fall . . . .

The tent was damp, cold, and fetid with the stink of unwashed men. The floor was covered with duckboards layered with filthy straw. The men shivered and coughed, wrapped in all the clothes they owned plus their blankets. All suffered from fever and dysentery. Some of them mended gear or polished metal. Hedde sat by himself peeling strips of rotting skin from his feet, seemingly fascinated by how much came off. Ralph the Red combed out his long ginger beard. He did this faithfully every day, then he twisted the beard in two plaits and tied off the ends with the tattered green ribbons.

"Why d'you spend so much time on that beard?" Egwulf asked him. Egwulf never touched his own beard; it looked like small animals could be living in there.

" 'Cause the ladies like it," Ralph told him.

"Case you hadn't noticed," Black John said, "there's no ladies around here."

"You never know," Ralph replied. "One might walk down the street any minute. You got to be prepared."

Slowfoot, who had been the fastest man in three counties back home, looked disappointed. "I thought there would be whores in the Holy Land. Magdalene was a whore."

"Maybe she was the only one," Mayne said.

Ralph was unfazed. "I'll have all the ladies I want once we conquer Jerusalem. I'll never have to buy a drink again after that."

Doughy faced Arcil mended a shoe. "I don't even care about Jerusalem anymore. I just want to go home."

Offa huddled on his bunk, crutches beside him, leg splinted. "Got a lass waiting at home, do you?"

"I got nothing," Arcil said. "My family's got ten acres divided among I don't know how many people. 'Twas my dad talked me into going on this crusade. I didn't want to do it, but he told me what a great opportunity it was going to be. A chance to better meself, all that ballocks. At home I got no future but as a day laborer." He shook his head. "I don't care. I just want to go back to my little valley. I want to be with my family, and I never want to leave again."

Uwen ran a sharpening stone along the edge of his dagger. "If I go back to my little valley, my Mum will kill me."

"Get out," said Blackie.

"It's true. 'Cause when I took up as a soldier, I signed on

with an English lord. She'd do it, too—even after all these years."

"Tough mum," Ralph the Red observed.

Uwen snorted. "You should see Grandmum. She's worse."

"What did you do back in Wales?" Slowfoot said.

"Cattle thieving, mostly. That's the family trade. We lived on the border, near Chester. My dad got himself killed on a raid into England when I was a youngster. I never really knew him. Grandmum was the family boss."

"Me and Blackie done a bit of highway robbery from time to time," Slowfoot allowed.

"How'd that go?" Uwen asked.

Slowfoot made a turned-down face. "It's mostly poor people you get to rob, and I didn't much like doing that. Anyway, we was always worried that Brock the Badger and his gang would get wind of us poaching on their turf and come after us."

Uwen nodded agreement. He squinted down the edge of his dagger, tested the edge with a finger. "All the thieving I done, and I hardly ever had two coins to rub together. And when I did, I spent it on a whore who was likely related to me—'twas that kind of valley. I reckoned this crusade would put things right. It's warm in the East, they said. Not like Wales, where it's cold and rains every day and there's no earth beneath your feet but only mud."

The men all laughed at that, with the uproarious laughter only suffering men can achieve.

When the laughter subsided, Blackie said, "Slowfoot here come on the crusade cause he got a girl pregnant. What was her name—Cirelle?"

"That's right," Slowfoot admitted.

"Was you the father?" said Ralph the Red.

"Devil if I know. She said I was, though, and that was reason enough to make meself scarce."

Black John and Slowfoot—whose real name was also John—came from the same village and had been inseparable almost from birth. As children, they got into mischief—nothing serious, just enough to make nuisances of themselves. As they got older, they dodged work and hung out in the woods and, later, in ale houses. Blackie was a ditcher and thatcher by trade, but he preferred playing raffle and hazard.

"What's that 'B' on your cheek for?" Will asked Slowfoot.

Slowfoot touched the ragged scar. "Stands for 'braconnier,' or however the hell you pronounce it. Means 'poacher' in French. Bastards couldn't even brand me in my own language."

Blackie said, "Bailiffs knowed he was poaching but he's so fast they could never catch him at it, so they branded him out of frustration." He went on, "Me, now, I come here on a lark. I was tired of gambling in the same old places, seeing the same old faces and playing for small stakes. 'This'll be different,' I told Slowfoot. 'This'll be fun.'"

"It won't be fun if we get killed," Slowfoot said.

"We ain't going to get killed," Blackie told him with the patience that suggested this wasn't the first time they'd had this conversation. "If you'd stayed at home, the bailiffs would have cut off your hand next. That, or Cirelle's brothers would have cut off your dick. This is a chance to start over. If we don't like it, we can always go back."

Ralph tugged one end of his braided beard thoughtfully. "You know, now you mention it, I don't know if I want to go back. Me dad's a miller, but I'm the third son. That means day labor, and fuck that. If I like being a soldier, I may stay on. What about you, Wulfie, you going back?"

"Ain't thought about it," Egwulf said. "Maybe, maybe not."

Offa said, "Well, I'm definitely going back. Hilda drives me crazy, but I kind of miss the old girl. The boys is old enough they can take over the charcoal burning—let them fry *their* hands for a change. Me, I'm going to open a tavern down to the crossroads. If there's no customers, I'll drink the ale myself."

Young Cole said brightly, "I'd like to go to school and learn things."

That brought an awkward silence; no one knew what to

say. Then Offa cleared his throat. "What about you, Roger? You going back?"

"I can't," Roger said. "I made a vow."

"Will?" said Offa.

"It's home for me," Will grinned. He turned to Mayn. "Father?"

"I'm staying," said gap-toothed Mayn. "If I can't become a priest, I'll take vows and join the Templars or Hospitallers."

"Hedde?" Offa said.

Hedde had finished pulling the dead skin off his foot. Now he stared at the oozing foot, wondering what to do with it next. "I'm not going back," he said.

"No family?" Offa said.

"They're dead."

Long Tom said, "I wouldn't mind staying on here, I guess, but the only thing I know how to do is keep bees, and that would put me right back where I started."

"Come work for me," Uwen told him. "I got the urge to be like that one-eyed cove, Henry. Have me a fort out in the desert where I can carry on the family business. Lots of money out here—silks and spice. No reason we shouldn't have our share."

"Tell you what I got my share of," said Ralph the Red, "lice." He reached under his sleeve, pulled one from the crook of his elbow, and cracked it with his fingernail. "Buggers."

Black John, whose mind never strayed far from the opportunity to place a bet on something, drummed his fingers on the helmet he'd been pretending to polish. "Lice, lice, what can you do with lice?"

"Eat 'em, I guess, if you catch enough," Slowfoot said.

Blackie flashed a grin. "I've got it! How 'bout a race?"

"With lice?" said Uwen.

"Why not?" said Blackie, suddenly animated. "We've naught else to do. Come on, it'll be fun. Each man will furnish one entry, and we'll bet—what? Five pence apiece? Winner takes all."

Egwulf scrunched his shaggy brows. "Where do we get five pence?"

Blackie said, "We'll bet against our next pay."

"Whenever that is," Offfa grumbled.

Despite Offa's cantankerousness, the men's enthusiasm flared as they were offered a brief respite from their boredom. Roger was as excited as the rest of them. "Where will they race?"

Uwen said, "Matthew's serving plate—it's big enough, and it's flat.

"And it's dirty, so the lice will feel right at home," Slowfoot added.

"When will we do it?" Will said.

"Now," Blackie said. "Come on—every man get a runner."

That wasn't hard to do. The men were instantly searching themselves. Mayne hesitated. "I'd better not—it's a sin to gamble."

Blackie winked at him. "We won't tell no one, Father."

That seemed to satisfy Mayn and he lifted his shirt, searching for an entry as eagerly as everyone else.

The racers were easy to get. Roger found one in his armpit. He held it out. "Here's mine."

Cole was next. "And here's mine."

"That's a flea," Blackie said.

"Oh," said Cole, downcast.

"Here, I'll help you," Roger told the boy.

Soon every man held one of the tiny grey creatures between his thumb and forefinger. Bald Matthew fetched the serving plate.

"All right, everyone hold your entry over the center of the plate," Blackie said. "When I say, 'Go,' drop 'em and may the best bugger win."

Hands were extended over the wooden serving plate, men jostling each other for advantage.

"Go!" said Blackie.

Each man placed his louse on the plate. There was yelling

and shouting and pounding of fists as the tiny creatures hopped, or ran, or in some cases did nothing. Roger's louse started strong, heading straight for the edge of the plate, then he turned around and started back to the center.

"You're going the wrong way!" Roger yelled at him. "Turn around!"

Suddenly the tent flap was pulled aside and a page entered, dripping from the rain. It was the same snooty-looking boy who had carried the earl's banner the day the soldiers had left Trentshire. He looked like he'd grown an inch and lost ten pounds since then.

The page spoke in a high-pitched voice that he tried to make deeper. "I'm looking for Roger. The one from Huntley."

Chapter 25

Roger removed the hood of his newly acquired cloak and turned. "I'm Roger."

The boy sniffled, trying to stem a runny nose. "The earl wants to see you."

"The earl?" said Roger, surprised. "What does the earl want with me?"

The page sniffled again. "You'll find out when you get to his tent."

Behind Roger the shouting and yelling and cursing went on. Roger took a look at the race. He'd completely lost track of his tiny entry.

"You'll miss the end," Blackie warned him.

Roger shrugged. It couldn't be helped.

"Ask the earl if he can find us some food," Egwulf told Roger over the noise, while keeping one eye on the race. Supply ships had been unable to reach the army because of the weather, and the infantry had been put on half rations.

"See if he can make the rain stop, while you're at it," added Will.

As the page sighed impatiently, Roger tossed his cloak and blankets on his cot. He put on his helmet against the rain and followed the page from the tent.

They headed for the Toron, their boots squelching and making plopping sounds as they pulled their feet from the glutinous mud. As always, when he was outside the tent, Roger looked for Ailith. Common sense told him that it couldn't have been her he'd seen that night, yet he could have sworn that it had been. He spent much of his free time wandering the camp and searching for her, but to no avail. He'd begun to think his alcohol-sodden mind had been playing tricks on him.

Their passage was delayed by a Breton funeral procession. The hymns of funeral processions had become never ending these days, so much so that Roger only noticed them when they stopped. Nearby, a long-bearded cleric knelt in the mud, hands raised to Heaven, beseeching God's forgiveness for the army's sins, while a small group of people watched. Across the street, a knight's possessions were being auctioned off. The mists lifted briefly, giving Roger a glimpse of the distant hills. The number of tents out there seemed to diminish with each passing day as Saladin's men went home for the winter. *Lucky bastards.*

The funeral procession passed, and Roger and the page continued on their way. They went down the Concourse, whose walkways had been duckboarded by the merchants to facilitate passage by potential customers. Then it was into ankle-deep mud again until they reached the bridge to the Toron. The ditch below the bridge had filled with water, which threatened to rise to the level of the bridge itself, so a cursing work party was trying, with little success, to dig a drainage ditch through the mud. Crossing the bridge, Roger and the page weaved their way up the hill through the pavilions until they reached a small complex of tents over which the red dragon banner drooped in the rain.

The page led Roger inside the largest tent. The tent was crowded and noisy. It smelled of wet wool, wet fur, wet men. Straw was piled thick on the floor to keep the mud from rising. There was relative warmth in here, fed by charcoal braziers. There was also food—stale bread, moldy cheese, sweetmeats, nuts, and half-rotted fruit. To someone as hungry as Roger, it looked better than the Christmas feast at Huntley. He took bread and cheese from a startled servant, who no doubt wondered whether he should be giving the earl's victuals to such a ruffian—save for the guards at the entrance, Roger was the only common soldier in the tent.

The page looked at him disapprovingly. "Hurry up," he said as Roger ground his teeth into the hard bread. When Roger reached for more food, the boy slapped his wrist. Roger didn't know whether to laugh or turn the boy over his knee and spank him. In the end, he did neither. He took more cheese and nuts and stuffed them in his pockets, while the boy watched, incensed.

Finally, the page grabbed Roger's arm and pulled him through the crowd, rather like a child walking a large, obstinate dog. Every few minutes one of the men around them hurried outside the tent to deal with an attack of dysentery, but no one paid notice. Ahead, Roger saw the earl slumped in a camp chair near one of the braziers, his tall form wrapped in a fur cloak, fur cap on his head against the cold, his retainers clustered around him.

As they were about to enter the open area before the earl's chair, the page put out a skinny arm, halting Roger's passage. There was a commotion at the front of the tent, and a party of richly dressed prelates came through, led by a frail but intense old man wearing purple robes. With a start, Roger realized this was the archbishop of Canterbury. Roger was surprised by how much the old man had changed. He looked worn and sick.

The archbishop drew up in front of the earl and rubbed his gloved hands together—jewels on each finger—like a teacher who has just caught a student trying to hide from him. "Ha, Trent—there you are! I heard you were finally awake. I've had great need of you. Whilst you've been lying abed, I've been left to contend with the political situation."

Geoffrey of Trent had been thinking about his brother Hugo. The first thing Geoffrey had learned upon awakening was that Hugo had succumbed from his wounds.

Geoffrey and Hugo had not been particularly close—not since they were small children, anyway. Hugo had been gloomy and pugnacious and ambitious, as befitted a second son, but Geoffrey still missed him. Hugo's death hadn't been

Geoffrey's fault, not in reality, but Geoffrey had commanded the attack and he felt responsible. Hugo had gone down early in the fight, pressing ahead as usual without waiting for men to support him.

Would things have turned out differently had Hugo commanded the Trentshire forces, as had been the plan before Bonjute's meddling? There was no way of telling. Now here came this fool of an archbishop, prattling about politics. Geoffrey didn't like politics and he didn't like the archbishop. No one else liked the archbishop, either—his own cathedral chapter had objected to his being appointed to the archbishopric. And now the old goat was practically accusing Geoffrey of neglecting his duty.

Geoffrey shifted in his chair and tried to act interested. "How so, your eminence?"

"Do your people tell you nothing?" There was a rheumy quality to the archbishop's voice that hadn't been there a month ago.

"I've been unconscious due to a wound, and I've just learned that my brother is dead, so I really haven't had time for camp intrigue. Now what bothers you?"

"Queen Isabelle has been 'persuaded' to marry Conrad, that's what bothers me."

If the archbishop expected outrage from Geoffrey, he was disappointed. "What of young Humphrey, Isabelle's husband?" Geoffrey asked.

The archbishop's unruly white brows came together. "The bishop of Beauvais gave Humphrey a large sum of money to renounce the marriage, and Conrad promised him extensive lands when Conrad becomes king. Humphrey is scared to death of Conrad, so of course he agreed. Formal suit was then brought for annulment of Isabelle's marriage, but as president of the council of bishops, I refused to hear the case. Told the suitors that I would excommunicate everyone involved in the scheme—Conrad, Ibelin, the Papal legate—the lot of them, no matter what their rank."

160

Geoffrey scrunched his eyes. He still suffered from headaches and blurred vision. His flat steel helmet had been battered onto his head so hard by the blow from the mace that they'd had to pry if off. He was glad it was raining, because if the sun was out, he was afraid its rays would blind him.

Baldwin leaned in, his face preternaturally sallow. "So what do you think Conrad and his friends did next? They went behind my back and got the other bishops to issue a Decree of Council, which effected the annulment."

Geoffrey fought off a wave of nausea. He wondered if he was ever going to get better and he longed for the soothing touch of his mistress. "Please get to the point, your eminence. What do you want of me?"

Baldwin said, "I should think that's obvious. King Richard could put a stop to this travesty, but he has been detained in Sicily and won't get here till spring. So it's up to you and me to do it, and we must act quickly. Conrad and Isabelle could be married any day now. I can excommunicate them, but it may take more than that. You must get off your sick bed and do something."

Geoffrey sighed and sat straighter. "Why? The nobles of Outremer want Conrad for their king. It's *their* kingdom, after all."

"*Why?*" Baldwin stiffened. "Guy of Lusignan is kin to King Richard, that's why. You and I are duty bound to—"

"Guy is an ass," Geoffrey said. "He led the kingdom to near destruction once. Make him king, and he'll finish the job. He's damn near destroyed the crusade with this siege. I'd say the kingdom is well rid of him."

Baldwin's eyes, the whites of which had turned a sickly yellow, grew to a width Geoffrey had not deemed possible. "I cannot believe I am hearing this."

Geoffrey rose, fighting the nausea and temporary loss of balance that action produced. "Really? Well, here's what I can't believe, your *eminence*. I can't believe that your men failed us during the assault on the city. If it wasn't for you, the army would be warm and snug in Acre right now instead of sitting here in the rain. Your men should have been trained to use that belfry—but, no, you thought that beneath your precious dignity. I've been told that two of your knights offered to fight one another for the right to go first on one of the belfry's ladders, each claiming preference by right of birth. This, while my men were dying on the city walls, waiting for reinforcements that never came. My brother Hugo is dead, so is my squire Henry, and many more. Had we taken the city, they might have died for something. As it is, they died for nothing, and why? Because of you, sir."

Geoffrey's voice seemed to echo in the sudden silence of the great tent. Baldwin glared at Geoffrey, breathing hard.

Geoffrey sat, calm again. "What are you going to do," he asked the flummoxed Baldwin casually, "excommunicate me?"

"I could," Baldwin threatened. He added, "Living with a woman who is not your wife is a Mortal Sin."

Geoffrey raised his brows in a mocking gesture. "Are you jealous?"

Baldwin drew himself up and his voice was frosty. "King Richard will not be pleased to hear your views."

Geoffrey made a dismissive gesture. "So what? We'll all be dead before that fool gets here." He knew he shouldn't have used those words, but they slipped out. In a way, he didn't care.

The archbishop harrumphed and gathered his purple robes. He beckoned to his equally scandalized coterie of prelates, and the party swept from the tent.

Geoffrey closed his eyes. His head throbbed. His physician leaned in. "Would you like me to bleed you, my lord?"

"No!" Geoffrey pushed him away. "I'm tired of being bled. Have someone bring me wine, hot and spiced. And lots of it"

While he waited for the wine, his page Eustace—son of his good friend Baron Shortwood—approached, bowing. "The soldier called Roger is here, my lord."

"Ah." Geoffrey's spirits lifted and he beckoned with his fingers. "Bring him here."

The page motioned imperiously. As a servant handed Geoffrey the wine, a tall, sturdily built soldier removed his helmet and came forward. Geoffrey heard a gasp from his chronicler—perhaps because the soldier was so dirty. The soldier was being scrutinized by men of far greater rank, but he did not seem overawed by his situation. There was a confidence in the way he carried himself. He was young, with intelligent blue eyes, a thatch of straw-colored hair, and a darker beard. As he reached Geoffrey's chair, he bowed.

Geoffrey sipped the wine, feeling its warmth diffuse through him. He spoke to the soldier, using the English he had learned as a lad, playing with the servant boys. "You are the one called Roger? From Huntley?"

The soldier answered in French. "I am, my lord."

Geoffrey was surprised. "You speak French?"

"I do, my lord."

"However did you learn it?"

The soldier shrugged. "I picked it up while working at the abbey."

Geoffrey nodded, then got to the point. "I'm told I owe you my life, Roger."

The soldier spread his hands. "I only did what anyone would have done, my lord. And it was as much Egwulf and Will of my company as it was me. More so, perhaps."

"That's not what I hear. The lord of Deraa left me a report before he departed. He was much impressed by your actions."

"That was most kind of him, my lord."

"I understand your section lacks a vintenar."

"That's so, my lord. Our vintenar, Unferth, was killed in the attack."

"I'm making you vintenar to replace him."

Now it was the soldier's turn to be surprised. "My lord, I've only been a soldier for a few weeks. I'm hardly qualified to be a—"

"I say you *are* qualified," Geoffrey interrupted. "Do you dispute my judgment?"

163

"No, my lord. Of course not."

"Very well, then. Vintenar it is."

"Thank you, my lord. Thank you very much."

Geoffrey gestured with his hand, indicating the soldier could leave. The soldier bowed and turned away. Interesting fellow, Geoffrey thought, sipping more wine. He had the accent of an educated man; he must have picked that up from the monks at Huntley, as well. Geoffrey wondered what kind of work he had done there.

Back to more serious matters. Geoffrey beckoned his chronicler. "You'll make note of what the archbishop said?"

The young man bent close. "I will, my lord." He held up a finger, wincing, "But could I be excused for a moment?"

Geoffrey nodded, assuming he suffered an attack of dysentery. To Geoffrey's surprise, however, the chronicler hurried through the crowd after the retreating soldier.

Roger heard his name called. He turned and saw a grinning young cleric pushing through the crowd toward him.

"Roger," said Fauston, taking his hand and shaking it, "am I glad to see you."

Chapter 26

Roger's jaw fell. Fauston's long beard had been cut short, and in place of his curly locks there was now a shaven tonsure. The worn green cloak and ploughman's clothes had given way to a white tunic with a red cross on the shoulder and the earl's dragon badge on his breast. Roger recovered and wrung Fauston's hand with delight. "Fauston! What are you doing here? You're supposed to be in Chartres."

"I might ask you the same question," Fauston replied.

"You knew I was going on the crusade."

"Yes, but I didn't know you were going to be the hero of the thing."

"I'm no hero," Roger said dismissively. He clapped Fauston's shoulder. "You've changed."

"As have you, believe me." Fauston looked behind him, toward the earl, and said, "Come, let's go outside."

He led Roger from pavilion, into the rain. In the distance waves smashed the now-deserted beach. On the Accursed Tower, the green flag still flew defiantly. There were few people abroad on the Toron in this weather, and most of those were servants.

Roger said, "I thought I saw Ailith the other night."

"You probably did," Fauston told him. "She's here."

Roger's heart missed a beat. He grabbed Fauston's arm. "Where? I have to see her."

Fauston gave him a level gaze. "She's with the earl."

"With the earl?" Roger frowned, uncomprehending.

"She's his woman—his mistress, for want of a better term."

Roger was numb. Ailith—the earl's mistress?

"I'm sorry," Fauston said.

Roger had thought about Ailith every day since he had last

seen her. The memory of the kiss they had shared had never left him. Indeed, it had magnified itself out of all proportion until it had become the great event of his life. He'd always hoped he would see her again one day, as foolish as that hope had seemed. Now she was here, but she was another man's woman. A hundred thoughts raced through his mind; a hundred emotions tugged at his heart.

They stopped beneath the entrance awning of a nearby crimson tent, and Fauston drew his cloak about him in the cold, pulling the hood up. "Bloody tonsure—I hate getting my head wet."

Roger's joy at seeing Fauston was offset by the news about Ailith. "How did you and Ailith end up here? With the earl? The last I saw you, you were taking her to Leicester."

Fauston drew a deep breath. "Well, we went to Newton, and I gave the priest that money, like I said I would. We left there and started for Leicester, but we got stopped by some bailiffs who were hunting Brock the Badger. They accused me of being Brock and Ailith of being my woman."

Roger laughed. "You! Brock the Badger?"

"It's funny now, but it wasn't then," Fauston said. "They were going to hang us. Right there—no trial. They threw ropes across a tree limb and mounted me and Ailith on horses with nooses around our necks."

"Good God," Roger said.

"They were about to whip the horses from under us when the earl of Trent showed up, along with his squire and few of his knights."

"But the earl left for the crusade days before that," Roger said. "I saw him. What was he doing there?"

"He was taken ill, he said. Something to do with a surfeit of lampreys. He'd spent a few days recovering at the convent of Our Lady Of Mt. Carmel. Anyway, he asked the bailiffs what was happening, and the lead bailiff told him. Before the fellow could finish, Ailith starts crying and going on—you know how Ailith can be—saying that we weren't part of Brock's gang.

That her husband had died, that his brother took her husband's land and turned her out of her house. That she was trying to get to Leicester to start a new life, and she met this kind man on the road and he was helping her.

"The bailiff wasn't having any of that, but the earl, he was staring at Ailith, and you could tell he was thinking what a shame it would be to hang such a looker. 'I'm putting this lady under my protection,' he announces, all gallant.

"The bailiff argued, of course. There's a big reward for Brock and his woman, and the bailiffs didn't want to lose it. Finally the earl called the bailiff an impudent dog and threatened to hang *him* and the rest of his men, too, if they didn't let Ailith go."

"And that stopped them?" Roger said.

"Too bloody true, it did. It was funny—when the earl wasn't looking, Ailith stuck her tongue out at the bailiff. The earl cut the rope from Ailith's neck himself and freed her hands. He offered to escort her to Leicester or said she could go to the Holy Land with his party and he'd find work for her there. As you know, Ailith was never all that keen on going to Leicester, so she said she'd go with him."

"What were you doing all this time?" Roger said.

"I was still sitting with a rope around my neck, hoping the horse didn't decide to go for a walk. The bailiffs still swore I was Brock the Badger and they wanted to hang me. But Ailith pleaded with the earl and said I was innocent, so the earl, he cocks an eye at me and says, 'What kind of work do you do, fellow?'

" 'I'm a scholar,' says I. 'Which is what I've been trying to tell this lot. There's my bag of books to prove it.'

" 'A scholar, eh?'" says the earl." Fauston mimicked the earl rubbing his chin thoughtfully. "Then he says, 'You know, scholar, I've had it in mind to have a chronicle written about my crusade. Is writing a chronicle something you could do?'

"I was still worried about the horse running off, so I said, 'Of course. Love to.' "

" 'Splendid,' says the earl, and he made the bailiffs let me go, too."

Roger grinned. "Well, I'm certainly glad to see you. Writing the earl's chronicle is a great opportunity."

"Oh, it would be, without a doubt," Fauston replied. "Save for one thing."

"What's that?"

"I can't read or write."

Chapter 27

Roger stared. "What do you mean, you can't read? You're a gyrovage, a wandering scholar. You can't be a scholar and not read."

For a moment, the only sounds were the distant crashing of the surf and the rain beating on the tent's awning. Then Fauston cleared his throat. "Actually, I'm not a scholar."

Roger stared harder.

"It's a pose," Fauston explained. "It lets me travel from place to place without attracting attention."

"But your books—your Donatus, your *Doctrinale?*"

"I carry them for appearances. The fellow I took them from told me what the titles were."

" 'Fellow you took them from?' If you're not a scholar, what the Devil are you?"

Fauston made an airy gesture with his hand. "Sometimes I'm a priest, sometimes a knight. Sometimes I'm a merchant, other times a beggar or a ploughman on his way to market. Some men know me by one name and some by another, but mostly they know me as Brock the Badger."

Roger's jaw fell. "*You're* Brock the Badger?"

"S-h-h-h! Not so loud! You want to get me hung?"

"But that's not possible," Roger said, his voice lowered. "Brock the Badger has terrorized Trentshire since I was a boy. You're too young to be him."

"I'm just the current holder of the name. There's been a Brock in Dunham Wood since before the French came. I'm sure there will be one long after I'm gone. Who knows, you might even be Brock one day."

"No chance of that," Roger said. He paused, trying to come to grips with what he'd just heard. "So when those bailiffs were going to hang you . . . ?"

Fauston smiled. "They had the right man."

"Does Ailith know?"

"No, and don't tell her. I'll be strung up in a trice if the earl or any of his staff learn who I am."

Roger still couldn't believe it. "But—you don't look like a criminal."

"And what does a criminal look like? That fat churchman we robbed on the way to Keslow Priory was certainly a criminal, but did he look like one?"

Roger didn't know. This was all so unexpected. "Is Fauston your real name?"

"It is."

"How did you become a robber?"

"A man has to eat," Fauston said. "Steal or starve, that's the choice. There's plenty like me, too—runaway villeins, men outlawed for no good reason." Then he grinned, those blue eyes twinkling. "Anyway, I'm too lazy to be a ploughman."

Roger remembered the blood-curdling tales he'd heard about Brock the Badger. "Have you killed anyone?"

Fauston avoided a direct answer. "Fortunately, most of our victims give in willingly."

Roger said, "So that night you found us in the wood. You weren't searching for a pedlar, were you?"

Fauston hesitated. "I was searching for the members of my gang. Our camp had been attacked that morning by the sheriff's men—yes, the same ones that tried to hang me later. Ironic, isn't it? Our rendezvous in case something like that happened was the eremite's chapel." A wistful look crossed Fauston's face. "Poor fellows, I suppose most of the ones that weren't killed in the attack are hanged by now."

Roger asked the obvious question. "Why are you telling me all this?"

Fauston brightened and clapped Roger's shoulder. "Because, my monkish friend, I need your help. I need you to compose the earl's chronicle for me. The earl has given me until Christmas to present him with an up-to-date version. I've had some chap over in the Genoese camp working on it—can't hire anyone from our lot or the French for fear the word will get out. It's cost me most of my allowance from the earl, and the Genoese fellow's only produced a couple of pages of what I'm pretty sure is rubbish. Fortunately, the earl can't read or write, either. I've told him I've got the story in my head, but he wants to see filled pages. He wants to see progress, or . . .'"

"Or what?"

"Or he'll remove me from his entourage. Kick me out of camp. Come on, say you'll do it."

Roger shook his head. "No."

"Why? You were a chronicler at Huntley. You're perfect for the job."

"I have a job."

"You're not doing much right now except sitting around in the rain. You do owe me, you know. I saved you twice in the woods."

"But you're a criminal!" Roger said, as though that trumped any argument.

"So are you," Fauston shot back. "You're wanted by the Church, in case you've forgotten."

At that moment, the tent flap opened and a woman wrapped in a fur-trimmed robe came out. "Fauston, what's going on out here? Why are you making all this—?" She stopped when she saw Roger.

Roger's heart jumped at the sight of her. It was all he could do not to take her in his arms and kiss her. She was breathtakingly beautiful. Her dark green robe was trimmed in sable, her once-tangled blonde hair was brushed straight back, brushed till it seemed to glow, accentuating her sculpted cheekbones. She smelled of some exotic Eastern perfume. Her blue eyes were as riveting as ever.

Ailith stared at him a long moment. Hesitantly, she said, "Roger?" Then she shouted, "Roger!" and flung her arms around him, and the feel of her warm body against his made

171

him weak in the knees.

After a minute, she let him go and stepped back. "I'm so happy to see you. How are you?" There was more distance in her voice than he might have expected—or was he imagining that?

"I'm well," he replied. "And you?"

"Better than I could ever have dreamed."

"I'm glad to hear it."

She beamed at him. "I didn't recognize you, you've changed so. I swear, you've grown. And that hair!" She took off his helmet and mussed his thick hair.

"You've changed, yourself," Roger said. "You look a proper lady. Speak like one, too. I saw you, the night the rains began."

"I know. It was quite a shock. I wish I could have stopped."

"I've been looking for you ever since."

"And now you've found me." Ailith took his arm and led him into the tent out of the rain. He saw a blanket-covered bed, the blankets mussed as though she had just gotten up. "What are you doing on the Toron?" she said.

"I was called up here by the earl."

She furrowed her brows. "Really?"

"He made me a vintenar for saving his life."

"During the attack on the city? That was *you*?"

"Me and some friends. More them, really, than—"

She hugged him. "Oh, thank you, Roger. You have my eternal gratitude. Geoffrey was unconscious for so long, we feared he would die."

Roger felt a pang in his heart. This was not going the way he had expected it to. But what *had* he expected? Had he a right to expect anything?

He stared at the straw-covered floor. "I—I still think about that kiss we shared when I left England." He looked up. "I think about it a lot. I thought there was something . . . something special between us."

She blushed. "Perhaps there was. But things have changed since then." She took his hands in hers. "We'll always be friends, won't we?"

Friends. Roger struggled to keep his eyes from misting. "Of course."

"I'm glad."

She kissed Roger's cheek and it felt like he'd been branded with a hot iron. Then she ushered him toward the tent entrance. "You'd better go. I must attend on Geoffrey. We'll talk more later."

Outside, Fauston was waiting. "How did it go?" he asked sympathetically.

Roger shrugged, looking away.

They started walking, and Fauston said, "So, will you write the chronicle?"

Roger was too devastated by what had just happened to argue. Besides, Fauston was right—Roger owed him a debt. "Curse you, you knew I would."

Fauston laughed heartily.

Roger stopped and held up a forefinger. "I'll do it, but there's something I want in return."

Chapter 28

"Compliments of the earl!" Roger shouted as he entered the tent.

He carried two canvas sacks, one larger than the other. He put the larger sack down, and from the smaller one he began pulling the scraps of food he had collected at the earl's pavilion, along with others Fauston had found for him. That was the bargain they had made—Roger would write the chronicle, and Fauston would supply him with whatever food he could scavenge from the earl's table.

The men in the tent stopped what they were doing and mobbed Roger, pushing each other aside in their eagerness to get to the food. "God be praised," said gap-toothed Father Mayn as he squirmed his way through the others. "It's a miracle."

Uwen tried to grab the larger bag for himself. Roger yanked it back and held up a hand. "Stop! There's enough for everybody, but we'll give it out fairly."

He waited till the men had settled down, then he handed out the crusts of bread, pieces of cheese, nuts.

"Is this why the earl sent for you?" Egwulf asked, his voice muffled by the crust of bread he had crammed into his cavernous mouth. "To give us food?"

"And to make me vintenar," Roger said, feeling embarrassed.

Munching his scrap of bread, Will slapped Roger's back. "Congratulations. Well deserved."

Long Tom pounded Roger's back, as well. "You'll do a good job," he assured Roger.

Egwulf and Cole and all the others save one crowded around and offered their congratulations. "Could you try for some ale next time, too, your worship?" Black John asked Roger.

"And some women?" said Ralph the Red.

Uwen was the only one who failed to congratulate Roger. "Why didn't they give the job to me?" he growled. "I been a soldier close on ten years. I deserved it more than him."

Roger had expected this. Someone with more experience, like Uwen, was bound to be resentful of Roger's fortune. Roger might have felt the same way had their places been reversed.

"He keeps bringing us food, they can make him commander of the whole army," Egwulf said.

Leaning on his crutches, Offa turned to Uwen. "Maybe they ain't promoted you 'cause you don't deserve it."

"And maybe I'll break your other leg for you," Uwen told him.

"And maybe you won't," Egwulf said, moving forward.

"All right! All right!" Roger said, stepping between them. "None of that. Let's just be happy we have something to eat."

Will said, "Speaking of food, what's in that other sack?"

Grinning, Roger opened the sack and from it drew a cow's rib. There were still scraps of meat on the rib and, more importantly, fat. He put the bone back and opened the sack wide so the men could look in. More bones were inside. "The earl's servants slaughtered one of the draft animals because there was no grain to feed it."

The men laughed and punched one another on the arm; even Uwen looked pleased. They could boil the bones—no shortage of water with all the rain—till the marrow came out and make a broth.

"That's not all," Roger said mischievously.

The men waited. Roger let the suspense build, then, from his jacket pocket, he produced . . .

An onion.

The men went wild. It was a small onion, shriveled and black in places, but an onion nonetheless. Roger handed it carefully—as though it were a particularly delicate egg—to

175

Bald Matthew, the cook. That would go in the broth, as well.

The atmosphere in the tent was merry. Then Roger remembered something. "Hey!" he yelled above the din. "Who won the louse race?"

Young Cole held up a hand. "Me," he said proudly.

Black John playfully mussed the boy's hair. "Can you feature it? Of all the bloody luck. Won it going away, too. Little bugger's rich now."

"Be buying himself a house in London and all," Slowfoot chimed in. "Hiring us as his servants."

Grinning in spite of himself, Cole took more cheese to go with his bread, ignoring the mold on both. "Ain't you going to have none for yourself?" he asked Roger.

Roger was still hungry but he shook his head. It wouldn't be fair for him to have more. "I had my fill at the earl's pavilion."

Cole started to say something else, then he saw someone behind Roger, and he went silent and backed off. Before Roger could turn, a guttural voice said. "Well, well, the queer has food."

Roger turned. It was Dirk.

The shaven-headed Brabanter stood with his good hand on his hip, the broken hand still muffled in a dirty bandage. He had lost weight. His cheeks were hollow, and there were dark circles under his eyes from where Roger had broken his nose. The nose itself was flat and misshapen.

"What's it to you?" Roger asked him.

"I want some," Dirk said.

The tent went quiet. "Sorry," Roger told Dirk. "The food's only for the men in this section."

Dirk said, "I am the new centenar of axe men. I can order you to give me some."

"You can give me orders on the field of battle," Roger corrected, "but you can't tell me what to do with this food."

Dirk sneered. "Did you steal it?"

"How I came by it is none of your affair."

"I could turn you in, you know. The Council of Barons has decreed a death sentence for anyone caught stealing food."

Roger had heard that something like this was being discussed. He didn't know it had gone into effect, though.

Dirk smiled. "Now, you will give me food?"

"No," Roger said.

The two men faced each other. Dirk was trying to hide his rage from the men looking at him. Roger enjoyed having the Brabanter at his mercy. At last Roger said, "Maybe if you asked politely, I would reconsider."

Dirk ran the back of his hand across his mouth. He looked right and left at the men who were watching. Then he gave a hearty chuckle and tried to make it seem like the confrontation had been a joke. "All right, then, can I have some of your food?"

"You forgot something," Roger said.

"What?"

" 'Please.' "

Dirk's eyes narrowed. His breath was shallow. In a flat tone he said, "Please?"

Roger handed him the sack. "Help yourself."

Dirk rooted in the sack and fished out a crust of black bread. He looked at the bread like he had just found the Holy Grail and gnawed it with what teeth he had left. The tension in the tent dissolved.

"Why'd they make you centenar?" Roger asked him.

Dirk seemed friendly enough now. "They wanted a man with experience now that Warin is dead. I cannot fight yet, but I can give the correct orders." He ripped at the bread like a wolf tearing at its prey. "There is a new commander of footmen, too. Payen of Beaufort. A knight. No one knows from where he comes."

Roger remembered the old foot commander, James of Claire, bent over on the walls of Acre, an arrow in his eye. "What's this Payen like?" Roger said.

Dirk made a noncommittal gesture. "We will find out tomorrow night—we have been assigned to camp guard." Dirk

177

finished the bread, peered in the sack and gave Roger a questioning look.

Roger nodded. Dirk reached in again for a piece of cheese. He picked dirty straw and other things off the cheese, ate it. "Maybe," he said, "maybe we have gotten off on what you English call the wrong foot."

Roger said nothing.

Dirk went on; this was difficult for him. "I would like the bygones to be bygones between us. I need it to be that way. We must work together now that you are vintenar, and it won't do us any good if we are at each other's throats. I have dreamed of being centenar for a long time, and I don't want to do a bad job."

Roger still said nothing.

Hesitantly, Dirk held out his left hand, the uninjured one. Roger paused, then shook the proffered hand with his own left hand. He was surprised that Dirk didn't try to crush his hand.

"One more thing," Roger said.

Dirk raised his eyebrows.

"Don't call me 'queer' again."

Dirk waved it off. "I won't. It was just a joke, eh?"

Roger turned away, headed for the tent entrance. As he left, Offa hobbled up to him on his crutches. "You trust him?" Offa asked.

They looked at Dirk, who was now talking to his friend Uwen.

"No," Roger said. "He's right, though. He and I have to work together. I'll wait and see how things go from here. Right now there's somewhere I must be."

Chapter 29

The sick tent stank of damp and decay, of pus and urine and feces. Because of the rain, the area outside the tent had long since been cleared. Most of the wounded had been returned to their section tents; only a few remained. Roger looked here first because the man had been so badly injured he was afraid they hadn't been able to move him.

Roger didn't know why he was doing this, except that he felt compelled to. It was as though it had not been his decision to make.

He moved deeper into the large tent, eyes adjusting to the gloom. One of the washerwomen, a huge, mannish woman named Delva, attended the patients, giving them water and changing their bandages.

Roger saw the man. He lay off by himself on a cot, covered by a thin blanket.

Roger had learned what he'd come to learn. The man was still alive. Roger should have left. But he moved forward, once again as though lacking control over his actions.

Roger made no sound as he approached, yet Tatwine divined his presence and turned his head. Tatwine's face had been red with blood the last time Roger had seen him, so he seemed completely different. His hair was a deep reddish brown and he had a wispy chin beard. But it was his eyes that drew attention—they were dark, feral, cunning.

Dangerous.

"It's you," Tatwine croaked.

Roger felt awkward. "Glad to see you're still alive," he said. Tatwine's head wound had been sewn, none too expertly; the wound in his side was hidden beneath the blanket. "I guess you're too weak to return to your section tent?"

"They didn't want me back," Tatwine said.

That made things even more awkward. Tatwine reached up and took Roger's hand. Tatwine's hand was hot; his grip was weak. "You saved me," he said, "you and God." He caught his breath and continued. "When I was laying in that tower, wounded, with the flames licking at me, I told God that if I lived through this I'd mend my ways, that I'd make up for all the bad things I done before." He swallowed. "I didn't expect Him to listen to me, but He did. I knew it would take a miracle to save me, and a miracle is what I got." He paused for breath again. "I intend to live up to that vow I made. I was a sinner before, none worse, but I've changed."

"I'm glad to hear that," Roger said, looking for a graceful way to end this interview. He wondered what had ever possessed him to come here.

Tatwine's bird-like grip on Roger's hand grew stronger. "When I get out of here, I want to be in your section."

Roger hadn't expected that.

"Please," Tatwine begged. "I want to make up to you for what you done for me. Nobody ever done nothing like that for me before. You won't regret it, I promise. I won't give you no trouble. I told you, those days are done."

Of course he wanted to be in another section, Roger thought. His old section wouldn't take him back.

"I know what you're thinking," Tatwine said, "but you're wrong."

"It's not—" Roger had started to say the decision wasn't his to make, but he was vintenar now, so presumably he could let anyone into the section that he wanted.

Tatwine's feral eyes held Roger's. "Please," he said.

Forgiveness, Roger thought. *That's what Christ preached.*

He took a deep breath. "Very well."

"Thank you, thank you. You won't regret it."

"See that I don't," Roger said, trying to sound authoritarian and knowing that he was failing badly at it.

Tatwine lay back down, sweating heavily despite the damp chill.

Roger turned and left the tent, wondering what he had gotten himself into.

God's plan.

Chapter 30

Fauston waited for Roger by the Toron bridge, stamping his feet and beating his arms about his chest in the cold "What took you so long?" he said.

"I had to visit a sick man." Roger wondered what Tatwine would say if he found out that Roger knew Brock the Badger. Tatwine probably worshipped Brock.

Fauston nodded to the guards, who let him and Roger cross the bridge. The two men wound their way through the pavilions, whose once-gay colors had faded from exposure to the elements. Many were mended or patched. The rain had stopped. Watery sunlight broke through the clouds, and it seemed as though half the camp was suddenly scurrying about on neglected business.

"Where are we going?" Roger asked Fauston.

"Ailith's tent. I'm supposed to work in the earl's chancery with his chaplain, Stephen, but that won't do with you around. We need privacy. The earl isn't in Ailith's tent that much—he spends most of his time with the council of barons or with his own lords. Ailith will warn us any time he's coming."

"I still can't believe you're Brock the Badger," Roger said in a low voice as they walked.

"*Was*," Fauston corrected, looking around to see if anyone had heard. "Wouldn't be surprised if there's not a new Brock by now. Brock the Badger and his jolly robbers. Well, he's welcome to it. Let me tell you, living in the forest isn't as glamorous as the singers make it out to be. It's damned cold in the winter. Wet, too."

Roger went on. "Is it true that you only rob the rich, and you give the money to the poor?"

Fauston barked a laugh. "Not much use robbing the poor

now, is it? I rob the rich and give the money to myself." He saw disappointment in Roger's face and added, "Of course I give some to the poor. It's good business. I pay them more than the bailiffs do for information about me, so that when the bailiffs come snooping around, the villagers look out for me."

They had reached Ailith's small crimson tent. They went in. Compared with the chill outside, the tent was warm. It smelled of hair and perfume and warm skin . . . of Ailith. Roger looked at the bed, tried to picture Ailith and the earl on it, tried to picture what they . . . He shook his head, came back to reality.

In one corner of the tent were a couple of camp chairs. Next to the chairs were two trunks. From the larger of these, Fauston pulled a writing board. "Ailith told me I could put your things in here."

"*My* things?" Roger said.

"Your writing implements—all right, *my* things if you must be particular about it."

Roger took off his helmet and armor-plated leather jack. He seemed to live in them, and it felt strange not having them on. He sat in one of the chairs and placed the heavy writing board on his lap. It was unwieldy and uncomfortable, but it would have to do—one could hardly expect to find a fully equipped scribe's carrel, with its cushioned, high-backed chair and perfectly slanted desk, out here.

"Here's the parchment the earl got for you."

Roger shot him a look.

Fauston rolled his eyes. "For me," he corrected.

Roger took the parchment. The large folded sheets, called gatherings, had already been cut into pages. Roger would have preferred that not be done because it would take longer to rule the pages this way, but there was nothing he could do about it. "You should see how many quills I've prepared," Fauston said. "Took a while to learn how to cut them proper, but I'm pretty good at it now, if I say so meself. Had to do something to pass the time."

Roger fingered the parchment. It was average quality, a bit thicker than he was used to. At least it didn't have hair on it, as inferior parchment sometimes did. He held a sampling of the sheets to the light, turned them both ways. The parchment was white, from a sheep, not the brown that Roger preferred. Brown parchment, which came from cattle, had more interesting color variations than did white. Here and there on the parchment could be seen the outlines of the animal's veins, ridges from old scars. Only one sheet had a hole, made during the drying process, and that had been stitched before it got too large. Roger wondered if the earl had purchased the parchment locally or brought it all the way from England. He smiled to himself, remembering how old Brother Paulinus could look at a sheet of vellum and tell you where the cow—or sheep—had come from within twenty miles. Roger had never mastered that knack.

He put a sheet on the board and rubbed it with a pumice cake to even out the irregularities and remove any remaining oils. "Watch what I'm doing," he told Fauston. "It will be a lot of help if you can prepare the sheets for me ahead of time."

Fauston had found—or stolen—a metal ruler, and Roger used the ruler to draw lines on the parchment, scoring them lightly with the back of his knife. "Be careful you don't tear the sheet when you do this," he told Fauston, "else it will be ruined." Roger hadn't done it this way himself in a while. At Huntley these days they used the new method of ruling sheets, drawing lines on the parchment with thin pieces of metallic lead.

When he had ruled several sheets, Roger checked the ink. It was thin but serviceable—he would mix his own later. He seated the inkhorn securely in its hole on the writing board, knowing from experience how easy it was to knock over an inkhorn. He picked up one of the quills; it was black and white, made from a seagull's feather. Roger sighted down it. The quill curved slightly to the right—good for a right-handed scribe. The tip was firm, hollowed out. The nib had been sliced vertically, shaped along the sides, and cut across the top.

"This is good work," he told Fauston. "Who taught you how to do it?"

"A Pisan friend of mine, before he died. Showed me how to wet them and dry them in hot sand to make the tips hard. I haven't had much else to do, so I been preparing quills to pass the time and make myself look busy."

Roger shook his head. "What would you have done if I hadn't turned up?"

"Legged it, most likely. Try to steal some money and go where they don't know me."

"You wouldn't have become a soldier?"

Fauston made a face. "I'm not the soldiering type."

Roger cut off about a quarter of the quill's length, felt the balance, was satisfied. He dipped the quill in the ink, and at the top of the first page he wrote, *Lege Feliciter*," using the prescribed three letters per dip of ink.

"That the title?" asked Fauston, looking over his shoulder.

"No," Roger said, "it means, 'read this happily.' "

Fauston grunted. "Don't see much around here to be happy about."

"The story will have a happy ending when we take Jerusalem," Roger explained.

"If you say so."

Roger began, forming each letter carefully, with broad strokes, as Brother Paulinus had taught him to do in what seemed like another life. He started with the Creation, as all good chroniclers did, passing rapidly through the Old and New Testaments to modern times and the earl of Trent's heritage. From this point, he had to rely on Fauston, who had been given the information by the earl.

Geoffrey of Trent was descended from a prominent Norman family. His ancestor Eustace of Thaon had distinguished himself at the battle of Hastings—which Fauston obstinately referred to by the English name "Senlac"—and had been rewarded with estates in Trentshire and elsewhere in

England. Eustace's son, Hugo, had been given the earldom for services rendered to the first King Henry. Roger glossed over Richard's rebellion against the second Henry and the earl's part on the losing side, concentrating instead on the disastrous battle of Hattin, its aftermath, and Geoffrey's heroic decision to take the cross and set himself against the Saracen champion, Saladin.

By the time the story got to the earl's arrival in the Holy Land, it was dark outside. The tent's straw floor was littered with used quills—at Huntley, Roger had sometimes gone through sixty in a day. The inkhorn had been emptied half a dozen times. Roger shook his cramped hand, flexing his fingers. "That's enough for one day."

Fauston said, "You'll be here tomorrow, right?"

Roger shook his head. "My company has guard. I have to be sure my section is ready—weapons sharpened, armor polished, that sort of thing."

"I need this done by Christmas," Fauston reminded him.

"It will get finished. Pour me a cup of that wine, will you?"

As Fauston poured, the tent flap opened and Ailith came in, followed by a morose, broad-shouldered serving woman.

Roger tried to act casual, though he tingled all over at the sight of Ailith. She sauntered over to the writing board and glanced at the inked pages, casually laying a hand on Roger's shoulder. "You've done a lot," she told Roger.

"Yes," he said. His voice cracked as he spoke, making him feel like an idiot.

She took the hand from his shoulder, and he found himself missing her touch. She spoke to Fauston, worry in her voice. "What will happen if Geoffrey finds out about this?"

"What will happen if I don't have anything to give him by Christmas?" Fauston countered.

Ailith nodded. She hummed a tune as Roger and Fauston returned the writing materials to the trunks.

"You seem in good spirits," Roger remarked.

"I am," she told him. "The wedding's coming."

"Wedding?"

"Conrad and Isabelle—don't you men know anything?"

"I'm just a soldier. They don't tell us about weddings."

She twirled to imaginary music. "It will be the grandest affair the camp has seen. All the high nobility of Christendom will be there—well, all but the Lusignans and their friends. I've practiced my dancing for a month. I can't wait to try out the steps I've learned."

"You're not worried?" Roger said.

She made a face, "Me? I was the best dancer in my village— the best for miles about, so I'm told. If I'm worried about anything, it's that the dancing won't go on long enough." She twirled again. "Perhaps I'll get to dance with Conrad himself, the future king of Outremer—though I'm glad it's not me that's marrying him. Or with Frederick of Swabia, the emperor's son. Or with the count of Champagne—he's so handsome."

Fauston cleared his throat. "Not to put a damper on things, but aren't we supposed to be among the Lusignans' friends?"

Ailith made a dismissive gesture with her hand. "Geoffrey doesn't care a fig for that. With the archbishop sick like he is, Geoffrey can do as he pleases. He thinks Conrad will make a proper king."

Roger remembered the archbishop's wasted appearance when he was in the earl's tent. "What's wrong with the archbishop?"

Fauston shrugged. "A fluctuation of the humors, they call it. The physicians have prayed over him and bled him and fed him small amounts of boiling oil, but nothing seems to do any good. If he dies, the earl will command the entire English force until King Richard gets here."

"I pray Richard gets here soon," Roger said. "He'll sort out this mess."

"If you say so," Fauston said.

Roger's eyes widened. "You don't doubt Richard's abilities, surely?"

"I'd like to know what's taken him so damned long getting

here."

"I'm certain he has a good reason."

Fauston looked skeptical. "If you say so," he repeated.

Chapter 31

Roger and Fauston bade Ailith good night and left the tent. Ailith watched them go. Roger looked back once, wistfully it seemed to her, then exited through the tent flap.

Ailith let out her breath and scraped a foot across the tent's dirty straw floor covering. She hadn't told Roger, but seeing him in the rain that night had made her heart stop. She had wondered if he was in the camp, and part of the reason she had accepted Geoffrey's offer to join his company was because by doing so she might get to see Roger again. He was even better looking than she remembered, more manly somehow. When she'd laid her hand on his shoulder just now a jolt had gone up her arm and she'd thought for a moment that she was paralyzed. It was what she imagined being struck by lightning must feel like—that kind of jolt. It had taken all her willpower to take her hand off him, even more to pretend it was done casually.

She looked around her—at the tent, at the rich clothes she wore, the fur coverings on her bed, all of it a far cry from her thatched house at home and the flea-ridden straw sack she had slept on next to her parents, brothers, and sisters.

When Geoffrey had saved Ailith from the sheriff's men, the plan had been for her to join his washerwomen. But the journey to catch up to Geoffrey's troops had taken weeks— Geoffrey's party having been delayed by bad weather in the English Channel. It had been a small group: Geoffrey and his squire—now dead—a handful of knights—some of them now dead, as well—Ailith, and Fauston. Ailith and Geoffrey had been thrown together; as the only woman in the party, it was inevitable. They had talked—at night over campfires, as guests in the halls of monasteries or castles, or in seaside inns. But most of all they had talked while riding. They seemed somehow alone there, the two of them, under the endless panorama of sky and field and forest, even though others accompanied them. The talk had gradually led to something else—love, infatuation? She wasn't sure, but she knew that when she had given herself to him—one night in a forest glade—she had done it willingly, and she still did. Seeing Roger again had made her question what she had done. It had made her feel guilty. Roger had a strange effect on her. She felt natural around him in a way she had never felt around anyone else. She could be her real self with Roger in a way she could not be with anyone else, even Geoffrey.

Geoffrey was committed to Ailith, and she to him. She had to be. Geoffrey was handsome and charming and kind. He offered her a good life—maybe not as a wife, but he would be far from the only man who kept a woman to whom he was not married. It was the way of the world. Geoffrey said he loved her, and she believed him, just as she had believed herself when she said she loved him—until she'd seen Roger again.

So where did Roger fit in? He didn't, she told herself. He couldn't. He was a friend, and that was all he could ever be. Geoffrey offered the life that Ailith had dreamed about. Roger was a common soldier. Ailith owed Roger her life and her heart—he would always have her heart—but Geoffrey offered her the future she had dreamed of.

From the hidden folds of her dress she produced her purse and stared at it. It held the fifteen pounds that had been her share of the forest robbery. She had not spent a penny of that fifteen pounds. She planned never to spend it. She would keep it, though. She would keep it as long as she lived.

She realized her servant Margaret was speaking to her. Hastily she replaced the purse. "I'm sorry," she told Margaret, "what did you say?"

Margaret was an imposing woman of indeterminate age. Geoffrey's steward had picked her from the washerwomen to be Ailith's servant. She'd had a "husband" with the spearmen, but he had died of the bloody flux on the army's journey to the Holy Land. She'd lost at least twenty pounds since Ailith had first seen her and God knows how many since she'd left England. Flesh hung in loose folds on her big arms. "I *said*, I suppose the earl will be coming by tonight?"

"Yes, he will. And he'll be staying. Pour me some wine, will you, then straighten up in here."

Margaret gave her a look, then began halfheartedly making the bed. She didn't pour the wine, but Ailith didn't make a point of it. Ailith looked around the tent. "This straw needs to be swept out, but . . ," she saw Margaret's expression, "but I suppose you can't do that. Not right now."

"That's right," Margaret said.

Ailith saw the cups from which Roger and Fauston had been drinking. Geoffrey would want to know who had been here. Ailith had no friends among the few women on the Toron, so it would have to have been men, and Geoffrey might question that.

"Stop what you're doing, please, and go rinse out those cups," Ailith told Margaret.

Margaret acted like she hadn't heard; she kept fussing with the bed.

Ailith raised her voice. "Margaret!"

Nothing.

Ailith wasn't going to stand for this. She stood tall. "Margaret! Rinse out those cups!"

Margaret turned slowly and fixed Ailith with a baleful eye. "They're your friends. You do it."

Ailith paled. "You dare speak to me like that? Might I remind you that you're a servant?"

Margaret's face hardened with contempt. "And might I remind *you* that you're a jumped-up village trollop? You may go around here and give yourself airs and *'La-di-da, I'm going to dance with the king, isn't he the lucky one?'* but you don't fool nobody. You've slept with the pigs, same as me, and not so long ago, neither. You'll never lose that, no matter how hard you try."

Ailith breathed heavily. "I'll tell the earl about this. He'll—"

"He'll what? Send me back to the washerwomen? That's where I want to be. Not up here with the likes of you."

Margaret turned and started from the tent.

"Where are you going?" Ailith demanded.

Margaret said nothing. She parted the tent flap and left.

"Come back here!" Ailith cried.

But Margaret didn't come back. Shaking with anger and humiliation, Ailith splashed wine into the cup Roger had used. She raised it to her lips but couldn't drink. With a little cry, she hurled the cup at the tent entrance. Then she sank upon one of the camp chairs. She buried her face in her hands and began to cry.

Chapter 32

The men huddled in little groups in the dark, talking and trying to stay warm. Dirk had told Roger not to worry about trouble tonight. Because of the cold weather, nothing bad was likely to happen.

Roger paced back and forth, shield over his back, axe and dagger in his belt, cloak drawn close around him, the hood drawn over his head and held tightly in place by his helmet. Beneath his armored jack, he wore his other jack. It was a cumbersome arrangement, and one that did little to keep out the cold. It was a raw, damp cold, the kind of cold that ate right through you, no matter how many layers of clothing you wore. The cold was made even worse by the never-ending hunger. It gnawed at the pit of Roger's stomach like there was a small animal digging away down there, rooting for sustenance.

Roger's men were guarding a section of the long ditch that protected the Christian camp from Saladin's army. The ditch had been constructed with enormous effort during the early days of the siege, when it seemed as though the camp would be overrun at any moment by the Saracens. The ditch had steep sides and was narrow at the bottom, so that attackers would be crowded together down there and become easy targets for Christian arrows. Sharpened stakes had been placed at the bottom, as well, facing anyone sliding down from the Saracen side, waiting to impale them. The ditch was half-filled with icy water right now from all the rain. Anyone crazy enough to attack the Christian camp would have to wade across.

Roger was thinking about his first meeting with Payen of Beaufort, the new foot commander. Payen was a barrel-chested, prematurely grey-haired fellow, who, despite months in the Holy Land had somehow not acquired a tan. He'd come here with a contingent from Burgundy, but his lord had died, so he had taken service with the earl of Trent. He had inspected Roger's men before they had gone on guard, strutting back and forth in front of them like he'd just been made king. "Are these guttersnipes of yours ready?" he asked Roger.

"Yes, Captain," Roger said.

"Yes, what?" Payen snapped.

Roger had no idea what the man was talking about. "Yes, Captain, they're ready."

"You will address me as 'my lord,' " Payen told him.

Roger had never called James of Claire "my lord," and he didn't see why he should do it for this fellow. Payen might be a knight, but he wasn't Roger's lord. "Why?" Roger said.

"Because I'll have you flogged if you don't, you impudent hound!" Payen said. In the background, Dirk caught Roger's eye and shook his head in warning.

Roger grit his teeth. "Very well," he said.

"Very well, *what?*"

Roger's teeth grit even harder. "Very well .., my lord."

"That's better." Payen leaned toward Roger. "I'm watching you, Roger. I'll see if a man like you, with no experience, deserves to be vintenar. My opinion is, you don't. Do we understand each another?"

"Yes," Roger said. Reluctantly, he added, "My lord."

That exchange still rankled Roger. He hadn't asked, or wanted, to be made vintenar, but he didn't want the rank taken from him by somebody like Payen. The muddy ground squelched as Roger walked. To one side were the lights of the Saracen camp, warm and inviting. To the other side was the vast tent city of the Christian army. Lights shone there, too, but not many, not even on the Concourse, the busy merchants' street. Precious firewood had to be conserved. The camp looked ghostly under the new moon, acre upon acre of spread canvas, as far as the eye could see, with dark gaps where lay the horse and animal lines, wagon parks, and barriers between the various nationalities.

Beyond the camp was the sea, whose phosphorescent breakers rolled onto the shore with a never-ending crash. And, of course, there were the looming walls of the city, almost an afterthought now, as the Christian army struggled to survive.

"Conditions must be terrible in there," Will said, coming up beside Roger and gazing toward the city. Only the faintest glow emanated from behind those high walls. No doubt firewood was at even more of a premium over there than it was in the crusaders' camp. Will's boyish face had grown gaunt. "I feel sorry for those poor devils, infidels though they be. I can't imagine they have any food left—they've been blockaded since the beginning of the year."

Roger shivered. "Everyone says they'll surrender soon. Within days, maybe."

"I wish they'd get on with it," Will said.

The two men stood silently for a moment. "What manor do you come from?" Roger asked Will.

"Winstead," Will replied.

"I know Winstead—it's not far from Huntley."

Will nodded. "There was another lad from Winstead with the spearmen, but he's gone now, died in the attack on the city. And the lord's son Peter is with the knights." He paused. "You know it's funny, but when I think of home, it's always sunny and warm there, and the people are always friendly. I wonder why that is?"

Roger shrugged; he didn't know. In his memories of the abbey, he was always an outcast.

Will went on. "Was I was home now, I'd be snug in my cottage, eating porridge with some bacon thrown in as a treat now that the animals are slaughtered. Washing it down with Agnes's good ale, my dog Horsa lying at my feet. Raised Horsa from a pup, I did. As fine a hunting animal as ever you'll see."

Roger grinned. " 'Hunting'—you mean poaching?"

Will cleared his throat noncommittally.

"I know your wife is pregnant. Do you have any other

children?" Roger asked.

Even in the dark, Roger could see Will's hunger-hollowed eyes sparkle. "A boy and a girl," he said proudly. "The new babe will be born next month. Wonder how big he'll be when I finally get home."

"Who was the girl who wanted a Saracen princess for a slave when the company was marching off?"

Will frowned, then remembered and laughed. "That was my sister Mary. She said 'slave,' but what she really meant was 'playmate.' "

Will sighed. "I miss home, Roger, truly I do. I miss the land—that good soft earth that turns beneath your plough. The woodland, the streams. The people. Most of all, I miss Agnes. God save me, but I miss her more than I can put into words."

Roger said, "If you miss it so much, why are you here?"

Will looked sharply at him. "Same reason we all are. Has to be done, doesn't it? We have to recapture Jerusalem—it's our Christian duty." Then he said, "What about you? Do you have a family at Huntley?"

Roger hesitated. Will had become Roger's best friend, and he decided to confide in him, to tell him the truth. "No family. Actually, I was a monk, up at the abbey. I killed another monk, and I ran away and came here to atone for my sins."

Will's mouth dropped open. Then he laughed and pointed at Roger knowingly. "That's a good one. You almost had me believing you for a moment. Come on, what were you really?"

"I told you, a monk."

Will laughed again, and Roger said, "You don't believe me?"

Will shook his head. "Have it your way."

Will stared out to sea for a bit. "It's sometimes hard to believe we're really in the Holy Land. That Christ Himself might have once stood where we are now. There's so much I can't wait to see. Jerusalem—the Holy Sepulchre, the Mount of Olives. There's also Nazareth, Bethlehem, the Sea of Galilee— so many places."

"Not Acre?" Roger said.

"Any place but Acre." Will shook his head. "I'll tell you what, once I get home, I'm never leaving again. I've got thirty acres in the fields and an option for more. I'll be hayward when I get back. With luck, they'll make me reeve one day." The reeve was the manor's head man; he worked with the lord's steward.

Roger said. "At least you have something to go back to."

"And you don't? Oh, that's right—you were a *monk*." He laughed. "We'll probably find out you were really Brock the Badger or something."

Near them was a small group of men, shapeless because of all the blankets and spare clothes with which they had covered themselves. One of them was Offa. Payen had given Roger the Devil about letting Offa come up here on his crutches, saying how useless he'd be if something happened, but Roger didn't care. Offa wanted to be with his friends; he was tired of standing tent guard. Right now, Offa had to piss something fierce. Leaning on his crutches, he fumbled futilely in his voluminous garments. "I can't find my dick," he said.

"He said the same thing on his wedding night," Egwulf told the others.

"No wonder his wife's so mean," said Ralph the Red.

"She couldn't find it either," Swift John said.

"His dick—or hers?" Ralph said.

"Hey!" roared Offa, and the others laughed.

Suddenly Roger put up a hand. "Shhh!" He listened. "What was that?"

"What was what?" Egwulf said.

Roger put a finger to his lips.

"Did you hear something?" Will whispered to Roger.

Roger strained his ears. "I'm not sure." He heard the noise of wind and surf, fainter noises from the animals in camp. Far away, a dog barked. There it was again—he didn't know what the noise was, but instinct told him it shouldn't be there. It seemed to come from the far right of his line.

"Look to your weapons," he told his men in a low voice.

197

"Full alert. Spread out and watch the ditch. No talking unless you see something. Uwen, you're in charge here. Egwulf, you're with me."

He felt like a fool for worrying about staying warm when he should have been doing his job. Of course, this could still prove to be nothing. He hoped to God it was.

He felt for the axe in his belt and led Egwulf along the parapet. They passed the other men of his section, spreading out from their groups. It was nearly impossible to see in this darkness; the new moon was blotted out by clouds. They came to Arcil, the next to last man in Roger's line.

"Did you see or hear anything?" Roger asked Arcil.

"Not sure," Arcil said. "Maybe." Arcil sounded scared; his eyes were wide. "Kind of like somebody choking." As if to reassure himself, he added, "Didn't hear nothing from Tom, though. He'd of called out if something was wrong."

Long Tom was Roger's last man. There was a gap past Tom, then a company of Flemings held the line. Roger and Egwulf hurried on. Roger stepped on something soft in the dark, nearly tripping over it. He knew without looking that it was a man.

"Tom?" Roger knelt and put out a hand, and the hand came away covered with a warm, sticky liquid.

Roger swore. It was Long Tom, right enough. His throat had been slit.

Chapter 33

Egwulf knelt beside Roger. He looked at Long Tom's body and swore. "Poor sod. All he wanted was to get away from the bees."

Hot bile rose in Roger's throat. He remembered Long Tom bellowing "Girls of Falaise" off key. He remembered Tom congratulating him when he'd been made vintenar. "You'll do a fine job," he had assured Roger. And now Roger had gotten him killed—a dark gash across his pale throat, blood spilling down the front of him, clotting in his beard and forming a pool beneath his body.

"How many d'you reckon?" Egwulf said.

Roger shook off his thoughts, came back to the moment. "Not many, else we'd have heard them. A raiding party."

"Sound the alarm?"

"Not yet. Too many places they can hide if they hear the alarm. They can shed their weapons and armor and pretend to be camp servants or laborers. We'll have a better chance of catching them if we take them unawares."

Roger unslung the shield from his back as he talked. He removed his jack and took off the second jack he had been wearing beneath it. Suddenly he didn't feel cold any more. "Go back to Arcil," he told Egwulf as he redonned his armor-plated jack. "Tell him to pass word down the line to be on the lookout for raiders. Have Uwen send a man to alert the Flemings and then have him tell Dirk and Payen what's going on."

"What about you?" Egwulf said.

Roger drew his dagger. He left his shield with the second jack. "I'm going after them. Join me when you're done."

Egwulf turned away and Roger started toward the sleeping crusader camp. Did he believe what he had said about taking the raiders unaware, or was he trying to make up for his mistakes by playing hero? He didn't know. Why had he listened to Dirk? His first action as a vintenar—not even an action, just guard duty—and he had gotten one of his men killed, slaughtered like a farm animal.

It was perhaps three furlongs between the ditch and the line of latrines and wagon parks that formed the outer edge of the Christian camp; the first tents were a half-furlong beyond that. The horse lines used to be out here, too, but because raiders had killed so many of the animals last summer, most units had moved their animals behind the tent lines, making it harder for Saracen infiltrators to get at them.

Roger moved quickly, sweating now, despite the cold. As he reached the latrines, he heard running footsteps in the mud behind him.

He turned and crouched, dagger ready.

The running stopped. "Roger!" a voice hissed.

Roger relaxed. "Here!" he said in a loud whisper.

Egwulf loomed up in the darkness. He was accompanied by Will. "Couldn't let you two have all the fun," Will grinned. Will had left his helmet behind; he brushed his thick blond hair from his eyes.

Roger motioned them forward. They crossed the line of open latrine pits—the stench was lessened because of the cold. To their right was a wagon park. To the left was Resurrection Road, so named because at the end of it lay Saladin's army and a quick passage to Paradise.

As they moved across the uneven ground, Egwulf snapped his fingers once. The others turned, and Egwulf pointed to his feet, where lay a dark shape—a body, face down.

"Bad time for him to get the shits," Egwulf muttered.

They neared the tents, whose conical tops stretched into the darkness. Banners flapped in the fitful offshore breeze. Roger thought this part of the camp belonged to the Germans, but he wasn't sure.

He held up a hand. The party stopped and listened.

Nothing.

Then a noise. To the right. Another. Footsteps in the mud? Men moving stealthily?

Roger thought. What could the raiders be planning? It would be too dangerous for a small number to enter a crowded tent, even if the occupants were sleeping. Starting fires? That had been a popular tactic during the summer, but everything was too wet to burn now. What then? The horse lines—kill a number of valuable horses? All the camp animals were under heavy guard because men had been stealing them and killing them for food, but the Saracens might not know that. Or were the raiders headed for the knights' tents at the head of the camp street? There weren't as many men in those tents, and it would unnerve the common soldiers to have their leaders murdered. That's what Roger would do, if he were them.

"We'll cut them off," Roger whispered. "Be quiet as you can."

He, Will, and Egwulf hurried up the camp street, parallel to the direction from which they had heard the noises. If Roger was wrong—well, he didn't want to think about that. They passed tent after tent, moving lightly as possible. One tent to go before the break and the knights' tents. Roger motioned his men to the right, to the next dark street, to wait.

They had barely settled themselves when they heard footsteps approaching. Against the sky Roger made out dark shapes. He saw the outline of a conical helmet, unlike any helmet the Christians wore.

The shapes came closer. They were right in front of Roger and his party.

"Now!" Roger said.

Egwulf beat him to the first one, grabbing the man and thrusting a knife into his breast before he had time to react. The next man turned and ran. Will threw a knife at him. The knife stuck in the man's back, and the man stumbled and fell. Before the man could do anything else, Ralph ran up and struck him across the spine with his axe.

More footsteps. Running away. Roger started after.

He ran parallel to the steps, hoping he wouldn't trip over a tent rope in the dark and break his neck. Around him there were cries and shouts as men roused themselves from sleep.

Roger got ahead of the steps. He crossed over, down a camp street, emerged just as a form ran by. He never broke stride, putting his shoulder into the man's side and sending both of them into the mud. As the man rolled over, Roger raised his dagger to plunge it into the man's throat.

"*Nein!*" cried the man. "Halt—I am Christian!"

Excited as he was, it was all Roger could do not to drive his dagger into the man's neck. He had to force himself to hold back. The fellow was young, with a greasy blond beard. Roger lowered the dagger; he was shaking, breathing hard. "I nearly killed you," he said. "What are you doing here?"

"Chasing Saracens, you idiot," snapped the man, sitting up. "I was right behind one of them. If you've made me lose him, by God I'll have your hide."

"I'm sorry," Roger said, helping the German to his feet. "What do you want me to do?"

The German pushed him aside. "Stay out of my way. Try not to cause any more trouble while I—"

There was a *thunk* and a crossbow bolt slammed into the German's face, just above the bridge of his nose, shot from such close range that its point punched through the rear of the German's skull. The German's blue eyes went wide, then the light in them faded. He staggered, half turned and fell on his back.

Terrified, Roger turned. In the darkness he saw a hooded figure with a crossbow.

"He was a spy," said the hooded figure. The figure was a woman.

The woman moved forward. She was tall and athletic, with dark hair and eyes that might once have been merry but now gleamed with a strange light. Her cloak and hood were dark green, and there was a yellow cross sewn on her shoulder. A small crowd was forming around them. Some men recognized the woman and drew back.

The woman looked at Roger. Her French had a heavy accent. "His name was Rollo. He was a knight from Mundt, not far from my husband's lands. He deserted us during the march across Anatolia. We thought he was captured. Praise God, who led him to a part of the camp where he would be recognized. I guess Rollo did not know we had recently moved our tents to this spot."

"How do you know he deserted?" Roger said. "Maybe he *was* captured and escaped. Maybe—"

"Look at him. Does he look like a man who had been held prisoner for six months? He is reasonably well fed and his clothes are in decent repair. The camp is full of men such as he, men who have turned against their God to work for the Paynims."

"But—did you have to kill him? Couldn't you have taken him prisoner?"

The woman fixed a baleful eye on Roger. "I do not believe in taking prisoners."

More men hurried up. "Good work," said a man wearing an embroidered nightshirt and holding a sword, a stocky, square-jawed fellow who looked like he'd be good in a fight. He looked at Rollo's body contemptuously. "These men were no doubt here to kill nobles in their sleep, then retreat to their own lines. It is a common tactic of the Paynims, employed to spread fear among our men. I must admit, it is effective, too. We saw enough of it in Anatolia." He turned to Roger, "If not for you, I might now be dead. He inclined his head. "I am Leopold, who are you?"

Roger told him.

"Who is your lord?"

Roger told that, as well. "Geoffrey of Trent?" said Leopold. "I've met him—an excellent fellow. I'll see he hears of this."

Just then, Egwulf and Will appeared. "Did you get all of them?" Roger asked them.

Will made a face. "I thought I heard another one headed back for the ditch, but I'm not sure."

"Maybe our lads will pick him up when he tries to cross," Egwulf said.

Roger turned back to the woman, but she was gone. "Who was that?" he said to nobody in particular.

"Helvise," said Leopold. He chuckled. "You want to stay clear of that one."

One of the bystanders said, "What should we do with the bodies, my lord?"

"Take them to the catapults," said Leopold. "They'll find a use for them."

Roger wondered what use the bodies could possibly be to the men at the catapults, but he didn't ask. He turned to Egwulf and Will. "There's nothing more we can do here. We'd best get back to the company."

❖ ❖ ❖

"How did they sneak through our lines?" Payen fumed. "Weren't you watching?"

Roger cast a glance at Dirk, who looked worried. Roger thought about saying that Dirk had told him he could relax discipline, but decided against it. In the end, the fault was his, not Dirk's. "Not well enough," he admitted. The raider Will thought had gotten away—if indeed there had been one—had not been caught re-crossing the ditch.

"Not well enough?" Payen shouted. "Not well enough? Do you know what 'guard' means, you useless turd? It means keeping a lookout for the enemy."

Roger said nothing, and Payen went on. "God's balls, my Arab manservant would make a better vintenar than you. My horse would make a better vintenar than you. While you were swanning about, one of your men got killed. A good man, if what I hear is true."

"Yes," Roger said, and added, "my lord." God, it galled him to add that.

"That man's death is on your head. Yours alone."

"I agree, my lord."

"I intend to make this the finest unit of foot in the army, and I can't do it with asswipes like you commanding my men. Now get out of my sight while I decide who's to replace you."

"Yes, my lord."

Payen moved off. Roger's shoulders slumped. He was a failure. How could he face his men after this? How could he face himself?

Dirk came up beside him. "Thank you for covering for me," Dirk said.

Roger shrugged, not looking.

Dirk went on. "It would have been my head if you'd told him what I said, and me with the bad hand. Don't know I'd have found work, else." He paused and cleared his throat, as though what he was going to say was difficult for him. "I guess—I guess you are not so bad, after all. I'm sorry I made all that trouble for you."

Roger looked at him now. The truculence was gone from the big man's features. "It's all right," Roger said.

Dirk nodded toward the retreating Payen. "I'll have a word with him. See if I can calm him down."

"I warned you he was incompetent, my lord," Dirk said to Payen.

"Yes, you did," the gray-haired foot commander acknowledged. "I need to replace him before he does any more damage."

Dirk scratched the back of his close-cropped skull. "That might not be so easy, my lord. The earl loves him, him saving the earl's life the way he did. The way the bastard's luck runs, I wouldn't be surprised there's not word going back to the earl now, telling him what a great job Roger did killing those raiders."

Payen swore, because what Dirk said was probably true.

After a moment, Dirk went on. "There *are* other ways of getting rid of him."

Payen cast an eye at the big Brabanter.

"War is dangerous," Dirk said, spreading his hands innocently. "There are accidents. Men get killed."

"True," Payen admitted. Then he said, "What do you propose?"

Dirk smiled. "Leave that to me, my lord."

Chapter 34

They buried Long Tom the next morning on the plain, which was becoming an endless expanse of graves, a city of the dead—no, more than that, a country of the dead. The earl's chaplain, Stephen FitzNele, said the funeral service. Tom was buried in an unmarked grave with another of the earl's men, an archer who had died the previous day from the bloody flux.

The soldiers marched back from the grave in loose order. The weak winter sun hung low in the sky. The air blew chill off the sea. Dirk caught up to Roger, who was walking with Will. "You are still vintenar," the Brabanter told Roger. "I talked Payen out of demoting you."

Roger stared. "Thanks," he said at last.

Dirk gave a little shrug. "I did it for me as much as for you. Despite what Payen says, you have done a good job so far. That makes my job easier."

Dirk dropped back down the line, to talk with Uwen. "Nice to see you and Dirk are such chums now," Will told Roger with a smirk.

Roger made a rude gesture and Will laughed. Then Will said, "You look upset."

"I am upset," Roger said. "I got Tom killed."

"Stop blaming yourself. We all make mistakes."

"My mistake resulted in a man's death."

"That comes with rank. The higher your rank, the more men die because of your errors. That's why a lot of soldiers don't want rank. They can't accept that kind of responsibility."

"Then maybe I should give up the rank."

"And have more of us die because the next vintenar makes even bigger mistakes?"

As Roger thought about that, Will went on. "Besides, it's

almost Christmas. Cheer up." He looked around at the bleak plain and the camp, and he sighed. "Doesn't look much like Christmas, does it? At home, now, me and the lads would be getting in the Yule log, putting it on a sledge and dragging it up to the manor house. Agnes would decorate our house with holly and mistletoe. Mom would brew some of her special Christmas mead. We'd poach some of Lord William's rabbits— or a deer, if we could get one—for the feast. Lord William didn't care, not at Christmas, anyway."

Roger remembered Christmas at the abbey, remembered the warmth and cheer of the huge Yule log burning in the chapter house through the dank winter twilight. He'd never given much concern to the men who had felled it, or dragged it there. He started to say something when, from the tents ahead, a small bell began to toll. The bell was joined by another, then another, until bells were tolling all through the camp.

"Now what?" said Arcil, plodding behind them next to Mayne.

Roger knew instinctively what had happened. "The archbishop of Canterbury is dead."

❖ ❖ ❖

Baldwin of Canterbury's funeral was the biggest the camp had yet seen. Every person of noble blood attended, and all vowed that, when Acre was taken, they would exhume the archbishop's remains and build a chapel to house them in the church of St. Andrew—a vow that Geoffrey of Trent, now in command of the English force, found both amusing and hypocritical, since just about every noble in camp was secretly overjoyed to be rid of the old pest.

Two days after Baldwin's funeral, Conrad of Montferrat was married to Isabelle of Jerusalem. No amount of pomp and feasting could conceal the terror that the 18-year-old bride felt for her new husband, her third. Isabelle was a beautiful girl, but years of being knocked about as a political pawn had taken all the spirit out of her. In the midst of the celebration, Conrad called for quiet.

As silence fell over the packed pavilion. The shaven-headed Conrad addressed the crowd. "I have important matters to attend to," he said, casting a side glance at the lissome Isabele. "There is a break in the weather, and I intend to take advantage of it and take my new bride home to Tyre." He bowed and made a farewell gesture. "Enjoy yourselves this winter, gentlemen." He gazed at Isabelle again with anticipation. "I know I will."

❖ ❖ ❖

"Did you attend the wedding?" Roger asked Fauston.

They were in Ailith's tent. It was Christmas Eve, and Fauston's chronicle was due. Ailith was with the earl, exercising the horses. "Me? No, I'm just a chronicler. I'm not important enough," Fauston replied. In answer to Roger's unspoken question, he went on. "Ailith said she had a wonderful time. Apparently her dancing skills were every bit as impressive as she imagined them to be. She said the young men—and the old ones—were lined up to partner her."

Roger said nothing, appearing to concentrate on smoothing a new parchment sheet with pumice.

"Hurry," Fauston said, changing the subject. "We don't have much time."

"I'm nearly done. I just need to add something about the archbishop's death and how much he'll be missed, and bring the story of the siege up to date."

Roger had been writing about the siege for several days. He had not imagined the tale would take so long, but writing was a tedious process and there was much to relate. The siege of Acre was a year and a half old. It had begun when Conrad of Montferrat refused to let Guy of Lusignan into Tyre, blaming

Guy for the disaster at Hattin and saying that Guy was no longer worthy to be king of Jerusalem. Infuriated, and with nowhere to go, Guy took the few followers remaining to him and placed them before the walls of Acre.

It was a bold move; but, as usual with Guy, not a terribly intelligent one. The Acre garrison outnumbered Guy's force, so he had no hope of taking the city by storm, and his men were too few to mount a blockade. Twice in those early days, Guy was saved from annihilation—first when Saladin, beset by illness, passed up the chance to destroy Guy's little army in the narrow pass of Scandalion, the second time by the arrival of a fleet under the Fleming James of Avesnes just as Guy's camp was on the point of being overrun, James' men going directly from the ships to the fighting.

By rights, Guy and his men should have perished at Acre and been long forgotten. But a strange thing happened. As successive waves of crusaders reached the Holy land, they decided to go to Acre, where there was actual fighting, instead of to Tyre, as they had originally planned, where nothing was happening. As more and more crusaders crowded ashore to besiege Acre, Saladin brought up more and more men to besiege them, until there were huge armies on both sides and the entire dynamic of the crusade had changed. The crusade, which was supposed to be about recovering the Holy City of Jerusalem, had in essence become about capturing Acre.

Fighting at Acre was conducted on a scale undreamed of at home. Pitched battles at home were skirmishes here. The crusaders assaulted the city, Saladin attacked the crusaders' camp, there were battles at sea. Casualties from battle and disease were enormous, but men kept coming from the West to make them good—large armies and small parties from all over Christendom, princes and humble men who asked only to fight for their Heavenly King.

During the first summer of the siege, ten thousand foot soldiers, frustrated at the lack of progress, had attacked Saladin's camp on their own, without support from the knights.

"Ten thousand?" Roger had asked Fauston. "That can't be right. That's more than the population of London."

"That's the number I was given," Fauston said. "I've no reason to believe it false."

The foot soldiers had been massacred almost to a man on the plain, and afterward Saladin had their bodies gathered up and floated down the Belus River, which provided the source of the Christian camp's drinking water. The bodies had jammed in the narrow river, where they had swollen and burst in the sun. Many men in the camp were stricken with disease after this, and the crusaders were forced to burn the bodies to cleanse the putrefaction.

Roger wrote about many battles, but always the story returned to Guy and Conrad. Guy who had lost the kingdom of Jerusalem, Conrad who saved what was left of it. Their rivalry had taken so many twists that it seemed lost in time. Their dispute split the crusader camp down the middle. If Venice was for Conrad, Genoa was for Guy. If the Templars supported Guy, the Hospitallers favored Conrad. Making the story even stranger, Guy had saved Conrad's life in battle when he could have let him be killed.

Now Roger was down to his final paragraphs, at least for a while. "How many do you think are in the camp?" he asked Fauston as he trimmed what he hoped would be his last quill.

Fauston stood looking out the tent flap, quaffing arrack. He'd been drinking since before Roger's arrival; there wasn't much else to do. "Some say ten thousand, some say a million. If I had to guess—and it's only a guess—I'd make it maybe a hundred and fifty thousand, less of course the thousand or so who will die today. It's a good thing they die so fast. The commissariats wouldn't be able to feed them else." He watched yet another funeral procession winding onto the gloomy plain. "Madness."

"What do you mean?" Roger said, looking up from his writing board.

Fauston turned. "Isn't it obvious? All these men are dying for nothing."

"What do you mean?" Roger repeated. "They're dying for a cause—the greatest cause imaginable. They're dying for God."

"Men come here and they're dead from disease a week after they get off the ship. How does that please God? How does it get us any closer to Jerusalem?"

Roger said, "We must have faith—"

"I have faith, I have bags of faith. I have faith that our so-called leaders are imbeciles. I have faith that we'll be lucky if any of us leaves this place alive. If God approves of this, there's something wrong with God."

Roger stiffened. "What you're saying is dangerously close to heresy."

"So what?" Fauston said. "What are they going to do, kill me? We're all going to die here anyway."

Roger found Fauston's remarks deeply disturbing. How dare any man question God? "Everything is done according to God's plan," he told Fauston, explaining it as one might explain it to a child. "It may seem strange to us, but there is a reason."

Fauston jabbed a finger toward the sprawling camp. "What could possibly be the reason for so much suffering?"

"Perhaps we're being punished for our sins."

"Our sins." Fauston spoke with a bitter, mocking tone. He poured more arrack, sloshing some over the lip of the cup. "Yesterday I saw a page, he couldn't have been more than twelve. He was lying in the mud, dying, shivering uncontrollably and shitting blood. What sins was he being punished for?"

"We're being punished as a group, not individually. As Christians. For not having loved God enough."

"I love God enough, I just wish he'd show some love in return. This is one hell of a way to get to Heaven."

"I agree that we're suffering, but remember—Christ suffered for us, as well."

"You sound like a priest," Fauston told him.

212

"And you sound like a man who cares only for his own safety. Perhaps you've spent too much time in the forest with your outlaw friends—"

"And perhaps you spent too much time in your abbey. Perhaps you need to see how the rest of the world lives. Have you ever gone hungry up there in your pleasant little world of prayer and contemplation and goodness-me-what-songs-shall-we-sing-today? Have you ever had to eat grass in July while you waited for the harvest to come in? Have you ever eaten tree bark?"

"No, but—"

"You want to know the real reason I became an outlaw? I was lying a-bed one winter's night, trying to sleep but not able to do it because I was so hungry, and I heard my father and mother talking in low tones about how they might have to kill the new baby so that the rest of the family would have enough to eat. I left home the next day."

Roger put down his quill. "Perhaps I did live in a pleasant little world, as you call it, but I had no control over that, so don't try to make me feel guilty about it. At least you know who you are. You know who your parents are and from whence you come." He held up his left hand. "All I have is a ring."

Fauston's anger seemed to dissipate. He let out a long breath. "You and that ring. That really bothers you, doesn't it?"

"I never stop thinking about it," Roger admitted. "It's like a void inside me, an empty space that should be filled in but never will be. It's like I have no past, like I just came into being. Like I was created by some sort of alchemist."

The two men were silent for a moment. Then Roger removed the writing table from his lap. He hung the sheet of parchment upon which he'd been working to dry on a line that he and Fauston had rigged across the tent.

"When the sheets are dry, put them together as I showed you and take them to the earl."

Fauston looked abashed. "Thanks." He looked like he

wanted to apologize for his earlier outburst. Instead, he handed Roger a sack. "Sorry it's so light. Scraps are getting hard to come by."

Roger nodded, understanding. He clapped his friend's shoulder, then he returned the writing materials to the small trunk and left Ailith's crimson tent.

Roger felt confused and worried. Fauston no longer believed in what they were doing here; he had become disillusioned, tricked by the Devil. If Fauston felt that way, how many others must feel the same? How many more would succumb to Satan's ploys if the siege dragged on?

It never occurred to Roger to doubt the righteousness of what they were doing. He believed that God guided them, and if God put obstacles in their path, it was to make them better men. He believed that, in the end, the army's suffering would be rewarded, and that God would see His Holy City restored to the True Faith. There could be no other outcome. God would not permit it.

❖ ❖ ❖

Roger didn't head directly to his tent. The days were precariously short just now, but there was still a bit of light, so he wandered down to the German catapults. He was curious to see what it was they did with the dead bodies. This was the first chance he'd had to go down there—since the night of the raid, Payen had kept his section busy with extra duty.

The catapults were operating on a limited basis because of the weather. The thick mud made it difficult to transport the rocks they used as ammunition. The Germans had two catapults—called mangonels. These mangonels—there were at least a dozen different kinds with the army, but all followed the same general construction—were squat machines on big wooden wheels. They consisted of a rectangular frame and an upright crossbar, which was heavily padded with layers of twisted rope. Attached to the frame was a long pole, also heavily padded with rope, at the end of which was a bucket. The pole was winched down and ammunition was placed in the bucket. When the pole was released, it flew up and hit the crossbar, which stopped the pole's progress and released whatever missile was in the bucket. The crossbar needed to be made of very stout wood to resist the blows it received from the pole. The pole needed to be strong, as well, so that it didn't snap upon making contact with the crossbar.

As Roger approached, he saw bodies laid out some distance in front of the mangonels. The bodies had apparently been bound hand to foot right after they died, while they were still pliable. Now they were swollen, decaying balls of flesh. The artillerists wore masks across their faces because of the stench. Roger told the Germans why he had come. One of them, the captain, recognized him from the raid and was happy to explain.

"We send the bodies into the city," said the captain. "To spread disease."

"Disease?" Roger said.

"Of course," said the captain, a hard-bitten fellow of many years' service. "Anything to kill the bastards, or make them give up faster."

"That's right," chimed in one of his charges, who didn't look much older than Cole. "Won't be long now till they surrender. They must be dying like flies in there."

The captain motioned Roger to accompany him toward the bound bodies, which had been stripped of valuables and all clothing save their drawers. Pressing the back of his gloved hand across his nose to mitigate the smell, Roger followed. There were about a dozen bodies in all. Among them, Roger recognized the two Saracens that Egwulf and Will had killed the night of the raid. The traitor Rollo was there, as well, his bloodied blond beard conspicuous among the dark hair and beards of the Saracens.

"We cannot use Christian bodies," the captain explained. "It is against God's law—Christians must be buried. So we use Saracens or the bodies of native servants. That one—" he pointed to Rollo—"was a traitor, so it's all right to use him."

Some of the bodies were relatively fresh; others were hideously swollen, covered with a slimy, greenish film, their mouths formed in round "o"s. The eyes were long gone, pecked out by seagulls, which, along with the occasional rat, had also consumed some of the flesh. The Germans tested the swelling bodies, gently poking each with a gloved finger, the way a man might poke a cut of cooked meat to see whether it was done. "The trick is to use them right when they are ready to burst," the captain went on. "Sling them too soon and they do nothing, and the Turbans just burn them. Too late, and they burst on you—ask Johann about that." He grinned at a mustachioed fellow, who made a face at him. "The boys you killed now, they are not *quite* ready, but these two here should do nicely."

He indicated two of the bodies—dark haired, impossible to discern their features any more, they were so swollen. His masked assistants placed the bound bodies on boards, being extremely careful about it, and carried them to the mangonels. Roger nearly gagged from the stench as they went by.

"In the summer we did this with pigs," the captain said. "That was great fun. Scared to death of pigs, the Goat Fuckers are—something to do with their religion. But the pigs are just about all gone now, and the few that are left we need for food."

Of the two mangonels, one had a longer pole and higher crossbar, which would give its missile more elevation and range. There were different sizes of buckets scattered about— some leather, some wood—for varying types of missiles. A large shallow bucket was attached to the bigger mangonel's pole. The artillerists winched down the pole and locked it in place with an iron bar. They took the first body and loaded it into the bucket, placing it on its back, with the hands and feet facing up.

"Stand clear!" called the captain.

Everyone took a step back. The captain yanked the

restraining bar free. The bucket flew up. The pole hit the crossbar with a resounding *thwap!* and the body was propelled into the air. It flew through the air, a diminishing dot. The artillerists leaned in expectation. The body passed just over the battlements and into the city, to much shouting and laughter from the artillerists.

Roger spied a postern gate in the wall not far from the mangonel. "That gate—couldn't the Saracens sally out and attack you?"

The captain inclined his head toward a company of bored-looking spearmen huddled in a trench not far away. "Wish they'd try. Then we could kill some of the bastards."

Another man spit derisively. "They only come out at night. They slit a few throats, then scurry back into their holes like rats."

The mustachioed artillerist named Johann pointed. "Look."

Beneath the city's nearest tower was a curl of smoke, accompanied by glints of steel, as from spear points.

"I bet they're trying to get warm up there," Johann said.

The captain chuckled and nudged Roger. "Watch this."

The captain shouted orders in German. He and his men unlocked the mangonel's wheels. Using iron levers, they maneuvered the mangonel around in the mud. The captain lined it up with the tower and the wheels were locked again. The captain did some calculations in his head, marked a spot on the winching rope with chalk. "Fifteen years I have been doing this," he told Roger. "It is nice when you can have fun with it."

The Germans winched the rope down to the spot the captain had marked. They loaded the second body into the bucket. The captain checked his aim one last time.

"Stand clear!"

The men moved back. The captain yanked away the locking bar.

Again the bucket's pole thwapped against the crossbar. Again the body flew through the air. It hit the turret with a sickening splat and exploded in a mess of slime and rotted flesh, showering the men gathered beneath the walls there.

The artillerists erupted in hooting and pointing and laughing. "That got them!"

"Happy Christmas, Goat Fuckers!"

There were angry yells and curses from behind the parapet. One Saracen showed himself through a crenellation and waved a fist at the artillerists. Suddenly the man was struck in the chest by an arrow. He cried out and dropped behind the parapet.

Roger looked for the source of the arrow. Amid the detritus of wrecked siege engines, broken wagons, crates, dead animals, weapons, and articles of clothing, he saw a line of pavises. Some of the pavises had been smashed by missiles hurled from the city walls, others were intact. In the shadows behind one of these was a figure in a green-hooded cloak, holding a crossbow.

"Helvise," Roger murmured in surprise.

"You know her?" said the captain. "But of course you do, you were there when she killed the traitor."

"She sits out there all day," Johann said. "The Goat Fuckers dare not show themselves on account of her."

"Guess that last one forgot," said another man with a short beard.

"Christ's mercy," Roger suddenly realized. "She's the Woman in Green."

"She is," acknowledged the captain with a smile.

The Woman in Green was famous throughout the army, even among those who had never seen her. Her lonely, one-person war against the Saracens had become the stuff of legend. And here she was in the flesh.

The front of Helvise's pavise was studded with arrows where the Saracens had tried to hit her. Roger guessed that the crushed pavises were also attempts at killing her; she must have to change her position constantly. She was reloading the crossbow, one foot in the stirrup to hold the bow in place while she winched the string back. She saw Roger watching her. Their eyes met. Then she turned away, notched another iron quarrel in her bow and resumed her watch on the city wall.

"Cool one, isn't she?" said the catapult captain.

"She scares me," said the younger man.

Johann said, "I heard she's a witch."

Another witch. It seemed that any woman who went against the norm was suspected of being a witch. Roger gave a last glance at Helvise, then started back to the English camp.

"We are quitting now to celebrate Christmas," the captain told him as he left. "We will be sending that traitor Rollo over the wall in a day or two, though. Come and watch if you like."

The light was fading fast as Roger reached his tent. Soon darkness would envelop the camp. On most nights, without firewood or candles for light, there would be nothing to do but lie in bed through the long winter night, try to ignore the cold and hunger, and sleep. This was Christmas Eve, though. Tonight there would be bonfires and feasting.

Laughter and shouts came from Roger's tent. He opened the flap and stepped in, grateful for the clammy warmth produced by body heat. The men were gathered in a knot around someone. When they saw Roger, they moved aside, welcoming him.

"Roger—look!"

The center of attention was Tatwine. Roger had worried whether Tatwine would be accepted when he joined the section. The men knew who he was and they might resent his being placed with them. Apparently, he'd fit right in. In one hand Tatwine held someone's brimmed helmet, in the other a paint brush. With a gleam in his feral eyes, Tatwine showed the helmet to Roger. On the front right quarter of the helmet's crown, Tatwine had painted a skull in red. A vertical line beneath the skull represented a spine, two lines across the spine stood for ribs.

"What do you think?" Tatwine said.

Clamoring for his attention, the other men—Egwulf, Offa, Will, all of them, even Uwen—showed Roger their helmets. On each was the same red death's head, with the spine and ribs beneath.

Tatwine gave the finished helmet to fifteen-year-old Cole, who examined it like it was he greatest thing he'd ever seen. "Your turn," Tatwine told Roger, hand extended.

Roger demurred. "I don't think I—"

"Come on," the men around him urged. "You're our vintenar, you have to."

Reluctantly, Roger removed his helmet and handed it to Tatwine. There were cheers and laughter.

Roger gave the bag of food scraps to Bald Matthew, and he stepped away from his raucous men. He pictured Ailith gaily dancing the night away, pictured Helvise behind the pavise with her crossbow. He pictured men shooting dead bodies into the city. Death's heads on helmets.

Maybe Fauston had been right.

Madness.

Chapter 35

The earl's tent was crowded as Fauston entered, which was fine with Fauston because a crowd meant warmth. Fauston had tied the chronicle's parchment sheets together with a wood binding—hard to find wood that hadn't been burned—as Roger had showed him. He wished he hadn't drunk so much arrack; he was a little woozy on his feet. He couldn't help it, though. He was sick of Acre, sick of the crusade. Could no one see what a waste of treasure and humanity this was? Roger was as bad as the rest of them—worse, even, because Fauston had thought that Roger had good sense. Fauston would have given anything to be back in the forest, dodging the sheriff's men. At least that life seemed to have some purpose.

Earl Geoffrey was at his table. He looked sick, but so did most of those present. One who didn't was Ailith—grown thinner, maybe, but radiant in a gown of red velvet. She sat to Geoffrey's right, while the earl's marshal, Blaise, sat to Geoffrey's left, in the spot formerly occupied by Geoffrey's brother. William the seneschal sat to Blaise's left, and Stephen FitzNeale, the long-faced chaplain, was to the right of Ailith. Bet he liked that, Fauston thought. Stephen was a humble, pious man who dressed in plain clothes. His only vice was drink, and when he indulged it, he quickly regretted it.

Geoffrey was in the act of raising a silver cup to his lips when he saw Fauston approaching. "Well, well," he exclaimed, "it's my long lost chronicler. Just in time, too. Believe in cutting it fine, don't you?"

Fauston bowed his head. "My lord, sometimes there are things beyond—"

Geoffrey pointed to the bundle under Fauston's arm. "Is that it?"

"It is, my lord."

Geoffrey beckoned Fauston forward. Geoffrey held out a hand and Fauston gave him the slender book. Geoffrey leafed through it, turning the thick pages slowly, savoring the smells of ink and parchment, looking in wonder at the carefully printed letters whose meaning he did not know.

"Very well," he said at last. He handed the book back to Fauston. "Read it."

Fauston's guts tightened. He saw Ailith flinch. Trying to keep his voice steady, he said, "Now, my lord?"

"Yes, now," Geoffrey replied impatiently. "I want to hear what it says."

Fauston cast a quick look at Ailith, but she couldn't think of a way to help him out of this. He cleared his throat. "If it's all the same to you, my lord, I prefer not to read my own work. I find it a bit—" what was a good word?— "presumptuous. Perhaps if someone else were to—"

"*I'll* read it," said Father Stephen. Stephen thought the earl's chronicle the worst kind of vain extravagance. He also thought Fauston was a sluggard, and on more than one occasion he had voiced his desire for Fauston to do plain chancery work, where Stephen could have control over him, instead of working independently on the chronicle. He added, "I'll wager it's rubbish."

" 'Tis not for me to pass judgment," Fauston said humbly.

"No," Geoffrey said, "it's for me to do that." He made an impatient motion with his hand. "*Somebody* read the damned thing."

Father Stephen took the book, opened it with a long finger, and examined the title. "*The Song of Geoffrey of Trent and Saladin.*" With an involuntary eye roll, he turned the page, read the inscription. " '*Lege Feliciter*'—'Read Happily?' " He cocked a scornful eye at Fauston. "Do you think everything that's happening here is a joke?"

Damn Roger. Then Fauston remembered Roger's answer when Fauston had asked that same question. Smoothly, he said,

"Circumstances are bad now, my lord, but I'm certain the story will have a happy ending."

Ailith touched Geoffrey's arm. "He's got a point."

"Mm," said Geoffrey, "let's hope you're right." To Father Stephen, he said, "Go on."

Stephen grumbled and kept reading. The words flowed easily, and as the chaplain read on, Fauston could see that he was impressed in spite of himself.

Geoffrey leaned forward on the table, chin resting on his fist, listening intently. "Good, good," he murmured from time to time. Ailith listened as well, smiling, pleased by the quality of Roger's work.

Father Stephen came to the part about the recent assault on the city. " 'Then did the soldiers of God ascend the great tower. Geoffrey of Trent, no man bolder, went first, to vie with the Infidels on the walls of the city. There you would have seen blows given and blows received. You would have seen heads split open, bones cracked, teeth shattered. You would have seen blood in such abundance that men marveled from whence it came. Now did Geoffrey press forward, noble of mien. Now did he lead his men, driving the sons of Satan before him. Just as the battle seemed to favor the Host of God, Geoffrey was smitten such a blow upon the head as would have killed a less holy man. He sank to his knees in swoon. At this sight, a portion of our men lost heart and, sad to say, retreated from the walls. The valiant Geoffrey rallied the rest, aided by the lord of Deraa, Henry by name. They fought with hearts inspired by the Holy Spirit, slaying Infidels in great profusion, but Satan, curse him, set our tower on fire, preventing the men of God from receiving reinforcements. The Devil then summoned his minions in such numbers that our brave men were at last forced to relinquish the city walls, with Geoffrey and the lord of Deraa being the last to leave.' "

"Splendid! Splendid!" shouted the earl, getting to his feet and clapping his hands. "You make it sound as though you were actually there."

Fauston bowed indifferently, as though 'twere all in a day's work.

Geoffrey wagged a finger at him. "But you flatter me unduly—I wasn't last off the walls. And you should have mentioned that fellow who saved me—what was his name?"

"Roger," said Ailith.

"Roger, of course. How could I have forgotten? Can't remember things like I used to since I got knocked on the head." He cast a sudden look at Ailith. "How did you know his name?"

Ailith lifted her brows. "You told me," she replied innocently. "Or have you forgotten that, as well?"

Geoffrey rubbed his red-bearded chin. "Mmm. Suppose I must have." He glanced at her again, then he dug into his purse and flipped Fauston a coin. "Excellent work, my boy. Sorry I ever doubted you."

Fauston bowed again. "Thank you, my lord. My apologies for so long, but sometimes it takes me a while to get going when I'm writing."

Father Stephen sat, summoning a hungry looking clerk to read the remainder of the book. Geoffrey listened happily while the book was read, nodding at parts he especially liked, now and then looking at Ailith to see what she thought. She always nodded agreement with what he liked. Once or twice she caught Fauston's eye, and a corner of her mouth turned up.

When the clerk reached the last page, which described the archbishop of Canterbury's death and funeral, Ailith murmured. "Poor old fellow."

Father Stephen leaned close and spoke in a silky voice so low that only Ailith could hear. "Yes. He always had a kind word for you, my dear."

Ailith's face turned nearly as red as her dress, and she said no more.

"Excellent work!" cried the earl at the chronicle's conclusion. "Now, let us eat!"

Food was brought in, more food than Fauston had seen in

many a day. As each dish was placed on the table, the seneschal William, who was in charge of feeding the earl's retinue, fretted more. "There have been no grain ships since October, my lord," he pointed out, "and none are expected. At this rate, we won't have a bite left by Twelfth Night."

Geoffrey waved him off. "We're going to starve anyway, we may as well enjoy ourselves for Christmas." He turned to Ailith, "Don't you agree, my lady?"

Ailith had recovered from the insult delivered by the chaplain. She inclined her head to the earl. "I always agree with you, Geoffrey."

Behind Fauston, a man murmured, "Did you hear that the earl has taken up music?"

"Indeed?" replied a companion.

"Yes, he plays the strumpet."

Fauston resisted the urge to turn and drive his fist into the speaker's mouth. At that moment, a roast pig was carried into the tent, its tantalizing smells wafting over the crowd, people "o-o-h"-ing and "a-h-h"-ing at the sight. During the warm months, pigs had wandered the camp, feasting on whatever they could find, including the dead; but as the animals' numbers dwindled, they had been placed under guard, until now there were but a few left in the camp. This pig was the earl's last.

The earl's butler carved the pig, and servants carried slices to guests at the table, who ate eagerly. Ailith saved much of her portion for the poor. Shavings that had fallen on the trencher from the carving were fought over by eager hands, including Fauston's. He battled for a piece of bread, as well, soaked it in the pig's juices on the trencher and jammed it in his mouth. In better times, the dogs would have gotten the bones when the carving was done, but now men and women took them, gnawing them until they were clean, sucking them to drain out the marrow. Fauston was lucky and got a rib. He sucked on it, holding it in one hand, while with the other hand he pocketed a bit of bread and moldy cheese for Roger. Roger's predilection for giving the food to his men, rather than keeping it for himself, would have seemed mad to some, but Fauston understood. Life had been hard in Dunham Forest, especially in the winter, and Fauston—or Brock, as he was called then—had always made sure his men and women were fed before he ate anything himself.

"Eat up!" cried Geoffrey with his mouth full. "Soon it will be time for Mass."

As midnight approached, the greatest nobility of the camp assembled at the church of Our Lady of Mount Carmel, in the French lines. Ubaldo of Pisa, the papal legate, said the Mass, wearing vestments so heavy with gold and precious jewels that he could hardly walk. Four archbishops and twenty bishops were numbered among his assistants. The church was hastily built and soggy from recent rain, but who was not impressed by the glory of the service? Garlands and wreaths covered the walls and plank floors; incense filled the cold night air. Never, it seemed, were so many candles burned in one place; they gleamed off the gold plate with such brilliance that Geoffrey and Ailith, who were near the front, were forced to narrow their eyes against the glare. Thousands of voices lifted themselves to Heaven, and there was a determination in them, an iron purpose that would admit of no defeat. Men who had formerly been discouraged now came alight with the flame of God. Bells were run all over camp, and it was an odd back down which shivers did not run that night.

When the Mass was ended, men lit torches and an impromptu procession made its way through the camp, singing Hosannas and Te Deums. Nobles and commoners mixed together in a flood of humanity, dukes in robes of the finest velvet rubbing shoulders with men in rags. The clouds parted for the first time in days, and a full moon, which some swore to be the star of Bethlehem, gave an ethereal cast to the proceeding, reflecting off the sea and bathing the walls of the besieged city in a soft, greenish glow.

Roger and his men joined the procession, as did nearly

every person in camp, save Fauston, who watched from the Toron, drinking arrack, alone and dispirited. The procession wound its way slowly through the tent city—men, women, and children, nobles and commoners and servants, all singing and crying with joy. At the intersection of the Toron High Road and Paris Street, Roger caught sight of Ailith. In the press, she had become separated from the earl. Roger waved and caught her eye. She called to him, but he couldn't hear what she said because the singing was so loud. He forced his way through the slow-moving mob of people, trying to get close to her. She was laughing with the sheer joy of it all. He fought his way nearer; she moved toward him as best she could. He reached out a hand to her; she reached out her hand, as well. Their fingers touched for a second, then she was borne away on the river of humanity, looking back at him helplessly.

Ahead, someone shouted "Jerusalem!" The cry was repeated, and soon the entire camp was chanting as one as they marched. "Jerusalem! Jerusalem! JERUSALEM!"

❖ ❖ ❖

And in the hills, Saladin's guards watched, and listened, and shook their heads in wonder.

Chapter 36

Young Henry of Champagne coughed heavily into his sleeve. There were flecks of blood on the blue velvet; he hadn't seen that before. "My men are dying so fast, I'd have trouble raising a force if there was a battle."

"Most of my men died a long time ago," said hulking James of Avesnes wistfully. The long-jawed Fleming's arrival two summers previously had saved the Christian army from destruction, and had saved the siege in the process. James, who was so big his shoulders stooped, drank from a silver cup, tilting it to one side because if the arrack hit a certain tooth on the other side of his mouth it sent waves of pain through his head. "God forgive me, but I often think we would have been better off had I had arrived here a day later."

Balian of Ibelin idly rattled a pair of dice and let them drop onto the table. "Things would be different if you had, that's certain. There's many a brave man buried on that plain who would still be alive."

"Aye," said Geoffrey of Trent, "the army might be warm in Tyre now, instead of dying a slow death here."

"Tyre?" James said. "With a bit of luck, we'd have been in Jerusalem by now. Funny, isn't it, the difference little things can make? Just one day of contrary wind, and all this suffering would never have happened."

Balian said, "It's just as well our missing kings aren't here. There'd be no food for their men."

They were in Balian's pavilion. It wasn't a council of barons, just friends passing the time. There hadn't been a grand council since Christmas. The four men sat at Balian's table, looking out of place because the huge table held ten times that many, quaffing arrack and gnawing pieces of hard bread. The stores had run out after Christmas for all but those with money to purchase more. Acceptance of food these days required one to reciprocate. Geoffrey was calculating how much money at today's rates—tomorrow's rates were likely to be higher—it would cost him to feed Henry, Balian, and James of Avesnes, who looked like he could eat a cow all by himself. Geoffrey's funds were not inexhaustible; indeed, they were dwindling rapidly. Perhaps he should not have spent so much on jewelry for Ailith. He might have to sell some of that jewelry soon, just to keep his household fed. He wondered what Ailith would say to that.

Balian tossed the dice again. Like the others, Balian was gaunt. His once-swarthy tan had become mottled. "The bishops are organizing a relief campaign for the common people."

James snorted. "Much good that'll do them. There's no grain."

"Guy of Lusignan blames Conrad for that," Henry of Champagne said. "Guy says Conrad's holding the grain ships at Tyre till he can get a better price."

"Don't listen to that fool," Balian counseled. "Conrad's no saint, but he wouldn't deliberately starve his own supporters."

"More likely there's no grain to send," Geoffrey added. "Where's it supposed to come from? Europe? I doubt there's that much surplus there. Even if there were, they couldn't get it here because of the storms."

Geoffrey's long face looked even longer now because it was so hollowed out, and there was grey in his red beard that hadn't been there before. He still suffered from headaches, though they did not come as often.

Henry of Champagne worried at a loose tooth in his sore gums. He had lost four teeth since landing at Acre last summer, and he was afraid this one would soon follow. He didn't fancy going through life without his teeth. "Why doesn't the city fall? How much longer can these damned pagans hold out?"

"It can't be long," James of Avesnes said. "Days—hours, even. Everyone in there must be dead or near dead of starvation or disease."

Geoffrey said, "At least the weather's decent for a change. God's blood, had I wanted to be cold and rained on every day, I would have stayed in England."

There was laughter; James banged a hand on the table in approval.

"Another round of arrack?" offered Balian.

Geoffrey slid his cup across the table. "Please God it were a round of beef."

"Amen to that," James said.

As more drink was poured, the men became aware of a commotion outside. There were cries and shouts around the camp. Several of the men started to rise, and as they did, one of Balian's servants burst into the pavilion. "My lords! My lords! Come look!"

At that moment, in the English camp, the barber was cutting Cole's blond hair short. It was an order from Father Stephen, who was also the earl's chief physician. Stephen had hit upon the idea that short hair and beards would somehow improve the army's health. The barber wore leather gauntlets to protect his hands and arms from the lice and fleas escaping from the hair.

The barber finished Cole's hair. "You can go," he said.

"What about my beard?" Cole asked.

"Come back when you've got one," the barber told him.

As Cole slunk away, the barber eyed Ralph the Red. "You're next, Red."

"No!" hollered Ralph. "No! I won't do it!"

"You have to," Roger told him. "It's orders."

"Who cares? We'll be in the city in a few days. I'll get clean then."

The barber dipped his gloves in a bucket of arrack, held

them there a moment, then put them back on. The surface of the bucket was thick with the tiny corpses of lice and fleas that had been killed by the alcohol. "Let's go," the barber told Ralph impatiently. Ralph was last in line; the other men of Roger's section had already been shorn.

"No!" Ralph protested. "I been growing this beard for years. I won't get it cut."

"You've no choice," Roger said.

Ralph swore thunderous oaths. The other men were holding their sides and laughing at him. Laughing himself, Roger was just about to order them to hold Ralph down when there were cries from outside.

"I'm saved!" Ralph said, casting his eyes to Heaven.

The men ran out of the tent. All around them men, and a few women, exited tents or stopped work. The intermittent thump of the mangonels had ceased. Everyone stared out to sea.

In the distance, a fleet of ships could be seen sailing toward Acre. The ships were in single file, keeping good order. They were painted green, with furled lateen sails and double banks of oars.

"Egyptians," swore an Italian sailor nearby. "You can tell by the green hulls."

A collective groan swept over the Christian camp.

As the morning passed, the green-painted Egyptian fleet made its way closer and closer to the city. One by one, the ships rowed past the Tower of Flies and turned smartly into the safety of the harbor. One of the galleys misjudged its passage and an errant wave dashed it against the mole, crushing the vessel's oars, staving in its side and sinking it, to the delight and cheers from the watching Christians. The cheers soon died, however, as the remaining ships tied up at the quays, where they unloaded livestock and other foodstuffs—supplies to last the garrison a year or more. Worse still, the ships unloaded fresh troops, thousands of them, while the Christians watched in silent dismay. The city's old garrison, what remained of it, was embarked. The last man out wore a blue sash on his helmet. "Qaymaz," Roger murmured, his anger rising because he remembered what Qaymaz had done to Deaf Martin.

The ships untied and rowed past the Tower of Flies, heading south ahead of a new storm rising in the west, its clouds dark against the sky.

The men were dispirited. They had been so confident of entering the city. Several sat down in the mud, as though they lacked the strength to do anything else. Arcil was crying.

Ralph the Red turned and strode back into the barber's tent, untying the green ribbons that bound the plaits of his beard. "Cut it," he told the barber. "Cut the damned thing, or I'll do it myself."

❖ ❖ ❖

On the Toron, Balian of Ibelin let out a long breath. "All our efforts, all the dead—all for naught. The Saracens have a fresh garrison and supplies. I am no faint heart, gentlemen, but as God is my witness, I wish to spend no more time before these walls. Last winter was bad enough. This year there are four times the men and not a whit more food—barely a whit of food at all, in fact."

"We couldn't leave even if we want to," James of Avesnes pointed out. "Saladin's got us blocked in."

"We could sail away in the spring," Geoffrey suggested, "those who are left. We could go to Tyre, or to Ascalon—or to Jaffa, close to Jerusalem. Any place but here."

"No," said Henry of Champagne," showing decisive leadership for one of the few times since he'd been made commander. "We'll take this city no matter what the cost. We'll show Saladin that he cannot beat us."

The men around him, most of them, growled approval. They were hard men and proud, men who did not like to acknowledge defeat, no matter how temporary. Geoffrey thought about arguing, but he knew it was no use. These men were letting their hearts overwhelm their heads, and there was no arguing with that.

Henry went on. "Tomorrow we start work on a new belfry. We'll sheath this one in copper. By God, let's see the pagans burn that."

"Where will we get copper?" someone asked.

"There's some around camp. We'll get the rest from Cyprus in the spring. As soon as the ground dries, we'll begin mining the Accursed Tower. We'll take this city if it takes us a dozen years."

More growls of approval, louder. Geoffrey could only shake his head.

A voice said, "We may not have to wait till spring, my lords." It was Geoffrey's blond, curly-haired marshal, Blaise.

The others turned to look, and Blaise flashed a big grin. "I have an idea."

Chapter 37

The Death's Heads were making stew.

That was what Roger's section called themselves now, after the red skulls that Tatwine had painted on their helmets.

They were celebrating the date of Egwulf's birth—the day after the octave of Epiphany, or so Egwulf had been told. That was enough for Roger, who declared they should have a feast. Roger had no idea what his own feast day was, and that made him all the more determined to see that Egwulf enjoyed himself.

The men had not eaten in two days. There was no food in camp, not for those without money to buy it. Dirk, the centenar, wasn't around much, so Roger filled his unit's time with weapons drill and work details. The men complained, but it took their minds off how hungry they were, if only for a little while. Roger had observed that the best disciplined—and healthiest—units in camp were the ones that kept busy. This was in contrast to men of some other units, who roamed the huge camp in packs, looking for plunder. The lords of these men—those who cared—were powerless to control them, and many an unlucky fellow was murdered or severely beaten by them.

Preparations for the meal had been dampened by the arrival of the Egyptian fleet, but now they went on, the men determined to salvage something from a bad week. They had been out scrounging for the feast all morning, and as the afternoon waned, they brought their treasures to the cook pot, which stood under Bald Matthew's supervision outside the tent.

Water for the stew was no problem at this time of year; the men caught rainwater in a barrel. They had to guard the barrel, though, lest somebody steal it for firewood. Their own firewood for today was old headboards that Egwulf and Blackie had taken from graves out on the plain. Will and young Cole and Slowfoot came in with armloads of dried grass.

"Where'd you find that?" Hedde asked them. "Animals have ate all the grass hereabouts."

"Other side of the ditch," Will told him, "near the Saracen camp."

"Dangerous out there," Father Mayn observed.

A drop of blood trickled from Will's nose; he wiped it on his battered glove. "We did run into a Saracen patrol. They were as cold and miserable as we were. Nobody felt like fighting, so we exchanged a few pleasantries and went our separate ways. They seemed like pretty decent fellows, actually. One of them gave us this."

From a pocket of his leather jack he pulled a turnip and a small clove of garlic, and the men around the cook pot howled with delight.

"Anybody seen Tatwine?" Roger asked. Tatwine was the only one not back.

"No," said Will.

"No," said Offa, leaning on his crutches.

"Like as not, the sod's run off," Uwen said. "No more'n you'd expect from a fellow like that."

Will and his companions brushed as much dirt off the grass as they could, then piled the grass by the pot, which was just starting to boil. Nearby, leather goods belonging to the unit's dead men had been stacked. There were jacks with their linings ripped out and the armor plates removed, along with belts, worn-out shoes, and a bridle and set of reins someone had found. Arcil and Mayn were cutting the leather with shears, shaping it as best they could into uniform pieces.

"That's Long Tom's jack, ain't it?" said Ralph the Red, peering over Arcil's shoulder. "Look at all that sweat salt—the thing's white."

"It'll add taste," Offa assured him.

When Arcil and Mayn were done, Bald Matthew, assisted by Hedde, scraped up the leather pieces and dropped them in the boiling pot.

Egwulf picked at an oozing sore on his cheek, just above the edge of his now-short beard. "How long do you cook it?" he asked Matthew.

"How do I know?" Matthew said. "I never cooked a belt before."

When the leather was going good, Matthew added the grass, stirring it into the pot with a long spoon. He chopped the turnip and garlic into as many pieces as he could and threw them in, too, following them with a fistful of bread crumbs he had picked off the ground or out of the filthy straw of the tent over time, crumbs he'd been saving for a special occasion. Axe men from the other sections, along with a few spearmen, stood at a distance, watching enviously.

At that moment who should swagger down the company street but Tatwine. "Look what I got!" he cried, and he held something aloft.

It was a rat.

The men cheered and did little dances and slapped first one another, then Tatwine, on the back. "He's a beauty," Egwulf said, peering at the dead rodent. "Where'd you get him? Ain't seen rats around here lately."

"Found him rooting around the graves," Tatwine said proudly. "Bashed him with a rock." He held the dead rodent by the tail. "Fat 'un, ain't he? Kind of messed up his head with the rock, but that's by the by."

Tatwine handed the rat to Bald Matthew, who gutted and skinned it. Normally, Matthew would have tossed the guts on the ground for the stray dogs to fight over, but there were no more stray dogs or cats—like the rats, they had all been eaten— and anyway these were not normal times. The guts and heart went into the pot, followed by the animal's crushed head, its tail and legs. Matthew cut up what remained. There were thirteen men left in the section, counting Matthew, which meant the rat had to be cut into thirteen equal pieces, with each man getting one piece. The men clustered round Matthew, watching him critically as he worked.

"Here, that piece looks small," Uwen said. "Don't give me that one."

"Shut yer trap," Matthew told him. "I know what I'm doing."

"Yeah, let him work," said Ralph the Red.

The small pieces of rat meat went into the cook pot. The pot bubbled and greasy foam rose to the top. The smell was odious, but the men rubbed their hands in anticipation. They were filthy and emaciated, covered with lice and fleas, skin red from the bites, short hair and beards matted. There were so many lice in the blankets they held round their shoulders, it felt as though the blankets were alive. With a start, Roger realized that he must look the same way. In his mind's eye, he had pictured himself as clean and fresh shaven, as he had been at Huntley, when in reality he must smell like a midden, and he'd probably lost a good two stone in weight, maybe more judging by the way his clothes fit.

Just then, Roger saw the earl's young page come down the street, and he groaned inwardly. The page, whose name was Eustace, only came here when the earl wanted Roger. The page's hair was lank and dirty. He was all skin and bones, eyes sunk deep in his head, and his clothes hung on him. He walked funny, with short steps. He caught Roger's eye and, sure enough, he cocked a hand for Roger to follow him. Before Roger could move, a strange look came over the page's face and he bolted for the nearest latrine. No one gave the boy's plight any mind; they'd all had similar experiences.

Egwulf stood beside Roger and shook his head ruefully. "Bad timing. You'll miss my feast."

Roger pointed to the bubbling pot. "Save my share."

Will blotted more blood from his nose. "Don't worry. We'll see you get some."

❖ ❖ ❖

A number of powerful nobles were gathered around the earl as Roger entered the tent. Roger knew who some of the nobles were, others he didn't. Most weren't English, so he guessed something big was up. Fauston was in the back of the crowd, looking worried. Payen was there, as well. He saw Roger and frowned. "What the Devil is that on your helmet?"

Roger said, "The man call it a—"

"I don't care if they call it the Virgin Mary, get it off. Now."

Roger bristled. "My whole section has them. They—"

"Tell them to find some sand and scrub them all off. And be damned quick about it. This is the army, not a troupe of mystery players. You're in charge of those fellows, man. You're supposed to have—"

"No, no," said Earl Geoffrey, coming forward and examining the red design on Roger's helmet. "I like that. Shows somebody in this army still has spirit. You say all your men have them?"

"They do, my lord." Roger cleared his throat, a bit embarrassed. "They call themselves the Deaths Heads."

The earl chuckled. "Ha! Good name. I like it." He motioned to his marshal, Blaise. "Tell Roger your plan."

Blaise was a cheerful, athletic fellow, the type who never gets discouraged. His family were hereditary marshals to the earls of Trent. "A quick attack," he told Roger. "Tonight, while the new garrison is still settling in. One ladder. Me, another knight, and ten footmen. We'll get over the wall, fight our way down the Green Tower and open the gate before the Turbans know what's happened. The count of Champagne's men will be waiting outside. When the gate's open, they'll storm the city."

They were all staring at Roger, all those great lords, like they valued his opinion, like he had any idea what he was doing. "Well?" said the earl.

Roger thought for a moment. "Ropes," he said, the word

seeming to burst from his mouth of its own accord.

"Ropes?" said the earl.

Roger scrambled to keep up with his thoughts. "Yes, my lord. I remember how, when we practiced on the belfry, we slid down on ropes. Instead of fighting your way down the tower, and maybe raising the alarm, you could tie ropes to the balustrade and slide down. It would be quicker, and quiet. I think you'd have a better chance of getting to the gates."

"No one cares what you think," Payen said. "Leave those decisions to your betters."

"No, wait," Blaise said. "I like it." He turned to the earl. "I like it a lot. I think it might work."

"All right," said the earl. "Ropes it is."

Blaise gave Roger a big grin. "Are your Deaths Heads up for the job?"

So that's why they had called for him. "We'll try, my lord."

"Don't *try*, you fool," Payen cut in. "Do it."

"Yes," Roger said, and he paused before adding, "my lord." He always added that pause before saying "my lord," to Payen because he knew it drove the Frenchman crazy.

Blaise smacked Roger's shoulder, like they were old friends. "Good fellow."

Earl Geoffrey added, "There's a gold piece for each of you when the gate's opened."

Roger wrinkled his brow. "I think right now my men would rather have a piece of bread, my lord. Or an egg."

"Ha! They probably would at that," the earl agreed. "We'll see what we can do."

"Thank you, my lord." Roger saw Payen watching him with a predatory smile, like a cat eyeing a trapped bird.

Blaise grew more serious. "Ready your men. We go tonight, after matins."

Chapter 38

They reached the city ditch.

Wind gusts brought rattling sheets of rain. The wind and rain made it seem even colder than it was. The body of the storm had stayed out to sea, but its heavy breakers boomed on the shore, covering the noise of the party's approach.

In the dark, Roger half slid, half fell into the ditch. The Saracens had partially dug out the ditch since the Christians' last attack, and Roger landed in several feet of freezing water, standing in mud and on top of things whose identity he did not want to think about. The earl's marshal, Blaise, followed him, wearing an old conical helmet and a plain jack instead of his hauberk, shield slung over his back.

Above them, Will and Peter of Winstead, the party's other knight, lay on the edge of the ditch and lowered one end of the long ladder. Peter was the son of Will's lord, and he'd reacted with delight when he'd seen that Will was to be one of the assault party. "Will! Good to see you! Glad you're with us. We'll show them what's what, eh?"

Will had grinned; the two men had known each other since childhood. "That we will, Lord Peter."

Now, fumbling in the darkness, Roger and Blaise took the heavy ladder and maneuvered it upright while the rest of the men scrambled into the wide ditch. When they were all there, they carried the ladder across the ditch, then Roger and Blaise climbed out, took the ladder and pulled it up.

The remainder of the party emerged from the ditch. They had daubed their faces with mud before they started, for concealment; now the rest of their bodies were covered with mud, as well. Every second man had a long coil of rope slung across his chest. There were Blaise and Peter and ten of the

Death's Heads; Roger had left Bald Matthew and Cole at the camp, along with Offa and his broken leg. Young Cole had complained bitterly, to no avail. Roger sniffled; his nose had not stopped running since the beginning of Advent. He wiped it on the side of his muddy glove, the skin raw and tender against the harsh leather.

Carrying the ladder, the party moved forward, the walls of Acre looming above them, blotting out the storm clouds, St. Martin's gate to their front, rain spattering on their helmets. Roger chewed a piece of cooked leather from dinner, working the tasteless morsel around his mouth. Matthew had boiled the stew until it was thick, then strained it. The stew had been hot and greasy, if not particularly filling. After they drank it, the men took their morsels of rat meat and offal, following that with the grass, which they chewed to a pulp and swallowed, as though they were cattle. After that, they had sucked the tiny rat bones dry, then gnawed on the leather.

They reached the foot of the wall, barely able to hear themselves over the rain and the roar of the surf. Above them there was no movement, no sign they had been detected. Blaise had been right—it was the perfect time to do this. The Saracen relief garrison would be settling into unfamiliar surroundings; they wouldn't have established any routines yet. That plus the bad weather should put them well off their guard.

The men raised the ladder against the wall. Long and heavy, the ladder was unwieldy, its balance bad. It caught a gust of wind and swayed to one side and outwards and looked like it was going to fall, but the men regained control of it by sheer force and it hit the stone wall with a sharp thump. Everyone stood still and held his breath, but there was no sign they had been heard.

The plan was simple—climb the ladder, tie the ropes to the wooden balustrade and slide down, get to the gate and open it. Beyond the ditch waited the main assault party of Champenois, followed by Burgundians and English. Blaise would go up the ladder first, followed by Peter of Winstead, then Roger. Red-haired Peter was Blaise's lifelong friend. In more peaceful times, they had ridden the tourney circuit together.

Blaise grasped the sides of the ladder. He looked up, took a couple deep breaths and crossed himself. Then he turned, winked at the men behind him and grinned. "All right, Death's Heads. Let's be heroes."

He started up the ladder. Peter followed. Like Blaise, Peter wore no hauberk. He had left his shield behind and his sword was slung over his back. Roger spat out the leather and went next, shield over his back, axe and dagger at his belt. Uwen stepped in front of Will so that he could go behind Roger. Tatwine followed Will, then Egwulf, then Ralph the Red and the others.

"I should have known this would happen," Slowfoot cracked. "Whenever they give us a good meal, it's right before a fight."

They moved as quickly as they could, the scraping of their mud-caked feet on the ladder rungs drowned out by the angry surf. Roger was scared but he couldn't let the men see it—as their leader, he was supposed to set an example. Anyway, this was better than staying in camp and waiting to die from sickness.

Blaise neared the top. Then, from the corner of his eye, Roger glimpsed movement between one of the nearby crenellations. He looked and nothing was there, and it took his brain a second to register what it was he had seen.

A face.

His spine became an icy rod. His senses throbbed with life. "Trap!" he yelled up at Blaise. "It's a trap!"

But Blaise was through the crenellation and onto the parapet. Peter was nearing the top right behind him.

There were sounds of a struggle from the other side of the crenellations. "Get down!" Roger shouted. He turned and motioned to the men climbing behind him. "Down! Down! It's a trap!"

At the top of the ladder, Peter had heard Roger and

hesitated. He tried to start back down, but, from behind the crenellations, two men grabbed his arms and a third took hold of the rope around his shoulder and they hauled him up, struggling, onto the parapet.

Behind Roger, the men were getting off the ladder. Those closest to the ground jumped. The others clambered down as fast as they could, muddy feet slipping on the rungs. The sibilant hiss of arrows surrounded them in the darkness.

There was a sudden searing pain in Roger's left calf. He almost let go of the ladder but held on.

He hadn't been hit by an arrow, he realized; he had been stabbed.

By Uwen.

Uwen grabbed Roger's uninjured leg and tried to yank Roger off the ladder. Roger was holding on only by his hands. He kicked down, made contact, heard Uwen swear as he lost his dagger. Roger flailed with his legs to find the ladder rungs. He got one foot on a rung, then the other. He kicked down again, but Uwen was gone, for his own safety. To fall from this height meant certain death.

Roger slid down the ladder, gripping the sides with his hands, braking himself with the insides of his feet, as he had done as a sailor on the *Quail*. More arrows flew around him. Suddenly the ladder leaned away from the wall, pushed from above. It teetered, then fell outward. Shouts and cries from all sides.

Roger let go and dropped into the blackness. He hit the ground before he expected it, landed on his back, and just had the wits to roll over as the heavy ladder crashed onto his back and shoulders.

The breath was knocked out of him. His wounded leg was on fire. Nearby, yelling men ran away from the walls. Roger heard his name called—by Egwulf, by Tatwine, by Will. He pushed the long ladder off him and was about to reply, when he stopped. Against the stormy sky, a hulking form approached, attracted by the noise of the moving ladder.

It was Uwen. He was looking for Roger, and he was carrying his axe at the ready.

Roger lay still. He waited until the dark form was past him. Then he leapt to his feet—or tried to, because the pain in his calf kept him from being as fast as he would have liked. Uwen heard him and turned, axe raised. Roger lowered his shoulder and drove it into Uwen's gut. The two men went down. Roger grabbed Uwen's head by the chin and back and twisted sharply. Uwen's neck snapped and he went limp.

Roger dropped Uwen's head. Biting his lip against the pain in his calf, Roger rose and limped toward the ditch. Arrows thudded into the ground nearby, but the Saracens up top couldn't see in the darkness and the rain; they were shooting blindly.

"Egwulf?" Roger cried. "Will?"

"Here!" came a voice.

Roger followed the voice, slid into the stinking ditch. His men gathered around him, some still gasping for breath. Roger took a quick head count. Everyone was there. No injuries save for bruises and a few sprained ankles. "What happened?" Will said.

"They were waiting for us," Roger said. "They got the two knights."

"Hey," said Blackie, looking around the group. "Where's Uwen?"

"Dead," Roger said. "Broke his neck when he fell from the ladder." He started out of the ditch, but he couldn't plant his right foot to climb. "Give me a hand, would you?" he told Will.

Will boosted Roger's leg. "You're wounded," he said.

"I must have fallen on something. Let's go."

❖ ❖ ❖

The next morning, Blaise the marshal and Peter of Winstead were seen hanging by their necks from the city walls, their eyes gouged out, their naked bodies horribly cut up and bruised.

Roger and his men observed the sight from the safety of the Christian lines. Roger forced himself to look, tried to imagine the torment the two men had endured before they had been mercifully killed. Anger raged deep within him.

"Guess this means the siege won't end any time soon," Tatwine observed.

"That's not all it means," Roger said grimly. "It means there's a traitor in our ranks. A traitor who needs to pay for this."

Chapter 39

"It was a trap, my lords. They were waiting for us."

The assembled nobles exchanged glances—most of them dubious, a few worried. Roger was in Earl Geoffrey's tent, facing the most powerful barons in the camp, including Henry of Champagne, the army's commander. The barons were seated at Geoffrey's table or standing behind it, cloaks wrapped around them against the cold. Roger went on, telling them what had transpired during the ill-fated attack. When he got to the part about seeing the face between the crenellations, Guy of Lusignan interrupted. "A face? What kind of face? How many?"

"One, my lord," Roger said.

Guy still wore the gold circlet about his head. He had been with the assault party waiting behind the ditch. This had been his chance for vindication, his chance to replace Conrad as leader of the native Christians. "Did anyone else see this face?"

"No, my lord. It was dark and raining, and it was only there for a—"

"So," Guy interrupted again, "on the basis of this—this *thing* which you may or may not have seen, you, a mere vintenar, justified aborting the attack and sending your men back down the ladder?"

Roger said, "My instinct told me that—"

"Your *instinct?*" Guy paused for effect, looking around at the other barons. "Was it instinct—or cowardice?"

Roger grit his teeth. "What I say is true, my lord. Peter of Winstead tried to retreat, but the Saracens reached out and dragged him over the wall."

"Can any of your men verify that?" said Henry of Champagne. Henry's beard and the front of his tunic were flecked with blood from his coughing. He sounded doubtful, and Roger suddenly realized that he was on trial here. A misstep might well end in his death.

"No, my lord. They were behind me on the ladder. They wouldn't have had a good angle."

"What about the man directly behind you?" Henry said. "Wouldn't he have seen?"

Roger hesitated. "He was killed falling from the ladder."

"How convenient," purred Guy of Lusignan. "Come now, Master Vintenar, you don't really expect us to believe this nonsense about a trap, do you? Why, that would mean there is a traitor in this company."

"Yes, my lord," Roger agreed.

An uneasy silence fell over the tent.

Big James of Avesnes leaned across the earl's table. "And who would that traitor be?" he said with a throaty growl.

"I've no idea, my lord."

"Then why do you say there is one?" said Balian of Ibelin.

Roger held his ground; he couldn't show weakness or irresolution. "Because the Saracens couldn't have been waiting for us unless they had been warned we were coming."

Henry of Champagne tapped a finger on the table. "That's assuming they *were* waiting for you."

"The camp is full of Saladin's spies, you know that," James of Avesnes told Henry. "Half the native servants are in his employ."

"Yes, but they wouldn't have had time to get word to the garrison," Guy of Lusignan said smoothly. "Only a few people even knew of the plan—most of them in this tent—and to suggest that one of us somehow warned the Saracens is absurd."

Roger shifted his weight, wincing from the pain in his bandaged calf. On his way here, here had run into Ailith. Fauston had told Ailith about the coming attack and Roger's part in it, and she had been awake all night, uneasy for Roger's well-being. She had seen Roger's wound, still covered with the mud and filth of the city ditch, and she had insisted on dressing it. She wiped it with a cloth that was reasonably clean, then washed it out with fresh rainwater, squeezing water into the wound again and again until all the dirt was gone. Then she held the wound open and poured arrack into it.

"Have a care!" Fauston cautioned. "That's good arrack you're wasting."

Ailith paid him no heed—Roger had practically jumped through the tent roof from the pain, and she was busy holding him down.

Fauston went on, still lamenting the loss of the arrack. "That's not how the barbers would fix his wound. Are you *sure* you're not a witch?"

It was a trick Ailith had seen native surgeons—whom most crusaders strenuously avoided—use. She began winding a bandage around the wound. "Men. If it was up to you, you'd bind the wound with cow dung. It's a wonder any of you lives to be twenty."

Fauston thought she had chosen a poor example. "Actually, cow dung is said to have excellent restorative qualities—"

"Be quiet and hold him still."

Now Payen of Beaufort stepped before the assembled barons and waved an arm in Roger's direction. "My lords, it pains me to say this because Roger is in my charge, but I submit that he is a coward. I submit that he ordered his men back down the ladder when a bit of dash might have carried the day. If not for him, we would now be in Acre. If not for him, Blaise FitzMaurice and Peter of Winstead might still be alive. As punishment, I ask that he be stripped of his rank and hung."

Roger felt the eyes of the council upon him again. He stood straight, as though sure of himself, but his mind was racing.

Had he seen the face? It had been there but an instant, and he'd only glimpsed it from the corner of his eye. Was it possible he had imagined it? Could Guy of Lusignan be right? He tried to gauge who was on his side and who was against him. Henry of Champagne and Guy of Lusignan were against, that was certain. James of Avesnes had seemed friendly. Earl Geoffrey, Balian of Ibelin, the others—it was impossible to tell.

"Hanging's too easy," submitted Guy of Lusignan. "He should be drawn and quartered as an example to the other men."

There was grumbling and nodding among the barons, and it looked like there might be agreement with what Guy had said, but Balian of Ibelin stayed them. "The earl of Trent is this man's lord, let him make the decision."

Balian looked to Henry of Champagne for approval. Henry tapped his finger again. "Very well. I suppose that's fair."

Now all the attention was on Geoffrey, who stroked his beard as he studied Roger. Roger met his gaze unflinchingly. Geoffrey seemed to have aged ten years since he had arrived at Acre; Roger wondered if he himself looked as bad. At last, Geoffrey sat straight. "Roger has proved his bravery ere this. He saved my life when he might have run—when many others *did* run. I believe his story."

Guy of Lusignan made a disgusted noise; Henry of Champagne shook his head. Payen protested, "My lord—!"

Geoffrey held up a hand, silencing Payen, and went on, addressing Roger. "I must say, though, the story does seem flimsy. A face that no one else saw, that you're not really sure you saw yourself, unless I miss my guess."

Geoffrey cocked his head shrewdly. Roger said nothing, his silence an agreement with the earl's words.

"As for your accusation that there is a traitor here . . ." Geoffrey looked around the tent. "That is something we must consider." He nodded to Roger with his hand. "You may go."

Roger let out his breath and bowed. "Yes, my lord."

He felt the assembly's eyes on him as he left. He limped out of the tent and down the Toron to his company area, knowing he was lucky to be alive. The cold sea breeze blew his hair. He had lost his helmet in the fall from the ladder; Tatwine had promised to find him another and paint a red death's head on it.

As Roger entered the company street, he encountered Dirk. The big Brabanter looked like he'd actually gained weight; Roger wondered where he was getting food. "What happened to Uwen?" Dirk asked Roger.

"Broke his neck," Roger said.

"Bad luck."

"Yes. Friend of yours, wasn't he?"

Dirk shrugged. "Comrade, more like. We soldiered together in France and Flanders." He nodded at Roger's leg. "You are wounded."

"Yes," Roger said.

"At least you are still alive. That is good for you."

"Yes."

Dirk kept going. Roger watched him. He hadn't told the council about Uwen's actions on the ladder. There hadn't seemed to be a need. Why had Uwen tried to kill him? Roger had never liked the Welshman, but he had never considered him an enemy. The fact that Uwen had broken in line to get behind Roger on the ladder meant that he must have planned to kill Roger all along, that it wasn't a spontaneous act.

Had Uwen acted on his own? Or had someone put him up to it?

Chapter 40

The rains came again, harder, if such a thing were possible. Corpses and skeletons of men long dead washed out of shallow graves and their remains floated about in grotesque abandon. When the rain stopped, the cold worsened. At night the ground and standing water froze, and damp clothing stuck to the skin and rubbed it bloody.

Sickness raged through the crusader camp. The cemeteries exploded across the plain. The list of great nobles who succumbed was lengthy: the archbishops of Milan and Besancon, the duke of Lower Lorraine, the counts of Amiens, Blois, and Clermont. The life of Henry of Champagne was despaired of. Minor nobles died by the hundreds and common folk by the thousand. Bianca Foligno, a noted Pisan madame, had brought fifty prostitutes to Acre as an act of piety to ease the men's suffering. By the end of January only three were still alive. Geoffrey of Trent's dysentery was so bad they cut away the seat of his drawers. It so weakened him that he had trouble breathing and was forced to his bed. His young page Eustace had become a walking skeleton.

The very air of the camp seemed poisonous. Incense hung like a fog; a man could not walk a furlong without encountering a funeral procession or death carts that picked bodies from the streets, stacking them like cordwood. There was food to be had on the Concourse, but there was no money to pay for it. The nobles were forced to eat their horses and dogs. Common men lived on five beans a day and counted themselves lucky. Grain was a hundred bezants for a small cask; an egg brought 12 pence of Anjou. In the end there were men who lived on nothing but wine, though they did not live long. And, of course, there were men like Dirk, men who seemed immune to starvation . . . .

❖ ❖ ❖

Dirk made his way across the dark plain. The moon was down and clouds covered the stars, as they most always did these days, so no one could see him. In his good hand he carried a shovel; over his shoulder was an improvised canvas sling filled with bits of dry wood. He had scouted the ground yesterday, so he knew where he was going. The faintest bit of grey light showed behind the eastern hills. This was the best time to do this sort of thing—before the Christian and Saracen camps were awake.

Dirk came from Haaspoort, a dreary crossroads near Breda, its only attraction an abbey notorious for its collection of sodomites. Dirk's father had been a carter, employing a huge dog to draw a cart full of grain or building materials or whatever people would pay him to carry. When the dog died, his father put the strap around his own chest and drew the cart himself. Haaspoort was the kind of place where a lot of boys went off to be soldiers. Dirk had no intention of drawing that damned cart, and he didn't mind a fight, so he ran away from home and joined up with the first lord who needed men.

Dirk had served on both sides during the English king Henry's wars with his sons. He had also served in Navarre, Burgundy, Italy—anywhere a good soldier was needed. Soldiering meant fighting, looting, enjoying the favors of women—willing or unwilling—and liquor. All the things Dirk liked. He was under no illusions about his end. He would never be a grandfather bouncing brats on his knee and pottering around the roses, but damned if he wouldn't have some fun before he died.

In the beginning, Dirk had seen the crusade as a great opportunity. He'd been in York when the Jews burned themselves alive to avoid persecution. He'd hoped to grab some of their gold, but King Richard and the Church got most of that, damn them. After that, Dirk had wandered south, doing some robbing and plundering to keep his hand in, till he joined the earl of Trent's men.

Dirk had reckoned there would be easy pickings in the Holy Land. Back in Europe, men had talked of sacking the wealthy cities of Damascus and Baghdad. No one had talked about sitting in the mud and rotting from fever and starvation. If Dirk stayed here, he'd end up feeding the worms like the rest of these fools. But while he was trying to figure out how to get away, he needed to keep himself alive.

It was just light enough to make out where he was going now. He headed to where he'd seen the funeral yesterday—the funeral he was interested in, that is. He found where turned-up earth signified the newest grave among the thousands surrounding him. He was aware of other furtive figures on the plain, doing the same thing he was doing. By tacit approval, none of these men ever acknowledged one another.

He took his shovel and began to dig. The ground was wet and easy to turn. He hadn't gone far when he found the body. Usually the bodies were stacked atop one another, but not this one. This one had been a bishop; he had been buried alone. Dirk tugged at the shrouded body and dragged it out of the muddy hole. He cut open the winding sheet—it had been a long time since there had been wood for caskets. Sometimes these Churchmen were buried with their jewels or relics, things Dirk could use to buy bread on the Concourse. Dirk was in luck— there was a huge gold ring, encrusted with jewels, on the corpse's right hand. Dirk tugged, but the ring wouldn't come off the stiff finger. So he took his knife, cut off the finger, and put it in his pouch. He could detach the ring later.

Dirk pushed back the shroud, exposing the pale body. The bishop had been old and grey haired, but there was no helping that. Dirk knelt and cut a long slice of meat from the corpse's leg, another from its buttocks—that's where the fat was. Clerics—especially high-ranking ones like this—had more access to food, so there was more meat on their bodies than on those of the common soldiers, or even those of the nobles. Dirk sliced the meat awkwardly with his left hand, because his right hand still hadn't healed. He was afraid it would never heal in this endless cold and damp.

When he was finished cutting the meat, he removed the bits of wood from his sling and started a small fire with flint and tinder. Here and there, similar fires dotted the plain. Dirk squatted and roasted the meat on a spit. He had to hurry, before the day's first funeral procession came out from the camp and he was identified. He tried to char the meat, so as to hide the bitter taste peculiar to human flesh. When the meat was cooked, he sat on his haunches and devoured it greedily. It was gristly, and he chewed the gristle to get the juices, then spat it out. If this went against the teachings of the Church— fine, let the Church feed him. Until they did, he—

Suddenly he stopped.

He sensed someone behind him. Slowly, he looked over his shoulder.

It was Roger. Egwulf was with him, and that crazy-eyed devil Tatwine, and Will, looking like scarecrows, all of them.

Dirk stood.

"Enjoying your meal?" Roger said pleasantly. "Anyone we know?"

"What are you doing here?" Dirk said.

"We've been wondering how you stayed so well fed. Thought we'd follow you and find out."

"A man has to eat," Dirk said defensively.

"True, but he doesn't have to eat his fellow men. Unless I'm wrong, that's a Mortal Sin." Roger stopped smiling. "It's also a hanging offense."

Roger's men spread out. "What are you going to do?" Dirk said, watching them.

"Turn you in," Roger said.

Dirk said, "You want money? I can give you money."

Roger's genial attitude disappeared. "Money's not worth

the pleasure of seeing you pay for what you've done."

The other three men glared at Dirk, disgust and hatred in their eyes.

Dirk shrugged and rose, as if resigned to his fate. Then he flung the piece of meat at Roger, turned and ran toward the hills.

Roger and his men ran after him. They gained a bit on him—Roger wished they had Slowfoot with them—but Dirk had been eating regularly so he had more energy than his pursuers. At last Roger held up a hand for them to stop. "Let him go," Roger said. He was bent double, breathing heavily from the unwonted exertion. "We'll never catch him. Go much farther, and there's too much chance of running into a Saracen patrol. I don't want any of us killed because of that bastard."

"What'll happen to him?" Egwulf said.

"Nothing good, I hope," said Tatwine.

Roger beckoned them to rebury the bishop, then something caught his eye on another part of the plain.

Chapter 41

Helvise was lost.

She had been exercising her grey gelding, Storm, on the plain, but she had gotten herself turned around in the dark, and the dim lights of the crusader camp had not been enough for her to re-orient herself. The camp ran in a huge semicircle from the seashore north of Acre to the River Belus, south of the city. Riding into an unfamiliar part of the camp, at night, could prove to be more dangerous than remaining out here.

She exercised the horse at night because it was safer—both for her and for the horse. Storm was one of the few remaining animals in the German camp. He had been eating grain that Helvise had purchased with what remained of her husband's money—grain Helvise could have used to feed herself—along with what dried grass she had managed to gather. Now that Frederick of Swabia, the German commander, was near death, Helvise didn't know what would happen to Storm. It was only because Helvise's husband had been a distant relative of Frederick's that Storm had so far escaped the roasting spit. Helvise had raised the horse from a colt; he was her best friend. Helvise had brought an old crossbow with her and a quiver of bolts, but that was mostly for show. Should trouble arise it was unlikely she would have time to dismount and load the bow. She needed to get Storm back under guard before the camp had risen.

She knew where she had gone wrong. In the dark, she had encountered a gully that didn't seem to have been there before. She should have turned around right then and gone back to camp, but she had stubbornly believed she could find her way once she got across the gully. She had been wrong, and now that the sky was lightening, she had no idea how far away the

German tents were. Gradually the city walls detached themselves from the still dark eastern sky. Helvise made out the Accursed Tower with its green flag, the landmark everyone used to orient themselves. She had gotten herself well to the north of where she should have been. She saw the Toron, now, as well, or fancied she did. At one time the fires on the Toron had blazed all night, now it was as dark as the rest of the camp.

Now that she knew where she was, she would give Storm a good gallop back to the lines, assuming he could gallop at all in his worn-down condition. The sky was just light enough. Helvise couldn't run him in the dark for fear of his stepping in a hole or some other declivity.

She was about to touch her heels to the horse's flank when she was aware of movement close to her right. Men. *Where did they come from?* They seemed to have sprung from the very earth. Her first thought was that they were soldiers on patrol, but she quickly realized they weren't. Many wore the red caps of the Proveneaux, but there were Moravians and Lombards among them, and men from other countries, as well. This must be one of the renegade gangs that plagued the camp.

She was scared, but before she could get away, one of the men leaped forward and grabbed Storm's bridle. Helvise reached for her crossbow but another man snatched it from her. The men surrounded her—there were at least two dozen. One of them raised a knife and hacked at Storm's haunch. The horse screamed and tried to rear, but other men held him steady. They swarmed him, slicing flesh from his haunches, his withers. Storm tried to buck, but they cut his hamstrings and he went down, screaming piteously, its eyes rolling in terror, pleading for help. The men fell upon the animal, cutting it, taking raw flesh and cramming it into their mouths.

As the horse fell, Helvise was dragged from the saddle. She tried to fight, but men held her limbs and pushed her down. Her jack was ripped off, her linen shirt torn in half. Men held her legs and pulled off her breeches. She was pinned to the ground. There was shoving and arguing, then someone mounted her and she smelled his terrible stench and she heard someone screaming and realized it was her. She struggled but her assailants held her fast, and the man drooled into her face, grunting and panting as he pumped, and she knew he was the first of many men. Suddenly the man gave a little cry and fell over. There was more shouting and something hot splashed Helvise's face, and it was blood . . .

❖ ❖ ❖

Roger and his men had a long run to where the woman was being attacked. They were already tired from chasing Dirk. Gasping for breath in their weakened condition, they saw the horse dragged down, chopped to pieces and eaten while still alive. They saw the woman pulled from the horse and raped. Roger got to the screaming woman first. He hit the man on top of her with the butt of his axe, driving the hard wood into the side of the man's head. The man cried out and fell. Another man, an African, thrust a dagger at Roger. Roger avoided the thrust, and Egwulf clove his axe into the African's skull, blood and brains splashing. *Where did they get an African?* Roger thought.

The men who had been attacking the woman backed off. Some of their friends who had been cutting up the animal joined them. Roger and Tatwine brandished their axes at the mob while Egwulf and Will lifted the woman to her feet. The woman was shaking, crying, her bare legs unsteady. Roger and his men formed a half-circle around her while the mob advanced on them. Some of the renegades had hands and faces smeared with blood from eating the horse. Others paid no attention to the woman and were still cutting flesh from the animal, which was in its death throes, legs kicking weakly.

"Back off," Roger warned the men.

"What if we don't?" snarled a gap-toothed Provenceaux, a huge man with a filthy beard.

"We'll kill you," Roger said.

"There's more of us than there are of you," the Provenceaux pointed out.

Tatwine drew back his arm and threw a knife, which struck the Provenceaux in the throat. The man collapsed to his knees, clutching his throat, then fell onto his side, gurgling blood.

"Now there's one less of you," Tatwine told the renegades. Tatwine was up on the balls of his feet, his dark eyes wild. "Come on, then, who's next?"

The mob hesitated. No one came forward. Tatwine was so worked up that Roger had to tug his arm to let him know they were leaving. Slowly the four men backed away, keeping themselves between the mob and the woman. The renegades followed them for a space, then stopped. There was arguing among the men, then somebody waved a deprecating hand toward Roger and his companions and the renegades went back to eating the horse.

Roger and his men kept moving. Roger removed his jack and put it on the woman to hide her nakedness. She was shivering, tears streaked her cheeks. Her short dark hair was tangled and full of dirt. "Th-thank you," she said weakly.

Roger hadn't looked closely at her before; now he gave a start. "Helvise."

"How do you know my name?" the woman said.

"Someone told me. I can't remember who."

She stared at him, sniffling and blinking away tears, as though trying to think of where he might have seen her before. Then she said, "I remember now." She sniffed again. "You were at the catapults. And that night we caught the spies in camp—you were one of the men involved."

"That's right. I am called Roger. I'm from Trentshire, in England. These are my friends Will, Egwulf and Tatwine."

The three men bowed. "Madame," "My lady," "Your ladyship."

She acknowledged them, tight lipped. They kept moving

toward the camp, glancing backwards from time to time in case the mob had changed its mind and decided to come after them. "Interesting morning," Will observed, "and it's not even breakfast yet."

"Not that there's going to be any breakfast," said Tatwine.

"Or supper," added Egwulf.

They crossed the camp ditch and headed for the German lines, ignoring the sick and dying, ignoring the people who stared at the four men and the bare-legged, bruised woman. "Are you all right?" Roger asked Helvise.

She nodded. "I think so." Tears started again. "Poor Storm, I . . ."

Roger put a comforting arm around her shoulder. "Try not to think about it."

They reached the German camp, one of the smallest in the army. Helvise led the way. She had stopped crying; she held Roger's jack tightly around her. Out of respect, her countrymen tried not to stare, but they couldn't help themselves.

"Is your husband here?" Roger asked her.

"He's dead," she said dully. "Killed by the Turks in Anatolia. Along with our child."

"I'm sorry," Roger said. It was the only thing he could think of.

They reached Helvise's tent, a large green structure. "Come," she said, leading them inside.

The tent was divided into two sections by a green curtain. "Big," Will said, looking around.

She paused a moment before answering. "It was constructed to hold my husband and me, plus our servants. The servants are all dead as well."

She bade them wait and ducked behind the curtain. Not long after, she came back out, wearing a long linen shirt and fresh green breeches. She handed Roger his jack. "I cannot thank you enough. Those men would have killed me."

"We were glad to help," Roger said.

In her other hand was a purse. "Take this."

Roger was tempted. The money in the purse would buy much-needed food for him and his men. But that money would also buy food for her, as well as protection for a woman alone among so many men.

Roger pushed the purse back, his companions nodding agreement at his action. Roger said, "We don't want anything. We were only doing our Christian duty. Have you anyone to look after you?"

She shook her head. "No. The duke of Swabia is my lord, but he is gravely ill."

"You shouldn't be alone like this. It's dangerous."

"I have grown used to it. I will be all right." She gave a small smile. "After all, I am the Woman in Green."

Will and Tatwine gasped. Egwulf stumbled backward. They'd had no idea.

"Very well," Roger said. He turned to his dumbfounded companions. "Come on, lads." The four men bowed and took their leave.

They headed back to their own lines, Egwulf and Tatwine in front. "The Woman in Green," Tatwine said. "I've heard about her, but I never thought I'd get to see her."

"Wait till we tell the others," Will said.

Egwulf was more pragmatic. "Wonder if there's any of that horse left? God knows, I could do with a bit to eat."

"That thing'll be naught but bones by now," Tatwine said. "I'll bet there's a hundred men been over that carcass, and another hundred waiting their turn."

"Humans is like buzzards when you get down to it," Egwulf said. "Worse, maybe."

Behind them, Roger shook his head. "Each time I think this siege can't get any worse, it does. Now we're killing each other. Eating each other. In God's name, what are we coming to? We're supposed to be Christians. Where is this going to end?"

No one had an answer.

Chapter 42

Dirk stopped running. That bastard Roger and his friends were no longer chasing him.

Dirk caught his breath, looking around him in the first rays of sunlight. Where could he go? He couldn't return to the crusader camp. If he did, he would be hung—maybe even burned alive—for his sin. Damn the Church, anyway. They'd tolerate an abbey full of queers, but they'd burn him for trying to keep himself alive.

There was only one course open. He wouldn't be the first Christian to desert to the Saracens. Starving men go where there is food, and being a soldier is much the same in one army as it is in another. The Goat Fuckers were said to have entire companies of men who had once been crusaders. Anyway, he reflected, it was better to be on the winning side, and right now that side looked to be the Saracens.

Dirk's main worry was his hand. It hurt all the time. With the cold and damp, the bones had not knit correctly, and Dirk was afraid he'd never be able to wield a weapon properly again. He could learn to fight with his left hand, but that would take time, and the Saracens might not want to waste food on him while he gained that time. He had seen what they did to their prisoners, and it wasn't pretty. Dirk might have enjoyed inflicting such pain on someone else, but he didn't want it inflicted on himself.

This was all Roger's fault. Because of Roger, Dirk's hand was unusable. Because of Roger, Dirk couldn't go back to the camp. Because of Roger, Dirk had lost his rank as centenar, a rank he had worked years to obtain—with a bit of luck he could have become a man at arms someday, maybe even a knight. It was all so unfair. Roger had won their fight by a stroke of fortune; any other time, Dirk would have pounded him to a pulp or, better yet, killed him. He should have killed him afterwards for what he'd done to his hand. He'd sent Uwen to do the job during that surprise attack on the city, but Uwen hadn't come back. Roger seemed to have a charmed life.

Dirk swore. He would make Roger pay. He didn't know how or when, but he would do it.

He had entered a series of low, scrub-covered hills. The going was more difficult here, the visibility limited, and Dirk was soon panting for breath, out of condition after his long run and months of sitting idle in camp.

As Dirk crested a small rise and started down the other side, he heard a noise behind him. He turned and in the middle distance he saw a party of lightly armored horsemen carrying lances and short bows. The men saw him at the same time.

Saracens.

His instinct was to run, and he had to fight to overcome it. He faced the men and raised his hands as they approached. "Friend!" he yelled in French. "Friend! *Ami!*" Maybe some of them were familiar with the language of the native Christians. Even if they weren't, they might be accustomed to seeing deserters. "Friend!"

The horsemen cantered up, surrounding Dirk and prodding him with their spears, the tips of which were razor sharp. He felt them through his jack, whose armored plates they pierced with every jab.

"Friend!" Dirk cried

One of the Saracens yelled at him in a tongue he didn't understand. The man pointed and indicated Dirk should start moving in that direction.

Dirk started walking. He kept his hands up, half expecting one of those spear tips to slide deep into his back at any moment. The horsemen drove him to a camp, one of many Saracen camps dotting the hills around Acre. There was a lot of yelling and gesturing in the camp when Dirk appeared, and eventually a nobleman of some sort appeared, accompanied by an aide. The noble was in his mid-thirties, Dirk guessed, tall and handsome in a cruel sort of way; with a long, thin nose. He looked intelligent and thoughtful. Something about his lower lip, a certain thickness, bespoke licentiousness, as well. He wore a blue silk robe embroidered with gold thread along with baggy white trousers tucked into leather boots. A curved sword hung at his belt; on his head was a conical helmet with a blue sash wrapped around it.

The noble looked Dirk over, paying particular attention to his injured hand, then he said something in a smooth, rich voice to the man next to him. Dirk had not paid much attention to the second man before this, but now he realized that the fellow was European. Though tanned and dressed in Arab garb, he had brown hair and beard, along with watery blue eyes. *Another deserter*, Dirk thought.

The European indicated the Saracen noble; he spoke with a northern French accent. "This is the great emir Sarim al-din Qaymaz al-Najmi."

Why do the Goat Fuckers all have names that end in "al-din" or "ad-din?" Dirk thought. *How the hell do they tell each other apart?*

The European went on. "I am—or was—called Lambert." It was easy to see why Lambert had deserted; you could read the weakness in his face. *Gutless clerk*, Dirk thought contemptuously.

Dirk said, "Tell Qaymaz—tell Lord Qaymaz—that I am an experienced soldier. I have fought in many battles and held high rank." No harm embellishing things a bit. "I have seen the error of my ways in supporting the crusaders, and I now wish to serve Qaymaz."

Lambert said something to Qaymaz, who kept his dark eyes on Dirk. When Lambert was finished, Qaymaz gave an amused smile and pointed, as Dirk had feared he might, to Dirk's injured hand. Still smiling at Dirk, he said something.

Lambert translated. "The Emir Qaymaz does not think you will be much use to him with that hand." He spoke with the haughty sneer common to hypocrites. "He is not in the habit of feeding and clothing men who cannot fight. You had best pray to your God, because Qaymaz is going to have you killed."

Soldiers reached for Dirk's arms.

"Wait!" Dirk said to Qaymaz. "I can pay my way!"

He fumbled in his jack and pulled out the ring he had taken from the dead bishop. The ring was still on the finger, and there was an awkward moment as Dirk yanked at it. He had to crush the bone to get it off. "See?" He threw the finger away and pressed the jeweled ring toward Qaymaz. "I can give Lord Qaymaz something until my hand has healed enough for me to wield a sword and earn my keep again."

Qaymaz crooked a finger impatiently and Dirk handed him the ring, smelling scented oil from the emir's hair and the perfume with which he adorned himself. Qaymaz turned the ring over in his hand. He examined the jewel, then spoke in a bored tone.

"Lord Qaymaz asks, why should he not take the ring and kill you anyway?"

"Because he is an honorable man," Dirk said, standing straight and proud, soldier to soldier.

Lambert repeated what Dirk had said. Qaymaz considered this. He gave a slight nod, and spoke again.

"What else can you do for the Lord Qaymaz? "Lambert said.

Dirk said, "What does he like?"

Qaymaz smiled lazily and said something.

"Women," Lambert repeated.

And suddenly Dirk smiled, as well, because he had a splendid idea.

Chapter 43

Cole was the first to die, buried before his sixteenth birthday. Black John, the gambler, came next, followed by Bald Matthew, the cook.

There was an occasional small issue of grain, and the men mixed it with sawdust to make bread, and that kept them alive, along with the few bits of food that Fauston was able to give Roger from the earl's table. A man in the next tent went blind and blamed it on the grain and sawdust mixture, but Roger was of the opinion that the man had drunk too much bad arrack. Roger tried to keep his own men busy, but finally had to give up because they were too weak to work, too sick. Everyone had fever; everyone suffered from dysentery, which was even more painful because with so little to eat, it felt like they were shitting out their insides. The latrines were re-sited when they filled up, which was frequently, especially with all the rain. Ralph the Red got drunk one night and fell in, and the men wouldn't let him back into the tent until he cleaned himself up.

Eventually men gave up the effort of going to the latrines, they were there so often. It was nothing to see them squatting by their tents or even in the company streets. The rags with which they cleaned themselves wore out and fell to pieces, leaving them begrimed with their own feces, which ate at their skin, turning it red and sore. In desperation, some of the men cleaned themselves and their soiled clothes in the frigid sea; but the salt agonized their irritated skin even more, so others washed with rainwater or in the River Belus, side by side with men drawing drinking water . . . .

❖ ❖ ❖

The tent had once been white but was now stained greyish brown from the weather. The fabric was much patched and mended, the varicolored patches giving it a deceptively festive air. The tent's conical top and seams had been painted with tar for waterproofing, but the hot tar had burned holes in the top, resulting in yet more patches. The guy ropes had broken and been spliced again and again. Inside, the tent was mildewed, and water dripped from the mildew. The ancient straw was wet and black and full of bugs, but there was no fresh straw to be had. The men had saved all the grain sacking they could find, and they had sewn layer after layer of it to the inside of the tent walls for insulation from the cold. More sacking had recently been sewn together and placed over the straw as a kind of carpet. The men had taken to piling their mud-caked shoes at the tent entrance, to avoid spreading any more dirt than they had to.

Roger sat on Will's filthy bed. He gave Will water but Will vomited it up, splashing it over his worn blanket. Blood dripped from Will's nose, trickling down to his mouth. Roger wiped it away. He held Will's bony hand; Will's grip was weak as a baby's.

Roger remembered the good-looking young man who had so confidently marched off to war. Will had lost a third of what he weighed then, maybe more. His skin had dried and shrunk until his face took on the outline of the skull beneath it. His lips were drawn back, revealing swollen, blackened gums; many of his teeth had fallen out. The whites of his eyes had turned red. He could no longer leave his bed, even for the latrine. He tried to void himself but nothing came out of him now. His urine was dark brown and foul smelling.

The tent flap parted, and the earl's chaplain, Stephen FitzNele, hobbled painfully in, still weak from his own last bout of illness. Roger had sent for him. The foot soldier's chaplain, the young priest who had welcomed Roger to the earl's company, was long since dead, so Father Stephen had assumed his duties.

Father Stephen wore his stole; he had a jar of olive oil and his breviary with him. He stood next to Will's bed. There was no expression on the priest's face; he had done this too many times since he had arrived at Acre. He dipped his thumb in the jar and made the sign of the Cross on Will's forehead, reading from the breviary as he did.

Will had been dozing; his eyes fluttered open at the priest's touch. "What's that?"

"Nothing," Roger told him in what he hoped was a soothing voice. "You've got a scrape there, and Father Stephen is putting salve on it to make it better."

Roger wiped more blood from Will's nose. He put his hand on his friend's head; it was burning hot. Will's thatch of blond hair was thin and lank. It felt not like hair any more, but like . . . what? Dried grass. Will took a deep breath and fixed Roger with those bloodshot eyes. "When you . . . get . . . to Jerusalem . . ." He paused to regain strength. "Mount of Olives . . . pray for me."

Roger gave his friend's hand a squeeze. "I'll pray there, all right, and you'll be right beside me when I do."

Will shook his head, almost imperceptibly. Then he said, "Tell . . . Agnes . . ."

"Tell her yourself," Roger said. "You'll be good as new in a month or so, you'll see. This weather will break soon, and we'll all get well. You'll be complaining about the heat before you know it."

Will's lips drew farther apart, showing his few remaining teeth in a macabre grin. His chest rose and fell, and as it did, a whistling noise that sounded remarkably like the chirping of a small bird came from deep in his throat. He looked away from Roger and stared at the conical roof of the tent. "Tell . . . family . . . I'll be waiting . . . Heaven."

Roger bit his lip. He tried to keep the tears from his eyes. After a while, he said, "You need to drink some water."

He held the water jar to Will's drawn lips and poured a bit. The water rolled out the side of Will's mouth and down his cheek. Roger realized Will wasn't breathing.

Roger lowered his head. He made no effort to keep the tears back now. Around the tent, men were staring at him—Slowfoot, Offa, Hedde, all of them.

Roger pressed Will's eyes closed. In his shrunken condition, Will seemed to have become part of the cot on which he lay, of a piece with the blanket and bedding.

Roger thought about Will's wife, Agnes. The baby would have been born by now. There would be no news from the East—how could there be?—and every day Agnes would walk to the front gate thinking, "This is the day. This is the day Will comes back." And as the months dragged into years, she would gradually realize that day was never going to come, that she would never see Will again. Maybe there would be news finally, as the few survivors returned home—if there were any survivors—or maybe she would never learn what had really happened to her husband, and he would just become a dim memory from another time.

Fauston had been right. If there was a God, he would never allow His people—any people—to suffer this way. This crusade was for nothing. It was a waste of men's lives. What were they accomplishing here?

Roger should have stayed at Huntley. He should have taken his punishment for killing Auberie and died as a man, quickly. Maybe Roger was being punished for his sin by being here, but what sin had Will committed? Or Blackie, or Bald Matthew, or poor Cole, who hadn't even been old enough to grow a proper beard?

Roger hated all of this.

Maybe this wasn't God's plan.

Maybe God didn't exist.

The men were still looking at him. They expected him to do something. What did they want from him? Why did he have to be in charge? Why couldn't they just let him be?

He rose from Will's bed. "Let's get him buried."

Chapter 44

Following Dirk's disappearance, Roger was made centenar, commander of the axe men. It was the earl's decision. Payen protested—and Roger understood his protest, because there were lots of men in the company with more experience than he had—but the earl wouldn't listen. The men themselves—even the other four vintenars, each of whom could reasonably have expected the job for themselves—seemed to have little problem with Roger's promotion.

The first result of Roger's advancement was that those axe men in the other tents who had not already done so now got Tatwine to paint death's heads on their helmets. A good half of them had begun wearing the devices even before Roger's promotion. The entire company called themselves Death's Heads now, though Roger's original section zealously maintained that they would always be the true Death's Heads.

Being centenar entitled Roger to have his own tent, but he preferred to remain with his old section. He felt at home there, he didn't want to be by himself. He didn't want this new rank, either; he didn't want the responsibility—not now, not when he no longer believed in the cause—but he couldn't turn it down, just as he couldn't reveal his true feelings about their situation because that would undermine discipline. He felt like the worst kind of hypocrite as he pretended to be cheerful, encouraging the men to do their work, to keep their gear and tents clean, drilling them as much as he could when no one had eaten a real meal in weeks.

He felt even more like a hypocrite because, incredibly, morale in the crusader camp remained high. Grounded ships were broken apart and, under enormous spreads of oiled canvas, their wood was cut and pre-joined for the new siege engine. Workers hammered out plates of copper sheathing; archers shaped arrows; armor was repaired against the day it would again be needed.

The Death's Heads were as bad as the rest, dogged in their determination to finish the job they had come here to do. Hedde, a carpenter by trade, worked on the siege engine. The work seemed to make him happy, the happiest he had been since arriving in the Holy Land, though he still had little to say. Egwulf, the blacksmith's son, helped with the copper.

What was wrong with them, Roger wondered. Couldn't they *see* what was happening? Didn't they care whether they lived or died? It was one thing to die in battle in the service of Christ; it was another thing altogether to sit in the mud and perish from disease and starvation.

From time to time, plays—tales from the Bible—were produced, and the men and women in camp gave them great attendance. A permanent stage was erected in an open space near the intersection of the Toron High Street and Chartres Road. It was covered with a canvas roof from which flew a banner belonging to the lord whose men were producing that day's play. For Twelfth Night, the count of Artois' men presented the Conversion of St. Paul, a favorite everywhere, though the most popular version had little to do with the actual story. Two burly fellows played St. Paul and Satan (who, at Acre, was always portrayed as a leering, mustachioed Saracen). Meeting perchance on the Road to Damascus, these two gave a series of declamatory speeches delineating the other's faults, at first serious, then with comic invention, demeaning one another's ancestry, courage, and sexual proclivities. If part of the audience didn't understand the language, they could follow the trend of what was being said through the actors' pantomimes and exaggerated gestures. When the speeches were concluded, Satan and St. Paul engaged in a wrestling match, which started when Satan attacked Paul from behind. The two men threw each other around the stage, each slamming his opponent onto his back, pretending to strike him

271

in the face and stomach, getting him in all sort of apparently painful holds, headlocks, and arm bars. The crowd cheered St. Paul, who fought fair, and booed Satan, who cheated, gouging Paul's eyes and using a cudgel he had secreted at the rear of the stage. On a raised platform to one side sat an actor representing God, who from time to time commented, usually in ribald fashion, on the action. Because he cheated, Satan was able to beat Paul unconscious. He dragged Paul across the stage and was about to throw him through a painted wooden head with a gaping red maw that represented the entrance to Hell, when Paul made a miraculous recovery, reversed the hold, and—to the cheers of the crowd—pushed Satan through the maw instead.

A fortnight later, on the feast of St. Sebastian, the count of Sancerre's men presented the tale of Noah. In their version of the story, Noah's wife was an old shrew who refused to board the Ark until Noah induced her to do so by giving her a good thumping, much to the enjoyment of the audience. After that, the animals, portrayed by wrestlers wearing crude masks and headdresses, battled over who was to board the Ark first. This comic mayhem took up the entire stage, and while an exasperated God left his seat and attempted to sort out the confusion, two serpents—Satan's representatives (played by children)-- slithered toward the Ark unseen. The audience frantically tried to alert God about what was happening. At last, God heard the crowd and turned, but He was too late. The serpents were out of sight; they had secreted themselves aboard the Ark. God looked around and shrugged, as if he could not fathom why the audience had been yelling. To provide the play with a happy ending, the author had Noah give his wife another hiding.

Geoffrey of Trent enjoyed these presentations immensely, as did Ailith, so as a present to her, Geoffrey volunteered to give a play to celebrate Candlemas. Fauston, whose chronicle continued to praise (and please) the earl, was chosen to write the play, which in effect meant that Roger was chosen to write the play. Roger sat in Ailith's tent one rainy afternoon, while Ailith and Fauston tossed out ideas for a subject.

"David and Goliath?" Fauston said. "I saw that once in Badford—chap on stilts played Goliath."

Ailith said, "The martyrdom of St. Sebastian might be fun to do if you get archers who can shoot straight."

"How about the battle of Jericho?" Fauston said. "Lots of action there."

Roger's mood had not improved since Will's death. If anything, it had blackened. He sat, only half listening, as Ailith and Fauston came up with story ideas. Suddenly he snapped his fingers. "I've got it."

"What?" said Ailith and Fauston.

Roger told them.

Fauston frowned. "That's not a Bible tale."

"It has to be a Bible story," Ailith told Roger. "Plays are always Bible stories."

Roger said nothing. He was determined.

Ailith tried another approach. "Fauston will get in trouble if it's not a Bible story."

Roger looked at Fauston and waited.

"Oh, go ahead," Fauston said at last, rolling his eyes. "I suppose I owe you that much. Anyway, how could things be any worse than they already are?"

Ailith shook her head. "Fine. Do what you want, then. Don't come to me when the Church has you two burned for heretics."

Fauston brightened. "If they do, it will be the first time I've been warm since Advent."

Roger spent the best part of two days writing the play, with suggestions from Fauston. It turned out that one of the earl's spearmen, a strapping fellow named Ceolred, had actually been a travelling player before he joined the crusade, so Roger cast him for the lead part. He filled the rest of the roles from the Death's Heads who weren't too sick and with men from the earl's other units.

❖ ❖ ❖

Candlemas—when Mary formally presented the baby Jesus at the Temple to complete her ritual purification—was celebrated on the second day of February, forty days after Christmas.

The day was bright, sunny, and cold. In the distance, the sea sparkled. The wooden stands where the nobles sat and the surrounding area where everyone else stood filled up early, men and women wrapped in whatever they could find to keep warm. At home, vendors would have made their way through the crowd, selling pies and cakes and ale and wine, but that was not the case here. It had been a long time since anyone had seen a pie. There was arrack to be had, of course, made from God knew what at this point, and many availed themselves of it.

As the play's sponsors, the Death's Heads and the rest of the earl's men had good spots up front. Roger had a fever, but he'd had a fever since Christmas. His stomach hurt, though, and his guts rumbled and twisted, and he hoped he'd be able to make it through the performance. Looking at the stands, he saw Ailith sitting with Earl Geoffrey, the two of them with their heads together, laughing. Fauston stood not far from the stands, with what survived of the earl's chancery. Roger caught a glimpse of green among the women. It was Helvise, with a cloak wrapped round her. She saw him looking and she smiled and raised a hand in acknowledgement.

The makeshift curtain parted and God (played grumpily—how else?—by Offa, who was by now off his crutches) left his seat and stumped to the edge of the stage. Offa made a great show of looking first at the sun, then at his shadow. Then he shook his head in an exaggerated gesture of frustration and sighed. The English contingent and some of the others erupted in laughter. Many were puzzled though.

"What does this mean?" said one of the earl's Flemish mercenaries.

Arcil answered. "Back in England it's a tradition that if a man sees his shadow on Candlemas Day, it means six more weeks of winter. If the weather's cloudy, it means an early spring."

"Just our bloody luck," said Slowfoot. "First sunny day in a month."

God raised a hand for attention. When the crowd settled down, he intoned in a loud voice. "Greetings, my lords and ladies. To celebrate the great feast of Candlemas, the earl of Trent's men present: 'The Common Soldier of Acre, Tempted by Sin.'"

That announcement set off an excited buzz of commotion. No one had ever seen, or heard of, this kind of play before. God gestured to his right, introducing the first character. "My lords and ladies—the Soldier of Acre."

Ceolred staggered onto the stage to a roar of approval. Roger had to admit, Ceolred looked the part. He was stooped over, wrapped in a blanket, barefoot, his jack and breeches in tatters, carrying a bucket in case he needed to relieve himself suddenly. From somewhere Ceolred had found makeup, and he had darkened his cheeks and the skin under his eyes to make himself look even gaunter than he actually was.

As Ceolred wandered the stage, moaning from hunger, God introduced the first Sin—Greed, played by Tatwine. Tatwine was stuffed with blankets to make him appear outrageously fat. He wore a bishop's purple robes and carried a large sack of what was supposed to be money. The bishop's robes were real; Roger had no idea where Tatwine had gotten them and he didn't want to know. Greed tempted the Soldier with the money, promising him every earthly delight, promising to share his many mistresses, if only the Soldier would help him sell indulgences and make the sack grow even larger. The crowd loved it when the Soldier rained denouncements on the Bishop and threw his money into the ever-present mouth of Hell. They loved it even more when the Bishop jumped in after because he couldn't bear to be parted with his money. In the stands, many of the attending prelates squirmed, while others, like Father Stephen, frowned darkly.

Drunkenness came next, portrayed by Egwulf, who seemed to have researched his role with a bit too much thoroughness. Drunkenness plied the Soldier with arrack and tried to make him renounce his faith and surrender his soul to Satan. The Soldier grabbed Egwulf by the collar and the back of his jack, ran him to the mouth of Hell, and tossed him in. He kept the arrack, though, which he downed at a large gulp when God wasn't looking, belching and wiping his mouth with the back of his hand.

It was illegal for women to perform on stage, so Lust was represented by Payen's Arab servant boy, whom everyone called "Bug," as in buggery. There had been a lot of suspicion about Payen and the boy initially, but nothing was ever proven to be amiss. It was the only thing Roger admired about Payen. Payen had found the orphaned boy, taken him in, and contrived to keep both of them alive through illness and starvation. Bug had a cheerful personality, and he had become a great favorite among the soldiers.

To portray Lust, Bug wore a wig made of rope painted yellow. Huge balls of cloth were stuffed in his dress to represent breasts. He paraded around the Soldier, batting his dark eyes and flaunting his wares. He turned and flipped up the back of his dress, exposing his bare bottom. The Soldier stroked his chin, thoughtfully at first, then heatedly as his desire built up, but he got control of himself and reluctantly dismissed Lust, who said she would be waiting in Virgins Alley—where Bianca Foligno had once plied her trade—in case the Soldier changed his mind. The soldier turned to God and solemnly proclaimed his chastity, thus earning God's blessing. Then the Soldier turned to the audience and gave a large wink.

Sloth and Pride were represented as well. Pride provided the excuse for the obligatory wrestling match, with the Soldier taking on a man who by his fine dress and lisping accent was clearly intended to represent a noble. Many of the nobles in attendance, including Earl Geoffrey, were less than amused when the stage noble had to resort to cheating in order to overcome the virtuous Common Soldier. They were even less amused when the Soldier at the last moment defeated the noble (to God's overt show of approval). The commoners and Ailith loved it, though.

The twisting in Roger's guts grew worse. They rumbled unceasingly, groaning like a water wheel. Roger clenched and unclenched his fists. He needed to lie down. He did not feel at all well.

Now Satan appeared, played with swaggering braggadocio by Ralph the Red. Satan, as always, was portrayed as a Saracen. Ralph wore a black wig and fake beard and, as a touch, Roger had him wear a blue sash around his helmet. As Ralph strutted around the stage, God strode forward and announced. "The greatest Sin is saved for last—Gluttony."

For the sin of Gluttony at Acre, Satan tempted the Soldier with—one bean.

The audience went wild. The Soldier rolled on the ground, wrestling with himself. He prayed, he ran around the stage in anguish. He got on his knees and beat his fists on the stage floor. At last, he took the bean from Satan, eyed it longingly, hesitated, then threw it into the mouth of Hell, whereupon a number of other men came from offstage and dived in after it, fighting among themselves to be first.

The Soldier presented himself to God, who proclaimed him sinless. The Soldier paid formal homage to God, then announced to the audience *sotto voce*, that he was going to Virgins Alley and swaggered offstage to roars of applause.

As the crowd cheered around him, Roger caught Ailith's eye, and she smiled. The noise in Roger's guts swelled with the noise of the crowd. Suddenly he was bent double by a contraction in his gut and he vomited blood.

Chapter 45

From a distant hill, Saladin and a group of men watched the sprawling crusader camp. Snatches of cheering and laughter floated up to them on the sea breeze.

"Truly, the Feringhees are a strange race," frowned Qaymaz, the long blue sash on his helmet—he wore the helmet more for decorative purposes than because any action was imminent—fluttering behind him. Qaymaz had wanted to remain in Acre when the old garrison had been relieved, but Saladin had ordered him to leave because he could not afford to lose such a valuable man should the city fall. "Were I in their situation, I doubt I would find things so amusing," he said.

"Nor would I," agreed Al-Afdal, Saladin's heavy-faced eldest son. People called Al-Afdal "the Bull," and it was a name that suited him.

Al-Adil, Saladin's younger brother and chief confidante, nodded. Like Saladin, Al-Adil was lean and distinguished looking. He had come up from Egypt, where he was governor, to observe the progress of the siege. "What motivates such men?" he wondered.

"Their religion?" suggested Saladin's second son, al-Aziz, called "the Reader" because of his affinity for books and learning.

"If that is the case, their god is a poor general," quipped Qaymaz.

All but Saladin laughed. Al-Adil said, "You were right, brother. Setting the Emir Guy free was a brilliant move. He has led the Feringhees to their deaths at this place. Who knows what might have transpired had we kept him imprisoned?"

Saladin seemed to have aged since his triumph at Hattin. There was more grey in his hair and short beard, and he had lost weight. He was not in good health, worn down from years of constant campaigning and trying to keep his fractious empire intact. In addition for the usual propensity for empires to fragment, Saladin was distrusted, if not actually disliked, by many of his subjects because he was a Kurd, not an Arab or Turk. He suspected that he did not have long to live, and he feared that when he died, the mercurial al-Afdal would prove to be a poor ruler, and that he and his brother al-Aziz would eventually contend for power. Qaymaz might well hold the balance in such a struggle, a fact of which Saladin was sure that Qaymaz was only too well aware.

Outwardly, the Christian camp below them had changed little in the past year, but Saladin knew that appearances belied the truth. Most of the men who had occupied the camp at this time last winter were dead; most of the newcomers who had replaced them were dead, as well. Usually when he came here Saladin saw ant-like processions winding onto the plain to bury the dead and the breeze carried the Infidels' strange religious chants. Not today.

Another distant roar of laughter and applause, the loudest yet.

"Perhaps the Feringhees have gone mad," marveled Al-Adil.

The Bull, Al-Afdal, spoke to his father. "Qaymaz's new prisoner says the Feringhees are all weak from sickness. We should attack them. We could overrun their camp with ease."

"Why take the risk?" said the Reader. Al-Aziz looked nothing like his brother. The Bull took after the men of his mother's family, with his bulk, heavy beard and thinning hair. Al Aziz looked scholarly, like his father, and many thought him weak. But many had thought Saladin weak, as well. Al-Aziz went on. "If they chose to commit suicide here, why should we stop them? Let them die of their own stupidity."

The Bull made a dismissive gesture. "You talk like a woman."

"Really?" The Reader smiled. "Yet one of us counseled

flight before Hattin, and it was not I."

Enraged, the Bull was about to say something, when Saladin held up a hand, silencing them.

Qaymaz spoke, trying to ease tensions. He was an experienced soldier, and both brothers respected his judgment. "It is not easy to gather and supply our forces at this time of year, and, while the Feringhees are weak, they may yet have bite. Better we wait until spring to attack."

In a voice strangely devoid of triumph, Saladin said, "It is sad to see brave men, even Infidels, die in such fashion. Better to have beaten them as men, on the field of battle."

The Bull pressed his idea. "Then why not strike them now? There are more of them to come—many more, if our spies are to be believed—including the king called Rik, said to be the mightiest warrior in all the lands of the Feringhee."

Saladin perked up. "Ah, yes, I have heard of this Rik. I should like to meet him. It is sad, is it not, that war makes enemies of men with whom we might otherwise have been friends."

The Bull drew back. "Friends? Who would be friends with an Infidel? They are dirty and they smell bad, and their women are even worse."

"I don't know," Qaymaz said with a smile, "when you get the women cleaned up, some of them can be most attractive." He smoothed his trim beard. "And hellcats in bed . . ."

As always, Saladin's brother Al-Adil was more practical. "We do not know when this Rik will get here, or if he will ever get here—there have been rumors of his coming for over a year and no one has seen him yet. For all we know, he may be a myth, designed to frighten us. In the meantime, we have a new problem. Guy no longer leads the Feringhees. They have a new king, Con-Rad—the same man who defeated us at Tyre. This Rik does not worry me, but Con-rad may prove a formidable foe in the days and years to come."

Saladin's smile grew even sadder, as though what he was

about to say was distasteful to him. "That problem has already been taken care of."

❖ ❖ ❖

Far from Acre, in the hills near Homs, a boy named Hakim tended his family's goats. Hakim was not good with the goats, nor was he good with the orange trees or the olive trees, nor with the thin wheat that his father and his father's brothers grew. What he was good at was thinking. Hakim was intelligent far beyond his years. He was devout, as well. He longed to study, to teach, to inspire others, to become a great *sufi* or an imam. His family lacked money or influence for him to be educated, however, so Hakim thought he might one day become a soldier and fight the Infidels, as his father had done in the time of Zengi. His father, who was proud of his military service, always scoffed at that idea. "You are too consumed with affairs of the mind, boy," he would say. "You would be so busy thinking about something, you would not notice that the Feringhees were cutting off your head."

The day was grey and chill, and a thin drizzle fell as Hakim returned home, the bells of the goats tinkling as they ambled along. Hakim hated the goats. They were forever straying. It was difficult to concentrate on anything because the goats were forever demanding his attention with their waywardness. He would have beaten them but they were too stupid for a beating to have any effect.

Outside his small house, Hakim stopped. Standing there was a sleek black horse, richly caparisoned. Hakim frowned. He penned the goats, giving the last one through the fold a good thwack with his rod, then he went inside. He found a tall man drinking tea with his father, while his mother huddled dutifully in the background and his brothers and sisters watched in awe.

The tall man's robes and turban were of black silk. He sat cross legged and across his lap lay a curved sword. Like his robes, the sword was devoid of jewels or ornamentation, but Hakim could tell that it was a finely crafted blade, in a scabbard of rich leather. A man such as this had never been to Hakim's village, much less to his home. What could such a one want with Hakim's poor family?

The man rose gracefully as Hakim entered, and it was strange, but Hakim immediately felt comfortable in the man's company. "Ah," said the man, smiling, "this must be Hakim."

Hakim bowed. The man was well formed, with a handsome face and trim beard, and he carried himself like one used to wielding authority. He placed a strong, yet friendly, hand on Hakim's shoulder, and his voice was deep and smooth. "I have come a long distance to meet you, Hakim. It is said that you are most faithful to Allah and that you can recite large parts of the Koran from memory."

Hakim looked at his father, who urged him to answer. Hakim turned back to the stranger in black. "That is true, lord."

"I have been talking to your father." The stranger indicated Hakim's father, who took an involuntary step back. "I would like to offer you a chance to perform a service for the Faith, a chance to become a hero of Islam."

Hakim didn't know what to say. "I . . ." he stammered. "What must I do?"

"That I am not at liberty to say. I can promise you, however, that should you be successful, Paradise will be your reward."

Paradise.

"However, should you fail . . ," The man spread his arms.

"I will not fail," Hakim said hastily.

"So you will do it?" the man asked.

Hakim's father nodded to his son nervously. Hakim's mother bit her lip.

"It means you must leave home," the man in black added sternly.

Leave home? Hakim had never been farther than the hills where he tended the goats. "Where shall I go, lord?"

"To a great palace, where servants will attend your every desire."

Hakim grew excited. A great palace. No more goats, no more pruning olive trees. "I will do it, lord."

The man in black beamed, showing strong, white teeth. "Excellent."

"When do we leave?"

"Now."

Hakim had not expected such a sudden break. "But I—I must get my things."

"You will have no need of them. You will be given new raiment, such as befits your new station." The man's smile faded. "Say goodbye to your family, Hakim. You will not see them again."

Hakim's knees buckled. Not see his mother again? Not see his father? Not see his brothers and sisters, with whom he had shared his entire life? He might have reconsidered if he'd had the chance, but he had said he would do this thing, whatever it was, and he could not back down now. He bade farewell to his father, then to his sobbing mother and his siblings. As he broke from the tearful embrace of his two sisters, he saw the man in black remove a purse from his belt and place it on the crudely wrought table in front of his father. The purse jingled.

The stranger salaamed to Hakim's father. "Come," he told Hakim, and he strode from the house, hand on the hilt of his sword, black robes billowing behind him.

As Hakim followed, he realized that the man in black had never even given him his name.

Chapter 46

Roger lay on his bed. He had the bloody flux, the most dreaded of camp diseases. Dysentery twisted his stomach muscles until they tore and he cried out. He was too weak to get up, and his vomit and bloody stool fouled both himself and his bedding.

Ailith nursed him. Fauston swam into Roger's blurred vision from time to time, looking worried. So did Egwulf, and Tatwine, and the other Death's Heads. They came and went, but the constant was Ailith. She gave him watered wine and broth that she made from whatever food she could get hold of; she cleaned his body. When he was teeth-chattering cold, she wrapped him in blankets; when he was burning hot, she put cool, wet cloths on his forehead and cheeks. Somehow she managed to find fresh bedding for him. He reeked of feces and blood and piss and she pretended not to notice.

"Leave me," he told her, as she rolled him over to clean him after he had soiled himself yet again. There were tears in his eyes. "I don't want you to see me like this."

She scoffed at him. "Five bothers at home—think I ain't seen worse than this?" though both of them knew she hadn't.

There were other sick men in the tent—Hedde, Slowfoot, and Ralph the Red were the worst, but all were ill to some degree—and Ailith tended them, as well. Sick men from the other tents begged her to help them, too, and she did. She was spending most of her time in the foot soldiers' camp. She grew haggard but remained cheerful—she had to be, for the men's sake. And when one of them died, she wept as though the death had been her fault. Some nights she did not return to the Toron at all but stayed in Roger's tent, sleeping on an empty bed frame that had once belonged to Deaf Martin.

The Death's Heads were starving, all the footmen were, so Ailith sold the jewels that the earl had given her and used the money to buy grain on the Concourse. The money, and there was a considerable amount of it, didn't go far. When that was gone, she prepared to do something she had sworn never to do. She was going to use the fifteen pounds she had hidden in her dress. It never came to that, though, because the food ran out. There was no food to be found in the camp at any price. What little they had would keep the Death's Heads alive for a few more days. After that, they faced starvation. The entire army did. There were no more rats to be eaten, no more cats or dogs, no more horses, oxen, mules, or camels. Like locusts, the crusaders had devoured every blade of grass for a league around the camp. Every boot and jack that could be boiled, had been. There was nothing. In a week, most of the army would be dead; in two weeks, the army would be a memory. The crusade was over. Nothing remained but death, and prayer.

The little bit of food Ailith had found didn't help Roger. He couldn't keep anything down. He had voided so much blood that he grew pale and could no longer lift his head.

On a rare evening when Roger was sleeping comfortably, Ailith stumbled back to her tent on the Toron, her legs weak from hunger and lack of sleep. There would be no food at the tent, but at least she could get a good night's rest for once, in a relatively clean bed, even if she did have to put up with her servant Margaret's rudeness and refusal to work. If anyone had to get sick, why couldn't it have been Margaret, Ailith thought, then immediately regretted wishing such a horrible fate on anyone, even Margaret—though with death staring them all in the face, how they died no longer seemed important.

Ailith pushed aside the crimson tent flap and entered. Geoffrey stood there, clothes hanging off of him because he had lost so much weight, his cheeks hollow, his lips a thin line. He looked to have been there a good while.

"Where have you been?" he demanded.

Ailith wasn't expecting this, though she realized she should have been. She wasn't supposed to leave the Toron unescorted—it was too dangerous for a woman to be alone about the camp. The threat of punishment wouldn't keep men from attacking her because they would all be dead soon. She hesitated. Behind Geoffrey, she saw Margaret poke her head into the tent then quickly withdraw.

Geoffrey went on. "I've been here five times in the last three days—including three times at night—and you haven't been here."

Did he think she had a lover? "It's not what you—"

"You've been in the footmen's camp, haven't you? Nursing Roger."

She paused. "How did you know?"

"Payen told me."

Ailith didn't recall seeing Payen when she was in the footmen's camp. His servant boy, the one they called Bug, had been around Roger's tent, though. "Payen seems to know a lot of things that aren't his affair."

"Payen commands the footmen. It is his job to know what goes on in their camp."

Ailith straightened. "What if I have been nursing Roger? He's an old friend."

That news came as a surprise to Geoffrey. He lost his momentum for a second, then went on. "It's not your place to tend common soldiers, Ailith. There's a barrier between the common people and us, and it's not to be crossed. You, if anyone, should know that."

"Why? Because I crossed it when I took up with you?"

"Yes, exactly for that reason. It doesn't look good for you to be down there—for you or for me. You're my—" he struggled for the right word "—my consort. You need to behave like it."

" 'Consort.' " She turned the word over in her mouth. " 'Consort.' That's a pretty term for mistress, isn't it? And mistress is a pretty term for whore."

"You're not a whore," Geoffrey said. He let out his breath. "I wish it could be different, Ailith. I wish you could be my wife, you know that. But that can't happen. We may not have much time left, and I want you to spend it with me."

"So do I, and I'm sorry. But Roger is sick. He may be dying. There are other sick men down there, as well. They need me. I feel like I'm doing good when I'm there, like I'm more than an ornament on your arm."

He started to say something, but she went on. "We're supposed to be Christians. How can we—"

"Because it's not your place! Let the common people look after themselves. It's what they do." He drew himself up. "You are to make no more visits to Roger's tent."

She drew herself up, as well. "That is a command I won't obey."

"You dare to defy me?"

"If I must."

There was a long silence, then Geoffrey said, "Are you in love with him?"

"With Roger? Don't be foolish. How can you even think such a thing? I love you, I've told you that."

"Then why—?"

"Because Roger saved my life. I wouldn't be here if it wasn't for him."

Silence. Then Geoffrey swore, more in amazement than from anger. "God's bones, is there any person in this camp whose life that fellow *hasn't* saved? Why don't we just make him a saint and be done with it? How did he save *your* life?"

Ailith looked down. "I wasn't turned out of my house by my husband's brother, like I told you I was."

Geoffrey waited. Ailith related how Roger had saved her from being tortured for being a witch, though she didn't mention that Roger had been a monk at the time and that he had killed another monk while helping her get away.

"Why didn't you tell me this when I first met you?" Geoffrey said.

Ailith shrugged. "I thought you wouldn't save me from the bailiff's men if you knew that people called me a witch."

Geoffrey shook his head slowly. "You're wrong there. I don't believe in witches, and I've no patience for those who do. What about Fauston—does he know who you really are?"

"No," Ailith lied. "He thinks the same as you did."

Geoffrey cocked his head to one side. Something about Ailith's appearance didn't seem right. "Where is the gold necklace I gave you? The one with the sapphires and rubies?"

"In my trunk," Ailith said. "I don't like to wear it when I go—"

"Show me."

"Why?"

"Show me!"

They faced each other. She made no move.

"Very well, I'll see for myself."

He moved forward and opened the trunk.

"All right!" she said. "They're gone. I sold them."

Geoffrey straightened. "You did what?"

"I sold them. To buy food. For the soldiers."

Geoffrey's face reddened. "The soldiers! Why—?"

"Because they would die otherwise."

Geoffrey looked her over and saw other things that were missing. "Your rings, your bracelets—did you sell them, as well?"

Her silence told him all he needed to know.

"That jewelry cost me a lot of money."

"Aren't the lives of your men worth more than a few trinkets?"

"Perhaps, but that is a decision for me to make."

"You gave those jewels to *me*, remember? I didn't realize there were conditions with them."

Geoffrey's voice was cold, colder than she had ever known it. "You try my patience, Ailith. Should you violate my instructions to you about visiting Roger's tent, you risk your place in my camp."

Ailith lifted her chin stubbornly. "I'm not one of your servants, Geoffrey. I'll go where I will."

"Then go, and be damned to you."

Geoffrey turned and left the tent.

Ailith knew she had gone too far, and she started after him. "Geoffrey, I—"

But he was gone.

Ailith sank onto a trunk, head down, too tired to cry.

She remained that way for some minutes. She felt a comforting hand on her shoulder and she started, because she hadn't heard anyone come into the tent. "It's all right," Margaret said. "Drink some o' this."

Margaret handed Ailith a cup of warm spiced wine. "Took it from the earl's table," Margaret said. "Serves the bugger right."

Ailith stared at the wine, hesitating.

"Go on," Margaret said. "It ain't poisoned."

Ailith sipped the wine. The warm liquid felt good. She sipped again. "Thank you. Why are you doing this? You don't like me."

"I heard what you done for them boys down in the camp," Margaret said. "You're a brave woman to go down there. You're a good woman, too, and I ain't ashamed to say I misjudged you. Come to it, there's no one I'd rather serve, and proud to do it. I hope you'll take my apology."

Ailith smiled and squeezed the big hand that still rested on her shoulder. "Of course."

Geoffrey returned to his own tent. He regretted speaking to Ailith the way he had. After all, what difference did it make what she did now? Barring a miracle, they would all be dead in a few days.

Chapter 47

Roger was dying.

He barely knew what was happening around him. At times he was not aware of anything, but existed in a strange half-world where his vision was blurred and voices came to him in distorted snatches, as though he were hearing the speakers from under water.

"... send for ..."

"... how do we ..?"

"... be different if King Richard ..."

The camp was quiet. Even the catapults had fallen silent. The starving army was conserving energy, so that it might live an hour longer, a day longer, while it waited for a miracle.

Roger had come to the Holy Land to die, to be a martyr for the Faith and have his sins forgiven, but now that the hour of his death was at hand, he wanted to live, he wanted it desperately. He touched the ring on his finger. He could see the silver and niello ring in his mind's eye as clearly as if he were able to focus on it for real—the stylized animal, the cruciform decoration on the bezel, the letter "A" inscribed on the inside. Old English work, Fauston had said.

Roger sighed. He would never know who he really was. He regretted that, but he doubted that he would have ever learned it, anyway. It was foolish for him to have thought that he might find his father here, after so many years. It no longer mattered. Nothing mattered. In a few hours, a few minutes, Roger would be a lump of decaying flesh.

He lost consciousness. When he came to, his surroundings were a blur, as before. Sound was still distorted. Ailith was there, but he felt her more as a presence rather than saw her. A shadow loomed over him. Something touched his forehead. An oily finger. Drawing a pattern—a cross. There was a droning that sounded like prayer, and though Roger didn't recognize the voice, he knew it was Father Stephen.

He closed his eyes—or did he? He couldn't tell.

Diffuse white light surrounded him, like fog with fire burning behind it. Roger saw the young Saracen he had killed on the walls of Acre. The Saracen's face was whole, and he was smiling.

He saw Will. And it was Will as he used to be—stocky, bright eyed and ruddy faced, straw-colored hair ruffling in the breeze.

"Will," he said.

Will gave him a big grin and reached out his hand.

Roger smiled. He reached out to take Will's—

"You're not going to die!" Someone was shaking him by the shoulders. It was Ailith. "I won't let you!"

Will disappeared. Drops of warm liquid splashed onto Roger's cheeks.

Ailith came into view, dimly at first, then more clearly. Fauston was behind her, so were the Death's Heads.

Ailith shook him again, hard. "Do you hear me?"

Roger nodded, and she lay him back on the bed. "If you die, I swear, I'll kill you!"

Roger's cracked lips moved. He spoke with difficulty. "In that case . . . I better live . . ."

Ailith sobbed and wiped her eyes.

Somewhere a church bell tolled. "For me?" Roger joked. "Didn't know . . . I was that . . . important." He regretted that he hadn't spoken to Will.

Outside, the bell kept tolling. It was joined by other bells in the camp. Men started cheering—a few at first, weakly, then more, with gathering strength, until the entire camp was yelling and screaming as though everyone in it had gone mad.

Arcil poked his head through the tent opening. "Grain ships!" he cried. "Grain ships have come from Tyre!"

They had gotten their miracle. The army was saved.

Part III
A GATHERING OF KINGS

Robert Broomall

Chapter 48

Spring came to the Holy Land overnight, or so it seemed to those in the massive crusader camp. The days grew soft; the country took on an unwonted greenness. White and yellow wildflowers blossomed on the plain, while the hills blossomed in a different manner as the tents of Saladin's army reappeared. The sandy soil, which for months had been a quagmire, dried up. The familiar thumping of the catapults resumed; skirmishing broke out on the plain. Protective canvases were rolled back and the new assault towers, four of them, including the great copper tower—the Invincible Tower, men were calling it—were assembled in the sun, in full view of the city walls, so that the defenders would know what awaited them. Men began filling in sections of the camp trench to provide the towers a way across . . . .

Roger and Ailith were walking on the Concourse. Roger moved slowly, recovering his strength; Ailith matched his pace. The sun and fresh air felt good to Roger after weeks of confinement in the fetid tent. With the coming of the warm weather, the flies and mosquitoes had returned, as had the stench of dead bodies and excrement and animals and thousands upon thousands of unwashed men. It was a measure of how long Roger had been here that he barely noticed them.

Roger's recovery, after his near brush with death, had been slow. Ailith had stayed with him throughout, only leaving his side to tend to the other men in his and the neighboring tents—feeding and cleaning them, praying with them, making their bodies ready for the grave. In addition to grain, the relief ships had brought fruit, and Ailith had made infusions of orange and lemon which seemed to greatly aid the sick men in their recovery.

"So, you're returning to duty tomorrow?" Ailith said. "Do you think you're well enough?" She was haggard, with dark circles under her eyes. It was a miracle she hadn't fallen ill herself, having been exposed to so much sickness. She'd lost a lot of weight, and her naturally high cheekbones had become even more prominent.

"I'm well enough," Roger said, though in truth he felt weak and dispirited. "Wulfhere, from the second section, has commanded the company in my absence. He's done a good job, too. He's the one who should have been made centenar, not me. I'm no soldier."

"The men don't mind you being centenar," Ailith pointed out.

"That's because they don't know I'm a fraud," Roger said bitterly. "They don't know I was once a monk."

"All of us were someone else once," Ailith said. "Fauston was a gyrovage, your friend Egwulf was a blacksmith. I was . . ." She let the words drift off, as if the past was too painful for her to remember.

They passed two querulous beggars playing chess. A man whose leg had been cut off at the knee limped by on crudely made crutches. In a bewildering variety of languages, merchants hawked wares to the soldiers, nobles, sailors, and servants who thronged the Concourse. Supplies were plentiful once more, not only grain, but fruit and eggs and meat, as well as wine and arrack, spices, silks, jewels, horses and camels, the horrors and privations of the previous winter seemingly forgotten as though they had never happened.

They reached the end of the Concourse and stopped. The shore and the sun-sparkled sea beyond were once more filled with vessels. There were warehouses on the beach again, along with transient camps where units waited to be assigned permanent camping spots and men who had come to the Holy Land by themselves pitched tents until they had found lords to hire them.

Prominent among the ships were six large galleys belonging to King Phillip of France, who had just arrived with his friend the count of Flanders and the vanguard of the French army. Supplies were still being unloaded from the ships, and the sea breeze brought the sounds of cursing, shouting, laughing men.

"Philip is finally here," Roger said, watching the French vessels. "But where is King Richard?"

"No one knows," Ailith said. "The rumor on the Toron is that he's been lost at sea."

They stood like that for a few minutes, gazing at the water, then Roger turned to Ailith and said, "You know I can never find words to express my thanks for what you did for me. Without you, I would have died."

Ailith pursed her lips. "I was only being a good Christian."

"Surely it was more than that?"

Her voice held a note of caution. "What do you mean?"

Roger drew a deep breath. He had been rehearsing this, waiting for the right moment to say it. "Ailith, I love you."

Ailith's features softened. Her lips parted, but before she could speak, Roger pressed on, afraid that if he didn't say his piece now, he'd never be able to. "I've been in love with you since we parted in England, when you kissed me. There's scarcely a day since then that I haven't thought about you. All the time I was crossing France, all the time I've spent here as a soldier—my one regret was that I might never see you again. And then I did see you, and it was like an answer to my prayers."

Ailith paused. "And now what do you want?"

Roger thought that was obvious. "I want you to leave the earl and be with me."

She waited a long moment, emotions playing across her face. At last she said, "Geoffrey would never let me stay with you, Roger. He would punish us if I did, you know that, you more than me."

"Then we'll run away," Roger told her.

"Run away where?"

"Anywhere, who cares?"

"What about the crusade?"

"I don't care about the crusade any more. I don't care about anything but being with you."

He reached for her, but she moved back. "You have nothing to offer. No money, no station in life."

"I can offer love."

"Geoffrey loves me, too. And he can give me everything I've ever wanted."

Roger didn't understand why she was being so reluctant. "He's married."

"What of it? He had no say in who he married. He doesn't love his wife—what man of his station does? He loves me, and he'll do anything to keep me near him."

"You're willing to accept that kind of life? Being a rich man's mistress?"

Ailith stiffened. "As opposed to being a poor man's mistress?"

"I don't want you to be my mistress. I want to marry you."

Ailith stared at him for a long moment, then gave him a wistful smile. "I won't go back to being poor, Roger. I can't."

Roger felt like he'd been sliced open with a knife. She had hurt him and suddenly he wanted to hurt her in return. "Your children will be bastards," he taunted. There was no doubt the earl would give her babies, unless she was barren. It was a miracle she hadn't gotten pregnant already.

Her reply was cold, formal, and Roger knew he had gone too far. "If I have children, Geoffrey will provide for them."

"He told you that?"

"Not in so many words. But he's a good man, he'll do the proper thing."

Roger had never expected Ailith not to come with him. He

had convinced himself that she was as besotted with him as he was with her. He had planned this moment, and it had come out nothing like he had expected. "Do you love him?" he asked her.

"Yes." She said it firmly.

"Then why did you stay with me all that time I was ill? Why did you bring me back from the dead?"

"I told you, I was being a good Christian. Besides, I owed you a great debt. If not for you, I would have been tortured and killed for being a witch. I would never have met Geoffrey."

They stared at each other. Roger felt like his heart had fallen out of his chest. After a minute Ailith spoke in a quiet voice. "I think you had better find a place other than my tent to work on Geoffrey's chronicle."

Roger said, "Ailith—"

She held up a hand. "Geoffrey is already angry with me because I spend all my time with you. You're well now; my debt to you is paid. I'll always be your friend, Roger, but I can't be seen with you anymore."

Roger was dumbfounded.

"Goodbye," Ailith said. She turned and started for the Toron.

Chapter 49

After Ailith left, Roger wandered aimlessly. He left the bustle of the Concourse and eventually sank onto a low rise not far from the German lines. Here he had a good view of the shore and the city of Acre, wreathed in dust from catapult strikes. He was surrounded by the sights and sounds and smells of a siege that seemed to have no beginning and appeared likely to have no end.

He saw the broad sweep of the crusaders' encampment, with its many-colored tents, behind which lay the hills where Saladin's army camped. Dust rose from the plain in between, where mounted patrols clashed. Not far away, business was being conducted on the Concourse as though this was a giant market fair and not the middle of an ongoing battle. All around were music and singing and prayer. The cries of gulls mixed with the whinny of horses and the braying of donkeys and mules, with the shouts of soldiers, the jingle of horses' bells, with hammering and the creaking of heavy wheels. Smells of spices and cook fires mingled with the stench of war. And, of course, there were funerals. Always there were funerals.

A company of newly arrived French spearmen tramped by, singing jauntily. *That won't last*, Roger thought. Roger wanted to feel sorry for himself, because of losing Ailith, but he couldn't. Not after what he had been through. He had been dead, and he had been pulled back from the dead.

He had been spared. Ailith had been part of it, of course, but only a part. Roger had been spared by God. Why? Why had God chosen Roger, a sinner, to live, when He had allowed so many innocent men to die? It made no sense.

A shadow fell over him.

Roger looked up. The sun was haloed behind the

newcomer, so that all Roger could make out was the person's outline, tinted green from the person's clothing. Roger thought he made out a crossbow, as well.

He realized who it was and scrambled to his feet.

Chapter 50

Halfway up the Toron, Ailith could go no further. She stopped and choked back her sobs, staunching her eyes with her sleeve.

That talk with Roger had been the hardest thing she'd ever done in her life. When he'd told her he loved her, she had been overjoyed. She had dreamed of hearing those words, and her first instinct had been to throw her arms around him and reply in kind.

Then she had stopped. She had forced herself to consider her position. With Geoffrey she had everything she had ever dreamed of, ever longed for. Was she ready to give all that up to go off with a penniless commoner, a man wanted by the Church for murder?

Of course she was, and she would have gone with Roger right then and gladly, but there was another, darker, consideration. Ailith wasn't worried about her own fate, she was worried about Roger's. She was afraid Geoffrey would have Roger killed if Roger took her from him. Geoffrey was a good man, but he was a great lord, and to be cuckolded so blatantly by a lowly foot soldier might be more than his honor could withstand. The news would be all over the Toron, all over the camp. Geoffrey would be a laughingstock among both nobles and common folk alike, and he might feel compelled to act. In truth, he might have no other choice, because if he didn't act the whole fabric of society would be threatened. And if he didn't kill Roger, some hotheaded knight—outraged at the impudence of this commoner—might well do it for him.

Roger had talked about running away, but the reality was that there was nowhere to go. The only way out of this camp was by ship, and with Roger a deserter and Ailith the runaway consort of an earl, the beach was certain to be watched, if only for the reward, which was certain to be generous.

As she wiped more tears from her cheeks, someone stopped beside her, head lowered in concern. It was Geoffrey's friend Balian of Ibelin. "Are you all right, Lady Ailith?" Balian said in his smooth voice. "Can I be of assistance?" He handed her a dry kerchief.

"I'm fine, thank you," Ailith said, taking the kerchief and putting it to her eyes. She sniffed, and there was a break in her voice as she added, "I'm happy, that's all."

Ailith's heart was breaking, but leaving Roger was the best thing she could have done for him. She loved him too much to be the cause of his death.

Chapter 51

"Lady Helvise," Roger said, bowing.

The German noblewoman smiled, teeth white against the deep tan of her face. Across her back was slung a rectangular pavise; in her hand was her crossbow, with a quiver of arrows at her belt. "By the Virgin's grace," she said, "it *is* you—Roger, the Englishman. I saw you taken ill at your earl's play last winter. I thought you long dead, so it came as a shock when I saw you sitting there. I am so glad that you have survived."

"As am I," Roger said, returning her smile.

Helvise's green jerkin and hose were faded and stained with sweat. There were patches on the jerkin's shoulders and sleeves; the hose were much darned, especially at the knees, with threads of grey and black. "Your three friends, they are well?"

"Tatwine and Egwulf are." Roger paused, not liking to dredge up the memory. "Will is dead."

"I am sorry to hear it." She unslung the heavy pavise and placed it on the ground along with her crossbow. The scarred green pavise had a yellow cross painted on it, matching the tattered cross on Helvise's shoulder. The rich cherry tiller of her crossbow—much worn, but oiled and varnished—was decorated with intricate carvings all along its length, and just below the bow stave it had been carved into the likeness of a dragon. Helvise ruffled her sweaty hair, which was cut severely and thick with dust.

Roger said, "I am glad you survived, as well, my lady."

Helvise nodded her thanks. "I was very ill, of course—who was not?—but it was not so bad for me. The same cannot be said for the rest of my people. We are down to a few hundreds now. Out of all those thousands who started from Ratisbon . . ."

She was lost in the memory for a moment, then she shook her head, letting it go. "As you may have heard, my liege, the duke of Swabia, is dead."

"Yes," Roger said. The Emperor Barbarossa's son, Frederick, had recently succumbed to illness.

"The archduke of Austria is here now, though. I have offered my services to him, and he has graciously accepted." She studied Roger, cocking her head to one side. "You look different without that helmet of yours—less threatening, perhaps?"

Before Roger could say anything, she went on. "Our soldiers know of your men."

Roger frowned. "They do?"

A corner of her mouth turned up. "I think the whole camp knows of them. That skull painted on your helmets is very distinctive. Some of our fellows are jealous of it."

Trying to change the subject—he still felt awkward about the death's head symbol—Roger indicated her crossbow. "How go your efforts at harassing the enemy?"

She shrugged. "The Paynims have learned not to show themselves so much on the walls, so I have learned to be more patient." She gestured. "But what are you doing here—sitting by yourself so far from your tents?"

"I don't know. Thinking, I guess."

"About what?"

"About all this." He waved a hand in the direction of the besieged city. "Do you think it will ever end?"

"I think it must," she said. Then she said, "You are well spoken for a soldier. I noticed it before, when you saved me from—" there was a hitch in her voice— "when you saved me from those men. You could pass for a man of education."

Roger wondered if he should tell her, decided it wouldn't hurt anything. "Actually, I have some education."

"Really?" She cocked her head again. "How unusual. How did you manage that?"

Roger took the plunge. "I used to be a monk."

She stared. "No."

He nodded his head.

"You cannot be serious," she said.

"I am serious."

She spread her hands. "But—how did you end up here, a common soldier?"

Roger knew he was taking a chance, but he told her anyway. He wasn't sure why, really; it just felt good to tell someone, to unburden himself of his secret. "I killed a man, another monk, and I ran away. I came here to atone for my sin."

Helvise studied him for a long moment, then shook her head. "If you killed a man, you must have had a good reason."

"How can you say that, my lady? You know nothing about me."

"I know you are not a murderer. I can feel that. And you needn't call me 'my lady.' I am a soldier like you."

There was a burst of shouting near the city walls. They turned, but nothing untoward seemed to be happening. Roger watched a mangonel hurl a block of stone at the Accursed Tower. The stone hit the tower but did no appreciable damage.

Helvise appraised him. "You don't look like a monk. You look too . . . too strong."

Roger laughed. "I spent a lot of time chopping wood."

"Was that your job?"

"No, it was punishment."

"Punishment for what?"

"For a lot of things. For not wanting to be a monk, mostly. When I wasn't being punished, I worked in the scriptorium, copying books."

Helvise's eyes widened. "Then you can read? And write?"

"I can."

She appeared to debate with herself for a moment, gnawing her lower lip, then she said, "I realize that you barely know me, but would you think me impertinent if I were to ask you a great favor?"

"I cannot imagine anything you could do that would be impertinent, my lady," Roger replied. "Ask what you will."

"Could you teach me to read? Perhaps even to write?"

Roger hadn't expected this. "I—whatever for? I mean, you're a woman. What use has a woman for reading?"

"I want to read the Bible," Helvise explained.

"But you have priests to do that for you."

She shook her head vigorously. "It is not the same. I want to read it for myself. I want to see God's Word and be able to understand it. To have the Word spoken directly to me, not through a priest. I do not like people doing things for me."

Roger passed a hand across his bearded chin. "I don't know . . ."

"Please," she said. "Learning to read has been my dream since I was a child, but I could never get anyone to teach me. My parents were aghast at such an ambition—they begged me to tell no one. And my husband—I loved Welf more than anything in the world, but he would not hear of me learning to read. Forbade it. Said people would think me a witch."

Roger wasn't sure. "A woman, reading? It's unheard of."

The edges of Helvise's mouth began to droop.

Hastily Roger said, "All right, I'll do it." He remembered rescuing her from the gang of men who had tried to rape her, remembered her horse being eaten alive. Remembered that her husband and child were dead. This woman had been through enough. What harm could it do to let her read?

Helvise's face brightened and she clapped her hands, but before she could say anything, Roger held up a warning finger. "I must tell you, I don't know how good a teacher I will be. I've never done anything like this before."

"You will be a good teacher," she assured him. She grinned broadly, this fierce slayer of Saracens looking suddenly girlish, and with a start Roger realized that she was in fact little more than a girl. She was probably close to his own age of twenty-one, though he had thought of her as being much older because of her title and her fearsome reputation as the Woman in

Green. The almond-shaped eyes that gave her that vaguely Asiatic look were shining. "Oh, I can't believe I'm finally going to learn to read," she said. Then her grin faded. "I cannot pay you much, I'm afraid."

Roger waved her off. This would be an interesting challenge, though he could get in trouble if he was caught—the Church looked askance at women with learning. "I wish no money from you."

She looked relieved. "When can we begin?"

Roger thought. "I'll have to get materials—parchment, ink, quills." He would have to ask Fauston to provide them from his supplies; he couldn't go to Ailith's tent and take them anymore. He felt a twinge in his heart at the thought of Ailith, but he put it aside. "Would tomorrow evening be all right? That's if my company doesn't have duty."

"Tomorrow would be wonderful," she said. "Do you remember where my tent is located?"

"I do, my—" He started to say "my lady," then caught himself and smiled. "I do."

"Come after vespers, then."

"All right."

"Thank you. Oh, I am so happy. This is a dream come true." She was beaming so brightly, she looked like she might float off the ground.

"It will be a long process," he cautioned. "You can't learn to read overnight."

"All the more reason to get started," she said. She bent to collect her gear and, as she did, trumpets sounded on the Toron.

They both turned. The trumpets kept blowing, and they knew what that meant.

"They are calling a council of the barons," Helvise said. "Something is happening."

Chapter 52

"When will I see more of the chronicle?" Geoffrey demanded of Fauston.

The two men were headed for Balian of Ibelin's tent and the grand council, Geoffrey thinking that attendance at the council might spur his wayward chronicler to action. Fauston had anticipated this question and he replied smoothly, "My lord, there's been nothing to write about. Everyone has been sick."

"Then write about that."

"Yes, my lord," Fauston said. Roger had picked a bad time to go off and nearly die. Fauston needed to get him working again.

The earl stopped and faced his chronicler. "See here, Fauston, you have a serious responsibility. Years from now, when you and I are dust, people will want to know what happened on this crusade. It's your job to tell them. Tell them the truth."

"I will, my lord."

"Another thing—don't put the emphasis on me any longer."

Fauston's eyes widened. "My lord?"

The earl waved a hand. He'd only arranged to have the chronicle written to make his wife happy, but now he saw a real purpose for it. "This crusade isn't about me. It's about all the men here, not only the nobles but the common soldiers, as well. I want their sacrifices to be remembered for all time. I think that's important. I think they deserve that, and that's your job."

Fauston wondered what had gotten into the earl. "Of course, my lord."

The trumpets blew again as they resumed walking. The French king had called the council, and Geoffrey was curious as to what he would say. It was a warm day, and the bottom half of Balian's pavilion had been rolled up to let in air. Geoffrey and Fauston passed the guards and went inside.

The pavilion was packed. To the din of talking were added the smells of sweat and perfume, of wine and sweetmeats being served to the guests, and the cinnamon that men and women chewed to sweeten their breaths. They passed shaven-headed Conrad of Montferrat. "Congratulations, Marquis," Geoffrey told him, inclining his head politely. "I hear your wife is with child."

"Be a miracle if she wasn't," Conrad replied, showing rare good humor. "I ploughed that field day and night last winter."

Henry of Champagne was there, as were Guy of Lusignan and Leopold of Austria, also newly arrived. There were a lot of other new faces, as well. The newcomers were easy to spot, with their long hair and fresh clothes. Like most everyone else who had been in the Holy Land for any length of time, Geoffrey wore his hair and beard short now. Geoffrey saw King Philip's cousin and good friend, the count of Flanders, barely off the boat and already so ill he was forced to sit, while a youthful servant knelt beside him and fanned his pallid face.

"Geoffrey!" It was the big, burly Fleming, James of Avesnes. James had been ill and Geoffrey hadn't seen him in some time. James looked older; he had lost a lot of weight and most of his teeth had fallen out. "How the Devil are you?" James said, pounding Geoffrey's back, and Geoffrey couldn't help but laugh because without his teeth, James' deep voice sounded like he had mush in his mouth.

"Go ahead," James retorted. "It's all very well for you to laugh—you still have your teeth. Four months I've waited for meat that hasn't been ridden first, and when it finally gets here, I can't eat it."

Geoffrey laughed heartily. As he did, strong hands clapped both men on the shoulder, and they turned.

"Good day, gentlemen!" It was one-eyed Henry of Deraa. "I trust you had an enjoyable winter!"

"Most enjoyable," Geoffrey replied dryly. "I haven't stopped laughing since Christmas."

James added, "I grew so weary of stuffing myself with food, I decided to get rid of my teeth."

Henry grew serious. "By God, 'tis glad I am to see the both of you above ground." He noticed Fauston. "Still got that scribbler, eh, Geoffrey?" He punched Fauston's shoulder playfully, which meant that he hit Fauston near hard enough to fell an ox. Fauston rocked on his feet but stayed upright. "Good-looking specimen," Henry said. "I'd make a soldier of him were I you."

Fauston tried to look as though he took that as a compliment.

"He's more valuable to me where he is," Geoffrey told Henry.

Henry said, "Ah, well, each to his own. Now if you'll excuse me, I must greet some old friends."

Geoffrey and James of Avesnes watched the tall, rangy Henry swagger through the crowd. He was met with disdainful looks by some, with hearty handshakes and cries of welcome by others, while the newcomers from Europe just stared at this one-eyed apparition in wonder. Fauston grimaced and flexed his shoulder. He was going to have the Devil of a bruise there.

Balian of Ibelin made his way through the crowd. He wore colorful silk robes, his graying dark hair and beard were oiled, and there were gold rings in his ears.

"God take me, you could pass for Saladin himself," Geoffrey told him.

Balian dismissed the comparison. "Old Sidesaddle doesn't dress nearly as well as I do." He thought about telling Geoffrey that he'd seen Ailith crying earlier, then decided against it. If Geoffrey knew, he seemed unconcerned. If he didn't know, maybe there was a reason he shouldn't. Instead, he said, "Have you met the king of France?"

"I've not had that privilege," Geoffrey admitted.

Balian took Geoffrey's arm and led him to where the count

of Flanders was sitting. "Sire?" Balian said.

The young man who had been fanning the count looked up.

Chapter 53

Geoffrey was so startled that he missed a step. He had supposed the young man to be a servant. The man was dressed plainly, with no display of jewels or mark of rank. His nose and cheeks were red and peeling with sunburn. Long, stringy hair had left an oily stain on the shoulders of his worn blue bliaut.

To the count, King Philip said, "You'll excuse me?"

"Yes, yes," said the count in a raspy voice, "I'll be all right."

Philip rose and handed the fan to a servant.

"Sire," Balian repeated, "this is Geoffrey, Earl of Trent, commander of the English forces in King Richard's absence."

Placing his right hand over his heart, Geoffrey bowed low. "Sire."

Philip smiled. It was a thin smile, the smile of a man not given to humor. "My lord Trent, I've looked forward to meeting you. Odd we've never met before, though I believe we've crossed swords—in the figurative sense, at least."

Philip was referring to his, and to then-Count Richard's, wars against Henry II of England. Philip and Richard had chased the sick old king and his army, of which Geoffrey had been a part, through France and taken much of his lands. Geoffrey still smarted from the humiliation of those days, but he forced a smile in return. "We have, sire. Please God we're on the same side this time."

The king nodded. Philip Capet was twenty-five; he had been king for ten years. He was the kind of man who passes unnoticed in a crowd, yet there was something in his eyes, a cold cunning, a steely determination. This was not a man to have for an enemy, as Geoffrey well knew. "We'll talk later," he told Geoffrey. Then he nodded to a liveried herald, who sounded a blast on his trumpet.

The tent quieted. Striding briskly, the French king took a place at the center of Balian's long table. Conrad assumed the place to Philip's right, much to the consternation of Guy of Lusignan, who still wore the gold circlet about his head.

Before Philip could speak, a jowly knight whom Geoffrey did not know forced his way to the open space at the front of the head table and bowed elaborately to Philip. He spoke with a Poitevin accent. "My name is William of Mello, and I bring news from King Richard."

The tent erupted. "Richard!" men shouted. "Richard! He's not dead then!" Heads strained this way and that. "Is he here?"

Philip raised a hand, quieting the tumult, then he said to William, "Well, sir, where is my cousin of England?"

"He's in Cyprus, sire."

Philip regarded William as he might regard a wayward child. "And what, pray tell, is he doing in Cyprus?"

"He's conquering it, sire," William said.

This news set off another uproar. "My cousin is supposed to be here, not in Cyprus," Philip pointed out.

William of Mello shrugged diplomatically. "The king says he will be here as soon as he may."

"How considerate of him," Philip replied.

Philip thanked William for his news and dismissed him. "Is there no message in return, sire?" William asked, eyebrows raised.

"No—no message." Philip spoke offhandedly, as though he deemed Richard's news unworthy of a reply, as though it were no more than Philip had expected.

William bowed stiffly and took his leave. Guy of Lusignan stopped him on his way out. The two men conferred briefly, then William left the pavilion.

Philip watched William go, then addressed the crowd. "I have called this council because I am taking command of the army. As the highest ranking noble here, that is my right. Does anyone dispute this?"

No one did, least of all Henry of Champagne, who looked

relieved to be rid of the duty. Henry and Philip were approximately the same age, but there the similarity ended. Henry was handsome, assured, well groomed. There was no mistaking him for anything but a lord of the highest rank. Philip, on the other hand, might be lucky to pass for a stable boy. Yet Henry was largely ineffectual as a leader, while Philip already had a long list of accomplishments to his name.

At the inception of Philip's reign, his possessions had consisted of little more than the territory surrounding Paris, and many had speculated that he would lose even that. The consensus had been that the kingdom of France was about to pass into history. That it had not was due to Philip. His goal had always been to make his country great. Many had laughed at that goal, but little by little Philip was making it come true.

Philip said, "I want everyone who does not command troops to leave the tent. Servants, heralds, squires, some of you clerics." He nodded to the few women in the audience. "*Pardon*, ladies, but I must include you, as well."

There was grumbling, especially from the women, many of whom had not yet had the chance to be introduced to the French king, but the tent emptied. Geoffrey motioned to Fauston, who made his way out with the rest, picking a bishop's pocket for old time's sake.

Philip turned to the count of Flanders, perhaps his only real friend in the world. "How do you feel?"

Sweat poured down the count's pale face, matting his grey hair and beard and darkening his wool bliaut. Now approaching fifty, the count of Flanders had at one time been the most powerful lord in northern Europe. He had also been Philip's guardian when Philip was a child. Philip had learned much from him, and although the exigencies of statecraft now made Philip the count's suzerain, the two shared a great affection for each other. "I just need some rest, that's all." This was the count's second crusade. On his first, fourteen years earlier at the height of his power, he had been offered the regency of the kingdom of Jerusalem. How differently things might have turned out had he taken it, Geoffrey thought.

To a pair of departing servants, Philip said, "See the count to his tent."

The servants helped the count from his chair. "I'll be by later, to see how you fare," Philip told him.

"That's kind of you," the count replied, and the servants assisted him from the tent.

Philip regarded the assembled nobles. "Gentlemen, I did not come here to dither. I intend to launch an all-out assault on the city."

"You're not going to wait for Richard?" cried Guy of Lusignan.

"I could become an old man waiting for Richard," Philip replied. "No, we go as soon as possible—the day after Easter."

"Easter Monday's but five days off," Henry of Champagne pointed out. "The copper tower won't be ready for another month."

"That's too long. The wooden towers will have to do. We have enough of them."

"What's your hurry?" said Robert de Sable, newly elected grandmaster of the Templars.

Philip looked at him coolly. "You will have perhaps noticed the extensive graveyards surrounding this camp. My hurry is that I do not wish to be interred in one of them. If you find pestilence to your liking, by all means remain in this camp as long as you will."

"What about Saladin?" Geoffrey said. "Every time we attack the city, Saladin attacks us, and because we must defend the camp, we can never mount an all-out assault on Acre."

"And he always seems to know exactly when we'll make our attack," added Bailian of Ibelin.

Philip tapped a bony finger on the table. "Saladin. You know, people at home call this knave 'the perfect knight.' If he's so damned perfect, let him give me back my falcon."

Geoffrey raised his brows. "Sire?"

"Right after we landed, my favorite falcon somehow got

loose and flew into Saladin's camp. I sent the fellow a note, asking him to return it, and do you know what he said? He said he liked the bird so much, he had decided to keep it for himself. Can you imagine such effrontery? 'Perfect knight.' The fellow's no more than a bird thief." Philip's eyes narrowed. "We'll bruit it about that we're attacking a week from Easter. The men won't be told the truth until the night before the assault. We'll see if we can't steal a march on our friend Saladin."

Square-headed Conrad of Montferrat nodded. "I like it."

"As do I," said Leopold of Austria in his heavy accent.

"And I," added the count of Champagne, through Geoffrey sensed more reluctance in him than in the others.

The bishop of Beauvais, famed for spending more time in armor than he did in his priestly robes, raised a practical objection. "It will make preparations difficult, since we'll be in church a good portion of those days."

"All the more reason for Saladin to think we won't attack then," Philip said.

"Richard won't like this," warned Guy of Lusignan.

"He should have thought about that before he decided to conquer Cyprus," Philip told him.

There were more protests, a number of the barons wanting to wait for King Richard. To break the impasse, Philip turned to Geoffrey. "What about you, my lord of Trent? Richard is your king. Think you that we should wait for him?"

Geoffrey's response was immediate. "I say go now, sire. Capture this damned city and be done with it."

There was a roar of approval. Next to Geoffrey, James of Avesnes chimed in. "Aye. I'd like to see aught of the Holy Land than this stinking camp."

Another roar.

Guy of Lusignan sulked. "I still think we should wait for Richard."

"Wait for him, then, and be damned to you," Philip snapped. "The rest of us attack the day after Easter."

Chapter 54

Vespers had been rung. It was Holy Thursday. Evening mass, celebrating the Last Supper, had been said, and now the camp was largely quiet, anticipating the greatest day in the Christian calendar.

Roger made his way to Helvise's tent. He carried a small pot of ink, a bundle of writing quills and a dozen sheets of parchment, rolled up. He had gotten the materials from Fauston, who had begged Roger to start working on the chronicle again. Roger had promised to help him on the morrow, when just about everyone else would be taking part in the huge Good Friday procession around the camp.

Helvise's big green tent seemed forlorn. Its fabric was frayed and faded, sewn together in places. It must take a lot of work for Helvise to maintain it. Roger pulled the flap aside. He didn't see anyone. "Madame?" he called hesitantly. He wondered if she had forgotten he was coming. "Lady Helvise? It's Roger."

"Come in," replied Helvise's voice from beyond the partition. "I'll just be a moment."

Roger stepped into the tent. The floor was covered with fresh grass. The tent smelled of must and sweat, but that was like perfume compared to the noisome quarters Roger shared with the Death's Heads. A curtain ran across the tent's middle. Like as not, the servants had once slept in the front part of the tent, but since there were no more servants, Helvise had converted it to a kind of antechamber. Her crossbow, oiled and freshly polished, hung from the center pole, along with her green jerkin and quiver of bolts. Her pavise leaned against the pole. There was a table with two candles on it, and a folding camp chair.

The curtain parted and Helvise stepped through. She wore a dress of dark green velvet with a small yellow cross sewn on the shoulder. The dress clung to her, revealing the outlines of her breasts and slim hips. She had brushed her dark hair clean. Roger suddenly realized how attractive she was.

Helvise held her arms out to the sides; the long sleeves of the dress dangled nearly to the floor, as was the fashion. "What do you think?" she said shyly, turning this way and that. "I haven't worn it since Christmas. It feels strange."

Roger wasn't sure what to say. "It's—it's most becoming, madame. I'd scarce have recognized you."

"Should I take that last part as a compliment or an insult?" she said.

"A compliment madame, most assuredly. You look—well, you look nice. Very nice. Beautiful, if I may make so bold."

She made a face, as if he was overdoing the flattery. "It's a change, anyway. I thought it would be good to feel like a woman again." She saw the materials in Roger's arm and flashed that girlish enthusiasm. "Can we begin?"

Roger motioned her to sit at the table. Where to start? He'd thought about that a lot since he'd agreed to teach her, and because he hadn't arrived at a satisfactory answer, he feared he might not be up to the task. He'd learned the basics so long ago, he'd forgotten how they'd been taught to him. "Language is composed of three kinds of words. There are nouns, which name a person, place or thing—'the *lady*,' for instance. Verbs, which describe action—'the lady *rides*.' And descriptive words—'the *young* lady rides a *black* horse.' Written words are formed with letters. There are 23 letters in the alphabet. The first is 'A.' "

He dipped a quill in the ink, leaned over the table, and carefully drew a capital "A" on a sheet of the parchment, followed by one in lower case. " 'A' can be pronounced in two ways—'ah' and 'ay.' "

" 'Ah' and 'ay,' " she repeated dutifully. Then she held out her hand. "Can I try?"

Roger gave her the quill.

She grasped the quill in her fist, holding it as one might grasp a knife when cutting up a dead animal. Her tongue pushed between her lips with concentration. In her eagerness to write something, she dragged the quill down the parchment and tore a ragged hole in it.

She turned to Roger, eyes wide. "Sorry."

"Not so hard," Roger said. "Here—hold the pen like this."

He stood behind her, leaning over her shoulder, trying not to touch her. He was aware of her smell, of her new-brushed hair, the oils she used to cover the sweat of battle, the heat of her body. Her breasts were right below his eyes, and he forced himself not to look at them. He guided her hand—callused from using the crossbow—onto the quill, placing her fingers in the proper positions. He had a hard time because her fingers were stiff and didn't want to stay where they should.

"It's uncomfortable," she complained.

"It takes a while to get used to it. Try again."

He guided her hand across the parchment. "Not so hard," he repeated. When her hand threatened to veer from a straight line, he gently steered it back on course. When they had finished, there was an "A," or something vaguely resembling an "A."

Again and again they practiced, Roger lightly guiding her hand.

"Try it by yourself now," he said at last.

Brows knit tight, Helvise practiced making "A's." Her capital letters looked like map outlines, veering into sudden coves and promontories and hitherto undiscovered boundaries. Her small "a's" resembled meandering streams, wandering all over the landscape before eventually reaching a confluence. More holes appeared in the parchment. Eventually, and a number of quills later, Helvise was able to form plausible "A's".

"Good," Roger told her. There were still declensions, participles, first and third person . . . Well, it was a beginning.

Helvise shook her hand, flexed it. "My hand hurts."

"That's natural," Roger said. "As I said, it takes a while. Now, let me show you a word."

He dipped a quill in the ink and on the parchment marked the letters "ad." "This is the word '*ad*.' It means 'toward,' or 'to,' or sometimes 'at.' "

"How do you know which?" she said.

"It depends on the context of what you're reading or writing."

That deflated her for a moment, then she was brimming with enthusiasm again. "Is '*ad*' a noun, a verb, or the descriptive thing?"

Roger looked sheepish; he wondered what else he had forgotten. "Actually, it's none of those—it's a preposition."

"A preposition?" she said, puzzled.

"It's complicated, we'll get into it later. Here—let me show you some numbers."

He inscribed the numbers "I" through "V." "You can practice writing these, if you like. Next time, we'll go to ten."

They took a break, and Helvise poured Roger a cup of wine. She used her left hand to pour because her right hand was still sore. Roger sipped the wine—white wine, the kind the Germans favored. "What is it like where you come from in Germany?"

Helvise drew a breath and stared at the opposite wall of the tent. "It's green," she said, and it was as though she were seeing it clearly in her mind's eye. "Bright green grass, deep green pine forests. Clear, deep lakes, sparkling rivers alive with fish. Distant mountains where the snow lingers year round. Air that is crisp and clear and bracing, and makes you feel glad to be alive. In the spring, the meadows are blanketed with wildflowers of white and yellow and purple. In the winter, it snows, and we ride on sleighs and make balls from the snow and throw them at one another. It is the most beautiful place on earth."

"Sounds as though you miss it."

"I do, more than you can imagine."

"Then why don't you go back?"

"I can't. I have made a vow to stay until Jerusalem is free."

"Vows are broken every day."

"Not by me. I mean to keep my word and avenge my husband and child." She looked at Roger. "You made a vow, as well. Why don't *you* go back?"

Roger turned the wine cup in his hands. "I have nothing to go back to. The abbey would hardly welcome me."

"Why do you have to go back to your abbey? Where did you live before that?"

"I was left at the abbey as a babe. It's the only home I've ever known."

"Oh," she said. "But surely you have family. Where were your parents from?"

Roger shrugged. "Of my mother, I know naught. My father abandoned me at the abbey and came to the Holy Land. All I have of him is this ring."

On impulse, he took off the ring and showed it to her. She turned it over in her long fingers, examining it by the candlelight. "It's beautiful."

"That doesn't help me know who I am or where I came from," Roger said.

She handed the ring back. "Have faith, Roger. Someday you will learn."

Faith, he thought bitterly, and he said, "I don't see how." He added, "Anyway, I've committed a Mortal Sin, and that can only be expunged if I die here."

She regarded him thoughtfully. "It is not hard to get yourself killed here. I'm sure you could have died already and had your sin forgiven."

"Yes," he admitted.

"Yet you've chosen to live. Why?"

"I'm not sure. When I was ill, I think I *did* die for a moment, but I came back. I was aided by a friend, it's true, but . . . perhaps I should have taken that last step." *Maybe if I had believed, I* would *have taken it. Maybe that's what held me back.*

Roger looked at the candle and was surprised by how low it had burned. "It's late," he said. "I'd better go."

"And our next lesson?"

"The next few days will be busy. The day after Easter should be quiet, though. My company has camp guard Easter night, but I'll be free afterwards. I could come at sext."

"That will be fine," she said. "Could you leave the parchment—that which I have not destroyed— and the ink?"

"Certainly." Roger bowed. "Good night, Lady Helvise."

She inclined her head. "Good night."

Roger left the tent. Behind him was the sound of a quill scratching parchment.

Chapter 55

Easter, holiest day of the Christian year. The altars uncovered. Solemn Mass at sunrise, processions, singing of hymns. Geoffrey of Trent revealed the new date for the attack on the city at a banquet he gave for the English commanders after services were finished. Setting the tone for the coming engagement, he raised his cup and said simply, "Jerusalem."

At Christmas, this same toast had set off wild celebration. Now, however, the assembled nobles repeated his invocation. "Jerusalem." No cheering, no upraised voices, no singing—just grim determination to finish the job.

Dusk.

The earl of Trent's footmen moved up Resurrection Road. Tramp of feet, creak of leather jacks, clink of armor and weapons and accoutrements. The Death's Heads were at the rear of the column, breathing the dust churned up by the spearmen. Payen always made the Death's Heads march last.

"Straighten that line!" Payen shouted at the Death's Heads. Payen was even more out of sorts than usual because his native serving boy, Bug, was sick, and Payen was forced to carry his own helmet and shield. "Look like soldiers," Payen went on. "This is the poorest excuse for a company of men I've ever seen. Damn your eyes, Roger, it's because of you and your misfits that we've been held out of the assault."

Roger didn't reply; he didn't even look at Payen. These remonstrances were a daily occurrence. If one were to believe Payen, the crusaders would be in Jerusalem by now were it not for Roger and the Death's Heads. As Payen moved up the line to inspect the rest of the men, Egwulf cuffed Roger's shoulder in a gesture of support. Tatwine, whom Roger had saved from the burning belfry all those months ago, made a rude gesture in Payen's direction, to muttered laughter from the rest of the Death's Heads. Payen acted like he didn't hear the laughter and kept walking.

The Death's Heads had been detailed to guard the bridge at the end of Resurrection Road. They relieved the guards, a mixed company of Swedes and Danes, the original units having merged when they became too small to be effective any longer. "Anything happening?" Roger asked their captain.

The light-bearded Swede—a hard-bitten fellow with a ring in one ear—shook his head. "Quiet as a choir of deaf mutes. You'd think 'twas the Turbans celebrating Easter, not us."

As the Swedes straggled off, the earl's men spread out to their assigned posts, centenars and vintenars giving half-hearted orders, or in some cases giving no orders at all. The men had done this many times before; it was routine. When the ditch surrounding the huge camp had originally been dug, the turned-up dirt had been used for ramparts. These ramparts had been reinforced with a palisade, and sharpened stakes had been planted in the bottom of the ditch to hinder attackers further. The palisade and stakes had mostly disappeared, burned for fuel over the winter. Rain had crumbled the ramparts, partially washing the dirt back into the ditch, which had also been used as a latrine and a dumping spot for refuse of all kinds, including the bodies of men and animals. Efforts to strengthen the ditch had been indifferent.

Four bridges crossed the ditch, spread at more or less equal distances along its length. These structures were made of heavy logs, wide enough to permit two horsemen at a time to cross. The bridges were kept under sheds covered with oilcloth, to protect them from the weather. When needed, they were run up to the ditch on wheels and manhandled across. Men crossed the ditch at all times, of course—spies, deserters, foragers—but because the sides of the ditch were so steep, horses could only cross using the bridges. Each bridge site was guarded by crude stone battlements to either side.

Roger set the watch and, as darkness fell, the men settled in. The nights were still cold, and the men wrapped themselves with blankets—there had once been guard huts here but, like everything else made of wood, they had been burned. The men munched bread, drank watered wine, ate anything else they had been able to scrounge. Sugared almonds were popular— the use of sugar being one vice nearly every man had picked up since arriving in the Holy Land. Dried camel meat was a staple, as well, though nobody liked it. A lot of the men pounded sugar into it to mask the taste.

Roger lay on his back and looked at the stars. What were the stars, he wondered. The souls of the saints, he had been told at Huntley, and maybe that was so. He wondered why they changed positions in the sky. Men said it was because they revolved around the earth, but why would the souls of the saints want to revolve around the earth? Why wouldn't they just stay in one place? Even more puzzling was that the stars here did not occupy the same positions in the sky as they did back in England at this time of year. Why? None of it made sense. Roger was still thinking about that when he drifted off to sleep.

He rose before dawn, to join the last watch. If there was trouble, it usually came at dawn. The stars were gone. Heavy mist from the sea lay upon the ground, damp and chill, muffling sound. Roger swung his arms, trying to get warm, as he approached the stone breastwork to the left of the promontory which would hold the bridge. Behind him, in the main camp, thousands upon thousands of men were rising and preparing themselves for the assault on the city.

Men from Roger's old section were at this breastwork— Egwulf, Tatwine, and a man who had just come to the section—a cheery, irreverent young fellow named Wat. Watford Wat, the men called him, not because he had anything to do with Watford but because they liked the sound of it. A shoemaker by trade, Wat had come to the Holy Land last spring with the company of Londoners. The Londoners were gone now, dead of disease or battle, and the few survivors had taken service with other barons. "Me and me pal Nosey, we joined a company o' the Archbishop's men," he'd told Roger when he joined up. "Northumbrians, they was, and weren't that above half a mistake for us. Couldn't make out a bloody word any of 'em said. Anyway, Nosey died, as did most o' the Northumbrians, so here I am."

Wat was badgering Tatwine as Roger came up—Wat always seemed to be talking. "When you going to paint me helmet, Tatty? That's why I joined this bunch—to get one o' them skull helmets."

"I told you, I'll paint it soon's I get some free time," Tatwine replied. "I promise. I run out o' paint, and I got to mix me some more. Stuff don't grow on trees, you know."

A distant trumpet sounded. The three men and Roger looked toward the crusader camp, its campfires a dull glow in the mist.

Wat spat. "T'ain't right, them newcomers getting ready to take the city while we—we who been here since Noah got off the bleedin' Ark—we sit out here in the cold."

"They want fresh troops for the attack," Roger explained. "We're too worn down."

Wat was unmollified. "All the good loot will be gone by the time we get into the city. The best quarters will be taken."

Egwulf growled. "We're foot soldiers, you lump. We don't get good quarters."

"Maybe not, but we can get loot," Wat said. "By the hair on St. Peter's ass, it just ain't fair."

"I didn't know St. Peter had a hairy ass," Tatwine said.

"That's cause you don't pay attention in church," Wat told him. "Why, I'd give anything to—"

"Shh!" Roger said suddenly. "What's that?" he pointed into the mist before them.

It was hard to hear anything. The mist deadened sound, and the growing rumble from the camp threatened to drown out everything else.

Roger stared. "Is something moving out there?"

Wat said, "A jackal, maybe."

Egwulf said, "Maybe it's St. Peter. Come to get you for making jokes about his ass."

"Quiet!" Roger said. "Listen."

There was a metallic clink. Another.

"Somebody's out there," Roger said.

The sounds came closer, or seemed to. It was hard to tell.

"Wake the men," Roger told Tatwine. "Alert the other posts."

Tatwine moved off and roused the sleeping figures, who stumbled from their blankets and grabbed their weapons.

More noise. "Who's there?" Roger cried into the mist.

"Friends," returned a voice in heavily accented French. "Is this the Rue de St. Pierre?" The Rue de St. Pierre was the next bridge site to the north.

"No," Roger returned. He wasn't going to give away their real position.

The voice swore, as though its owner had just learned that he was lost. "I am Gervaise of St. Cloud, man-at-arms with the duke of Burgundy. I've got a party of Turcopoles with me. We were on a raid, but we got jumped. We got away in the dark, but the Goat Fuckers are right behind us. Let us come up."

Something about the voice jarred Roger's memory but he couldn't say why. "How many are you?" he said.

"Six," said Gervaise from the dark and mist, and there was more noise as somebody slid down the far side of the ditch. "We're all hurt, three of us badly. We need help getting up your side. Hurry, before those bastards catch us."

Where had Roger heard that voice before?

"*Par Dieu, monsieur!*" pleaded the voice.

Roger's men were looking at him.

From the plain came the sound of galloping horses—

Saracens.

"Hurry!" Gervaise cried in terror.

Roger nodded to Egwulf. "Help them up." To Gervaise, he cried, "We're coming."

Egwulf and the rest of Roger's old section started down the steep side of the ditch. That gutteral voice nagged at Roger, nagged at him, and then he knew where he'd heard it.

He swore in disbelief, then yelled to his men, "It's a trick! That's Dirk out there! Get back!"

There was an angry cry from the bottom of the ditch. Roger's men scrambled back, and Roger realized why there were horses on the plain.

"Sound the alarm!" he cried. "They're after the bridge!"

As Slowfoot blew three ragged notes on a horn, Egwulf and his men scrambled back to the top of the ditch.

"Thought Dirk was dead," Egwulf puffed.

Roger said, "Bastard must have been captured by the Saracens and gone over to their side. He was trying to lure us into the ditch so his new friends could ambush us."

There were sounds of scraping, of dislodged stones and dirt as the Saracens began climbing this side of the ditch. It sounded like a lot of them. The rumble of horses was loud now as Saladin's cavalry reached the ditch's far side, waiting for the bridge to be run across.

"We have to hold the bridge!" Roger cried to his men. "If those horses get across, the camp is lost!"

It was dawn; the mist was lightening. Figures in pointed helmets could be seen in the ditch, climbing the steep sides. Up and down the ditch line, horns blew. There was the sound of men running into position, but it didn't seem like a general attack on the camp, not yet. There was no telling how many Saracens were out on the plain. If they got across the bridge, those horsemen could be at the backs of the men advancing on the city in a matter of minutes. Roger swore again. Somehow the Saracens must have found out the Christians were attacking the city today and hoped to catch them by surprise and destroy them.

The bridge abutment rested on a rocky promontory. On both sides of the abutment, the slope was steep. The Saracens were massing there, climbing both sides of the promontory; it was the logical place for them to concentrate their attack. Take the promontory and they would take the bridge. Unbidden, Egwulf ran to a position at the promontory's point. He wrenched the large stones from the breastworks and with his great strength began hurling them down on the advancing enemy, hitting men in the head, in the chest, knocking them back, bowling them into those who came behind. Egwulf hoisted the heavy stones easily, laughing at the Saracens, holding back the attack all by himself. When he ran out of stones within reach, Roger and other men formed a line and passed him more. Then a Saracen managed to climb close and throw a pot of something at Egwulf. The jar hit Egwulf on the shoulder and burst into flames—naptha. In seconds Egwulf was engulfed. He screamed and fell backwards, wreathed in fire, and began rolling in the dirt. There was a great cheer from the misty ditch and the Saracens surged forward.

At the sight of his friend on fire, Roger lost control of himself. He vaulted the breastwork and found himself sliding into the ditch amidst the enemy. He was yelling, eyes focused on the man who had thrown the naphtha. The man saw him coming, and his own eyes widened with fear. Roger was aware of other men swinging weapons at him but he didn't care. His feet hit the bottom of the ditch. The naphtha thrower had turned and started up the far side. Roger caught up to him and buried his axe in the back of the man's skull. The man fell, and Roger's own momentum and the uneven ground caused him to fall as well. He expected to be butchered by the Saracens while he lay exposed, but nothing happened. He was aware of more yelling around him, looked up and saw a helmet with a Death's Head.

It was Tatwine, with Ralph the Red beside him, and Offa, and Watford Wat, and the others. All of them yelling and swinging their axes at the startled enemy, who had never expected a counterattack from the outnumbered Christians. Roger struggled to his feet in the press of bodies. He couldn't find his axe, so he drew his short sword and picked up a round Saracen shield. He stood beside Tatwine, stabbing with the short sword in the close quarters fighting at the bottom of the ditch. He drove the sword into one man's neck. Another man's eye. Took a blow on his shield, reeled, bent and stabbed at the knee of the man who'd swung at him. The man fell and another lunged at him. He took the force of the lunge on his shield and pushed back, scrambling for footing in the narrow, blood-soaked ditch bottom, stumbling on the bodies of the dead and wounded. He stabbed at his attacker's chest and the sword's blade broke on the man's steel breastplate. The man shouted and launched a blow at Roger but Tatwine hit the man in the head with his shield and knocked him down. Roger bent to pick up a discarded Saracen sword, got bumped and lost his feet in the melee, and fell. Before he could rise, a body toppled onto him, then another. Hot blood spurted over his neck from above him. It ran around onto his face and into his eyes, and he wiped them with his muddy glove.

He shouldered the bodies off him and got to his feet with the curved Saracen sword. The Saracens in this part of the ditch were fleeing now, taken by surprise by the Death's Heads' counterattack. From nearby Roger heard trumpets and horns and cymbals, and he remembered why Saladin's cavalry was out there.

"Back up the side!" he told his men. "Get to the bridge."

They climbed back up the muddy side of the ditch. A bearded man, wounded, staggered at Roger from the right. Roger slashed at the man's face, felt his curved sword bite into bone, and the man fell away. Roger kept climbing, heard fighting above.

He reached the top. The left-hand breastwork was momentarily cleared of Saracens, but the men guarding the right breastwork, Wulfhere's section, were hard pressed.

Another party of Saracens had bypassed the fighting around the promontory and had dragged the wooden bridge from its shed. These men were under Dirk's direction; Dirk wore Saracen armor and carried a Christian sword in his left hand; his right hand was muffled with gauze. The Saracens heaved and rolled the bridge ponderously forward, while across the ditch their mounted comrades cheered them on.

Roger and his men charged the enemy who were rolling the bridge, taking them unawares, hacking with axes, slashing and stabbing with swords and daggers. Roger went after Dirk, but a big Moor got in his way. Roger struck at the Moor with the Saracen sword and hit him at the base of the neck. The Moor fell against him; Roger caught the man's heavy weight as blood sprayed his face. Roger stumbled backward and threw the man aside. Dirk was nowhere to be seen.

More Saracens were climbing over the top of the ditch, their armor proclaiming them dismounted horsemen come to aid their fellows. Roger and his men drove off the Saracens dragging the bridge, then formed a shield wall around the bridge. The Saracens threw themselves against it. Press of bodies, stench of sweat and blood and shit as men died and voided themselves. The curved sword was next to useless in this kind of close-in fighting, but it was all Roger had. The best he could do was to duck under his shield and slash at the legs of the men he was fighting. He and his men were forced backwards by the press of numbers against them. The man next to him fell and was trampled under the oncoming enemy. Roger glimpsed Dirk again, exhorting the Saracens on.

Roger and his men were pushed back until Roger's leg struck the thick log of the bridge and he could retreat no farther. "Hold!" he cried, but his voice was a thirsty whisper. His head swam with fatigue. They weren't going to make it.

Then there was a cheer and a wave of mailed horsemen smashed into the Saracens' flank and rear. Exhausted, Roger looked up to see one-eyed Henry the Lion, leading his knights. Henry's charger reared and trampled the terrified Saracens, crushing skulls and bones with its monstrous hoofs. Henry yelled and swung his sword at the enemy. Trumpets blew, more Christian knights arrived, and the Saracens ran.

The Saracens retreated into the ditch and up the other side. The knights followed them to the lip of the ditch, spearing them, hacking at their backs with swords. Tired as he was, Roger started after the Saracens, looking for Dirk. He saw Dirk in the ditch and went down after him, heedless of the fleeing enemy around him. Dirk reached the bottom of the ditch and started climbing the far side, moving fast for a big man. Roger realized he wasn't going to catch him. Bracing himself against the uneven side of the ditch, Roger drew his dagger, took careful aim, and threw.

The dagger's handle hit Dirk in the back and fell harmlessly in the dirt. Dirk turned, saw Roger on the other side of the ditch, and laughed. He gave Roger an ironic salute, then disappeared over the ditch's far side.

Chapter 56

As the Saracens fled, Roger climbed slowly from the ditch. He didn't think he'd ever felt this tired before. The weariness was like a weight on his shoulders, pushing him down, so that all he wanted to do was to fling himself onto the ground and sleep. But there was no time for that.

His old section seemed to have come through the action pretty well—Egwulf was gone, of course, and Roger didn't see Watford Wat. Arcil and Ralph the Red were wounded, but not so badly that they couldn't fight. "Where's Wat?" Roger said.

No one knew. Slowfoot said, "He jumped a fellow what was about to put a spear in your back when we was coming back up the ditch. That's the last I seen of him."

Roger's gut tightened. "Find him," he said. Then he added, "Red—you're vintenar now."

Ralph, who was winding a strip of cloth around the wound on his arm, nodded. He was still unhappy about having to wear his hair and beard short. He had taken the faded green ribbon that the whore had given him—the one he had used to use to tie his beard when it was long—and braided it around the side of his helmet strap.

Wulfhere's section had suffered more than Roger's. Wulfhere and four others were dead, with several more men wounded too seriously to fight. Roger appointed a tall fellow called Short Peter as vintenar to the survivors. The Saracen cavalry, several thousand strong, were still demonstrating before the bridge, but they were powerless to cross the ditch because Henry the Lion had sent his footmen to reinforce the bridge guard, and the earl's spearmen were there now, as well.

"Call me if anything happens," Roger told Ralph. "I'm going to check on the wounded."

Chapter 57

Images passed before Egwulf's eyes: a ploughman with a withered leg pleading with Egwulf not to take his cow . . . a widow begging for her hen . . . Egwulf carrying a family's table—the family's only possession—from their house, giving it to the bailiff to be smashed up and used for firewood . . .

More images: beaten, bloody faces glaring at Egwulf with hatred . . . the bailiff urging Egwulf on when Egwulf wanted to stop.

He remembered the sickening feel of his big fist against a man's jaw or in his gut. . . .

The images faded. The memories were gone. Pain washed through Egwulf like liquid fire. A river of fire. An ocean of it, breaking over him in ever larger waves. He bit clean through his lower lip to keep from crying out, but he could not feel it because of the pain from his burns.

He felt as though he were being consumed by the fires of Hell, and he prayed that he did not go to Hell because he could not imagine spending the rest of eternity like this. While the other men had battled the Saracens, Mayne had put out the fire engulfing Egwulf by covering him with a blanket then scooping dirt over him. Later, when there was a break in the fighting, they'd used the blanket to carry him here with the other wounded, near the shed, taking care because every step caused Egwulf agony.

Egwulf's beard had been scorched off. His blackened, blistered skin oozed blood. His jack and shirt and hose had been burned so badly they had fused to his skin along with pebbles from where he had rolled in the dirt, and everyone was afraid to cut any of it away because of the pain it was certain to bring him. He could only open one of his eyes, and that effort caused him intense pain. All he could see was shadows, anyway, so mostly he kept his eyes closed. Where his skin was exposed to the air and the sun it felt like it was still on fire. A puff of breeze was like someone dragging a razor across him. He was dying, and so he prayed . . .

Egwulf hailed from a manor called High Wycombe. His father was a smith, but Egwulf had an older brother to inherit that trade, so the bailiff had enlisted Egwulf as the manor's beadle. The beadle collected rents or services that were owed to the lord but went unpaid or unperformed. Big and strong—stronger even than his father or brother—Egwulf was well suited for this kind of work, and he had to admit, a lot of the delinquents had it coming. These were lazy, worthless, frequently drunken individuals who were trying to avoid their just obligations. There were always a few, though, who had fallen on hard times, who couldn't work because of illness, who couldn't render the lord's bushels because of a bad harvest, who couldn't pay the lord's eggs at Easter because a fox had eaten their laying hen.

The bad types usually gave in quick enough when Egwulf came around, but sometimes he had to "persuade" them. If they didn't pay or show up for work in Lord Ranulf's fields, he'd give them a hiding—a vicious one, because that's what the bailiff wanted. Other times he would confiscate their possessions in equal value to what they owed the lord.

Egwulf didn't like hurting people, he liked it even less when they were in arrears through no fault of their own. His job made him the most hated man in the manor. His strips in the common were dug up at night and his crops destroyed because of it; the girl he fancied wouldn't marry him; people refused to talk to him or even to acknowledge his presence when he was around. This treatment hurt Egwulf terribly because all he ever really wanted out of life was to be liked.

He tried to quit more than once, but the bailiff—Lord Ranulf's bastard son, who acted like he was the lord himself—wouldn't let him. If Egwulf didn't make the slackers pay, the bailiff promised to take it out on Egwulf's family. So Egwulf made them pay. The crusade had been a godsend for Egwulf. By royal decree, manorial officers like the bailiff were not allowed to prevent anyone from taking the cross, and so Egwulf had made a new start, only to have it end here.

❖ ❖ ❖

A shadow. Someone knelt beside him.

"Do you have any sins you wish to confess?" Mayne asked Egwulf. Since Father Stephen's death, Mayne had taken on the duties of company chaplain. Instead of vestments, he wore the badges he had gotten on various pilgrimages—the cockleshell of Santiago de Compostela, the keys of Rome, the badge of Our Lady of Rocamadour, and others.

Egwulf had sins, he had many of them, and he wanted to confess but he couldn't, because the pain was so bad. He groaned.

"It's all right," Mayne told him soothingly. He made the sign of the cross. *"Ego te absolvo."*

More shadows loomed. Two of them. One resolved itself into Roger. The other was Tatwine. Tatwine wasn't a bad sort, Egwulf thought, once you got to know him, nothing like what they used to say about him. 'Course he had greased his arrival in the section with a couple jugs of prime arrack, which hadn't hurt. *Wish I had some of that arrack now. Wish I had a bucket of it.*

Egwulf felt, rather than saw, Roger kneel beside him. Something was pressed to his cracked, swollen lips. Not arrack—water. Egwulf drank, the liquid cool and refreshing, but stinging when it spilled out of his mouth and over his burned chin.

"How are you?" Roger asked.

337

Egwulf had trouble speaking, and when he did speak his voice was a hoarse croak. "Hurts."

"Is there anything we can get you?"

Egwulf shook his head. He swallowed and moved a hand weakly. He had to know. "Tell me . . . something. Do you like me?"

"What kind of question is that?" Roger said. "Of course I like you."

Tatwine said, "We all like you, Wulfie."

Offa, who must have been standing nearby, though Egwulf couldn't see him, said, "No man in the company's more popular, ye great loon."

Egwulf sighed, lay his head back and relaxed. He felt better.

The pain came over him again, so intense that he cried out, "Oh, my God." Salty tears squeezed from his eyes, and the salt burned his skin. With a hand, he beckoned Roger closer.

Roger held his head near Egwulf's.

"Make it stop," Egwulf whispered to him. "Please."

Egwulf held Roger's gaze with his good eye.

"Please," Egwulf repeated, crying freely now.

Roger's eyes narrowed and he drew a long breath. He put his hand to his belt, but his dagger was gone.

"Want me to do it?" Tatwine asked softly.

"No," Roger said, "I'll do it. Lend me your dagger."

Tatwine handed Roger his dagger. Roger wiped his mouth on the back of his mailed glove, then he took Egwulf's right wrist, gently because the touch caused Egwulf pain—Egwulf could feel burned skin slipping off. Egwulf closed his eyes. He hardly felt the incision as Roger drew the dagger's blade down his right arm, opening the vein; this new pain barely registered above the agony he was already enduring. He felt Roger move the dagger to his left arm and repeat the process.

Egwulf opened his eyes and nodded thanks to Roger, flinching as a fresh wave of pain swept over him.

Roger's eyes never left him. "Just relax, old friend," he said.

Egwulf was aware of the others drawing closer—Tatwine,

Offa, Mayne. He felt at peace. He felt like he belonged.

Gradually the light around him dimmed, until all he could see was the blurred image of Roger above him. Then the light went out.

Chapter 58

Roger pressed Egwulf's eyes closed. He bowed his head and stayed like that for a moment. Then he rose and returned to his company, followed by Tatwine and Offa.

"Did you find Wat?" Roger asked Ralph the Red.

Looking glum, Ralph inclined his head toward the ditch.

Roger and Tatwine slid into the ditch. Slowfoot was there with Wat, who lay among the blood-soaked dead. Wat's body, especially his face, bore so many wounds it was nearly impossible to recognize him.

Wat had died saving Roger's life. He would probably be alive now had he ignored Roger's plight and continued retreating up the side of the ditch. How did you repay a debt like that? Roger was a sinner, had his life even been worth saving?

"Let's get him up top before the Saracens come back," Roger said.

Carefully, because Wat's left arm was nearly severed, the three men pulled Wat's body out of the ditch and laid him alongside the bodies of Wulfhere and the other Death's Heads. Tatwine went to one knee beside Wat. "Poor bastard, all he wanted was to get his helmet painted."

Tatwine removed his own helmet with the red skull painted on it, and he placed it on Wat's chest. He took Wat's hands and folded them on the helmet, as though Wat were holding it.

"Bury him with that," Tatwine said. "He earned it."

From the Christian camp came the sudden sound of trumpets, cheering, tumult. The assault on the city had begun.

* * *

The red oriflamme of France went forward, along with the new siege towers and a host of men. One by one, however, the siege towers were burned by Greek fire and collapsed in heaps of flame and timber. The Crusaders might still have carried the walls by ladder had they not been forced to direct so many men to defending their camp from Saladin's attacks. Unit after unit was recalled from the assault—veteran troops of Pisa, Genoa, and Hungary first, then newcomers belonging to the duke of Burgundy, the count of Dreux, and many others, until it seemed as though there was no one left to attack the city.

The fighting along the trench's three-mile length lasted all day. It was not a continuous attack. Saladin's forces seemed to arrive at the ditch piecemeal, as if they been assembled hurriedly and without coordination. They demonstrated and launched probing attacks, and at every point they appeared, the Christians were obliged to commit men to oppose them. The fighting was furious in places, as the Saracens found what they thought were weak points in the Christian line and attempted to punch through. There were two more assaults on the Resurrection Road bridge site, but these were largely met by Henry the Lion's men and the earl's spearmen. The Death's Heads suffered no more casualties.

As the sun set, the fighting died down. The Christians gathered their dead for burial on the plain. They piled the Saracen bodies and burned them, the skins of pigs being thrown on as many of the piles as possible.

As lord of the men who had defended the bridge at Resurrection Road from the surprise attack, Geoffrey of Trent was given credit for saving the camp. Geoffrey, in turn, gave the credit to his foot soldiers, led by Payen of Beaufort, who was only too willing to let Geoffrey and anyone else within earshot know that he had more or less saved the bridge all by himself.

While Payen was basking in his self-anointed glory, Henry the Lion rode over to Roger's position near the promontory. Seen in the soft, purplish light of dusk—it had actually been a beautiful day, Roger realized with a start—Henry's hauberk and dirty white surcoat were spattered with blood. There was blood in his grizzled beard, blood all over his horse. He reached down and smacked Roger's shoulder in that friendly way of his. As Roger struggled to regain his balance, Henry said, "Good work today, boy. That counterattack of yours held them off long enough for me to organize my men, and by doing that it saved the bridge. God's stones, it may have saved the whole army." He waved a disdainful hand in Payen's direction. "Don't worry, I'll make sure Lord Geoffrey knows the truth about what happened."

Roger shook his head wearily. "It was one of my men who saved the bridge, not me. His name was Egwulf, he—"

"Nonsense. I admire your modesty, but take credit for what you did."

Roger started to say something, then stopped. What good would it do to say that his "counterattack" had been an act of blind rage, that he'd lost control of himself, that he'd barely been aware of what he was doing? If everyone wanted to believe he was some kind of hero, they would believe it no matter what he told them. What good would it do to tell them he no longer cared, that he no longer believed? It would be even worse for his men to know that. For their sake, if for no one else's, he must pretend to be enthusiastic, to be the hero they wanted him to be. He must be a fraud. He would make sure Egwulf's name got in the earl's chronicle, though. He would make sure that his friend's act of bravery got the credit it deserved.

"Yes, my lord," he said.

"Good lad." The one-eyed knight thumped him on the shoulder again. "Now, I don't know about you, but I need a drink."

Chapter 59

"Lusignan's supporters are saying it was King Philip's fault," Balian observed. "They say Philip lacks ability as a commander, that he should have waited for King Richard to get here."

A group of nobles had gathered in Balian's tent, having removed their armor and cleansed the blood from themselves as best they might. Young Henry of Champagne, who had faced the same kind of criticism when he was the army's commander, nodded. "And now Guy has decamped to Cyprus to be with his cousin Richard. Convenient, isn't it?"

"That sack of weasel shit," muttered toothless James of Avesnes. He swilled more wine. The wine made the cavities in his gums where his teeth used to be hurt, but he didn't care. "Guy wanted Philip to fail because Philip supports Conrad as king of Jerusalem."

Geoffrey of Trent stared into his cup, disconsolate. "This time I thought it would work," he said. "This time I really thought we'd take the city."

Henry the Lion gulped more wine, the red liquid running down his chin into his grizzled beard. "You know why it didn't work, don't you?" he said.

Geoffrey nodded glumly. "Because my man Roger was right—there's a spy in our midst who warned the enemy of our attack. I guess I knew it in my heart all along, but I just didn't want to believe it."

The count of Champagne said, "The spy must be a Christian, and a fairly high-ranking one, because no one else knew the date of the attack."

James of Avesnes said, "So what are we to do?"

"About the spy?" said Henry the Lion. "Damned if I know."

"About the siege," James said.

343

"We keep fighting, that's what we do," said Geoffrey suddenly, sitting straight. "We hammer the bastards night and day until they give in." For the first time, Geoffrey felt fully invested in this crusade, in this siege. Before, he was here because his wife had made him come. Now he no longer wanted to sail away, even though he still knew that was the sensible thing to do. Now he was as determined to see the city fall as any man in the camp, no matter what the cost or how long it took.

Balian of Ibelin raised a dark eyebrow. "Welcome back, Geoffrey. I thought you'd lost interest."

"I guess I found it again," Geoffrey said.

In Saladin's tent, a similar scene was being enacted. The sultan sat on silk cushions, attended by his sons and generals. Like the Christians, they had doffed their armor and cleaned themselves, though they had done a rather better job at the last task than had their Christian counterparts. They drank sherbet made from lemon or pomegranate, tamarind or cornelian cherry, and ate from bowls of dates, figs, pears, and oranges.

"Your plan was a good one, Qaymaz," Saladin said. His voice was mild and reassuring, as though he were discussing a scientific experiment. "Had the feringhee attack on the city taken place six days hence, as we had originally been led to believe, we would have had all our forces but the Egyptians in place and we might have taken the Infidel camp. As it was, we had to form our troops and throw them into battle as they became available. Still, Akko was saved. That is the important thing. All praise to Allah that we received word of the attack when we did. If not for that, the city might well have fallen."

Qaymaz sat with one knee up, his other leg straight before him. He had changed to robes of blue silk, and his dark hair was combed straight back, giving his head a square look. "The traitor called Dirk did his part, I'll give him that. It was bad luck he was recognized by the bridge guards. We had taken the bridge, else, and maybe the Christian camp, as well."

There were nods around the circle, but Saladin's eldest son, Al-Afdal, the Bull, leaned forward. "Are you certain it was bad luck, Qaymaz? Are you certain this *Dirk* --" he spat the word— "did not betray us to the feringhees?"

Qaymaz regarded Al-Afdal patiently. He did not like Al-Afdal, but the young man stood to inherit his father's empire, so it was best to keep on his good side. "Dirk is too scared of me to betray us."

Several of the men in the tent laughed. They well knew the torments Qaymaz could inflict on those who fell afoul of him.

Saladin's second son, Al-Aziz, was fatalistic. "It was not God's will that we destroy the Infidels this day, that is all. Who can know the ways of God?"

The Bull snorted derision.

Saladin's brother, Al-adil, turned a grape in his fingers. To the sultan, he said, "We lost many good men today, brother. I was in favor of maintaining our army here while it seemed as though the Infidels might die from sickness. But they have survived. Indeed, they grow stronger with each ship that arrives from the west. Fighting the Infidels on fixed defenses as we did today plays to their strength rather than ours. Would it not now be better to let the city fall and withdraw our army to fight them in the open field, where we may better employ our speed and mobility?"

The Bull sneered. "You speak like a coward, uncle."

"And you speak like a fool," Al-Adil snapped. "I have fought in more battles than you have years to your life. Think twice before you call me such a name again."

The Bull growled and half rose, but Saladin held up his hand. "Enough." He motioned his son to sit, and his eyes seemed even sadder than usual. "Your advice is wise, brother, and at any other time I would agree with you. Unfortunately, we have staked too much of our prestige in this fight. To give way now, after nearly two years of this siege, would be a grave defeat, if not in reality, then in the eyes of the Infidels and, even more, of our own subjects. No, we must see to it that Akko does not fall. The city has become too much of a symbol." He sighed. "We must beat the Christians here or we risk losing everything."

Chapter 60

Failure did not deter King Philip. He had failed at things before in his young life, and always he had come back to be successful. He was patient and persistent, both as a king and as a military commander, and when he wanted something he kept after it. "When the Invincible Tower is finished, we shall attack again," he vowed, "and this time we shall succeed." Fresh copper sheeting had arrived from Cyprus, and construction on the Invincible Tower proceeded apace, Hedde and the other men now working on it by torchlight.

The fighting raged steadily now, with never a respite save on Sundays and Fridays, when by tacit agreement each side observed the other's holy day. Christian mangonels dueled with the Saracen catapults on the city walls, using building stones and marble columns for ammunition. Under cover of the archers, men and women labored to fill in the ditch around the city, while at night working parties from inside the city worked equally hard to clear it. Cornish and Picard miners drove shafts beneath the Accursed Tower. The Saracens countermined, and savage battles were fought in the blackness below ground. Italian ships repulsed an Egyptian fleet offshore, and a seaborne assault led by Conrad of Montferrat failed by a whisker of carrying the Tower of Flies and opening the harbor for the Franks.

Casualties were enormous. Mighty armies dwindled to companies. The contingent from the Northlands had numbered 12,000 on their landing two years earlier; there were not a thousand left. The Bugars, those strange, dark men Roger had encountered on his arrival at Acre, had disappeared entirely, their camp taken over by the remnants of the Irish, who were themselves down to little more than a hundred men.

The Pisans who had camped in the Belus marshes had been wiped out by disease, and that part of the encampment had been abandoned. Replacements were easily come by, though. Ships brought more men from over the sea almost every week, plus there was a steady supply of soldiers who had lost their lords and needed employment. In addition, there were clerks and servants and displaced colonists who had somehow found their way to Acre and who could be enlisted as soldiers or pressed into service as laborers.

Saladin's army launched daily probes along the length of the Christian lines. The city garrison sortied against the Frankish siege engines. The night rang with the din of fighting. During one of these clashes, Coelred, the spearman who had portrayed the Soldier of Acre in Roger's Candlemas play, received a deep gash in his lower leg. The wound festered, and Coelred's leg was amputated above the knee. The stump swelled and blackened, however, and his leg was cut off again, this time at the hip. Coelred died during the operation.

Roger and the Death's Heads were kept busy—Payen made sure that when they weren't defending the camp ditch or guarding the archers at the walls, they were drilling, and when they weren't drilling, they got the camp's dirtiest work details. When they had free time during the day—which was infrequently—the men took to going down to the beach and bathing in the warm sea water. Some of them rode the short waves with their bodies, arms straight to guide them, hooting and yelling. Sometimes noblewomen bathed at the seashore as well, and screens were erected to keep prying eyes from watching them. Common women, like the laundresses and camp followers, went naked in the water with the men. Some priests protested this fraternization, but to no avail. When they weren't at the beach, the men got drunk in the wine tents that infested the camp.

Roger spent his free evenings instructing Helvise in her letters. Helvise still took her place outside the city walls each day with the archers, then returned to her tent in the evening for her lessons. She had learned the alphabet and her numbers from one to ten, and she could recognize a modest amount of words. She could use a writing quill without tearing a hole in the parchment, and she was struggling with the first declension of verbs.

Helvise always wore the green dress for the lessons. A year and a half of battle and hardship had taken their toll on her. She was gaunt and complained of being tired—though she would miss neither a day at the city walls nor her lessons. One evening Roger once again brought up the subject of her going home.

"I confess," she said, looking up from her work, "I think about that more and more, despite my vow, but it is complicated. I have lands at home, it is true, but those lands are in the gift of the duke of Bavaria. Women cannot hold land in Germany, so if I go home, the duke will marry me off to someone of his choosing."

"Oh," Roger said. He hadn't considered that.

Helvise sat back and turned the quill over in her hands, studying it. "I don't want another husband, not one who is forced upon me, one I do not love. But if I refuse to marry, the duke can confiscate my lands." Helvise put the quill down. "As long as I am here, I don't have to make that choice."

"Still," Roger said, "being a soldier is no life for a woman."

"And what is a life for a woman? Who decides that—you? What is wrong with our society—shouldn't a woman have a say in her future?"

"Yes, of course she should," Roger said. "It's just . . ."

"Just what?" She made a face. "You don't want to teach me anymore, do you?"

"Of course I do. It's just—well, I've gotten to know you now, and I'm worried that you'll get hurt. Or killed."

She rested a tanned hand on his forearm. "That's kind of you, Roger, but, really, I can look after myself." She smiled. "Ask the Saracens."

Roger laughed and nodded. "You're right. We'd better get

back to the lesson."

As the days lengthened and grew warmer, Helvise's lessons continued, and Roger's friendship with her grew. And then one evening, as they had both known it would, the green dress came off, and there was no more talk of letters or writing.

Chapter 61

Helvise rolled onto her stomach. It was hot; she and Roger were naked, with no blankets to cover them. Helvise took Roger's right hand and toyed with his ring. "Have you ever been in love?"

"Once," Roger said. "At least I thought I was in love. The other person didn't feel the same way."

"She was a fool." Helvise spoke these words with surprising intensity. Then she grew curious. "Was this while you were a monk or after?"

"A bit of both, actually."

Helvise raised a brow, but Roger didn't elaborate. He also didn't tell her that the woman in question was at this moment on the Toron, only a mile away.

Helvise's tent was lit by a single candle. There was the smell of cinnamon. Outside were the sounds of a distant skirmish, but Roger's instincts, honed by experience, told him it was nothing to worry about.

Helvise went on, releasing Roger's hand and tracing a finger along his forearm. "Do you think that what we do is a sin?"

"No," Roger said.

"Neither do I. The Church thinks it's a sin, though, because we're not married."

"The Church is wrong."

"Don't tell them that. It would be worth your life."

Roger leaned over and kissed the nape of her neck. "Something that wonderful could never be a sin."

He ran a hand down the small of her sweaty back and across her firm buttocks. He didn't say anything and she looked up. "Is something wrong?"

351

"No, I'm just looking. You have the most beautiful body I've ever seen."

She cocked her brow again, playfully this time. "And how many women's bodies *have* you seen?"

Roger felt himself blush. "One." And that was the one who had robbed him in France. The other women he'd been with had just lifted their skirts. "Still," he rallied, "I can't imagine that there are any more beautiful than yours."

"Not even the woman you were in love with?"

"Not even her."

"You're sweet." Helvise lifted her head and kissed him. "So—how do I progress as a student?"

"Fine, I guess," Roger said. "I'm really not a judge."

She rolled onto an elbow, facing him. "I suppose *you* were an excellent student."

"Me? I was more interested in talking and horseplay than I was in my studies. I still have marks on my back from the master's cane."

Her eyes went wide. "Really?"

He laughed. "No, I'm joking. Those marks faded long ago. The master beat me when I was young, but as soon as I got old enough, they set me to cutting wood for punishment—we always needed wood at the abbey. I liked cutting wood, actually. It was a lot more fun than studying rhetoric and dialectic."

"I'm beginning to think you weren't all that fond of life at your abbey—what was its name?"

"Huntley," Roger said. He pursed his lips in thought. "It's not that I didn't like it there, it's more that I didn't fit in. Don't get me wrong—life at Huntley was good. We were secure from the dangers of the outside world, and there was always enough to eat, even in the bad times. I wanted to see what lay over the next hill, though, and the hill after that. I wanted to be out in the world doing things, not praying and copying books."

Helvise nodded, as though she could understand that, and Roger went on. "I didn't fit in with the other members of the chapter, either. Most of the boys I grew up with at Huntley were sons of nobles. They called me "Foundling" because I didn't know who my parents were. I got in a lot of fights because of that, which led to even more—"

"Wood cutting?" she ventured.

He grinned. "Fortunately, we had a large forest."

"Didn't you have any friends?" Helvise said.

He looked away for a moment, remembering. "Two. One was another boy from a common background, Gervaise. His father was a merchant—a very wealthy one, which was why Gervaise was tolerated at the abbey. The other was named Evrard. His father was a baron with estates in Oxfordshire. At one time, the three of us were more or less inseparable. They cut almost as much wood as I did."

"So what happened?"

"Both of Evrard's older brothers died, and he was granted dispensation to leave the order and become his father's heir. Gervaise's mother was sickly, and he was transferred to a house closer to his family home in Ipswich. After that," he shrugged, "I had friends, but no one I was close to."

Helvise grew uncomfortable on her elbow and sat up on the bed, wrapping her arms around her knees, a sheen of perspiration making her naked body glisten in the guttering light from the candle. "All this because you didn't know who your parents were?"

Roger moved closer and toyed with her knee. "Funny, isn't it, especially considering how the Church preaches that no man is better than another. Still, the abbot liked me, so it could have been worse."

"Did the abbot know who your parents were?"

Roger ran his hand along the outside of her thigh; her skin was smooth as silk. "He said my father wouldn't tell him. Said my father left me at the abbey with a bag of silver and rode away." He shifted his hand to her inner thigh, and that was just as smooth. "Enough about me, what of you? I know nothing about you."

She smirked. "Save that I have the most beautiful body you've ever seen."

"Save that," he corrected, and he slid his hand around her buttock.

"There's not much to tell. I had a very conventional life— no, 'conventional' is not the correct word. Most conventional lives are not happy. My sister Ermengarde, for instance, is married to a man twice her age, whose children hate her. I was not like that, I was happy. I was married to a man I had loved since we were children. I thought I had the perfect life. I thought I was blessed. Then came the crusade."

The tenor of her voice changed and Roger removed his hand from her body. She went on. "I couldn't bear to be parted from Welf, so I went on the crusade with him. I was not alone in that—many wives accompanied their husbands. We had the emperor with us, no harm could come to us, or so we imagined. We thought it would be over quickly, and we would come home and our lives would go on as if nothing had ever happened. It was going to be a lark, it was going to be fun.

"I was pregnant when we left home. I gave birth on the march. At first the journey was like a grand holiday outing, with lots of feasting and hunting. Then the emperor died and everything fell to pieces. There were constant attacks from the Turks. We suffered from the heat and lack of water. All round us men and women died, but we kept going. Then Welf was killed."

She paused. "I never got to bury Welf. I never even got to see his body; he had to be left on the battlefield. After that, my sole object became the protection of my baby. But it was not to be. He died in my arms, his tiny body wasted from thirst and sickness."

Helvise's eyes had become dark pools of hatred. "That is when I took up the crossbow. I had used one before, of course, for hunting, but now I hunted men. I dressed as a man and marched with the army's vanguard, killing any infidel who came within my range. Men died all around me, but I refused to die. I vowed to reach the Holy Land. I vowed to take revenge on the people who killed my husband and child." Her voice fell. "And so you see me."

"The child you lost," Roger said softly. "It was your first?"

She shook her head. "Before that, there were two miscarriages. That's why we were so happy when Oskar was born. He made our lives complete. Then came the march through Anatolia."

She wiped something from her cheek. "It's my fault. I should never have come."

Roger moved behind her and put his arms around her. "You couldn't have known what would happen. No one could have foreseen this."

She sniffed and eased herself against him. They stayed like that a long time, then she put a hand on his. "Will you stay the night?"

"I'd like to, but I can't. We have formation at dawn. If I'm late, God knows what kind of punishment Payen will inflict upon my men. I don't want them getting in any more trouble because of me."

She sighed with disappointment.

"I don't have to leave right away, though," he said.

"How long can you stay?"

He turned her and gently placed her on her back. "We'll see."

Chapter 62

When Roger was not on duty, he was with Helvise. He still taught her to read and write, and she was doing well at it, but that had become a minor part of their relationship. They spent their nights together whenever they could. On Fridays and Sundays they spent their days together, as well, strolling the crowded Concourse, marveling at the tents and sheds filled with expensive spices, perfumes, silks, pearls, and ivory, items that Roger and Helvise had never seen at home. They drank cooling fruit sherbets or ate the misshapen fruit called bananas or dates or oranges. Other times, they partook of peeled figs stuffed with almonds, ground pistachios, or cheese, then wrapped with bacon (the last part a Frankish touch); or they had lamb or goat ke-babs, or yoghurt with coriander and pine nuts. Later they might watch a mystery on the stage at the Toron High Street (due to Church complaints, the earl of Trent's men had been barred from presenting another play) or one of the musical performances that sprang up throughout the camp; or they might walk along the shore, taking in the bustle of ships and men, or wading in the surf. At other times they sat in the quiet of Helvise's tent, mending their gear for the morrow, content just to be in one another's company.

One night, Roger took Helvise down to the water. They slipped past the guards at the northern end of the transit camp and found a secluded portion of beach. They left their clothes on the sand and waded into the water, with the light surf lapping around them. The full moon cast a broad, silvery path across the sea and, enveloped in its glow, they made love.

Afterward, walking back to the German lines, her arm through Roger's, her head against his shoulder, Helvise said, "Is it right that we should be so happy in the midst of such misery?"

356

Roger leaned over and kissed her still-damp forehead, smelling the sea salt in her hair. "*Are* you happy?"

She looked up at him as though the answer was obvious. "Yes, I am. Incredibly so." She squeezed his arm. "Aren't you?"

Roger hesitated. Then he said, "Yes, but there's—there's something you should know."

She frowned and pulled away, still holding his arm. "What? You're not married, are you?"

"It's worse than that."

She let go of his arm now. This was a moment Roger had dreaded, but it could no longer be avoided. "I've wanted to tell you for a while," he said. He hesitated again and looked away from her, back across the moonlit sea. "When first I arrived at Acre, I was filled with the crusading spirit. The flame of God burned bright in my breast. But now . . ." His voice trailed off.

"But now?" she prompted.

"Now I no longer believe in what we're doing here. Now I no longer hear Mass." He turned and stared her in the eye. "I no longer know whether I even believe in God."

Helvise stepped backwards as though jerked by an invisible cord. "Are you serious?"

"Yes."

"How can you not believe in God?"

He was surprised by the vehemence of her reaction. "Of all people, I thought you would understand. Look at what you've suffered in God's name—losing your husband and child. Look at the death and disease around us. Look at the graveyards on the plain. If there was a God, He wouldn't permit this. He couldn't. Why should I believe in Him?"

In reply, Helvise grabbed Roger's arm and pushed him around to face the lights of the camp and the city walls. "No, Roger, you look, and stop being selfish. It's not about what God does for *us*, it's what we do for *Him*. What you see before you is an act of faith, the greatest act of faith the world has ever known. Every man and woman here, save you, is here for one purpose—to free Jerusalem. To restore the Holy City to the

True Faith. When we were eating grass and dirt last winter, it was our faith that sustained us, nothing else. Without that, we all would have perished. I call that a miracle, and only God works miracles."

Roger stared at the panorama before him, the moonlit sea, a fiery missile arcing toward the city wall, the twinkling lights of the camp, voices singing ribald songs. Priests chanting funeral dirges. The stomach-curdling stench of death. Hard to see that as a miracle.

Helvise went on, speaking earnestly. "Who are you—one man out of thousands—to doubt our cause? Who are you to doubt God? What makes you so special? You're always telling me what a sinner you are and how much you regret it—well, if you don't believe in God, then you don't believe in sin, and if that's the case you've done nothing wrong. Without God, there is no sin, there is no right or wrong. Everyone can do as he pleases and hang the consequences. That's anarchy, that's the realm of Satan."

Roger said nothing, and she went on. "You know that what you are saying makes you a heretic."

Roger nodded.

"The Church will burn you if they find out."

Roger said, "They might burn you, as well."

There, it was out.

Helvise stopped to digest this. "What are you saying?" she asked at last.

"I'm saying you could be at risk if we continue our relationship. Associating with a heretic is the same as committing the sin itself. There are many inquisitors who would be more than happy to consign you to the stake on those grounds. Are you sure you want to face that possibility?"

She waited a long moment, looking at him. Then she said, "Are you ending our relationship? Is that why you brought me here?"

"No," Roger said hastily, "I want to keep seeing you." He paused and added, "I want to keep seeing you forever."

"I feel the same way," she said. She paused, as well. "And I always will."

Roger's heart swelled. He placed his hands on her shoulders. "I couldn't bear for anything bad to happen to you, Helvise. I needed you to know that being with me could prove dangerous."

"I have faced danger before," Helvise said.

Roger sighed with relief and embraced her. After a second, she stepped back and took his right hand in both of hers. "Promise me one thing."

"What?"

"That you'll try to regain your faith. For your sake, not mine. Don't you see, Roger—without faith, you're nothing. Without faith, there's no reason to live. Please? Will you do it for me? For us?"

"I'll try," Roger told her, but he was doubtful.

Chapter 63

The next day the Acre garrison launched a dawn sortie intended to destroy the mangonels ranged opposite the Accursed Tower. A secondary target was the crossbowmen guarding the mangonels, especially the infamous Green She-Devil, who had caused the city's defenders so many casualties and upon whose head lay such a rich bounty.

The raiders filtered out of the city in darkness and silently crossed the ditch. They erupted out of the gloom as the mangonel crews were lighting their breakfast fires. The sentries had fallen asleep and the mangonel crews were taken by surprise. Those who couldn't flee resisted as best they could, but they were cut down and their catapults set afire or chopped apart with axes.

A second group of Saracens swept through the crossbowmen as they were straggling in from camp, still half-asleep, cutting them down like harvesters reaping grain and with about as much opposition.

"There she is!" one of the Saracens cried. "There is the She-Devil!" The Saracens abandoned the other crusaders and ran toward Helvise, eager to be first, eager to take the head that would make them rich.

Helvise had been thinking about Roger, worried for his soul, when the raiders burst upon them. She threw her heavy pavise from her back. She kept control of herself and loaded her crossbow, which was more than her fellows did, most of whom panicked and ran away. All this Helvise sensed rather than saw, because she was concentrating on what she was doing—foot in the stirrup at the curved end of the bow to hold the weapon steady, bend down and loop the bowstring over the claw in her belt, now rise, using the strength of her body to draw the bowstring taut and seat it in the trigger nut. The yelling of the enemy was loud as she placed a bolt in the track on the tiller. She raised the bow and fired the bolt into the chest of an onrushing Saracen no more than two feet away. The man dropped, but there was no time to load another bolt, no time even to draw the short sword at her belt. The mob of Saracens was upon her.

Helvise knew about the bounty on her head, and she was under no illusions about what was going to happen to her, but she was determined to die facing her enemies. She thrust the empty crossbow into the face of the first Saracen to reach her, breaking his nose, making him stagger backwards, nose gushing blood. His helmet fell off, and Helvise raised the crossbow with both hands, intending to bash the man's head in. But before she could bring it down, another Saracen rushed forward and slashed his sword across her left side. Helvise cried with pain, dropping the crossbow and falling to her knees.

Shouting *"Allahu akbar! Allahu akbar!* She is mine!" the Saracen lifted Helvise by the hair and lined up his sword for the blow that would take off her head. As he swung his arm, he was transfixed by a three-foot arrow. His arm followed through weakly and the sword skittered out of his hand. He let go of Helvise's hair and stared stupidly at the arrow in his chest, and then his own head was split open by a sword as the raiders were attacked by a party of English and Picard footmen sent to drive them off. Helvise was vaguely aware of fighting around her, of yelling and men falling, of blood welling from her side, then she toppled full length on the ground and lost consciousness.

Chapter 64

Roger went to Helvise's tent after vespers. He was tired because he and his company had spent the day hauling supplies from the beach, payback for some slight Roger was supposed to have shown Payen. Roger carried quills and ink and parchment, as he always did. He entered Helvise's tent and found two weary-looking Picard foot soldiers in the outer area. Helvise's green jerkin lay on the tent floor, rent and covered with dried blood.

Roger went cold inside. The writing implements fell from his hands, ink spilling onto the tent floor. "What happened?" he said. He was barely able to get the words out.

"Who are you?" asked one of the Picards.

"What happened!" Roger demanded.

"No need to get rude, *mon ami*. The lady was wounded. We're guarding her till—"

Roger yanked the curtain aside and burst into the rear of the tent. "Hey—!" shouted one of the Picards, but Roger ignored him.

Helvise lay on the bed, naked and unconscious, her torn shirt thrown over her breasts and private parts as a gesture to modesty. Bloody towels and bandages were strewn about the floor. Two men wearing black, with black skullcaps, bent over her, one sewing her wound, the other brushing away the flies that clustered around her. They looked up as Roger entered.

The first one straightened, a grizzled fellow with a long nose. "Who are you, sir?"

Roger couldn't bear to look at Helvise's wound, but at the same time he couldn't take his eyes off it. The ragged gash ran diagonally across her side. Her beautiful body had been sewn back together crudely, like a sack of grain. Roger's mouth was dry. "A friend," he answered at last. "What happened?"

The old man toweled blood off his hands and forearms while his companion finished the sewing. "She was hurt in an attack on the mangonels," the old man said. His companion snipped the end of the suture and stood. He was younger, with thinning fair hair and a sunburned nose. The old man passed him the bloody towel and he wiped his hands in turn.

Roger's legs were unsteady. He started closer but the older man waved him back officiously. Roger said, "Is she—will she be all right?"

The older man frowned. "That is the province of God, sir, not of man. If you wish her to survive, you would do better to pray for her than to stand there gawping like a peasant on market day."

The younger man bent and felt Helvise's forehead and cheek. "She's burning up, Father."

"A surfeit of choler," said the greybeard, nodding sagely. "I expected as much."

"Shall we bleed her?"

The greybeard nodded again. "We have no choice."

"Bleed her!" Roger looked at all the blood on the bed and tent floor. "Hasn't she lost enough blood already?"

The two surgeons spared him a condescending glance, then the younger one addressed his father. "We can open a vein. I have my scalpel."

Greybeard tapped his thin lips with a finger. He moved closer and indicated the swelling around Helvise's wound. "See how dark it gets here? Better to use the leeches, I think. Put them on this blackened area."

"Opening a vein relieves the pressure more quickly," the younger man pointed out.

"True, but leeches address a more specific area," the older man rejoined. He waggled a forefinger. "Never forget that, my boy. Leeches are a far more scientific form of treatment."

The younger man nodded reluctantly, as though he didn't really believe his father, and the older man motioned to a scabrous native boy sitting in the corner and looking bored.

"To my tent. Bring the leeches."

The boy got up and hurried out.

Roger stepped forward, "I don't think—"

"Did anyone ask what you thought?" the old man said.

"No, but I've seen—"

"No one cares what you've seen. We are the archduke's personal physicians, you have no say in this matter. Leave."

"Listen, you—"

"Go, I say!" the old man commanded, arm outstretched like an Old Testament prophet's, finger pointing. "Go, or I'll summon the guard."

Roger left. In the gathering darkness, he hurried back to his own lines. He reached his old section tent and burst in. "I need your help, men. Come armed."

The men had been lounging around, tossing dice, sleeping. They rolled from their cots and stumbled from the tent — Tatwine, Ralph the Red, Slowfoot, Arcil, Offa, Hedde and Mayne—arming themselves as they went, buckling on their helmets. "Where are we going?" Offa said, hopping along as he tried to put on a shoe.

"To save a life."

They hurried to the German camp, past the protesting guard and down the street into Helvise's tent. The two Picard soldiers were still there, helping themselves to bread, cheese, and wine from Helvise's stores. They saw the Death's Heads helmets and decided it was time to leave.

Roger and his men entered the back area of the tent to find the older man arranging leeches along Helvise's bare, swollen side. The younger man stood on tiptoe and watched intently over his father's shoulder. Five of the slimy creatures were already in place. With great precision, the Greybeard took a sixth leech from a pan and placed it on Helvise's discolored skin.

"Stop!" Roger ordered.

The two surgeons looked up, then went back to what they were doing.

Roger took a long stride across the tent and pushed the old man away from Helvise. "I said, stop!"

The old man confronted Roger, face red with anger. "This is an emergency, you fool. Her fever has worsened. We need to get it down immediate—"

"Shut up," Roger told him. He indicated the leeches. To his men he said, "Anybody know how to get these things off her?"

Tatwine—who else?—said, "I do."

As Tatwine took out his dagger and knelt beside Helvise, Greybeard advanced on him. "You're making a mistake."

Tatwine looked the older man in the eye. "You'll be making a bigger one if you get in my way."

Greybeard advanced no further.

Carefully, Tatwine slid the dagger blade under the head of the first leech and pried the creature loose from Helvise's skin. He repeated the process with the leech's back end. Then he picked up the leech and tossed it onto the tent floor.

"Be careful!" Greybeard cried. "Those leeches cost a lot of money!"

Tatwine gave the man a deliberate look, then he stomped on the leech, making it pop.

"You'll pay for that!" Greybeard shouted.

Tatwine pried the rest of the leeches from Helvise's side and dropped them none too gently into a pan, while Greybeard tutted over his precious creatures.

"Put her on a litter," Roger told his men when Tatwine was done.

"What do you think you're doing?" the younger doctor cried. "She can't be moved."

Slowfoot and Ralph the Red improvised a litter from blankets and spare tent poles. "Hurry," Roger said, "before the camp guards get here."

When the litter was done, the men gently lifted Helvise onto it, trying not to look at her naked form under the torn shirt. Helvise moved her head and moaned.

"Let's go," Roger said. Offa, Hedde, Arcil and Mayne took

the litter. Tatwine, Ralph the Red and Slowfoot acted as guards, axes drawn, Tatwine and Slowfoot going ahead of the litter, Ralph bringing up the rear.

Greybeard placed himself in front of the party, arms outstretched. "You cannot do this. As the lady's physician, I forbid it."

Roger shoved him aside.

"This is an outrage!" cried the younger physician.

"The duke shall hear of this!" thundered his father.

Roger and his men got outside. The way was clear. As they carried Helvise up the camp street, Greybeard and his son ran after them, as if to physically detain them.

"Help! Help!" Greybeard cried as he ran. "They are—"

Ralph contrived to "accidentally" extend an elbow which caught Greybeard flush on the nose and knocked him on his back. As his son bent over him, Roger and his men hurried away.

"I want to thank you men for helping me," Roger said as they made their way back to the English lines. "I shouldn't have involved you in my affairs, but this lady would have died if we hadn't gotten her out of there. She still might."

"Then it's as well we came," said Father Mayne.

Offa said, "We saved the m — " he couldn't pronounce the word "margravina" — "her ladyship once before, might as well do it again. Gettin' so it's our job, like."

"What are we going to do with her?" Ralph the Red asked Roger.

"Take her to my tent," Roger said.

Chapter 65

They carried Helvise to the centenar's tent. Roger still hadn't moved into the tent; he only used it to store equipment. They placed Helvise on the cot and Hedde fetched blankets. Helvise's breathing was shallow; her forehead felt like a blacksmith's furnace. Occasionally she moaned, moving her head back and forth.

"Now what?" said Ralph the Red.

Roger poured water onto a cloth and placed the cloth on Helvise's forehead, like he'd seen Brother Regimus, the abbey's physician, do at Huntley. "She needs a doctor."

Tatwine said, "You noticed how well that worked out the last time."

"There has to be one doctor in this camp who knows what he's doing," Roger swore.

Offa, the charcoal burner, rubbed scarred fingers across his bearded chin. "A few weeks back, I was in a wine tent and I heard some Frenchies talking about a native doctor what was supposed to be good. Saved the duke of Berry, they said."

"A native?" Mayne said, his eyes widening. "You mean a Muslim?"

Offa shrugged. "That's what they said."

The men looked at one another uneasily. Mayne, the company's unofficial chaplain, voiced their thoughts. "Having a Muslim doctor is like having Satan tend you."

"I don't care if he *is* Satan," Roger said. "If he can help Helvise, I'm all for it." To Offa, he said, "Who is this fellow, and how do we find him?"

"Didn't catch his name," Offa said. "Mebbe—"

"I bet Bug would know," Tatwine cut in. "Little beggar knows everything that goes on in camp."

"You're right," Roger said.

Tatwine said, "I'll find him."

After some searching, Tatwine located Bug and brought him to Roger's tent. Roger explained to the native boy what he needed. "Do you know the man we seek?"

Bug rolled his big brown eyes. "Hassan, yes," he said in his broken French. "I know him."

"Can you bring him here?"

Bug looked over at Helvise. They had taken the blankets off her because she was so hot from fever, and she was bloody and naked save for the shirt thrown over her, and Bug's big eyes grew even bigger. "Yes. I do it." He scampered from the tent.

He returned sometime later with a short, round—almost fat—man with a bulbous nose and neatly trimmed beard and mustache. The man had quick, dark eyes and pudgy fingers that belied their reputed skill. The man salaamed graciously for one of such ungainly form, and Roger bowed to him in return.

"You are the doctor?" Roger asked him.

"I am," the man replied. "You may call me Hassan al-Burq, though my actual name is much longer than that."

Roger indicated Helvise. "Can you help this woman?"

Hassan bent over the unconscious Helvise, raising one side of her shirt and examining her wound. There was uneasy shifting among the Deaths Heads as he did this. Hassan felt Helvise's forehead and lifted one of her eyelids. He pinched his lips in thought, then turned back to Roger. "I can help," he said.

"Can you save her?"

"Nothing is guaranteed, save Allah wishes it, but I will do my best." He paused. "My fee will be forty bezants."

Forty bezants—that was two month's wages for a knight, half a year's wage for a centenar of footmen like Roger. Roger's face fell in dismay. Teeth bared, Tatwine started toward Hassan. "How 'bout you help her or we slit your throat?"

Roger held up a hand to stop Tatwine, but Hassan was unfazed. "You may threaten me or torture me," Hassan said smoothly. "I have heard such talk from you feringhees before. It seems to be all you know. Torturing me will not cure that woman, however."

"He's right," Roger told Tatwine. To Hassan, he said, "I don't have forty bezants. I'll give you what I have, but it's not more than a few *sous*."

Hassan said nothing.

Roger swallowed. "I'm begging you."

"I am a doctor, but of necessity I am also a man of business." Hassan shook his head. "I feel sorry for this woman, but there are many sick and injured in camp. Were I to work for a few—*sous*, did you call them?—I would soon be tending every man in camp, and because there are so many who need tending I could not see to everyone, so I would have to see only the ones who could pay me more. I am sorry, but that is the way of the world. I have more than enough patients now. I take only new ones who can pay." His dark eyes drifted down to Roger's hand and narrowed. Then he said, "I will take that ring in payment."

He indicated the ring Roger had sworn never to give up, the ring that was all that connected Roger with his parents. The ring was worth considerably more than forty bezants, but Roger didn't care. He looked over at Helvise, her short dark hair lank with sweat. "All right." He began twisting the ring from his finger.

"Wait," said a voice.

Everyone turned. Fauston lounged in the doorway of the small tent, leaning against a tent pole in his cleric's white robe.

Fauston straightened and started forward. "I'll get your forty bezants," he told Hassan. "I'll get you eighty, an you make the girl live."

Roger said, "How—?"

"Don't worry about that," Fauston said. Then he grinned. "Getting money used to be a specialty of mine, remember?" To Hassan, he said, "Eighty bezants—have we a deal?"

Hassan eyed the ring regretfully, but he had already told

369

them he would help Helvise for forty bezants, eighty was an unexpected bonus. His honor forbade him to go back on that promise now. "We have," he said.

"Get to work then. I'll be back with your money."

Fauston turned and left the tent.

Chapter 66

Hassan returned his attention to Helvise. He pulled aside the tattered shirt that covered her, lifted the blood-stained bandage and examined her wound more closely, sniffing at it and frowning. "By the Prophet's beard, I have seen old shoes that were sewn together better than this. In fact, I doubt I have seen many shoes that were sewn this badly."

Although the surgeon's words rang true, Roger felt that they should sting his pride as a Christian. "The men who attended her were Archduke Leopold's personal physicians," he said stiffly.

"Then let us hope the archduke does not become ill, for his sake." Hassan held up a pudgy finger. "First we must bring down her fever." He turned to Bug, who had remained in Roger's tent out of curiosity. "Fetch my assistant, if you would be so kind, young man." As the boy scampered off, Hassan said to Roger, "I will prepare a draught for your friend and a plaster for the wound, but first we must bathe the patient in cool water—fresh water, not sea water. Can you see to that?"

"All right," Roger said. He'd seen Brother Regimus use a cold bath to bring down a patient's fever. "I'll get a—"

"I'll do it," said the newly promoted vintenar Short Peter, who had ducked into the tent. "Me and Tom will. You stay here, Roger—watch over things, like."

"I'll need vinegar, as well," Hassan said.

Roger frowned. "Vinegar?"

"Yes, vinegar. You've heard of it, haven't you?"

"Of course, but—"

"Then stop asking questions and get it."

Before Roger could say anything, Offa said, "I'll get some." He motioned to Arcil and the two of them left the tent. Mayne stood at the foot of Helvise's bed, hands folded, intoning

371

prayers of his own devising.

Hassan's assistant arrived. Short Peter and Tom, a skinny axe man from Peter's section, borrowed a tub from the washerwomen and fetched water from the River Belus. Offa and Arcil returned with a clay pot full of vinegar. Impatiently waving Mayne out of the way, Hassan motioned to his assistant—an alert, blond-haired lad who looked like a Christian—and the boy removed Helvise's shirt.

This occasioned more muttering and shuffling of feet among the men in the tent. "Dunno as I like watching a Turban touch a naked white lady," grumbled Ralph the Red.

"Then do not watch!" Hassan barked at him. Roger was surprised that the surgeon knew English. "Get out," Hassan told the men. "Get out, and let me do my job. Go on, all of you—out!"

The men looked to Roger. With his head, Roger motioned them from the tent. "You, too," he told Mayne. Mayne made a hasty sign of the cross over Helvise and followed the others. Roger was the last to go.

"I still don't like it," Ralph told Roger outside the tent. "What if he treats her and she dies?"

Roger had asked himself the same question a hundred times already. "She would have died for certain with those two Germans treating her," he said.

Gap-toothed Mayne placed a hand on Roger's shoulder. "We'll all pray for her." The other men nodded and murmured agreement.

"Yes," Roger said woodenly. "Prayer."

Prayer. The concept he had so loudly abandoned, so confidently renounced. He raised his eyes to Heaven and immediately lowered them again, feeling like the worst kind of hypocrite.

He left the men and wandered over to the archery butts, which were not in use at the moment. His company was scheduled to go up to the ditch after vespers, but that was not for a while yet. Roger took out his dagger and began throwing it at one of the straw-padded wooden figures. Harder and harder he threw. Tears clouded his eyes, and because he threw the dagger too hard it kept bouncing off the figure instead of sticking into it. That only made Roger mad, and so he threw it even harder, until it seemed as though he was trying to throw it completely through the wooden figure.

"What the Devil are you doing?" Fauston said.

Roger turned. He hadn't heard his friend approach. Wiping his eye, he picked up the dagger and told Fauston how he had missed a chance to kill Dirk at the battle for the bridge. "I don't want to make that mistake again." He threw the dagger once more, not so hard this time, but it still bounced off the target.

Fauston stared at the target. "I gave Hassan the money."

"Eighty bezants? Where did you find such a sum so quickly?"

"It's probably best you don't know."

Roger retrieved the dagger and turned it over in his hand. "I can't thank you enough," he told Fauston. "I'll pay you back, but I don't know—"

"Forget it," Fauston said. Then he grinned. "After all, it wasn't my money."

Roger didn't fall for his friend's nonchalance. "That's a big risk you took. You know the camp rules—you could be hung for what you did."

"They've been trying to hang me for years," Fauston said dismissively. "Good luck to them." He hesitated, "Anyway, I was happy to help. I know what it's like to be fond of a woman."

"Really?" Roger frowned. "You never talked about women before. I thought—"

"What, you thought I liked men? That's bloody great, that is."

"No, I mean—I mean I thought maybe you didn't care about women. You know, like a priest or something."

"Oh, I like women well enough," Fauston said. "Been with more than my share of 'em, too—that's one of the benefits of being Brock the Badger. Never stuck with any of them, though. Not till I met Mary."

He looked away. "Runaway, Mary was. Come from a manor where the bailiff reckoned the women were put there for his amusement. Summoned Mary to his bed when she was of an age. When she refused him, he threatened her family. She stabbed him then, killed him, and ran away to Dunham Wood."

Fauston sighed and let out a long breath. "Mary was the one I wanted to be with forever, the one I wanted to have my children with, the one I wanted to stop being Brock and have a normal life with." He turned to Roger. "It was Mary I was searching for that night I found you and Ailith in the woods."

He looked away again and it was like he was speaking to himself. "I wonder where she is now? Dead, like as not. Hanged by the sheriff. Or worse. But maybe she got away. Maybe she's out there somewhere. I hope so. I hope she's happy."

Roger said, "Will you go back and look for her when this is over?"

Fauston shook his head slowly, as if to say what was the chance of any of them ever going back.

"Why have you never mentioned her before?"

"Don't like to talk about it. Guess the memory hurts too much." He turned back to Roger and raised his brows. "So, now you know why I seem disinterested in women—not that there's many women around here to be interested in."

There was an awkward silence, then Fauston snapped his fingers. "Almost forgot the reason I came to see you—the chronicle. The earl likes the new pages. He wants to see more."

Roger groaned, and Fauston went on. "He was surprised to learn about Egwulf being the hero of the battle for the bridge. Accused me of making that up, swore it was you."

Fauston looked amused, but Roger felt a bitter taste in his throat. Why did they always want to give him credit for things he hadn't done? "What did you tell him?"

"Told him 'twas you I had the story from."

"What did he say to that?"

"Said you're being too modest. Told me to change the pages."

"I won't change them," Roger said. "Egwulf deserves to be remembered for what he did. I won't take credit for it."

Fauston nodded.

Roger went on. "Was Ailith there?"

"She was."

"Did she say anything?"

"No. Right after the battle, though, she asked me if you were safe. I told her you were, and she seemed glad to hear it."

Roger threw the knife again. His mind was on other things and once again he threw it too hard, and once again the handle hit the target and the knife dropped harmlessly to the ground.

Fauston said, "Are you trying to kill this fellow Dirk or give him a headache?"

"I suppose you can do better?" Roger challenged.

In one smooth motion Fauston drew his dagger by the hilt and with a backhanded throw sent it sailing toward the target. It stuck in the crude figure where the neck would have been had it been a man.

Roger's eyes went wide. "Where did you learn to do that?"

"In the greenwood. I'll teach you, if you like."

"I would," Roger said. Then he said, "Have you ever used that move on a man?"

"Once or twice."

"What happened?"

Fauston shrugged. "I'm still here. They're not. Shall we get started?"

"Later," Roger said. "There's something I have to do first."

"What's that?"

Roger looked back in the direction of his tent and set his shoulders. "Pray."

Chapter 67

Roger prayed.

An act that had once come so easily to him, had once been second nature, had once been as much a part of him as breathing itself, was now difficult—more than difficult, it was one of the hardest things he'd ever had to do in his life. He had to swallow his doubts. He had to swallow his pride. He had to humble himself.

"Dear God," he began haltingly, "I'm sorry for everything I've done—to You and to others." He wanted to say he was sorry for doubting, but he didn't know if he could truthfully say that. "I'm not asking forgiveness for me, because I don't deserve forgiveness. Helvise does, though. Helvise hasn't sinned. Helvise has never doubted You. She doesn't deserve to die. She deserves a long and happy life. She has sacrificed enough in Your name. I don't care what You do with me, but please let her live. Please let her survive and have the life she deserves. Please, God. If you do, I'll . . ."

I'll what? he thought.

And then he knew the answer.

"I'll believe."

He spent the rest of the afternoon on his knees, praying in a similar vein, saying *Pater Nosters* and *Credos*, reciting Psalms and other Gospel verses that he knew by heart. Then the camp church bells rang Vespers, and it was time to go on duty at the ditch.

Outside their tents, the Death's Heads fell in, then joined the earl's spearmen. Payen inspected them, wearing a hauberk without a surcoat—a surcoat would stand out in the dark—Bug strutting happily behind him, as always. Payen came down the rows of men, looking them over, lean and hard as only men who have gone a long time without proper nutrition can be, ragged and bearded and dirty, but with their arms polished and weapons sharpened. Payen stopped in front of Roger.

"I understand there's a woman in your tent, Roger."

Roger's eyes darted to Bug, who looked away guiltily, then back to Payen; and when he spoke there was a dangerous edge in his voice. "Why, are you going to tell me I'm not allowed to do that?"

"Not at all," Payen drawled, "not at all. It's your tent, do as you will. Any number of men have whores staying with them."

Roger started forward, but a voice inside his head stopped him. *Don't—it's what he wants you to do. Assault a superior and you'll be hung.*

Payen regarded Roger with a mocking smile. "You were about to say something?"

Roger grit his teeth so hard they almost broke. He glared at Payen. Payen probably knew that the woman in his tent was gravely wounded. He probably even knew that the woman was the famous Lady in Green. Roger forced himself to calm down, even forced himself to smile. "I'll say it to you another time," he told Payen. Then he added, "I promise."

"You promise what?" Payen demanded.

He wanted Roger to add "my lord," but Roger refused to do it. He matched Payen's stare, daring him to make an issue of it.

Payen gave in. He snorted derisively, as though the lack of respect meant nothing, and stepped back. "All right," he ordered the centenars, "get this lot moving."

The next morning, when they returned from guarding the ditch and the men were dismissed, Roger looked in on Helvise. She was asleep. Her dark hair was matted and damp; beneath her tan, her skin had a sickly pallor. Hassan was standing over her, and Roger wondered if he had spent the night there. The tent smelled of vinegar and liniment.

"How is she?" Roger asked, removing his helmet.

The plump physician yawned and spread his hands. "There is no change."

"Is that a good sign?"

"It could be. We should know soon."

Roger said another silent prayer. Then he went to his old section tent and got Offa and Tatwine. "I need to go to Helvise's tent and get her things. Can I get you two to help?"

They agreed. Arcil and Ralph the Red came, too. Arcil had lost his doughy look and grown hard like the other men. He wasn't homesick any more. He'd decided that he was never going to make it home, so there was no use worrying about it.

At the German camp, the group encountered curious stares and whispers. Roger thought nothing of it—he had been stared at by the Germans when he came over here often enough before. He thought they'd have gotten used to seeing him by now. Helvise's green tent smelled mustier than ever. It smelled empty, as well—empty and cold, like death. The men collected Helvise's chest with her spare clothes, along with her blankets and bedding, her crossbow, quiver, pavise, and her bloodied green jerkin, which still lay crumpled at the foot of the tent pole. Roger folded the stiff jerkin over his arm, smoothing it.

"Don't look like naught's been taken," observed Ralph the Red as they finished up and started toward the tent entrance.

"Honest bunch, the Germans," Tatwine marveled. "Your Scots, now—they'd have stripped this tent bare and sold the lot of it by now."

"Sounds like Jews," Arcil cracked.

Patiently, as though speaking to a child, Tatwine said, "That's 'cause the Scots is the lost tribe of Israel."

Arcil made a face. "They are?"

"Didn't you know that?" Tatwine said. "Where you been, son? Why'd you think their noses—?"

He stopped. They had emerged from the tent to find themselves surrounded by members of the camp guard.

The guards faced them with leveled spears. One of Helvise's German doctors—the younger one—stood behind the guards, smiling. The guards' leader was a brawny fellow with a badly bent nose and missing front teeth who wore full mail and carried a shield to go with his drawn sword. He turned to the young doctor. "These are the ones?"

The doctor nodded vigorously. "Yes, yes."

To Roger and his men, the guard said, "You will come with us, please."

There was no possibility of a fight. Roger and his men were outnumbered and their arms were filled. They'd be killed before they could even draw their weapons. Roger tried to brazen it out as best he could. "Why should we?"

The guard gave him a little smile. "Because you are under arrest."

"On what charge?" Roger demanded.

"Kidnapping."

Chapter 68

Leopold V, archduke of Austria, sat at a trestle table in the rear of his black and yellow pavilion. His yellow surcoat bore the black double-headed eagle of his house. He held a dagger on the table, point down, and he spun the weapon lazily, swinging his middle finger against the guard. The father-and-son physicians—who were named Bernhold and Tymo—stood to one side of the duke, looking smug, still in their black robes and skullcaps. Bernhold's nose was bandaged and splinted, and there were dark circles under his eyes.

Roger's men—even Arcil—stood straight. The Germans had not taken away their weapons, but it was plain they were not free to go. Roger had no idea whether camp law permitted him and his men to be arrested like this, but the duke didn't seem to care.

The duke spun the dagger once more, then looked at Roger. "You and your men are accused of kidnapping Helvise, Margravina of Halsbach."

Roger said, "My lord, I—"

"Kidnapping *and* robbery," added Tymo, the younger physician, with a pleased look on his sharp-featured face. "They were looting the lady's tent when we caught them. That was the real reason for this crime, my lord—to get Lady Helvise's wealth."

"The poor woman is probably dead as we speak," added Bernhold, the father, solemnly. "God knows what they'll have done with her body."

Roger tried not to lose his temper. "The woman in question lies in my tent, gravely wounded," he told the duke. "I did not kidnap her. I took her away so that these boobs wouldn't kill her."

Bernhold and Tymo protested in unison, "My lord—!"

The duke silenced them with an upraised hand. He was in his mid-thirties, well built, with blond hair and beard and bright blue eyes. To Roger, he said, "You realize these men are my own physicians."

"I am aware of that, my lord."

"And you still say they would have killed her?"

"Lady Helvise had lost a great deal of blood from her wound. Close to a fatal amount, I'd wager." He indicated the physicians. "Their 'cure' was to bleed her further."

The archduke turned to the physicians, eyebrow raised.

"We needed to draw down her fever, my lord," the older man Bernhold explained.

"It was imperative," Tymo added.

Leopold nodded and turned back to Roger. "Is the lady under medical care now?"

"She is, my lord."

"One of your English physicians?"

Roger was tempted to lie, but he knew better. He would be found out. He straightened, "The physician is a native, my lord, Hassan al-Burq by name."

"An infidel?" Tymo cried, wide eyed.

"I believe he is a Muslim—"

Bernhold interrupted, "My lord duke, you must send men to rescue her! She is in grave danger! Every moment is of the—"

Once again, Leopold held up a hand for silence. Calmly he said to Roger, "Your men wear the Death's Head."

Roger didn't have his helmet, but Ralph and Tatwine had worn theirs. "They do, my lord."

"Are you leader of these Death's Heads?"

"I— yes, my lord."

"That means your lord is Geoffrey of Trent?"

"It is."

"Excellent fellow. He supports my cousin Montferrat for the kingship over that swine Lusignan. Tell me, Death's Head, do you trust this infidel doctor?"

Did he? "I do, my lord, as much as I trust any physician. He is reported to have done great things."

"Cured the duke of Berry, he did," Offa piped up.

The duke gave Offa a look, and Offa took a step back, chastened.

Roger said, "My lord, I swear to you, Lady Helvise is free to return to her tent as soon as she is able. She is not being held against her will—you can send someone to check on her if you wish."

Leopold spun the dagger again, watching light reflect off its polished blade. "The margravina has pledged fealty to me. I am responsible for her, and I take my responsibility toward my vassals seriously. You seem like a worthy fellow, Death's Head, so here's what I'll do—return the lady to the care of my physicians, and no charges will be placed against you."

Bernhold and Tymo puffed themselves, preening.

Roger's mouth was so dry it was hard to speak. "I am sorry, my lord, but I cannot accept your offer." Behind him he thought he heard Offa sigh in resignation. He went on. "The lady in question is my friend. I will not see these two kill her."

Did the shadow of a smile cross Leopold's thick lips? "I thought you might say that. Very well, then. The lady may remain where she is, and if she lives, there's no harm done."

"And if she dies?" Roger said.

Leopold spun the dagger again. "If she dies, I will go to Earl Geoffrey and have you brought up on a charge of murder."

Roger stiffened.

"You may go," the duke said.

Bernhold said, "My lord, you're making a mistake!"

The duke gave Bernhold an angry look. The physician cleared his throat and said no more.

"One thing, my lord." Roger said. He indicated his four companions. "These men—they're only here on my order. They had no part in this. I would hope they would be spared the charge of any crime."

Leopold nodded. "That seems reasonable."

"Thank you, my lord." Roger bowed and left the pavilion, along with his men.

Ironic, Roger thought—he had come all this way to fight Saracens; now he was betting his life on one.

Chapter 69

For two days, Helvise remained unconscious. Roger slept on a mat next to her bed. When Roger was on duty, Hassan's young Christian assistant or Hassan himself took his place. Roger bathed Helvise as Hassan had instructed; he changed her dressing and put Hassan's specially made salve on her wound. He thought the ragged gash in her side looked better, but he couldn't be sure. The swelling had gone down a bit, and the skin around the wound wasn't black the way it had been before. Most importantly, the wound didn't smell or leak pus.

On the third day, Roger and his men came back from drill, hot and sweating. Hassan heard them and emerged from the conical tent, wiping his hands on a towel.

"How is she?" Roger said, taking off his helmet and armored jack.

Hassan folded the towel—he had them made specially—and mopped his brow. "The same."

There was a water butt at the head of the company street, near Roger's tent. Roger ladled water into a tin cup that was attached to the butt and drank. The water was warm and brackish, and he made a point of not looking at it for fear of what he might see growing or swimming there, but it was water, and in this hot land that was all that mattered. Someone had etched a Death's Head onto the side of the cup. Roger offered the cup to Hassan, who shook his head politely.

"Tell me," Roger asked the physician. "Why do you help us? You're a Saracen."

"I do it for the money," Hassan replied. "I am a poor man— or I was. I could not gain preferment with the emirs of Damascus, or Homs, or Aleppo. I went to Tyre but was shunned there because of my faith. Through circumstances too tedious to recount, I found myself a refugee in your camp, and here I have been able to put my skills to use—at considerable profit to myself."

Tatwine, Slowfoot, and some of the other Death's Heads gathered around, drinking water and dropping their gear in the dust. Their initial hostility toward Hassan had gone; they had come to think of him as a harmless coot who happened to have a gift for curing sick people. They liked to tease him and debate him about the merits of Christianity and Islam, and about which of them was the real infidel. Hassan, for his part, was good natured about the teasing, and because he treated the men's minor illness and hurts when he was in their lines, they welcomed his appearances.

Roger went on. "It doesn't bother you, helping your enemies?"

"Medicine is about healing, not about whom you heal," Hassan said. "I believe one of your Greek physicians, Hippocrates, said much the same." The Death's Heads shrugged or shook their heads; aside from Roger, they had never heard of Hippocrates. Hassan continued. "This does not mean I am on your side—far from it. Each day I pray to Allah that you will lose. Indeed, I know for a certainty that you will."

There were snorts and hoots from the men.

Hassan raised a hand. "Go ahead, laugh. And while you laugh, I will tell you this. The True Faith will one day hold sway in your own lands."

The Death's Heads laughed even more.

Undeterred, Hassan went on. "And when that day comes, your countries will submit to the True Faith willingly and not through use of force."

The laughs grew louder still. "Never happen in England, Hassan, me lad," Tatwine said. "We'll die before we become Goat Fuckers. The Frenchies, now, you never know about them. Bunch o' queers, the Frenchies are. Goats probably look good to them." He nudged Ralph with his elbow and the two of them laughed.

Hassan gave Tatwine an admonitory shake of the head and returned to Roger's tent, Roger following. As they entered the tent, they stopped.

Helvise was sitting up in bed, wearing one of Roger's long shirts. She smiled at them.

"You're—you're awake," Roger marveled.

"Of course I'm awake," she said. "You and your friends were making so much racket out there, no one could sleep through it."

"How do you feel?" Hassan asked her, frowning.

"Thirsty. Sore. Alive." She looked around. "Where am I?"

"My tent," Roger said. He recounted how he had stolen her from the German doctors and brought her here.

"Who are you?" she asked Hassan, taking in his strange manner of dress.

Roger said, "This is Hassan al-Burq, the physician who saved you."

Hassan salaamed. "It gives me great pleasure to see you better, lady."

Helvise's eyes widened. "You are Muslim?"

"I have that honor," Hassan replied.

Helvise laughed weakly. "What a world."

Roger dropped to a knee and took her hand; he felt tears splashing his own hand. He was aware of men crowding the tent entrance. They had heard Helvise speaking and were peering in. Roger wiped his eyes, rose, and motioned them forward. "Well, don't just stand there gawking, come in."

The Death's Heads filed in, paying their respects to Helvise, knuckling their foreheads to her, some of them, because she was a real lady. Most of them had never been close to a real lady before, much less spoken to one. "Pleased to see you're doing good, my lady," they mumbled shyly. "Glad to see you better, my lady. " "We was worried about you, my lady." The last two from Tatwine and Offa, who had been part of the group that rescued her once before. Helvise reached out and took each man's hand or patted their arms in appreciation.

As they moved past her, Roger gave thanks to God, as he had promised he would. But in the back of his mind lingered a nagging question—*Do I believe? Do I really believe?*

The fever had broken, but Helvise was still weak from lack of food. On Hassan's orders, Roger fed her first broth and then black bread soaked in broth until it was on the point of disintegrating. The day after she woke up, Helvise climbed out of bed and with Roger's aid walked unsteadily around. She stepped outside the tent, blinking at the unaccustomed sunlight, not caring that she wore only the long shirt, which came below her knees.

"I never imagined this camp could look so beautiful," she said. She stared across hundreds of tents at the sea, breathing the salt air, oblivious to the soldiers around her.

Offa fussily brought her a handmade camp chair. Roger helped her into it and she sat for a while, eyes closed, letting the sun shine on her face. Then she got tired and went back inside the tent, where she drank cup after cup of water, then asked for some of Hassan's broth.

"Hassan should have been a cook," she said, spooning the broth down. "He could make a fortune. Do you have any more?"

"Steady," Roger said. "There's only so much food in camp, you know. Save some for everyone else."

Helvise laughed at that; it was good to see her laugh again. She sat on Roger's bed and regarded him with those liquid, almond-shaped eyes.

Roger grew serious. "You must go home to Germany now," he told her. "You can't stay here any longer. You've done your part."

That faraway look came over her and resignation filled her voice. "Yes, I suppose I must." She turned to him. "Will you come with me?"

Roger dropped his gaze. "I can't."

There was silence. "Because you don't really love me, or because of your vow?" Helvise said at last.

"It's not because of my vow, I don't care about that anymore." *It was a solemn vow,* he thought. *If I truly believed, I would care.* With his head, he motioned toward the tent opening. "It's because of them—the men. I'm their commander—I didn't ask to be, but I am. I can't desert them. I have to see this through with them. I owe them that."

He took her hand. "I'll come when Jerusalem is taken, I promise. It won't be long. The copper tower is finished. Acre will fall soon, then we march on the Holy City. With luck, I can be in Germany by Candlemas—Easter, anyway." He squeezed the hand. "Can you understand that?"

"I can," she said. "And I admire your loyalty to your men. That sounds like something Welf might have said." She took his hand and pressed her cheek against it. "Will you really come when Jerusalem is taken? Or are you just saying that to make me feel good?"

"I'll really come," Roger said.

She kissed his hand. "I couldn't bear it if I never saw you again."

"You will see me, I promise. And you must promise me something in return."

"What?"

"No more crossbow. No more taking your place in the siege lines. You must remain safely in camp until you're well enough to travel."

Helvise looked at her crossbow, pavise, and arrow quiver, stacked at one edge of the small tent along with her green jerkin, which had been cleaned and mended. Those items had been a large part of her life for the last year and a half. They had been her instruments of revenge, but revenge had been burned out of her. She was finished with warfare. Roger was right, she had done her part. She was finished being the Woman in Green, she was ready to simply be a woman again. "I promise," she said.

Roger turned her chin and kissed her. Roger had never tasted anything as delicious as her lips. He ran his hand through her hair; it was dirty and matted, but it felt like spun silk to him. He kept kissing her, drew her to him and ran his hand --

Behind them, a man cleared his throat.

Roger and Helvise whirled in surprise.

A figure stood in the open tent flap. Roger heard horses outside—smelled them. The figure was stocky, with a yellow surcoat.

Roger rose in surprise and bowed. "My lord."

Helvise tried to rise, as well, but Archduke Leopold motioned her to remain as she was. "I came to see if you were getting better," he told Helvise. He raised his eyebrows in amusement. "Apparently you are."

Roger felt himself blush. "My lord, I—"

The duke held up hand. "No need to say anything. I was young once." He chuckled. "Send someone to check, you said, so I sent myself."

Roger said, "How did you find me in this huge camp?"

The duke planted his fists on his hips. "I am the greatest hunter in Austria. I have tracked red stag, ibex, boar—surely I can find one Englishman." To Helvise, he said, "How are you feeling, Margravina?"

"Much better, lord duke."

"I am glad to hear it." In the tent's dim light his blue eyes twinkled as he added, "For the record—you are **not** being held here against your will?"

Helvise looked at Roger and smiled. "Far from it, my lord."

The duke smiled back. "Is there anything you need? Anything I can do for you?"

"Not that I can think of," Helvise said.

"You will let me know if there is? I am serious."

"I will, my lord."

"Good. Good." He turned to Roger. "I am glad I did not have to charge you with murder, Death's Head."

Roger grinned. "No gladder than I am, my lord." He hadn't really given any thought to that until now; his thoughts had

389

been consumed with Helvise. Roger realized that Hassan had not only saved Helvise's life, he had saved Roger's life, as well.

"I shall bid you two farewell," the duke said. He bowed. "Good day, Margravina."

"Goodbye, my lord, and thank you for coming. I am most honored."

"Not at all, not at all." The duke smiled at her. He clapped Roger on the shoulder and left the tent.

❖ ❖ ❖

Three days later, on the Sunday after Whitsun, Helvise felt able to get outside for an extended period. It was a fine day, warm but not hot, fluffy clouds above, the sea breeze keeping down the ever-present smell of death and decaying bodies. A few passersby recognized the Woman in Green—even though she was not wearing her jerkin and breeches—and there were whispers, shoves, pointed fingers. Helvise and Roger ate fruit-flavored sherbet and yoghurt on the Concourse. Then they went to the square at the Toron High Street to watch the Sunday acts. There were acrobats and dog trainers, musicians, and a juggler who kept ten rings going at once, bouncing them off the ground, his knee, and the bottom of his foot, to the applause of the hard-bitten soldiers who formed the majority of his audience.

Some bored young knights had decided to hold a tournament on the plain that afternoon. Not to be outdone, the common soldiers organized wrestling matches and footraces in the square. Roger and Helvise won a lot of money betting on Slowfoot in the races—the cheering crowd called him "B" because of the letter branded on his cheek—then lost most of it when Slowfoot was beaten by a Moor off one of the ships in the harbor. They were setting up a rematch—at a longer distance—when shouting erupted from the shore.

The shouting grew and grew until it was a roar. The racers

stopped. People left the square and hurried toward the beach. Roger and Helvise joined them to see what was happening, Roger holding Helvise around the waist so she wouldn't get knocked down, Helvise laughing with the excitement of it all. They reached the shore and made their way through the swelling crowd until Roger wedged them a spot from which they could see.

Sweeping into the bay before them was a fleet of large galleys, at least a dozen. The leading galley was painted bright red and on its red sail were the three lions of England. As the crowd watched, the red sail was taken in. The bank of red oars flashed and dipped in the water. A man poised on the stern rail and leaped onto one of the oars. Balancing himself, he tried to skip across the moving bank of oars. He made his first jump, but missed the second and fell into the water. Two more men followed him but fared no better. Then a huge man, dressed all in red, copper hair bright in the sun, leaped from the rail onto the oars. Hands on his hips, the big man skipped from one oar to the other down the length of the galley, nimble as a dancer. When he reached the bow, he jumped back onto the ship, whose crew greeted him with a wild burst of cheering. The cheering was taken up by the rest of the fleet, then by the mob on shore, thunderous ovations that could be heard in Saladin's tent in the hills.

Such was the arrival of King Richard at Acre.

Chapter 70

Richard Plantaganet, by the grace of God king of England, duke of Acquitaine, count of Poitou, and lord of a dozen lesser places, stood on the forecastle of his great red galley, sweating from his exertion of walking the oars and stunned by the sight before him. Under the bright Mediterranean sun, the crusader camp seemed to go on forever, the banners of every noble house in Christendom flying from its pennons and tent poles. Richard had no idea how many men were assembled in the camp, more than he had ever seen in one place—perhaps more than anyone had ever seen in one place. He heard the cheering from the shore but he paid it little mind. He was used to people cheering him.

Instinctively, Richard's mind turned to military matters. Foremost was finding supplies for such a host—food, water, forage for the animals. The siege didn't concern him so much; he knew how to conduct a siege—the castle of Taillebourg was considered to be impregnable, and he had taken it in three days. But what if he had to lead all these men in open battle? He'd only been in one big open battle—at Ballans, where he had faced his father—but there had only been a few thousand men on each side at Ballans. With an army this size, he would not be able to see from one end of the battle line to the other. How would he know what was happening? How would he give orders?

For a moment, his heart sank, then he recovered his spirits. After all, how difficult could the task be? Saladin did it, and if an Arab or Turk or whatever he was like Saladin did it, Richard would surely find it manageable. Fun, even.

In lands he had never tred, men knew of Richard. His father had been the mightiest king in Christendom; his mother was the Queen of Love. At 32, Richard was the real-life hero of a hundred romances. Tall and handsome and mighty of limb, with red-gold hair and beard, he was regarded as the perfect Christian knight, the greatest warrior since Charlemagne, maybe since Alexander.

Richard's mother, Eleanor of Acquitaine, had held sway on the European scene for over a half-century; was it not natural that as her star waned, her son's should be in the ascendant? This was Richard's hour, and he was aware of it. No enterprise of this magnitude would present itself again in his lifetime, perhaps for many lifetimes to come. He knew that the world was watching him, and he liked that. He embraced the coming challenge—he was eager for it. Here was a stage worthy of his talents. He almost had to laugh with the sheer exhilaration of it all.

A hand touched his arm. "Sire? Are you well?"

It was Alart, count of Vouzan. Alart was a handsome fellow who liked music and hunting and war, as Richard did. He wore his dark hair slicked back, and there was a gold ring in his right ear. He was a loyal vassal and an even more loyal friend. He was good with money, too, a talent Richard prized (though some hinted that Alart had Jewish blood because of this skill). Richard had been seasick on most of the voyage from Cyprus, just as he had been on the voyage from Marseilles, and Alart was afraid the sickness had undermined his health.

"I'm fine," Richard said. "I was just thinking." He drew in a hearty breath, heedless of the stomach-churning stench, and pointed to the high walls of Acre. "So that is the city about which we have heard so much. I am glad it has not yet fallen. It is not right that such a city should be taken without us present—eh, Alart?" He backhanded Alart's shoulder playfully.

"Indeed, sire," said the count, smiling. Around them, other men grinned.

The ship ran aground. Instead of waiting for the landing plank to be laid out, Richard vaulted over the side, landing thigh deep in the surf. He waded in to shore, where the high nobles of the camp waited for him along with a cheering throng of knights, men-at-arms, and common soldiers. Richard was followed ashore by Alart and Guy of Lusignan, Guy looking especially arrogant as he basked in the glow cast by his illustrious kinsman.

As Richard neared the shore, the welcoming nobles moved closer, with greasy haired Philip of France at their head. Richard could not read Philip's expression. This was going to be tricky, Richard thought. Richard had been betrothed to Philip's sister Alice for nearly twenty years. The marriage had never taken place, and while in Cyprus Richard had broken the engagement and married Berengaria, daughter of the King of Navarre. Richard knew Philip would be furious at this rejection of his sister, especially after such a long betrothal. Philip would have to be placated somehow.

Philip had been Richard's ally against Richard's father, King Henry, but Richard didn't like him much. The fellow was too severe; he never wanted to have fun. He was obsessed by duty and the fact that he was a king. Maybe that was because being king didn't come naturally to him, Richard thought as he trod through the cool surf. To Richard, being king was second nature, as though he could be nothing else. If his elder brother Henry hadn't had the decency to die, Richard would have had to wrest the crown from him by force.

Richard stepped onto the beach. Before Philip could say anything, Richard cried, "Philip!" and embraced the French monarch as though they were long-separated brothers.

Philip looked even more constipated than ever. He obviously didn't like Richard's huge arms around him—he didn't like to be touched—but when Richard at last let him go, he graciously introduced the English king to the other lords present. Richard already knew many of them, of course. Others, like the heavy lipped duke of Austria and the grim count of Montferrat, he did not, but that would change as the days went on.

It was hard to hear what anyone was saying because of all

the noise. That was good because it delayed the inevitable confrontation with Philip over Alice. Held back by spearmen, the knights and common soldiers were shouting, cheering, vying for a look at the great king of England. Men reached over the guards' shoulders to touch Richard, and he laughed and waved at them, pointing and calling out a few familiar faces by name. They would have picked him up and carried him on their shoulders were it possible.

At last some kind of order was restored amidst the pandemonium, and, escorted by Philip of France, Henry of Champagne, and Conrad of Montferrat, Richard marched off the beach, to his destiny.

Chapter 71

Eustace the page ran along the beach as fast as his lanky legs would carry him. Eustace had grown several inches since Christmas, and his body was still adjusting to its new size. He was filling out, too, now that there was plenty of food to eat. He had remained on the beach to watch the arrival of the old queen, Eleanor, to see if she was as beautiful as they said, even at her advanced age—she wasn't—but now he had to get to the earl's pavilion as quickly as possible.

He passed a party of bare-chested Genoese stevedores, sweating and cursing as they unloaded one of King Richard's ships. The sand sucked at his feet, as if trying to hold him back, but he kept on.

Eustace was thirteen. He had been a page since he was seven. Normally he would have had to wait another year to be made squire, but the exigencies of war had hastened his promotion, and he would be formally appointed next month. Battles loomed in the months ahead, and it was just possible that Eustace could earn his knighthood in one of them. A knight at fourteen, even fifteen—wouldn't that be something? Plus, being knighted on the battlefield meant you didn't have to go through that stupid ceremony, with the Vigil and all the Holy Water and praying.

Eustace careened to a stop to let a seemingly endless string of camels go by, trying to ignore their rancid stench. When the camels took too long, he slid under the trace reins of one. The creature spat at him and missed, and Eustace kept going.

Eustace was the fourth son of Baron Shortwood, a close friend to the earl of Trent. He had originally been destined for the Church—per custom, the baron's first son would inherit the title, the second would be a bishop, the third would be a soldier, and Eustace was slated for an abbey—but Eustace had protested so much that his father had relented. Eustace would rather be a common merchant than go into the Church. All that singing and praying. And reading—how could any sane man stand such a life? The Church was full of hypocrites, anyway—that's what his father said. Like that jumped-up villein Thomas Beckett, who went from being a nobody to Archbishop of Canterbury, and then immediately started making trouble for the man who had raised him so high. Beckett had gotten what he deserved.

Eustace liked hunting and training with weapons. And he was pretty certain that he was going to like girls. He was eager to see the hayward's daughter Gwynneth again, at his father's manor of Sandholme. All the more reason not to go into the Church—though it was true that some clerics hunted more than the nobles did and more than a few consorted with women. Hypocrites.

He left the beach and made his way through the mob on the Toron High Road. He maneuvered around a company of newly arrived spearmen and bumped into a water boy, spilling half the boy's load. He forced himself through a knot of crippled beggars, men who had lost limbs—or eyes, as one of them was blind—during the siege. They yelled at him, but he made an obscene gesture and started running again.

Before leaving England, Eustace had been betrothed to somebody named Sedilon, who was a younger daughter of the count of Necy, in France. Eustace wasn't sure what marriage entailed, exactly, though most of the men and women he encountered didn't seem to like it very much. Eustace's father had settled several rich manors on him at the betrothal, as well as the title of baron, and his bride would bring several more manors as dowry, enough for the two of them to live comfortably. But Eustace wanted more than a comfortable life. He was determined to make a name for himself, a name his descendants would be proud of. There were lands to conquer and battles to be won, and Eustace intended to have his share of both.

Eustace vaulted a bale of fodder that had fallen from a wagon and was blocking the road—laughing at the fun of it. He pushed past washerwomen, bakers, cooks. He reached the Toron and raced across the bridge—the guards knew him and let him go by. He pumped his legs up the hill—he was a good runner and could run all day, though as a noble he preferred riding. He dodged dukes and counts and bishops, squires and messengers and servants. He ran around men erecting pavilions for new arrivals, and around men taking down the pavilions of those who had died.

He reached the earl's tent and went in. The sides were rolled up part way in the heat. The earl was in the rear, conferring with the chronicler, Fauston. Eustace ran up to them. "My lord!" he blurted, heaving for breath.

The earl turned sharply, frowning at this interruption. "What the Devil?"

Eustace gulped air. "It's your wife, my lord."

"My wife? What about my wife?"

"She's here."

The earl went rigid. "What?"

"She came as escort to King Richard's wife, Berengaria. They're down on the beach while the old Queen Eleanor unloads her baggage. They'll be here in a few—"

For a moment Eustace thought the earl had been struck dumb, such was the look on his face. Then he gathered himself. "Clement! Matthew!" he yelled. "Come with me. You, too, Eustace." As the two servants joined them, the earl said to Eustace, "You've done good work, boy. I won't forget it."

"Thank you, my lord."

Eustace and the two servants struggled to keep pace with the earl as he hurried from the tent. Behind them, Fauston looked worried.

Chapter 72

"Hold still," Margaret said.

She dragged the flea comb through Ailith's heavy blonde hair. When she was finished, she dipped the comb in a cup of arrack, held it there for a second, then pulled it out, wiped dead fleas off the tines and drew it through another section of Ailith's hair. "Be still," she repeated. "You're squirming like a hooked fish."

Ailith beat her fingers on her knee in an impatient rhythm. "Which do you think looks better?" she asked Margaret. "The green dress or the blue one?"

The dresses were laid side by side on the bed. They were both made from silk, that wonderfully smooth fabric the crusaders had discovered in the East. "I don't know," Margaret said, wrestling to hold Ailith's head in place, "but if you don't keep still, you're going to go to the feast with a big bald spot because I'm going to pull out your hair."

"Seriously, Margaret," Ailith said, "which one? I have to look the best I've ever looked tonight. I think I like the blue one."

Margaret couldn't help but smile at her charge's youthful exhilaration. Since the famine, she and Ailith had grown quite fond of each other. "Well, miss, since you ask, I believe the green dress might go better. The blue sets off your eyes, but the green matches your necklace and earrings, what with the gold and them red stones."

Ailith considered, then nodded. "You're right, as always." She clapped her hands in excitement. "Oh, Margaret, think of it—I'm going to meet King Richard. *King Richard.* This is going to be the best—"

At that moment, the tent flap was thrust aside and Earl

Geoffrey swept in, followed by his page Eustace and two servants.

"Take it down," Geoffrey said, waving an arm around the tent. "All of it. Quickly."

Ailith rose. "Geoffrey, what—"

"You have to leave," Geoffrey told her. There was a hard edge to both his voice and his look that she had never experienced before.

"Leave? What do you mean?"

"I mean leave. Get out. Now."

Ailith stood still, not comprehending. "What—"

"My wife is here. You need to get out of this tent and off the Toron—right now." Around them, the sides of the tent were coming down. "Make sure no trace of it remains," Geoffrey told Eustace and the servants.

Ailith started to say something, but Geoffrey spoke first. "Did you hear me? You have to go."

"Go where? I don't—"

"Anywhere, I don't care. Get your things and get out."

He wasn't joking. "But—I thought you loved me?"

"I do." He sighed, looking harried. "But Bonjute controls most of my wealth. She can make life very difficult for me if she wants to. Now, please, hurry."

Tears rolled down Ailith's cheeks. Around her the tent was coming down, her life was coming down. She heard laughter from some of the watchers outside.

Geoffrey tried to move her along. "You can keep the jewels," he said. When that produced no result, he untied the purse from his belt. "Take this, as well. Just get—"

Ailith flung the purse at Geoffrey. He tried to duck but he wasn't quick enough, and the heavy purse hit him flush on the cheekbone. "Ow!"

Ailith's tears had become tears of rage. "Is that what you think I am? Someone whose affections can be bought with a bag of gold?"

"Ailith, I swear—"

She snatched the jewels from the bed and hurled them at him as well. The gold necklace bounced off his chest, and he blocked the ruby earrings with his forearms, but a finger ring found its mark and left a cut on his forehead. "I wouldn't take your jewels if I was starving in the street," she swore. "Mary's milk, what a fool I've been."

Eustace and the servants had stopped. They were watching. So was a growing crowd outside, peering into what was left of the tent. Ailith began stuffing personal items into a sack, Margaret helping her and casting angry looks at the earl.

Geoffrey rubbed his cheek and moved hesitantly closer. A trickle of blood ran from the cut on his forehead. "Ailith, I care for you, I really do. Bonjute won't be here long. I'll send for you as soon as I can."

Ailith stopped what she was doing. She sniffed. "Really?"

"Yes," Geoffrey said.

Ailith's voice softened. "You promise?"

"I promise."

She smiled hesitantly and moved toward him. He reached to embrace her, and as he did, she drew back her hand and hit his face with such a resounding slap that it seemed to echo across the Toron. "You can send for me until Judgment Day, you miserable bastard, but I'll not come. I'd rather be with the Saracens."

She grabbed the sack and stalked out of the tent, followed by Margaret.

There had been a surprised roar outside when Ailith slapped the earl. Now the watchers scrambled aside as Ailith left, lest they incur her wrath as well. Fauston pushed some men out of the way and approached her. "Ailith," he said, taking her shoulders and bending to look into her face, "are you all right?"

Her chest heaved, her wet cheeks were red. "What do you think?"

"Come, I'll find you a place to stay."

"That won't be necessary." She drew herself up. "I know where to go."

Chapter 73

"I'll go to Roger," Ailith went on.

Fauston grimaced. "I don't think that's a good idea."

"Of course it's a good idea," Ailith said. "It's what I should have done all along."

Fauston said, "But Roger has—"

A hand tugged Fauston's sleeve. *Bloody Eustace.*

"The earl wants you," Eustace said.

Fauston said, "I'll be there in a moment. I'm—"

"Now," Eustace insisted. "He's on his way to meet the king."

Ailith said, "Go ahead, Fauston. I'll be all right."

"But there's something I have to—"

Eustace pulled Fauston by the arm. "Hurry. It's my hide if you're late."

Fauston tried to shout to Ailith, but she and Margaret were already disappearing into the hubbub of the Toron.

Ailith and Margaret made their way through the crowd. Ailith knew people were staring at her—her expulsion by Geoffrey had created quite a scene—but she tried to act like the attention didn't bother her. She said, "I'm sorry this had to happen, Margaret, for your sake. Where will you go now?"

Like Ailith, the big woman had a sack of belongings slung over her shoulder. "Me, I'll go back with the washerwomen. " 'Twere good enough for me before, 'tis good enough for me now. I'll stay with you till you get to Roger's tent, though. Just to see you're all right."

Ailith smiled. "Thank you, Margaret, you're a good—"

"Lady Ailith!"

A lean courtier caught up with them, slightly out of breath from running and dodging the crowd. The man had a trim beard and wore yellow silk spotted with old grease stains. He bowed low to Ailith, waving his right hand with a practiced flourish. "My dear Lady Ailith, his excellency Guy of Dampierre, constable of Champagne, sends felicitations. He has asked me to express his regrets over your present circumstances and to offer you the hospitality of his tent."

Before Ailith could reply, a squire appeared, hair fuzzing his cheeks and chin. He stepped in front of the first man, cutting him out, and bowed with a flashing smile. "My lady, your good friend Peter of Courtenay finds himself overcome with sorrow at your misfortune. Knowing your need for shelter, he offers you the sanctuary of his pavilion."

No sooner had the squire finished than a third man appeared, a crimson-clad clerk, bowing haughtily. "Garin Fitz-Gerold, baron of the English Exchequer, sends his compliments, Lady Ailith, and he wonders if you would do him the great honor of staying in his pavilion during this time of unpleasantness. Lord Garin's pavilion is one of the finest on the Toron, and he vouchsafes that it will provide your every imaginable—"

Ailith had heard enough. " 'Great honor!' That's a polite way of saying he intends for me to sleep with him, isn't it?"

The haughty clerk was taken by surprise. "No, of course—"

"The same with your master—" Ailith pointed to the first messenger, then the second—"and yours."

Peter of Courtenay's fuzzy cheeked squire stepped back in the face of her anger. The man in yellow silk attempted to remain unruffled. "My lady, I assure you—"

"Tell your masters they can go to hell, and they can take you with them. Now get away from me—all of you!"

The clerk in crimson got his back up at that. "See here, you. I'm not used to being addressed—"

"Now!" She advanced on him and he scurried backwards. If

she'd had a whip she would have taken it to him; she would have taken it to all of them.

The courtiers moved away, stunned, looking at one another in disbelief. There were still more courtiers on the way, and these now stopped, seeing what had happened with the first group. *My God,* Ailith thought, *it's like I'm being auctioned off.*

Ailith resisted the urge to wipe her eyes. She didn't want the courtiers, or the passersby who had stopped to watch, to see her cry. Peter of Courtenay, Guy of Dampierre—she knew these men. They had always been polite to her, they had treated her like a lady; but the truth was, she realized bitterly, they considered her a whore. A high-priced whore. This was the lowest moment of her life.

She turned to Margaret. "I feel unclean. Everyone thinks I'm whore. But I'm not. Am I?"

Margaret put her free arm around Ailith's shoulder. "You're no whore. You're a woman took in by a married man. Ain't the first time it's happened, 'twon't be the last. Let's get away from here. I never did fancy this place."

They went down the hill and crossed the bridge that led off the Toron. Ailith realized she was crossing the bridge for the last time and she turned around. The Toron had been her home for so long, now it was to be forgotten. Life went on up there, but she would no longer be part of it. *Good riddance,* she thought, and she turned away.

"I wanted to go to Roger all along," she told Margaret as they walked. "The only reason I didn't was because I was afraid Geoffrey would have him killed, but that won't happen now. Geoffrey threw me out—he no longer has any right to care where I go. Really, this is the best thing that could have happened to me."

Margaret was expressionless. "If you say so, ma'am."

"Please, don't call me 'ma'am.' I'm no better than you—I never was. My name is Ailith."

Margaret hesitated; routine was hard to break. "All right—

Ailith."

Ailith slipped her arm through that of the bigger woman and smiled, sniffing and wiping her nose on the sleeve of her free arm.

The two women reached the earl of Trent's infantry lines. The neat rows of tents looked picturesque from a distance, but up close they were falling apart, a motley of patches and rotting fabric. Aside from the guards, the camp was deserted; the men must be on duty somewhere. Ailith and Margaret approached Roger's tent. The tent flap was open. This felt good, Ailith thought, it felt right. It felt like coming home. "Come on," she told Margaret, "we'll wait for him to come back," and she went in.

She stopped, Margaret bumping into her from behind. A dark-haired woman in a green dress sat at a crude table, staring at them in surprise. The woman was a bit shorter than Ailith, and pretty, with exotic, almond-shaped eyes. Her deep tan indicated that she had been in the Holy Land for some time, though the pallor beneath it made it look like she was recovering from illness. In her hand was a quill with which she had been forming letters on a sheet of parchment. She raised her eyebrows quizzically. "Can I help you?" She spoke with a German accent.

"I—" Ailith didn't know what to say. She frowned, hoping against hope she had made some kind of mistake. "Is this Roger's tent?"

"Yes," said the woman pleasantly, "it is." She rose. "I am Helvise, Margravina of Halsbach."

The woman waited for Ailith to introduce herself, but Ailith just said, "Oh," in a small voice. Not knowing what else to do, she added, "I—I thought Roger was here by himself."

The woman lowered her eyes and blushed modestly, but also with pride, Ailith thought. "No." Quickly she added, "He will be back at dusk. You and your friend are welcome to stay. We have bread and cheese and some excellent Rhenish wine."

"No. No, thank you. We'll be going. I'm sorry to have

disturbed you." Ailith turned and started from the tent.

Puzzled, the woman said, "Shall I tell him you called . . ?"

Again she waited for Ailith's name, and again Ailith declined to give it. "No, that won't be necessary. Good bye." Ailith hurried from the tent, Margaret beside her.

Outside in the company street, Ailith halted, unable to go any further. She felt hollow inside. She didn't know if her legs would support her. Margaret put an arm around her. "You all right, ma'am—Ailith?"

Ailith swallowed and tried to make a joke. "I'm starting to think I should have held onto those jewels." Then she broke down, eyes welling. "Oh, Margaret, what will I do? I never dreamed Roger would . . ."

She started crying and Margaret folded her into her big arms. "You thought he'd wait for you?" Her tone was kindly, her voice tinged with experience.

"Yes. I mean, I don't know. I . . ." Ailith's voice tailed off again and she stepped back, wiping her eyes "Now what?"

"You can always come with me," Margaret said. She cocked her head. "Not afraid o' hard work, are you?"

Ailith sniffed. "Hard work? Hard work and bad luck are all I've ever known. Let's go."

The two women headed down the street, toward the washerwomen's camp.

Chapter 74

Geoffrey had hoped to be away from his pavilion, attending the king, before Bonjute got there, but that was not to be. Only moments, it seemed, after Ailith had departed the Toron, Bonjute arrived in a swirl of self-importance, catching Geoffrey just as he was leaving.

"Bonjute!" he exclaimed, trying to act overjoyed. "My dear, what a wonderful surprise!" He took her shoulders and kissed her cool cheeks. "I had no idea you were coming."

Bonjute stepped back and looked around distastefully. As always, she had not a hair out of place and her clothes were clean and unwrinkled. Geoffrey wondered how she did it. Her eyes touched on the open spot of ground where Ailith's tent had stood, lingered there for a second, then moved on. "Where is your whore?" she said.

Geoffrey gave what he hoped was a puzzled frown. "My dear?"

"Don't play innocent with me," Bonjute said. "You've had a whore with you on every campaign you've undertaken since we were married. You have whores stashed at hunting lodges all over England. And don't think I don't know about the Prioress of Mt. Carmel, either."

Geoffrey spread his hands. "The prioress! My dear, Prioress Cecilia is a lady of the utmost probity. You can't possibly think — "

"You're the one who doesn't think. Were your brains anywhere but between your legs, you'd be justiciar of England by now. Instead, I have to play nursemaid to that harridan Eleanor and Richard's so-called wife, Berengaria, so that you might one day get your chance."

Geoffrey cleared his throat and stood straighter. "Even if

what you say about me were true, you've no doubt observed that there's not many women here."

"If there was only one, you'd find her," Bonjute snorted. She looked around again. "Well, whoever she was, she's gone now. Lucky for you. And for her—saves me the trouble of having her flogged." She peered at his cheek, red where he had been slapped and swelling where the purse hit it, and at the small cut on his forehead. "What happened to your face?"

"We *are* in a war, my dear. A minor skirmish, nothing serious."

"No doubt," she observed sourly. She pushed past him, into the tent. "I'm in need of refreshment. Being closeted with Eleanor for five months will do that to you. She might have been the most beautiful woman in Christendom once, but if she was as much of a pain in the ass then as she is now, it's a wonder any man could put up with her. King Henry had the right idea—throw the bitch in prison. Well, are you going to stand there staring, or are you going to come inside and tell me how happy you are to see me?"

Chapter 75

They went into the tent's private quarters, where Bonjute took a long draught of wine. "Can't you afford better wine? This tastes like donkey piss."

Geoffrey cleared his throat. "I'd like to stay with you, my dear, but I must wait upon the king."

"That's been cancelled," Bonjute said breezily. "Richard's not feeling well and wishes to rest before the feast tonight. If you really wanted to see him so much, you should have been on the beach waiting for him like everyone else."

"I—"

"You never miss a chance to make things worse for yourself, Geoffrey." Bonjute quaffed another drink and looked around the tent. "God in Heaven, this place is a pig sty. And it stinks! You can't expect me to stay here." She raised her voice for the earl's steward. "Richalm!"

"Richalm is dead," Geoffrey said. "A man called Manier is in charge of the—"

"I don't care what he's called. Get him in here and get this place cleaned up."

Before Geoffrey could reply, there was a rustle at the tent entrance. Eustace was there with Fauston.

Geoffrey said, "Ah, Fauston. Turns out I don't—"

"Who is this?" Bonjute demanded. She eyed Fauston up and down appraisingly. Fauston returned her gaze. They stared at each other for a moment, then Bonjute turned and smiled at the page. "Hello, Eustace."

Eustace bowed. "My lady." He wasn't sure why Bonjute liked him, but he was glad she did.

To Bonjute, Geoffrey said, "This is Fauston, my chronicler."

Bonjute turned to Geoffrey in surprise. "You finally did something I told you? I'm shocked." She looked back at Fauston. "And how is the chronicle progressing?"

"It goes well," Geoffrey said before Fauston could reply.

To Fauston, Bonjute said, "What's wrong with you? Cat got your tongue?"

Fauston began, "My lady—"

But Bonjute was already talking to the earl again. "Are you keeping your deeds in the forefront of it like I told you?"

"Yes, dear," Geoffrey lied.

Having learned that, she no longer seemed interested in the chronicle, and at a look from Geoffrey, Eustace and Fauston discreetly withdrew. Bonjute poured more wine. "I see you no longer have that dreary priest Stephen."

"You shouldn't speak that way about Stephen. He was a very holy man."

"Bah, the old fool would have gone around in sackcloth and a hair shirt if you'd let him. Hardly suitable for a lord of your rank."

Geoffrey, who had liked Stephen, said nothing.

"Who is your chaplain now?" Bonjute asked.

"I don't have one. All the priests I brought from England are dead. I haven't had time to look for another."

"Haven't had the inclination is more likely. Well, I may be able to help you there."

Geoffrey tried to sound polite. "Indeed?"

"Yes, a fellow who came out with us from England. He was a bishop's aide before he caught the crusading fever." He'd also given Bonjute the distinct impression that he wouldn't have minded sleeping with her, but she had laughed at that. He was too far below her station. Now if King Richard wanted to get between her legs . . . but, alas, that could never happen.

She went on. "He makes a good show, the kind of chaplain a justiciar of England needs. I'll introduce you at the feast tonight if you're interested."

"Of course," Geoffrey said, "that would be wonderful."

411

Bonjute drank more wine and sighed, "I suppose you have to have sex with me."

Geoffrey said, "I—"

She drew her robe over her head. "Stop blubbering and get to work. I have a lot to do."

Chapter 76

That evening, the camp magnates assembled in Balian of Ibelin's tent for the feast to celebrate King Richard's arrival. Richard had brought some of the most famous troubadours in Christendom to the Holy land with him—Pere Vidal, Eble of Ussel, Peirol—and he had sent them ahead to entertain the guests. They strolled about the huge tent, the sound of singing and lute music a counterpoint to the buzz of conversation.

"What the Devil's taking him so long?" said Henry of Champagne. "Maybe he's not coming," said hulking James of Avesnes. "Maybe he's sick, like everyone else who comes to this place."

"He'll come," said Henry the Lion. He downed a cup of wine, wiped the spilled liquid off his beard, and wagged his chin toward the head table, where sat Philip of France, fingertips slowly tapping the table top. "He's making Philip wait, that's all."

"Doing a good job of it, I'd say," James observed.

One-eyed Henry, who, unlike the well-dressed men and women around him, wore a plain surcoat in need of repair, was philosophical. "Philip's like me—he hates to waste time. On the other hand, if we must waste time, this is damned fine wine to do it with." He beckoned a servant for more drink.

Balian, who as usual looked more like an Arab potentate than a Christian, said, "I don't understand why Richard erected his pavilion down below, with the men of Gascony and Poitou. We held a prime space for him here on the Toron for over a year, and he doesn't use it."

"Perhaps he feels more comfortable among his own countrymen," offered the young count of Champagne.

James of Avesnes frowned. "His countrymen? Thought that

was the English?"

Heads turned to Geoffrey of Trent, whose mind had been on other matters. Bestirring himself, Geoffrey said, "Richard has no connection to England, not really. He was born there but left as a babe. He's spent his entire life in Aquitaine, only returned to England for his coronation. Even then, he only stayed long enough to raise taxes. Far as I know, he doesn't speak a word of English."

Geoffrey didn't know why he had added that last part. There were any number of English barons—and their wives—who did not know the native language. Geoffrey had learned it as a boy, playing with the servants' children on his father's estates, but he hadn't used it in a long time—not until he met Ailith. Ailith . . .

Balian said, "I didn't see you on the beach today, Geoffrey. Have you spoken to Richard yet?"

"Haven't had the chance," Geoffrey replied. "My wife's here. I've been busy getting her settled in."

That remark occasioned knowing looks among the nobles. By now, everyone on the Toron was aware how—and why—Geoffrey had hastily evicted his mistress from her quarters. Geoffrey didn't care, not any more. Bonjute had been right, he'd always had a weakness for women. Ailith had been different, though. Geoffrey had felt for Ailith what he had never felt for another woman. Love? He didn't know; he wasn't sure what love was. He only knew that he wanted Ailith with him. After the crusade was over and they returned to England, he had hoped to establish her on a small manor of her own. He even had the estate picked out—Plaistow, not far from his seat at Badford Castle. He could visit her there when he was supposed to be hunting. When she bore him children, as she inevitably would, they would be taken care of. The boys would be knights with small freeholdings, the girls would go to a good priory.

Now it seemed that future was not to be. Lesser lords kept women openly. Geoffrey did not, for fear of his wife. Had he been younger, he might have risked all for Ailith, but now . . .

He sighed. For all his lands and power, for all his titles and feats on the field of battle, he was a weak man, made even weaker by feeling sorry for himself the way he did now. He despised himself at these moments. Sometimes he wished he been born a peasant.

There was a trumpet blast, and Henry the Lion nudged Geoffrey's ribs, taking him out of his reverie. "Richard's here."

Chapter 77

A red-liveried herald strode into the pavilion. "The king of England!" he cried.

"O-o-hs" and "A-h-hs" erupted and, as the excited crowd surged forward, Richard entered the tent. He gestured the audience for quiet and flashed a bright grin. " 'England,' " he announced. "That's a French word, meaning 'cold and always raining.' "

The pavilion erupted with laughter. Laughing with them, Richard moved forward, with his new queen, Berengaria, on his arm. Berengaria looked somewhat bewildered, her eyes large, as though she hadn't been prepared for what she had gotten herself into by marrying the most famous man in Christendom.

"Nice bit of fluff," James of Avesnes remarked.

"She's beautiful," the count of Champagne corrected.

"Has he got her with child yet?" said Balian.

Rotrou, count of Perche, stood next to Balian. Rotou was reckoned an old man at 47, but he still had an eye for the ladies. "I heard he hasn't even tried. She followed him across the Med for two months before he finally got around to marrying her, and they've hardly spoken a word since. They even came here on separate ships."

Balian frowned. "He needs to produce an heir."

Rotrou said, "If he doesn't want to get her with child, I'll be happy to do the job. God knows I could do with a bit of —"

"S-h-h-h!" Geoffrey hissed, because the couple was drawing near.

Richard and Berengaria moved past them. The candlelight burnished Richard's red-gold hair and beard; his white teeth flashed as he smiled. Behind Richard came the Queen Mother,

Eleanor of Acquitaine—the legend, straight backed and regal even though she was past eighty. Eleanor had been to the Holy Land almost a half-century earlier with her first husband, King Louis VI of France, when she was said to have had an affair with her uncle Raymond of Antioch and to have dressed like an Amazon and ridden bare breasted through Asia Minor. Geoffrey didn't know about the affair—Eleanor was supposed to have had affairs with just about every famous man in Christendom, and not a few of their wives—but he knew what the torrid Mediterranean sun could do to pale skin and he doubted the part about the bare breasts. If she had done it, it was like as not with painful results.

It was Eleanor who had arranged her son's match with Berengaria. The old queen was attended by Bonjute and three other English noblewomen. They were followed by Richard's coolly beautiful sister, Joanna, queen of Sicily, and a dark-eyed Greek princess named Anna, a hostage from the emperor of Cyprus. After them swaggered Guy of Lusignan, still sporting his gold circlet.

Richard was mobbed by men and women eager to touch him, to take his hand. He laughed in delight, pausing with a kind word for all who sought his attention.

At last he reached the head table, where stood King Philip—impatient, as always. "I apologize for being late," Richard told Philip and the rest of the guests at the high table. "I've been feeling ill." He went on, speaking to Philip. "I trust you enjoyed my gift?" On his arrival, Richard had sent presents to the great barons of the camp. His gift to Philip had been a magnificent white charger that he had purchased in Cyprus. It had taken him a month to find the perfect gift.

"It is the most beautiful animal I have ever seen," Philip said truthfully. *I shall ride him across the lands I take from you.* Graciously, he bowed to Berengaria and added, "Nearly as beautiful as your bride."

Berengaria blushed and Richard said, "Thank you, brother, truly." He edged close to Philip, so that Berengaria could not hear, and in a contrite voice, added, "I pray there are no ill feelings because of your sister."

Philip waved the idea away, as though it were not worth another thought. "These things happen. It is politics. You wish to protect Acquitaine's southern border, so you marry the king of Navarre's daughter. It makes perfect sense. I might only have asked that you had not kept Alice waiting so many years. Thirty-two is rather late for a man to get married, after all."

Richard frowned. "What are you trying to say?"

"Nothing. I am sure you had good reason for delaying marriage as long as you did. I was married at fifteen, with three children to show for it, so who's to say you weren't right? Now, of course, I must decide what to do about Alice. Perhaps a match with your bother John?"

"A good idea," Richard admitted, "but Mother would never hear of it."

"Ah, yes," Philip said, and the corners of his mouth twitched upward, "Mother."

Richard and Berengaria took seats at Philip's right hand and the feast began. Richard held out his cup for wine and looked up in surprise when he saw who was pouring. He had expected to see his friend Alart of Vouzan, but another had taken his place. "What are you doing, sir?"

The man bowed. "My duty, your majesty. As earl of Trent, I am the king of England's hereditary cupbearer."

"Ah, yes," Richard said, relaxing. "I seem to recall someone telling me that."

Geoffrey went on. "This is the first opportunity I've had of filling my office, what with the haste of your coronation and departure from England and my illness at the time."

Trent had supposedly missed the coronation because he had been sick abed. Richard's informants later reported that the earl had been "sick abed" with a certain abbess. Richard swirled the wine in his jeweled cup and smiled at Geoffrey lazily. "By the way, I understand you called me a fool."

Chapter 78

The pavilion went quiet. All eyes were on Geoffrey.

Geoffrey was in dangerous territory (he could visualize Bonjute rolling her eyes in exasperation). Richard was known to be a vengeful man, and if Geoffrey said the wrong thing now it could mean his title, maybe even his head. Too many people had heard him call Richard a fool for him to try to lie his way out of it. Better to tell the truth and let things fall where they may. Sweat trickled from his hair and down the back of his neck as he set the ewer of wine on the table and searched for the appropriate words.

"I did say it, sire."

Richard's face hardened, and Geoffrey went on. "I meant it in terms of your tactics last winter. Had you and your men been here, we had taken this city long since, and many good Christian souls would have been delayed their entrance to Heaven."

Geoffrey expected Richard to rise and strike him, or maybe to signal the guards and have him hauled away. As it was, Richard remained calm. He even smiled at length, though the smile contained little warmth. He spoke loud enough for everyone in the pavilion to hear. "You do not understand, Lord Geoffrey. Did I want to be here? Of course I did, but my pilgrimage has been dogged by obstacles and ill will. In Sicily, they murdered our men and threw their bodies in the privies. Could I let such insults go unanswered? Of course not, honor would not permit it. So I conquered Sicily. In Cyprus, the emperor imprisoned our sailors and threatened his queen, my own sister, Joanna. Could I permit such a thing? No. So I conquered Cyprus. The governor of Crete insulted me, as well. By all rights I should have conquered Crete, but I was in such haste to reach the Holy Land that I let the governor's remarks pass."

Richard rose. "So, you see, you spoke in ignorance of the true situation."

Richard was offering Geoffrey a way out, and Geoffrey took it. He felt cowardly for doing so, but for all he knew, what Richard said could be true. "You have my apology, sire."

"Accepted," Richard said. Then he broke out a big grin. "Damn me, but I like a man who speaks his mind, though." He embraced Geoffrey, pounding Geoffrey on the back with his hand.

The tension in the tent was released. Geoffrey saw Bonjute sag with relief. In the pavilion, conversation resumed, with laughter and calls for drink.

Richard let go of Geoffrey's shoulder and leaned toward Geoffrey's ear. "As for being my cup bearer, the count of Vouzan has performed that office these many years. I am comfortable with his presence and will not require yours— except on state occasions when we are back in England." He cast the dark-haired Alart an amused look. "Assuming I ever go back to England."

Alart smiled.

"As my lord wishes," Geoffrey said, bowing. He had never liked the office of cupbearer anyway. It was supposed to be a great honor, but it made him feel like a servant. Bonjute would likely complain about this abdication of his office, rolling her eyes till they fell out of her head. If she liked it so much, let *her* pour wine for Richard.

The feast went on, course after course of meats and stews and vegetables, most of it brought at no little expense from Tyre. The din inside the tent was excessive, the quantity of wine consumed, stupendous. The air was thick with the cloying smell of incense. Troubadours, jugglers, and jesters vied for attention.

"Thank God I'm only staying here a few days," Bonjute told her husband as he tore apart a leg of mutton and handed her a piece. "This camp is the vilest place I've ever seen in my life."

"That's one thing we can agree on, anyway," Geoffrey said. He wiped the mutton grease from his hands onto the back of a passing dog.

Bonjute went on. "What is the army doing *here*, anyway? What does any of this have to do with Jerusalem?"

"A lot of us have asked the same question."

"You should have done more than ask, if you want my opinion."

"Yes, my dear."

Bonjute put down the mutton, sucked grease from her fingers and beckoned to someone in the crowd. A man came forward. He was about average height with thinning blond hair. His skin hung on him as though he had lost a lot of weight in a short period of time. His scarlet robe was of the latest cut, though, far more stylish than Geoffrey's own, and he carried himself with an air of haughtiness.

"This is the man I was telling you about," Bonjute said. "I believe he would make you a good chaplain."

The man bowed. For a priest, he didn't have much of a tonsure. "My lord earl."

"What is your name?" Geoffrey asked him.

"I am called Otho, my lord. Otho of Malcherce."

Chapter 79

When the meal was over, Richard borrowed a lute from his good friend, the troubador Pere Vidal. He stood before the head table, facing his wife, and sang a song of his own composing. The song was an *aubade*, a dawn song sung by a lover as he departs for the wars. Richard's great-grandfather, William, the bloodthirsty ninth duke of Acquitaine, was generally acknowledged as the first troubador, and Richard had inherited that worthy's musical talents. Richard was a noted troubador in his own right; indeed, he was regarded as the finest singer in Europe. The song he sang now was slow and sad and sweet, and Richard deftly picked the lute strings to accompany his rich, mellow voice. As the song ended and the final notes of the lute died out, Richard moved behind the table, bent and kissed a surprised Berengaria on the lips. This act elicited rapturous sighs from the women in the audience (save for Bonjute, who of course rolled her eyes) and rousing applause from the men—led by Philip, who stood, clapping his hands in admiration.

At this point, the women left the pavilion for Conrad's tent, where Conrad's young wife, Isabelle, was hosting a party in honor of Berengaria and Queen Eleanor. The musicians and other entertainers accompanied the women. The nobles remained in Balian's pavilion for a council of war.

"Now to business," Richard said when the women were gone. "The first question we must decide is, who is to command the army? I've some thoughts on that, if you'll allow me. There are two kings in camp. I am the older, but my cousin Philip has been king longer. So I say the two of us should share command." He turned to Philip, "Does that suit you, cousin?"

Philip nodded graciously. What choice did he have? The

room roared approval. Richard beckoned Philip to stand. He raised the shorter man's hand and the two of them basked in the applause. Richard's face was flushed and sheened with sweat. He wiped his brow with his free hand.

When the noise died down, it was Philip's turn to speak. "Now that we have settled the matter of command, we must plan an immediate attack on the city. Every day we spend in this camp sends at least a hundred more good men to their graves. With a new army just arrived, the camp will be more overcrowded than ever." To Richard, he said, "Do you not agree, England?"

Richard raised a forefinger. "I think we should hold off a short while. The rest of my army has not yet arrived, nor have my new catapults."

"We have the Invincible Tower," Philip pointed out.

Richard nodded. "I inspected your copper tower earlier. Very impressive—the best I've ever seen, in fact. But I've brought the latest model catapult with me—trebuchets, they're called. These mangonels we have now can batter Acre's walls till Judgment Day and not make an impression, my trebuchets will knock those walls down. Together with the Invincible Tower, they will guarantee victory."

Heads nodded, there was a murmur of assent. Philip sensed he was losing the argument. He and Richard might be co-commanders, but Richard was the greatest warrior in Christendom, maybe in the history of Christendom. The nobles would do what Richard advised. Philip said, "We have waited here enough. We—"

Richard put up a hand and smiled. "Trust me, France. I know how to take a city. I daresay I've taken more of them than any man in this room. I will take Acre, as well—or I should say, *we* will take it. We just need a little more time."

Philip sighed in frustration. *A little more time.* He hadn't wanted to come here in the first place, but the Pope had made him. Now Philip's friend and mentor, the count of Flanders, was dead. Philip needed to arrange for the Flemish succession, but he couldn't do that from Acre. To make things more irritating, Flanders' life might have been saved, but the one man who could have done it, a Muslim doctor named Hassan something or other, had been forced to flee for his life by Christian physicians who had accused him of witchcraft. According to Philip's sources, he had only gotten out alive through the efforts of the famous Lady in Green and some English soldiers—an odd combination. Philip could not wait to be done with this place. There was nothing here but death.

Richard called for water. He was burning with thirst. He wished he could take off his heavy robes, he was so hot. His head was swimming and it was difficult to concentrate. "There is another matter we must settle," he told the assemblage. "I have heard stories of dissension in this army. We must have no more of it. Once and for all, we must determine the rightful king of Jerusalem."

"We already have," growled square-jawed Conrad of Montferrat. "It's me."

He and Richard glared at each other. "Forgive me, my lord, but that is not for you to determine," Richard said. He tossed his mane of sweaty red-gold hair. "In fact, having considered all the evidence, I believe that Guy of Lusignan has the best claim to the crown."

There was a groan from the crowd. If Richard had expected overwhelming approval of this decision based on his personal popularity, he had expected wrong. Guy smiled and preened, Richard's Poitevin barons "Hurrah'd," and there were expressions of approval from Robert de Sable, Grand Master of the Templars, and one or two others, but that was all. Conrad stared at Richard like he might take a bite out of him.

The rest of the pavilion was quiet. Richard looked over at Philip. He wondered if the French king had organized this response. He wondered if Philip was playing some kind of trick on him. Philip was devious that way, one never knew what he was up to. He wouldn't—or couldn't—fight man to man, so he resorted to trickery. Seeking a way to vent his frustration, Richard lighted on the earl of Trent, who looked glum. "You do not approve of my decision?" Richard asked him.

"No, sire." Absurdly, all Geoffrey could think about was what Bonjute would say when she learned that he had defied the king yet again.

Richard drew himself up. "You *are* one of my vassals, I believe?"

"And proud to be counted as such," Geoffrey replied.

"Yet it seems you never follow my lead."

"Your pardon, sire, but I have seen the results of Guy's actions, and they do not inspire me. Besides, the local barons wish Conrad for their king, and I think we should accede to their wishes."

Next to him, a rangy one-eyed baron in nondescript clothes said, "Well spoken."

Richard stared at the one-eyed man, then went on, addressing Trent. "I may like men who speak their mind, Earl Geoffrey, but you would do well not to try the limits of my patience."

"I shall bear that in mind, sire."

The one-eyed baron grinned, as if this were all a joke. Richard turned on him. "And who might you be, sir?"

The one-eyed baron bowed with a flourish so elaborate as to be just shy of insolence. "Why, I *might* be anyone, sire, but as it is, I am called Henry. I am lord of Deraa, beyond the Jordan River."

"You are one of my cousin Guy's vassals?"

"Your pardon, sire, but that is something I shall never be."

"You swore allegiance to me," Guy reminded him.

Henry said, "I swore my allegiance to Queen Isabelle, not to some French pimp. I'd swear allegiance to Saladin before I'd swear it to you."

Guy's eyes narrowed. "Suppose I take Deraa from you?"

"You're welcome to try," Henry told him. "Saladin couldn't manage the job, so I doubt I'd have much to worry about from a military midget like you."

Richard was about to say something, but King Philip interrupted. "For the love of God, gentlemen, can we forget the crown for once? Our most important task is to capture this city. We can decide who should be king afterwards."

Philip's words made sense. There were murmurs of assent—some strong, some reluctant. Richard realized this was not the time to push his cousin's claim to the crown. "I agree," he said. More murmurs of assent, stronger now. Richard flashed his big grin. "We still have to wait until we attack, however."

"Why?" Philip said, exasperated. "I don't—"

Richard's grin broadened. "Because I'm too sick to fight."

Then he fainted.

Chapter 80

King Richard was put to bed. Once there, he was too weak to leave. His physicians declared that he had contracted the leonardie. His lips swelled, his teeth and gums pained him terribly. His hair and nails fell out. Saladin learned of Richard's illness and, under a flag of truce, he sent the king fruited sherbet cooled with snow from Mount Hermon.

"We wait all this time for Richard, and when he finally shows up, he keels over sick," said James of Avesnes. "God may be on our side, but He's sure not making it easy for us."

James suffered the same symptoms as Richard, though they were not as bad. So did King Philip, so did many others. Indeed, every man in camp suffered from something. Great patches of skin, worn raw from stiff, filthy clothing, were never allowed to heal. Dirt and sweat bred suppurating, flaking sores. At home people were condemned as lepers for ailments that went unremarked at Acre. Even the noblest men and women were dimpled red with louse and flea bites.

As sole commander while Richard was incapacitated, Philip ordered a general assault on Acre to take place in three days. As they had the last time Philip ordered an attack, some of the commanders protested—Guy of Luisignan and his friends, along with Richard's newly arrived barons such as the counts of Vouzan and Perigord. They wanted to wait till Richard was well, but Philip would hear none of it. "We have the Invincible Tower—there is no way we can fail."

"What if Saladin learns of our plans?" asked the once-portly Papal legate, Ubaldo, whose heavy vestments now hung on him as though they had been fashioned for a much larger man.

427

"What if he does?" said Philip. "I may even send him the precise day and hour of our attack and dare him to stop it."

"He could cause much mischief if he attacks our camp while our full force is in front of the city, sire," Henry of Deraa pointed out. "He hasn't sent his entire army against us since early in the siege. This would be a good time for him to do it. Remember what happened the last time we attacked the city."

Philip took a deep breath and held it for a second. "You are right, Lord Henry. I'm afraid I let my emotions get the better of me. I still believe we should attack now, but we can't let our plans leak out."

Henry of Champagne started to say something, but Philip anticipated him. "Yes, I know—Saladin has a spy amongst our leadership. Double the guards on the camp ditch—triple them—to keep any messages from getting through." He grit his teeth. "I lose my best falcon and Saladin steals it and laughs at me. Richard gets a headache and Saladin sends him sherbet. Doesn't Saladin know I'm a king, too? If he doesn't, by Heaven, he'll soon learn. I'll give that camel merchant something to think about."

And Richard, as well.

Chapter 81

Otho of Malcherce made his way from the transient camp on the beach to the Toron. Behind him, two scrawny Arab boys lugged his heavy trunk, stopping every few minutes to readjust their grip.

"Stop dawdling," Otho snapped at them.

Otho should have been delighted to have found a position as chaplain to the earl of Trent, but he wasn't. Here, on the other side of the world, midst death and dirt and disease, was far from where he wanted to be. That robbery in Dunham Wood had destroyed his career. The story of how he had shown up at Keslow Priory stark naked, eaten alive by insects, slashed by thorns and vines, had preceded him back to Winchester and turned him into a laughingstock.

He'd been too humiliated to tell the truth, that he'd been robbed by a girl, a peasant and some kind of monk, so he told everyone it had been the notorious Brock the Badger who'd done it, at sword point, with his whole villainous gang behind him, but that had not spared him the laughter. His reputation in tatters, he hadn't been able to continue in his official duties because of all the negative attention he received. That attention impinged upon the bishop's dignity, and the bishop had hinted that Otho should go to the Holy Land to restore his honor.

The journey here had been horrible, as most journeys were, and it hadn't been improved by the suffocating presence of that hag Eleanor. On the plus side, Otho had met Bonjute of Trent. He'd given much to have bedded her, and though he had tried to make that sentiment clear without ever actually saying it, she wasn't having any of it. There was something about her cold attitude that excited him. He'd wager there was a fire in there waiting to explode were it stoked by the right man. She had introduced him to her husband, though, and her husband had offered him this position.

So here he was, a man who had once aimed at being justiciar of England, and right now the best he could hope for was being the justiciar's chaplain. It was galling. He hadn't told Trent why he was really in the Holy Land, of course. He'd said he felt constrained in Winchester, said he'd wanted to do his part in the crusade, thus had left the bishop's staff. Trent — whom he had seen before but never met — blathered on about how saintly his old chaplain Stephen had been and how Stephen had ministered to the common people after their priests died. "Would you be willing to do that?" Trent had asked Otho.

"Of a certainty, my lord," Otho said. "If I have time. Ministering to you and your nobles and overseeing your chancery — even one truncated by war — will be a large responsibility. But I'll undertake to look after the common folk, as well, should you see fit to take me on."

Needless to say, Otho had no intention of ministering to the common soldiers. Let them find someone of their own station. And it looked like something as seemingly easy as running the chancery might prove a problem as well. While in the transient camp Otho had made the acquaintance of Archbishop Rudolph of Mainz, who was too sick to carry on and was waiting for a ship to Italy, and thence home. When Otho had told the archbishop about his new job, the ailing man had assumed a look of horror.

"I don't envy you, sir," Rudolph had said. "Don't envy you in the least. A lot of work to be done there. A lot of work. That Trent fellow has a chronicler who wrote a Michaelmas play that was deemed by many of us to be heretical. Forbidden from producing more plays, Trent was. Fellow who wrote it would have been burned were it up to me — and I was far from the only one who felt that way."

Heretical plays? What the Devil was going on here? Otho needed to get this sorted out.

They reached Trent's pavilion, the two Arab boys panting and ready to collapse from carrying the trunk. Otho gave them each a coin, and they looked at him with faces filled with equal parts shock and anger because of the paltry sum.

"Go on." He shooed them away. "Go on, you little heathens, or I'll have the guards on you."

One of the boys made a rude gesture with his finger as he left. Enraged, Otho would have had them arrested, but here came the earl. The earl's page Eustace had gotten the chancery staff together, and the earl introduced Otho to them.

"Where is Fauston?" the earl asked, looking around when the introductions were done.

"Dunno, my lord," Eustace said. "Couldn't find him."

No one else seemed to know where this Fauston was, either.

"Fauston is my chronicler," the earl explained to Otho. "Splendid fellow. I'm sure he'll be along shortly." The earl rubbed his hands together. "Well, I'll leave you to it," he said to Otho and departed, while Eustace hung about to watch the fun.

Otho was laying down his rules to his new charges when a figure approached, apparently in no hurry, a tonsured young man of stocky build, with a short beard and wearing a cleric's white robe with a red cross on the shoulder. The man seemed to react with shock at the sight of Otho, as though he'd seen the proverbial ghost. He stumbled and came to a halt, then he recovered and came on.

Otho scowled at him. "Are you the chronicler, Fauston?"

"I am, Father," said the young man. He was English by his accent, a commoner. How did a peasant like this get to be an earl's chronicler?

"You're late," Otho observed.

"Sorry, Father. I just received news of your arrival."

"Where were you?"

"Down below, working on the chronicle."

Otho peered closely at the young man. There was something about him . . . "Do I know you?"

Fauston frowned. "Why, no, Father. We've never met."

Otho narrowed his eyes. "Are you certain? You look familiar."

Fauston shook his head. "No, Father. I'm sure I'd remember if we had."

Otho's eyes narrowed further. He paused for effect, then changed the subject. "I'm told you wrote an heretical play."

The other clerks who were present edged out of the way.

Fauston seemed surprised by the accusation. "I wouldn't call it heretical, Father."

"Really?" Otho said. "According to my source, you accused the clergy of selling indulgences, of lusting for money—of fornication, even. What is that if not heretical?"

"The truth?" Eustace suggested.

Otho whirled on the page. "Don't you have anything better to do?"

"No," Eustace replied. "Not really."

"Make yourself useful, then, and get me some wine."

"Sorry," Eustace said cheerfully, "can't do that. I'm the earl's page, not yours."

Fuming, Otho turned back to Fauston, and he could have sworn the chronicler had been grinning. "The play was meant to be funny," Fauston told Otho. "I guess some people took it the wrong way."

Otho drew himself up, breathing heavily. "You have an odd sense of what's funny. There will be no more such 'humor' while I am Lord Geoffrey's chaplain. Do I make myself clear?"

"Perfectly clear, Father."

"We have a remedy for heresy, you know." He paused. "A very warm one."

"Yes, Father."

"You would do well to remember that. Now — why is it that you don't work up here with the other clerks?"

Fauston spread his arms. "I've never been able to work in a group, don't know why. I need to be by myself."

"Well, you'll have to change," Otho told him. "I don't want

my people all over the camp. I like to have them where I can keep an eye on them."

"Yes, Father," Fauston said. "Is that all, Father?"

"For the moment." With a curt nod, Otho dismissed the young cleric. He watched him amble toward the pavilion's entrance, for all the world like he owned the place.

Where *had* he seen him before?

Chapter 82

Fauston stepped out of the tent into the blaring light of the Toron. The sky was clear. The sun baked sea and sand. The city of Acre basked in undulating heat waves, seemingly unbothered by the monotonous *thud* of rocks from the catapults hitting its walls.

Jesus Christ and the Twelve Disciples, what was Otho doing in the Holy Land, and how had he ended up with the earl of Trent? Otho had lost a lot of weight, but Fauston had recognized that smug face right away. Fortunately, Fauston's appearance had changed so much that Otho hadn't remembered who he was, but if he ever did . . .

Fauston would have to stay out of Otho's way as much as possible — even though Otho looked like he was going to make that difficult — and hope the bastard dropped dead of disease or found a better position elsewhere. He needed to warn Roger about—

"Pardon me," said a voice.

Fauston turned to see a good-looking man in a crimson surcoat. The man was just above middle height, thick chested, with slicked-back dark hair and beard, the beard beginning to grey. He wore a gold ring in his right ear. He said, "You are the earl of Trent's chronicler?"

"I am," Fauston admitted cautiously. *Now what?*

"I have heard good things about your work."

Fauston nodded his head. "Thank you."

"Allow me to name myself. I am Alart, twelfth count of Vouzan."

Fauston straightened and bowed. The count of Vouzan — that name was familiar. "I am Fauston, my lord, a wandering scholar—or I was before I found a position with the earl."

Alart said, "I was wondering if you might be of service to me."

Fauston made no commitment. "If I can."

"Have you any experience of relics?"

Fauston was about to tell the truth, that he had not, when Brock the Badger surfaced within him. Perhaps there was money to be made here. He hesitated, then said, "I have some familiarity with the subject. What does your lordship desire?"

Alart said, "The two queens, Eleanor and Berengaria, return to France within the fortnight. I have sworn to bring my wife a relic from the Holy Land, and I was hoping I might send something back with them. Queen Eleanor will deliver it for me when she reaches Poitou. I looked all over the—what do you call it?—the Concourse, but I could not find a dealer in relics. Your earl of Trent told me you were a sharp young fellow who might be able to help me."

"I can't promise anything, my lord, but I'll try," Fauston said. Where *had* he heard this fellow's name? "Within a fortnight, you say?"

"Yes. If it's any help to you, my wife went on a pilgrimage to Rome a few years past, and because of that she has become particularly devoted to St. Peter. Any relic would be good, but something related to St. Peter would be excellent. Money is no object—within reason, of course."

"I understand," Fauston said.

"If you find something, you will have my sincerest gratitude. My wife is very religious, and having a relic might help keep her happy until I return home."

Fauston wondered what he had gotten himself into. "I'll do what I can, my lord."

"My tent is in the Poitevin camp, next to King Richard's. See me when you have something."

Fauston bowed. Alart strode away, and as he did, Fauston remembered where he'd heard the name. Alart of Vouzan was the father of Auberie, the monk Roger had killed—God, it seemed so long ago. Fauston wondered if the count had learned of his son's death yet. More importantly, he wondered what the count would do if he found out that Auberie's killer was in the camp and that Fauston had been involved in Auberie's death as well.

Chapter 83

Roger couldn't sleep.

He shook off his cloak, got up and took a turn around the quiet encampment. The earl's footmen had guard duty at the camp ditch again, and those not on watch were bedded down near the bridge at Resurrection Road. Roger looked at the stars and made it to be well past Nocturnes. He shivered a bit in the night air, though the chill was a welcome relief from the torrid heat of the day.

To one side of him were the scattered campfires of the crusader camp and the bobbing lights of ships in the harbor, along with a thin glow from behind the city walls. To the other side, the banked fires of Saladin's camp flickered in the hills. Here, near the ditch, it was completely dark.

He swung his arms to warm up. Around him men tossed, snored, murmured in their sleep. He caught a distant snatch of music, probably from the Toron, where it seemed they never slept.

He had known that Auberie's father was in the camp, and now he had learned that the fat priest they had robbed in Dunham Wood was the earl's new chaplain. Would wonders never cease. It was one more thing to worry about, but Roger had more important things on his mind just now. The priest, in fact, scarcely registered.

Roger's thoughts were on Helvise—that was what had kept him awake. She was recovering nicely from her wound; she would be leaving soon. How long before he saw her again? She had become such a part of his life that he didn't know how he would get on without her, yet he knew he would have to. As the time for her departure drew near, their lovemaking had become more and more frenzied, as though each was trying to drain the last drop of passion from the other before they were separated.

That afternoon in Roger's tent Helvise had rattled on about all the things she was going to do when she got home, the old friends she was going to see. "And snow—I can't wait to see snow again."

"I've been thinking," Roger said hesitantly. Actually, he had been thinking about the subject for some while. "What's going to happen to us when I get to Germany? Didn't you say that your duke would have to find you a new husband in order for you to keep your lands?"

She faced him with a sparkle in those bewitching, almond-shaped eyes. "I've been thinking about that, as well," she said, taking his hands. "You could never be margrave, of course. So, with the duke's permission, I plan to relinquish Halsbach and retire to a small holding I have in my own name. It's not big, but it's enough to support us. You'll have to learn German and become accustomed to our ways, but you'll enjoy that."

Roger was dubious. "Will the duke give his permission?"

"I believe he will. He likes me. Besides, Welf has a cousin who can claim the title, so there will be no fight over the succession."

Roger drew her to him; her lithe body pressed against his. "Got it all planned out, haven't you?"

She smirked. "Does that bother you?"

"Not at all." He ran a hand through her short dark hair. "I can't wait till we're together for good."

"Neither can I. We'll have such a wonderful life."

Helvise was like a little girl, almost clapping in delight as she stepped away from him. Then she grew serious and pointed at him. "Promise me you won't get yourself killed."

He grinned and put his arms around her waist again. "I promise."

"Swear it," she said sternly.

He drew her close. "I swear."

She gave him a sultry look, then pushed against his

forearms, as if trying to extricate herself from his embrace. "I should practice my letters."

"We'll practice something else first," Roger said. He pressed her onto his cot and thus the afternoon passed . . .

❖ ❖ ❖

Now he stared at the sea. The light from the quarter moon spread across the calm water like a silvery road. The road to his new home.

But when would he reach that home? Despite what he had told Helvise, Jerusalem seemed as far away as it ever had. For all he knew, they might sit in front of Acre for the next twenty years.

He left the sleeping men and wandered along the camp ditch. As he neared the part of the ditch held by the Death's Heads, a familiar figure fell in beside him. "Can't sleep?" Tatwine asked.

"No," Roger admitted.

"Me, neither. The Pagan—" Payen's nickname among the men—"says we'll be in the city in a few days. That must mean an attack's coming."

"First I've heard of it," Roger said. People always said there was an attack coming.

They made their way in the dark, passing other men from their company. After that, there seemed to be no guards at all.

"Where is everybody?" Roger said.

"Dunno," Tatwine said. "The Pagan placed the guards himself — he don't usually do that. Maybe he forgot about this part of the line. Maybe he was drunk or he just don't care anymore. He reckons he's got his knighthood sewn up and he'll be with the horsemen when we move on Jerusalem, and that's all that matters to him."

They came to the end of the English area of responsibility. Walloons held the line from here on. The two sectors were separated by a crooked ravine that ran through this section of the line. The ravine, filled with water during the rains, was mostly dry now, choked with stinking weeds, brush, and jumbled rocks. The ditch could not be extended across this section of the line, so a breastwork of rocks had been erected to block up the ravine. It would be difficult to push a formation of men, much less horses, through the steep-sided ravine, so the crusaders didn't worry much about it beyond placing guards at the breastwork to watch for spies and deserters.

Roger saw no guards. On impulse he scrambled down into the ravine. Tatwine followed.

The two men picked their way along the ravine, moving slowly because of the jumbled rocks and thorny brush. It stank down here because men had been using the ravine for a latrine. They reached the point where the ravine intersected the camp ditch. The breastwork was mostly tumbled down now; no one worked on maintaining it.

Roger looked around. He was wasting time here, he didn't even know why he'd come. He needed to go back and get some sleep. He started to leave when Tatwine grabbed his arm.

Roger said, "What—"

"S-h-h-h." Tatwine put a finger to his lips. He pointed to his ear, then into the darkness, in the direction of the crusader camp.

Roger listened.

He heard a faint scrape. Something moving.

He looked at Tatwine and listened again. Whatever it was, it was coming closer. Slowly, cautiously. Was it an animal—a wild pig, a dog?

Or was it a man?

Closer the noise came. Roger's eyes strained into the darkness but he saw nothing.

Roger motioned Tatwine farther back, toward the breastwork. At the same time, Roger eased behind the nearest rock.

Roger heard the sound again. Closer. His heart pounded and he slid his dagger from its sheath.

The sound was opposite him now. It was a man, there was no mistaking the sound of footfalls. Roger made out a darker shadow against the gloom of the ravine.

The man moved past Roger, creeping toward the breastwork, stopping every few steps to listen. Roger stepped from behind the rock.

The man heard Roger and without looking behind him to see who it was bolted for the breastwork. Tatwine emerged from the shadows and blocked his path.

The man skidded and turned back—to find the point of Roger's dagger pressed against his throat.

"Please—no!" It wasn't a man—it was a boy.

Roger and Tatwine stared at each other because they knew the boy.

It was Bug, Payen's manservant.

Chapter 84

They were in Roger's tent, with Payen bound to the center pole. Tatwine paced back and forth behind Roger, breathing heavily, his feral eyes fixed on Payen, a serrated knife in one hand. Offa and Mayne had ushered Helvise away. This was not likely to be any place for a woman.

Outside, the Death's Heads formed an armed ring around the tent, holding back a crowd of off-duty spearmen. Roger and his men had grabbed Payen from his sleep and spirited him back to Roger's tent for questioning. Roger had hoped to get Payen out of the guard encampment before they were noticed, but one of the spearmen had seen them, and at least fifty spearmen had followed the Death's Heads in rag-tag fashion, with more streaming in as word of what had happened got out. Men from other units milled around, as well, curious to see what the commotion was about.

"I'm warning you, let me go while you still can," Payen told Roger. Payen wore only a shirt and hose; his greying hair was mussed. "You're in enough trouble already. I can have you hanged for this. No, not hanged—I can have you flogged within an inch of your life, and when you recover, I can do it all over again."

He was right. Roger's actions toward his commander warranted an automatic sentence of death unless he could prove they were justified. Roger didn't have much time to get the truth out of Payen, either. Somebody must have sent for the earl by now. The earl trusted Payen. Once the earl got here, Roger would have to untie Payen, and Payen would then have the leisure to spin any story he liked, a story whose end would likely feature Roger dangling from a rope. And if the earl didn't come soon, some of those spearmen outside might try to rush the tent and free their commander.

Roger forced himself to act calm, as though he had all the time in the world. "Admit that you're a spy," he told Payen.

"A spy!" Payen cried. "I'm no more a spy than King Richard is."

Roger regarded him steadily, with Tatwine's caged-animal pacing in the background. "Bug has already confessed," Roger said.

There was a flicker of something in Payen's eye, then he laughed. "Bug! He's a child, who's going to believe what he says? Certainly not the earl. Where is Bug, anyway?"

"My men have him in a safe place. He's admitted carrying messages to the Saracen lines. Messages given to him by you."

"Oh, for God's sake. He's saying that to save his skin, you camel's dick, can't you see that? The boy is a spy, and I'm sorry to hear that because I liked him. But now you've caught him and he's trying to save himself by saying that the real spy is me." Payen let out a long, exasperated breath. "Tell you what, let me go and you won't be punished. It was an honest mistake on your part—stupid, but honest."

A kernel of doubt formed in Roger's mind. What if Payen was telling the truth—what if Roger had grabbed an innocent man? Was he doing this because he really believed Payen was a spy or because he didn't like him? Then he dismissed the thought. "Bug knew our plans for attacking the city. How would he have gotten them if not from you?"

"Maybe he found them in his ass, how do I know? I'm giving you one last chance, Roger—release me."

Roger shook his head. "Confess."

Payen spat in Roger's face. "I'll confess nothing to you, you peasant bastard—no, you're worse than a bastard. At least a bastard knows who *one* of his parents is. You've sealed your fate, Roger. When the earl gets here, I'll have the skin off your back. I'll feed your balls to the pigs — that is, if they'll eat anything that small."

Outwardly, Roger showed no emotion. Inwardly, he knew he had to get this done quickly, and there was only one way to do that. It was a method Roger would have preferred not to use, but there was no choice. He looked to Tatwine and nodded. Then he left the tent.

"Where are you going?" Payen cried from behind him. "I didn't say you could leave. Come back here—come back, I command you!"

The crowd around the tent had grown. A few of the Death's Heads guards wiped their lips or shifted their hands nervously on the hafts of their axes. Some of the spearmen ranged opposite his men would be with Roger—the ones with the Death's Head symbol on their helmets for a start. Others would be neutral. But a number were loyal to Payen. They had grown to like not working; they liked having the Death's Heads do all the dirty jobs. Were there enough of these to rush the tent and overwhelm Roger's men? Would they try?

"What's going on in there?" one of the spearmen shouted. "What have you done to Pagan?"

"He's a spy for the Goat Fuckers," Ralph the Red shouted back.

There was an outcry from the spearmen. "What?" "I don't believe it." "Says who?"

"Bug," Ralph said.

"Bug! What's he—"

From the tent came a sudden, drawn-out scream of pain, and the crowd fell silent. Roger felt a sickened jolt to his insides, then he hardened himself as he thought of all the good men who had died because of Payen's treachery.

A pause, then another long howl of pain from the tent. It sounded like an animal was being torn apart in there. Roger didn't want to think about what Tatwine was doing to Payen. He remembered the earl's marshal, Guillame, and young Peter of Winstead, remembered their tortured, mutilated bodies hanging from the city walls.

Some of the spearmen loyal to Payen murmured. A few started forward, growling, fists clenched. "Red—don't let anyone near the tent," Roger snapped.

Ralph slapped the haft of his axe against the palm of his hand. "We won't."

Another gut-curdling scream of pain from inside the tent. A pause, then another, the worst yet. Roger forced himself to look stern yet nonchalant, like he ordered this sort of thing done every day.

There was the canvas crack of the tent flap. Tatwine appeared next to Roger, blood over the front of Tatwine's leather jack. With a piece of cloth that had once been Payen's shirt, Tatwine wiped blood and other things from the blade of the serrated knife. "He's ready to talk," Tatwine said.

Roger had to force himself not to let out his breath in relief, had to force himself to appear stoic. He nodded and ducked into the tent, Tatwine following.

Payen sagged against the tent pole, head down. Roger tried to ignore the blood, the pieces of Payen that were missing. "You admit you spied for the Saracens?" he asked Payen.

Payen sobbed. "Yes."

"Why?"

"Why do you think? Money, land. The sultan promised me an estate outside Damascus, plus gold." He looked over at Tatwine fearfully. "I did it, all right—I did it, and I'd do it again. Just don't let him hurt me anymore." He collected himself and added, "I wanted to be on the winning side. You fools have no chance of taking Jerusalem. Your bones will be left to bleach in the desert."

"That may be, but you won't be there to see it," Roger told him. Then he said, "How did you become a spy?"

Payen sucked in his breath, accidentally swallowed blood and coughed. "My real name . . . Boudin, from Villancourt in Artois. I was captured in a battle with the Saracens a year ago Easter. I had a choice—join them or be executed." He shrugged. "So I joined. I converted to Islam. I could have become a

445

soldier for them, like others who were taken, but I volunteered to be a spy."

"Because of the gold?" Roger said.

"Yes. The Saracens smuggled me across the ditch, along with Bug. I assumed a new identity and hired out to your earl as commander of footmen." Some of his old arrogance returned, though his self-satisfied smile did not go with the blood in his mouth. "I was fortunate to gain a position where I was privy to the army's plans."

"Weren't you afraid you'd be recognized?"

"At first, yes. That's why I didn't leave the English lines much. But now, since the famine, there's none of my old comrades left alive, and if there are one or two, they're not looking for me."

Tatwine stopped pacing and glared at the prisoner. "You betrayed Our Savior. How could you do that?"

"One god is much like another," Payen said. "At least my god keeps women in their place." He sneered at Roger. "Not like that whore of yours. She should be—"

Roger backhanded Payen's broken face with his mailed glove. Blood flew, and Payen sagged. Roger drew back his fist for another blow but thought better of it. "You're not worth it. We'll let the earl decide what to do with you."

"I already heard," said a voice.

Earl Geoffrey stood in the open tent flap, his hair and clothes tousled as if he had just awakened. One-eyed Henry the Lion was there, too. He had been on guard, seen the commotion and come to investigate.

Payen fell to his knees, awkwardly because his bloody hands were bound to the tent pole. "I beseech your lordship's mercy," he told the earl. "The Saracens forced me to spy. They said they'd torture me else, and I was too weak to resist them. Please, I beg of you, give me a chance to redeem myself."

Geoffrey stared at Payen as one might stare at a particularly repulsive form of insect. "There is no mercy for such as you. All that is left is to determine the method of your punishment."

Next to Geoffrey, Henry the Lion grinned. "I have an idea for that."

Chapter 85

"Let's go," Roger said.

Payen was slumped in pain on Roger's cot. He looked up. "Go where?" he mumbled through his grotesquely swollen jaw.

"You're going into the city."

Payen straightened. "Into the city? Really?" He couldn't keep the relief from his voice; he'd expected to be hung or beheaded, maybe even drawn and quartered. "Are they going to exchange a prisoner for me?"

"Just get moving," Roger told him.

Payen stood. His face was bruised; his mouth looked like there was a horseshoe crammed into one side of it. His clothes were crusted brown with dried blood. A thick, brown-stained bandage covered his right hand. But suddenly his spirits were high.

They exited Roger's tent. Two files of spearmen waited for them, standing at attention. Payen saw those ridiculous Death's Heads on some of the helmets, and he looked with scorn at the men who wore them. Men and a few women—the earl's old whore Ailith was one of them—watched from both sides of the company street, craning their heads to get a better view of the traitor. Roger motioned Payen to take a place between the files of spearmen. Wilbert, the grizzled centenar at the detachment's head, looked to Roger as if awaiting orders, and when he did that, Payen realized what had happened and he laughed through his distended mouth. "Don't tell me you've been given command of the footmen?" he said to Roger.

Roger didn't meet his gaze. "Yes."

Payen laughed again. "That's rich, that is. I can't believe it. Or maybe I can—that idiot of an earl has always had a soft spot where you're concerned. No wonder your side is losing the war."

Roger ignored the comment and motioned Wilbert to start the column off. A burly spearman behind Payen gave the prisoner a rough shove to set him in motion.

They marched through the camp onto the open ground in front of the besieged city—men, women, even children, watching or running alongside to see what was going to happen. Both camp and city were unusually quiet. A herald had been sent to the city walls under a flag of truce to inform the Saracens that one of their men was being returned to them.

They headed toward the German portion of the siege line. Directly in the little procession's path was a screen of footmen. To either side of the footmen waited many of the camp's great lords, mounted but unarmored. The breeze flapped their gaily colored banners; the sun glinted brightly off the sea. King Philip of France was there, looking grim as always, so were Leopold of Austria, Henry of Champagne, and the Papal legate Ubaldo, along with the earl of Trent, Conrad of Montferrat and others too numerous to mention. King Richard was too sick to attend, so the swarthy count of Vouzan served as his representative. Payen's heart soared at the sight and he squared his shoulders. Only an important personage rated this kind of attention.

❖ ❖ ❖

The footmen tramped along with spears on their shoulders, Roger marching beside them. Roger had tried to refuse his appointment to Payen's old position, but the earl wouldn't hear of it. "This spy has been a thorn in our side for a long time. You captured him—you've earned the promotion."

"It could have been anyone who captured him," Roger had protested. "I just happened to be there when he—"

"But it *was* you," Trent said. "I've told you before—don't question my judgment." He went on. "Your new position carries a considerable rise in social status, by the by. You're a man-at-arms now. With luck, you'll be a knight one day."

"Thank you, my lord." Roger felt guilty because he knew he had done nothing to deserve this rise in rank.

Trent continued. "As a man-at-arms, you're entitled to ride to battle and to wear a hauberk. Horses and hauberks should be easy to come by—cheap, as well—what with all the dead we've suffered."

Roger said, "If it's all the same with you, my lord, I'll just wear my old jack for a while. I've gotten used to it."

"And the horse? Do you ride?"

Roger remembered hunting parties in that long-ago world at Huntley Abbey. "I do, my lord, and maybe I'll get a horse later." He looked around the vast siege camp. "Doesn't seem to be much use for one now."

"As you will," the earl had said.

The procession's main attraction, Payen, couldn't contain his smile. The pain in his hand and mouth was so great it took his breath away, but he didn't care. He was going into Acre. He was going to live! The Saracens must have realized what kind of asset they had in Payen and decided to exchange him for a captive crusader—maybe even more than one. The fall of the city could prove a peril to him, of course, but only if the city fell. It had stood siege for over two years now, with no end in sight. Even if the city did fall, the sultan might be able to evacuate the garrison by sea. After that, Payen would have his revenge on Roger—and on Tatwine, the bastard who had maimed him. He'd make the two of them pay, and pay dearly. That was for the future, though. For now Payen was alive, and that was all that mattered.

He neared the high-ranking nobles who had come to watch him leave. He passed Geoffrey of Trent, and he met the earl's cold eyes with a smirk. His spying had prolonged the siege for months. It was not too much of a stretch to say that his efforts might have won the war for his new co-religionists. He was a great man. Once he had gotten his revenge on Roger, he would retire to his new estate outside Damascus and live a life of ease.

As the procession passed the nobles, the screen of footmen ahead of them stepped aside, revealing a huge mangonel. It was "Mad Meg," largest catapult in the crusader camp. The mangonel's crew stood by the weapon, impassive.

Payen stopped. His insides went queasy. Something was wrong. And here was that one-eyed monkey who called himself Henry the Lion, grinning like a peasant who'd made a penny on market day.

"Good morrow, Master Payen," Henry said with a mock bow. "As you know, we have informed the Saracens that we are returning one of their men. And so we shall."

Payen realized what was happening, and he almost voided himself. He stepped back. He would have moved back further had not two of his former men stopped him, grabbing the backs of his arms. Payen looked from the catapult to the city, whose distant battlements were crammed with watching figures, curious about the man who was being returned to them.

"No," Payen gulped, shaking his head. The smug pride in his accomplishments vanished, and he made one last attempt to save himself. "No," he told the nobles, looking around wildly, "I'm innocent. I swear it." Desperate, he jabbed his bandaged hand toward Roger. "It was him. He's wanted my job all along. Bug was the spy. Roger captured him and made up the charges against me. Why can't you see that?"

"Perhaps because you confessed?" King Philip pointed out.

"Only because they tortured me, sire." With what was left of his right hand he pointed at Tatwine. "You'd have confessed, too, if that maniac had done to you what he did to me."

Standing nearby, axe slung in his belt, Tatwine gazed

ahead innocently. Payen might have been talking about someone else for all the emotion Tatwine showed.

Henry the Lion's grin widened as he watched Payen's efforts to save himself. Henry turned to the nearest footmen and said, "Bind him."

"No!" Payen cried.

Strong hands shoved Payen to the ground. His ankles were bound tight with leather cord. "No!" His wrists were tied together beneath his thighs, so that he couldn't move.

"No!" he cried. "Don't. Please."

The mangonel's crew winched down the weapon's wooden arm and hooked it. Henry nodded, and three men lifted Payen and placed him in the mangonel's reinforced leather bucket.

"Please, I swear! It wasn't me!"

Suddenly all the repressed rage that Roger felt for Payen boiled up. He stepped over to Payen. "Enjoy your journey," he said. He inclined his head ever so slightly and added, "My lord."

Payen struggled in the mangonel's bucket but couldn't move. "Please!"

A herald signaled with a flag toward the city. Their man was coming.

"My God! I beg you—help me! Someone—help!"

Mad Meg's mustachioed commander looked to Henry. Henry gave Payen an ironic salute. "Say hello to the Goat Fuckers for me." Then he nodded to the mangonel's commander.

"Please, you can't do—"

The catapult's wooden arm was released. It flew upward and hit the wooden bar with a loud *thwack*, propelling the tied-up Payen into the air toward the city.

Up he went, a black spot against the blue sky, his thin scream trailing behind. Around Roger men were betting whether he would land inside or outside the city.

Downward went his trajectory. He struck the city wall, bounced off and hit the ground with a puff of dust, followed a second later by a muffled thump.

Some of the watching men cheered, others laughed. Still others turned away, sickened. Henry the Lion winced mockingly. "I bet that hurt."

Chapter 86

The great copper tower—the Invincible Tower—was wheeled out of camp and across the bridge that had been built for it, its axles squealing in their iron sockets. The bishop of Beauvais sprinkled the huge machine with holy water. Trumpets pealed, and the Invincible Tower started forward.

All morning the tower crept toward the spot where the city ditch had been filled in. The tower was heavy and slow, pulled by hundreds of sweating laborers chanting and trailing on ropes. The Saracens pelted the oncoming tower with everything they could think of, but they could not set it afire or impede its progress, though its once-smooth skin was crumpled and dented. They killed its laborers with arrows, stones, marble blocks, and quicklime, but more men — and women—leaped onto the ropes to take their place. And with every pot of Greek fire that burst harmlessly on the tower's copper sides, the derisive cheers of the Christian army grew louder.

❖ ❖ ❖

In a fit of pique, King Richard had ordered his forces not to take part in the attack, so the Death's Heads observed the assault from the camp ditch near Resurrection Road. The downward slope of the land gave them a decent view from there, though smoke and dust obscured the action.

Straw-haired Hedde, quiet Hedde, watched the Invincible Tower's advance as a proud father might watch a son perform his first test of manhood. Hedde's fingers unconsciously traced the beams and joists upon which he had labored so diligently over the winter and spring. He knew parts of the tower almost as intimately as he had known . . .

Hedde refused to complete that thought. He couldn't. Hedde was a carpenter, he liked building things. Building things gave meaning to his life. He had begun his trade in his village of Rumford, but as his skills progressed, his work took him further afield—to Badford for renovations on the cathedral and the earl's castle, then to Lincoln to work on the cathedral there, then to Belvoir Castle in Leicestershire. He made good money, enough to build a substantial house in Rumford, but he was of necessity gone from home for long periods of time.

On one of these occasions he had returned earlier than expected to discover that his wife, Emma, had taken up with another man, Guibert, the bailiff's son.

Hedde had loved Emma with all his heart. Everything he had ever done had been for her, every penny he had ever earned had gone to make her more comfortable. He hadn't wanted to take jobs far from home because they separated him from her, but he had done it because they paid more and enabled him to provide her a better life. Her betrayal tore him apart, especially with Guibert, who was good looking, smarmy and entitled. Everything that Hedde was not.

Hedde had waited until Emma and her lover were asleep in the house, Hedde's house. Then Hedde had blocked the door and burned the house down around them. He had fled the scene and, to atone for his sin, had joined the crusade, hoping to find God's forgiveness by helping to rebuild the Holy City.

Around him, men were cheering the belfry on, laughing and slapping one another on the back because it seemed the siege might finally be coming to an end.

❖ ❖ ❖

"No movement from old Sidesaddle at all," Offa marveled, looking back toward the hills. "Maybe we surprised them for once."

"Course we surprised 'em," the former poacher Slowfoot said. "Caught their spy, didn't we?"

Several men looked at Roger when Slowfoot said this, and there was pride in their eyes, as though Roger had tracked down the spy all by himself, as though he hadn't caught him by sheer accident. The earl's footmen had adjusted to having Roger named as their commander. As soon as he'd been promoted, most of the spearmen who didn't already have the red Death's Head on their helmets and cloth helmet covers got them painted on. A flag had appeared from somewhere—white, with the Red Death's head on it. Roger didn't need to ask who had made it. He felt faintly ridiculous about the gaudy banner, but the men were proud of it. They seemed to equate the symbol with Roger for some reason, as though he were a fearsome soldier, not a runaway monk who no longer believed in the cause he was fighting for. At Roger's suggestion, Bug had been allowed to pass through Saladin's lines following Payen's execution. He was only a boy, doing what he was told. There was no need to punish him.

Wilbert and the other centenars, all of them older than Roger, didn't seem to resent Roger's being given command of the footmen—or if they did resent it, they hadn't shown it so far. Roger had promoted Ralph the Red to be centenar of the axemen, and he'd made Offa vintenar in Ralph's place.

"Me!" Offa had yelled. "I don't want to be no vintenar. Satan's pizzle, you'll be putting me in charge of the bloody crusade next. It's gettin' so a man can't get no peace and quiet in this army."

The earl's footmen—collectively known as Death's Heads now—had gotten reinforcements, which was good since there wasn't much of the original companies left. In addition to new men who had come out from England, there were men from units that had been broken up after being destroyed by disease and battle. Roger now had Spaniards, Bohemians, Hollanders, a Basque, even a converted Moor in his command. There were the inevitable jostling and fights as the new men settled in. Roger had drilled the newcomers—with the help of Wilbert and the other centenars—until all of them could at least respond to basic commands in English.

All this kept Roger busy when he would much rather have been spending his time with Helvise. Each moment they had together was precious now because she would soon be departing.

Her wound had healed. To Roger, the long scar down her side made her even more beautiful than she had been before. That's what he told her as he had kissed its ragged length the previous night. "I'll miss you," he said fervently.

She tousled his short hair. "Don't talk about it. Let's enjoy the time we have left. We'll see each other soon enough, God willing."

So he stopped kissing the scar and went to other areas . . .

❖ ❖ ❖

He was thinking about last night as he watched the Invincible Tower belfry advancing on the city. In the sunlight the tower's copper sheathing flashed intermittently through the thick smoke and dust of the assault.

"I make it she's crossin' the city ditch about now," Offa remarked.

The men around him could scarce contain their excitement. "Think they'll be any women left for us?" worried one of the new spearmen, a youngster from Swinburne.

"Women!" roared Ralph the Red. "Where you been, boy? The Saracens don't like women. Don't you know what them heathens use for swyving?"

The boy thought. "Goats?" he ventured.

"Too bloody true, they do." Ralph winked at his comrades and leaned close to the youngster. "*You* don't fancy goats, do you, boy?"

"N-no, my lord."

"Had me worried for a bit. All right then. You're better off here, all snug and safe. Like as not, they've eaten all the goats by now, anyway. And don't call me 'my lord.' I'm a soldier, I work for my living."

"N-no, my lord. I mean, yes, my lord. I mean, yes, sir."

❖ ❖ ❖

The Invincible Tower was dragged across the city ditch. Arrows, rocks, and stones fell on the laborers heaving the ropes, but as fast as they fell, more took their place. Christian archers swept the battlements with their weapons. The tower was just yards from the wall now, cheers sounding from the archers on its top. The assault columns filed up to the rear ladders; the tower's drawbridge started its descent. Then a mangonel on the Accursed Tower smashed the tower with a flaming tree trunk. The roof and one side of the tower caved in, and, as the structure had been drenched with Greek fire during its advance, it erupted in flames and its occupants were roasted alive.

❖ ❖ ❖

Even through the dust and smoke, the Death's Heads could tell something had gone wrong. Cheering from the ground had been replaced by yells and trumpets and clanging cymbals from the city walls. Men who had been attacking the city began streaming back to the camp.

"It can't be," Father Mayne said, his mouth hanging open.

Hedde, who had been sitting, stood and moved forward involuntarily. "No. No! That tower was indestructible."

Through the dust Roger saw roiling black smoke. A gust of wind revealed the Invincible Tower in flames. Around him, men yelled and cursed and threw weapons and helmets in rage.

Hedde sank to the ground and buried his face in his hands.

Ralph the Red spoke for them all. "We'll never take that damned city."

Chapter 87

The destruction of the Invincible Tower was a serious blow to the crusaders. It was a blow to King Philip, as well. Twice Philip had led assaults on the city, and twice they had failed, and though his supporters blamed this latest failure on the lack of English support, Philip's abilities as a military commander had once again been called into question. "He should have listened to King Richard," the same men who had urged him to attack nodded sagely. "He should have waited."

The following day, King Richard had his litter placed near the burned-out remains of the Invincible Tower, in a shelter made of hide-covered mantlings. There Richard lay, propped on cushions, shooting his crossbow at Saracens on the battlements, whooping with delight when he hit one, laughing when the Saracens shot back at him and missed.

Two days later another fleet arrived, bringing the remainder of Richard's army under the earl of Leicester and Andrew of Chauvigny, who, like the count of Vouzan, was one of Richard's particular confidants. The fleet also brought Richard's siege engines. There were three of them, called trebuchets, the newest kind of catapult, which could throw a 300-pound projectile 400 yards. Specially cut stones for them were brought by ship from Messina and were dragged to the trebuchets on sledges pulled by teams of oxen. The biggest trebuchet was named "Bad Neighbor," the words painted on one of the support beams along with the three lions of England, the rest of the trebuchet painted red. Richard saw to the placement of the three machines himself, ranging them opposite the Accursed Tower. When the first projectiles from the trebuchets hit the city walls, the walls shook. Stone crumbled, cracks were seen. These walls, which had held out against the Christians for so long, suddenly seemed vulnerable.

The sight of the famed English king in action, even if he had to be carried everywhere on a litter, boosted the army's morale after the recent defeat. Richard distributed money freely, rewarding bravery, and many a knight and sergeant switched allegiance to his banner. As popular as his behavior was with the common soldiers, it was unsettling to some of the nobles, not the least of whom was King Philip . . . .

❖ ❖ ❖

"How dare he behave thus?" Philip complained to Geoffrey of Trent one evening as the two men strolled on a secluded area behind the Toron known as Kings Walk. "I am co-commander of the army, lord of half the barons in camp—including Richard for Acquitaine—but he does not consult me. He hires my own soldiers away from me. Setting his litter near the Invincible Tower was his way of mocking me. He acts as though I am a child, not to be taken seriously in military matters. I have been a king for ten years; I am not inexperienced in warfare."

Geoffrey said, "Richard's supporters are making much of the fact that you led the assault on the city from behind, while Richard places himself in front of the city walls."

Philip grimaced. "If I die in battle here, France has no king and there is chaos. France itself may cease to exist. If Richard dies in battle, he becomes immortal. The fate of his kingdom means nothing to him compared to that prospect."

The two men walked in silence for a bit, staring at the millions of stars overhead, listening to the sibilant rush of the surf on the beach. At last Philip said, "If the attack had succeeded, it would have enabled me to depart the Holy Land with a significant accomplishment. Ah, well—fortune does not always give us what we wish. The crusade is a worthy cause, Geoffrey, but it is not *my* cause. My cause is France, and I cannot further that cause by staying here."

Geoffrey's brows went up. "You're leaving?"

"Yes. I hold the crown, but it is a hollow crown. I have little money, and my writ extends no further than the Ile-de-France and some surrounding lands. Richard has the largest empire in Christendom. My goal is to create a country. Richard's goal is . . . Richard. So Richard can have the army and welcome to it. I only want to get away from this cursed land. I don't like being insulted by Richard, and I fully intend to repay those insults when I get home. I have not forgotten the shameful way he treated my sister, allowing her to waste her best years waiting for him and then betraying her. Richard can stay here, winning glory and fame. Let him see how much of his French possessions remain to him when the crusade is over."

Philip seemed surprised by the intensity of his own words, as though he were not used to revealing so much of his inner self. Not for the first time, Geoffrey wondered how much he was driven by his lack of noble looks and frame — how much that lack made him feel he had to prove himself.

"When will you go?" Geoffrey asked him.

"As soon as the city is taken. I shall say that two men cannot successfully lead an army such as this, and I shall cede full command to Richard, then depart so as not to be a distraction to him."

The two men stared out to sea, where the twinkling lights of ships filled the bay. Singing and shouts rang from Richard's camp among the Poitevins. Geoffrey said, "I will miss you, sire. You've been a voice of reason midst all the bickering here."

"I will miss you for the same reason," Philip said. Gravely, he added, "We shall likely find ourselves on opposite sides in the coming years, but I wish you well and I will always think of you as a friend."

"Thank you, sire. I appreciate that."

"You have estates in France, do you not?"

"I do."

"I shall attempt to look out for your interests there as best I may."

This was a huge gesture. If Philip was successful at recapturing Richard's French lands, he could easily confiscate Geoffrey's estates and give them to someone else—indeed, he would be expected to do so. "That's extremely kind of you, sire."

Philip smiled. "Call it a favor to an old comrade from the crusade."

The two men walked back to the Toron. "I wish Barbarossa had lived," Geoffrey said. "He would have commanded then. He would have put a stop to all this fighting among ourselves."

Philip said, "I wish the same, but it was not to be. And maybe it's for the best. Richard is the man everyone has been waiting for. They want to see a contest between him and Saladin. They've wanted that from the start. Were Frederick to have lived or were I to stay, we'd only be in the way. For better or worse, this is now King Richard's crusade."

Chapter 88

It was morning, and already blazing hot. Balian of Ibelin, Geoffrey, and one-eyed Henry the Lion lounged in the shade of Balian's wide silk awning. They were watching yet another emissary come out of the hills from Saladin's camp. They could not make him out yet; he was too far off and obscured by a second rider carrying a large white flag of truce.

"Think he's coming to visit Richard?" Balian asked.

"Of course he's coming to visit Richard," Henry said. "It's the only reason any of 'em come."

Geoffrey said, "God knows, there's been enough of them. Ever since Richard fell sick, Saladin's been sending him gifts, messages of friendship, hopes that he'll get well soon."

Henry pretended to have hurt feelings. "He never sent *me* a message of friendship when I was sick."

"He sent a few hoping you'd die soon, though," Balian reminded him.

They all laughed, and Balian went on. "Old Sidesaddle's trying to stir up trouble. I've met him—he's likeable but he's crafty. He knows there's friction between Richard and some of the other nobles, especially Philip and Conrad, and he's trying to drive a wedge between them. That's why he flatters Richard and pretends the rest of us don't exist."

"That's not the only reason he flatters Richard," Henry said. "He knows Richard supports Lusignan for the crown of Jerusalem, and of all the men who could bear that title, Lusignan is the one Sidesaddle would most like to see on the throne. As soon as you fellows from the west bugger off home, Saladin will crush Guy and his reconquest of the Holy land will be complete. Richard is too blinded by his own reflection to realize what's happening. He's a vain man, and vain men are susceptible to flattery. They believe others see them the way they see themselves. He doesn't understand that Saladin's trying to cause trouble amongst us. He thinks Saladin is simply giving him his due."

Balian shook his head ruefully. "Saladin must be amazed that a leper's foreskin like Guy could still be considered for the throne. Where Saladin comes from, you lose a battle like Hattin, and they don't make you king. They take you outside and slit your throat."

"That's what we should have done with Guy," Henry said.

Geoffrey stared at him. "Are you serious? That would have been murder."

"A lot of men would be alive today if we had," Henry said. "I don't call that murder, I call it common sense."

"You sound as though you would have been glad to do the job yourself."

Henry smiled. It was a chilling smile, and Geoffrey remembered Henry tossing a severed head into a council meeting. He could picture him doing the same thing with Guy of Lusignan's head and laughing about it.

Henry was about to say something, then he went rigid, staring at the plain.

Saladin's newest emissary had appeared from behind the white flag. Even at this distance, the men could see that from the emissary's helmet streamed a long blue sash.

Chapter 89

Qaymaz rode his black stallion through the Christian camp, a hooded falcon perched on his wrist. The stallion pranced under the eyes of the infidels, as though showing off. The falcon was a gift from the sultan to the feringhee emir Rik. It was a prized bird from the deserts of Arabia. Qaymaz had suggested that the sultan give Rik the falcon that the king of the Franks had lost upon his arrival at Akko, but the sultan had failed to appreciate the humor in Qaymaz's proposal.

The stench of the feringhee camp was so bad that Qaymaz had to breathe through his mouth, and even then his stomach turned. He did not know how the feringhees put up with the smell, but they were barbarians, so perhaps they were used to such things. Allah willing, Qaymaz would never have to visit their lands save with fire and sword.

Like his horse, Qaymaz held himself proudly, arrogantly, aware of the feringhee eyes trained on him. Under pretense of giving gifts to Rik, the Sultan was rotating all his commanders through the camp in order for them to know the camp first hand when it came time to attack it. Without appearing to, Qaymaz carefully studied the camp's layout. He noted the condition of the troops, which was surprisingly good despite the hardships they had endured. Perhaps, he reasoned, that was because most of these men were new, while those who had endured all the hardships were dead.

One of Rik's heralds, who had met Qaymaz and his flag bearer on the plain, directed them toward a large red pavilion near the camp center. It was odd that Rik did not camp on the hill with the rest of the feringhee leaders, Qaymaz thought, and he wondered what that might portend for—

He halted. Before him was a rider on a chestnut horse. The

rider wore no armor but on his arm was a plain shield, and across the pommel of his saddle rested a drawn sword. A patch covered the rider's left eye.

"Hello, Qaymaz," the rider said.

Qaymaz went still. This was the man he had sworn to kill above all others. Why did he have to come upon him now, when he was under orders to keep the peace? He smiled at the man without warmth. "Ah, it is Henry, the man the infidels call the Kitten."

To Henry, the herald said, "My lord, the emir is the guest of—"

"I know who he is," Henry growled with such intensity that the herald backed his horse away. Qaymaz's flag bearer did the same. To Qaymaz, Henry said, "It is a good morning to die, Qaymaz. Are you prepared?"

Qaymaz replied cooly. "I am prepared to die whenever Allah wills it. But even a one-eyed buffoon such as yourself can see I am here under a flag of truce."

"My seneschal Berold was under a flag of truce when you took him prisoner and tortured him to death."

"Your so-called seneschal was, like yourself, a brigand, and thus not subject to the courtesies of war."

Henry's eyes locked on those of Qaymaz. "Nor are you. Rid yourself of that bird and draw your sword."

Qaymaz made what he hoped was a bored face. "For one who styles himself a lord, your lack of manners is disappointing."

"You'll be more disappointed when I stuff a pig's balls in your mouth," Henry replied, "though I concede that will be an insult to the pig."

"The great sultan will not be happy if you interfere with one of his emissaries."

"Good. Have him come talk to me about it." Henry raised the sword. "You had your chance. Now I'm going to kill you."

He spurred his horse.

Qaymaz swore. He tried to draw his sword, but the cursed

falcon on his wrist got in the—

"My lord!" cried a booming voice.

It was King Richard, who had been summoned by the herald. With the aid of two burly squires, Richard placed himself in Henry's path, the squires supporting him by the elbows. With difficulty, Henry reined in his horse. The animal stopped feet from the king, stamping his big hooves, throwing dirt on the king's robe and red camp slippers.

Richard glared up at Henry. "This man is my guest, sir."

"This man is *my* sworn enemy," Henry replied, getting his horse under control. "He tortured my seneschal, and other good Christian men—and women—as well."

"Be that as it may," Richard said, "he is in this camp under a flag of truce. If you insult him, you insult me."

Nostrils flared, eyes wide, Henry stared from Qaymaz to the king. "Sire, you don't understand—"

"Damn your insolence! I don't care if the man is Satan himself, he is under my protection. Do you understand that?"

With difficulty Henry got control of himself. His breathing returned to something like normal and one side of his mouth curled up. "I understand, sire. I suppose this means you'll sing him a song? Maybe write a poem together?"

Richard's already sunburned face reddened further. "You will ask this man's forgiveness."

"That I will never do," Henry said.

"I command—"

"With all respect, sire, I am not yours to command. You are not my king." He turned to Qaymaz and bowed his head. "We shall meet another day."

Qaymaz placed a hand on his breast and bowed in return. "I look forward to it. The price on your head will buy me many infidel slaves."

"*Your* head I'll put on a post for the crows, after my dogs piss on it," Henry said. He looked at Richard and said, "Enjoy your picnic." Then he wheeled his horse and cantered off.

Chapter 90

As Richard's health improved, he took increasing control of the army, and of the siege. He set up ambushes at the postern gates to prevent nighttime sorties by the Saracens against the catapults. After the first few of the garrison's sorties were massacred and the heads of their soldiers displayed for the rest of the city's defenders to see, the Saracens stopped using that tactic.

Richard's wife and mother departed for Acquitaine, but he barely noticed, so obsessed was he with the siege. No detail, however small, escaped him. Under his personal direction, archers and crossbowmen continuously engaged the Saracens on the parapets, heedless of the casualties they themselves endured. Gradually they gained the upper hand on the defenders, and once that happened, laborers could work to fill in the city ditch for the final assault without fear of attack from the city walls. They filled the ditch with anything they could find—bodies of animals, trash, broken mangonels, planking from wrecked ships. Christian bodies were now used, as well, covered with layers of dirt and quicklime by men wearing strips of cloth over the lower portions of their faces, while horrified priests chanted dirges nearby. "No time for proper burial!" Richard cried to the priests from his litter. Casually, almost playfully, he lifted his shield to deflect a Saracen arrow directed his way. "God will forgive us—it's for the cause!"

All day, rocks from the trebuchets pounded the city walls, which were wreathed in dust. The Accursed Tower was beaten shapeless, its battlements a battered mess, but Meshtub's green flag still flew defiantly from a broken staff.

Though as a rule Richard didn't pay much attention to his army's English units, he became fond of a party of English archers. They were Yorkshire men from up around Barnstable—poachers, most of them, by their look. They carried the six-foot Welsh longbow, which shot an arrow measuring an ell's length, and they were consummately deadly with it. Richard marveled at the way these fellows seemed to hit anything they aimed at and the rapidity with which they got off their shots. They were led by a stout rogue called Rob. Indeed, it was this Rob who had shot the arrow that saved Helvise when she was about to be beheaded. Richard stationed Rob's men in front of the Accursed Tower. That was the most important point on the city walls, and everyone knew that, when the final attack came, it would come there. The only drawback to using Rob's men was that the arrows for their longbows needed to be hand made and fletched. The standard shafts sent out from England were too small. Rob's bowmen could shoot so rapidly that they were soon out of arrows, and were thus rendered useless until they had fashioned more.

Men sensed the end of the siege was near. Christian laborers filled in the ditch almost unimpeded now. Saracen archers hardly dared to show themselves, even with hoardings along the walls to protect them, because the Christian mangonels, of little effect on the stone walls, smashed the wooden hoardings and anyone in them. On the Accursed Tower and the towers flanking it, the Saracen mangonels, though shielded by mantlings, were under incessant barrage from arrows and stones. Both of the mangonels on St. James Tower were wrecked by a direct hit from the Bad Neighbor. The crews on the other towers couldn't be seen because of the mantlings, but their slackening rate of fire showed that the Christians were doing damage. At sea, catapults mounted in the waists of Pisan and Venetian ships battered the Tower of Flies. The port was securely blockaded so that no Saracen vessel could get in—or out. For the Saracens there were no reinforcements, no resupply, while the beach was lined with Christian ships bringing fresh men and supplies for the crusaders.

❖ ❖ ❖

When the Death's Heads weren't in the line, Roger drilled them. When Roger first joined up, he had been surprised by the amount of drill that was needed, marching in order, moving from column to line of battle—with the companies separated by gaps, the axe men covering the gaps and flanks—moving from line of battle to column. Wheeling a line left or right. Now, however, he had the men practice close order fighting— sometimes in a shield wall, sometimes in pairs, sometimes in groups of three—and he made them run, clambering up and down the camp ditch in full battle gear. Roger always took the lead, though he hated exercising as much or more than the rest of the men did.

"Why are we doing this?" the sweating men protested during a break.

"Because there's going to be a final battle, and we need to be in shape for it," Roger said.

"How do you know we'll be in the battle?"

"How do you know we won't be?" Roger said. "If we are, I don't want us to end up panting like a bunch of fat bishops when the collection plate is filled. Often as not, victory comes to the side that can stand up the longest." He didn't know that last part for sure, of course, and he felt like a hypocrite for acting like he did in front of the men, many of whom were battle-hardened veterans, but it made sense.

He added, "There will be plenty of time to rest when we're inside Acre."

"That's what you said a year ago," somebody shouted.

"A year ago, King Richard wasn't here," Ralph the Red shouted back, and the men cheered. Suddenly they didn't mind running.

❖ ❖ ❖

On the fourth day after the kalends of July, four years to the day since the disastrous battle of Hattin, Acre was almost finished. The walls trembled from their pounding at the hand of Richard's siege engines. Large mounds of broken stone formed at their base. And below the Accursed Tower, the latest mine neared completion.

King Richard had his litter carried to the mine's entrance, which lay in the ditch protecting the Christian camp on the seaward side. The Saracen counter miners hadn't discovered this shaft yet, but it wouldn't be long before they did, so there was no time to lose. Sweating men, bent double and stripped to their braies, carried thick wooden supports into the mine, passing other men who carried out buckets of dirt yoked to their shoulders. The mine's tunnel was braced with the supports. When the time came, the supports directly beneath the city walls would be set afire. When these supports collapsed from the flames, the walls above them would collapse, as well, and the city would be stormed.

A strange kind of life, Richard thought. Underground. He'd used miners before, and he'd always been amazed that men could live and work this way. He found them fascinating, as though they were beings from another world, which in a way, he supposed, they were.

The chief engineer approached, bowing. He was a wiry, grime-blackened fellow from Picardy who had been underground so long the dirt seemed part of him. "How long until you're ready, Master Miner?" Richard asked him.

The engineer calculated, scratching his head. "Three days," he allowed.

In three days the Saracens might discover the shaft, as they had discovered all the others, and block it. Richard flipped the fellow a gold coin. "Make it two, and there's one of these for each of your men, and ten of them for you."

The engineer grinned, his teeth unnaturally white against his dirty face. "Like I said, sire, we'll have it done in two."

Chapter 91

The sliver of wood was about five inches long and bleached so grey with age it was almost white. It sat on a red velvet cushion in a housing of chased brass. The wooden reliquary around it was enameled in blue and gold.

Alart of Vouzan tugged his earring. "It's from St. Peter's boat, you say?"

"From the mast," Fauston said. He handed Alart a small roll of vellum tied with a ribbon of red silk. "Here is a scroll attesting to its authenticity, signed by the archbishop of Tyre—there's his seal."

The count glanced at the scroll, which was inked in a good hand. The count couldn't read, so the scroll didn't mean much to him, but the silk ribbon and the seal looked impressive.

Alart held up the reliquary and examined the relic from various angles, being careful not to touch the ancient piece of wood lest he damage it. "How came you by this?"

Fauston raised his brows. "It took some doing, my lord."

Actually, it had been easy. Fauston knew a Greek named Gregory. Gregory looked like somebody's caricature of a Greek—swarthy, heavy bearded, gruff. Fauston had made his acquaintance months ago in a wine shop just off the Concourse, and over the course of the siege, they had become friends. Gregory claimed to be a merchant of some kind, and he was absent from the camp for long periods of time. He was the sort of fellow who knows everything and everybody, and he'd been one of the first people Fauston had approached in his search for a relic. Gregory had picked bits of food from his beard, popped them into his mouth and allowed that he knew where some relics might be found in Tyre, but that the cost would be high. Alart had advanced Fauston fifty bezants for the purchase. There was no danger of Fauston taking the money and running away with it—where would he run to? The same with Gregory—he was a familiar figure around the crusader camp. He wasn't going to jeopardize his business interests—whatever they might be—for fifty bezants.

The count continued examining the relic. It looked like an ordinary piece of wood to Fauston, but what did he know? The count was five years older than his friend King Richard, but they were much alike—handsome men with brilliant smiles, oiled hair and exquisitely trimmed beards.

"And the final price?" Alart said.

Fauston held his breath. "One hundred and twenty bezants, my lord." If the count agreed to this sum, Fauston's share of the deal would come to thirty-five bezants—not much to Gregory, perhaps, but a tidy sum in Fauston's world.

Alart considered, cast a shrewd eye at Fauston, then nodded. "That seems fair enough." And when he said that, Fauston swore to himself because he realized that Alart would have paid twice as much.

Alart closed the reliquary's lid. "Queen Eleanor has left, but there is a ship bound for Marseilles tomorrow. My wife will be thrilled with this. The mast of St. Peter's boat. Christ Himself no doubt touched that mast—He may have placed His hand on this very piece of it. Ellaire can have it mounted in her private chapel at Vouzan and pray over it every day and be as happy as ever she pleases. My thanks to you, Master Chronicler, you've done good work. By the by, should some of my friends desire relics, may I direct them to you?"

"You're too kind, my lord," Fauston replied much more glibly than he felt. He wasn't sure what he would do if the count sent someone to him and he couldn't find anything for them. It wasn't a good idea to incur the displeasure of King Richard's friends.

Still, Fauston left Alart's tent feeling good. He had a full purse and he hadn't been able to say that since his outlaw days. He remembered his life in Dunham Wood. He pictured the forest as it would be now—green and warm in the open areas, delightfully cool in the shade, birds calling, the deer sleek from eating summer foliage, the streams running clear and—

"Master Fauston!"

It was that damned page.

"Hello, Useless," Fauston said.

Eustace bristled. He didn't like to be called that. Before he could say anything, Fauston said, "I know, I know. The earl wants me."

Useless seemed to gain an inch in height every day. He was gangly now, with a few sprouts of whiskers on his chin and under his nose, which he preened with his fingers as though he had a real beard or mustache. "Hurry," he ordered.

Fauston fell into step alongside him. It was another hot day, another brassy sky. "The earl made you a squire yet?" Fauston said by way of conversation.

Eustace looked down his long nose, a move he seemed to have practiced since infancy. "I don't recall giving you permission to ask me questions."

Fauston stuck a foot between Eustace's long legs and sent him sprawling in the dirt. Eustace rose, his face beet red. "You did that on purpose."

"I'll do more than that if you don't keep a civil tongue in your head."

Eustace's hand went for the dagger at his side. Fauston grabbed the boy's left elbow, turned him, placed his foot against his backside and sent him sprawling again, at the same time taking the dagger from the lad's sheath.

Eustace sat up, rubbing his nose, which, along with one cheek, had been rubbed raw from contact with the ground. Fauston flipped the dagger, caught it by the blade, and threw it so that it landed between the boy's legs, missing his crotch by an inch. Eustace stared at the blade—and the near loss of his incipient manhood—wide eyed.

"Get up and stop playing in the dirt," Fauston chided him. "We're going to be late."

Eustace worked his dagger from the ground and hurried after Fauston.

Chapter 92

Geoffrey bent while a squire tugged his mail hauberk over his head. Geoffrey shrugged into the heavy hauberk, seating it on the leather haubergon worn underneath, wincing as the mail rings pinched his whiskers.

"Be careful, damn you," he told the squire.

"Yes, my lord," the squire said.

Geoffrey was arming himself preparatory to seeking combat with the Saracen cavalry out on the plain. This daily skirmishing was popular with the knights and men at arms, if for no other reason than it got them on horseback, where they felt more at home than on foot. Geoffrey had always thought it a waste of lives—enough men died from disease, why lose more to meaningless combat? He was in the minority, though, and as a great lord, he was expected to lead his men on these forays. It was like a tournament that never ended, a tournament contested with weapons whose edges had not been blunted. On the positive side, the Saracens had been reluctant to come out and give battle the last several days—they seemed to be losing heart now that the siege was nearing its end.

Geoffrey's new marshal, Thierry, and his higher ranking knights were in the pavilion, armed and eager to get going. His steward, Mainier, and his new chaplain, Father Otho, stood nearby, Otho looking almighty pleased with himself. He had sought an urgent audience with Geoffrey. "Something that can't wait," he'd said.

"This better be good," Geoffrey warned Otho. "It's your job if it isn't." He already wished he'd never made this pompous ass his confessor.

Otho bowed his head. "It will be, my lord, I assure you. Ah, here he comes now."

Fauston had entered the tent, followed by Eustace, whose face was all scraped up. "What happened to you?" Geoffrey asked Eustace.

Eustace glanced sideways, at Fauston. "Tripped, my lord."

"Hmm, better be more careful." Geoffrey beckoned Fauston forward. Then he nodded to Otho to begin.

The priest bowed to the earl and turned to Fauston. With a concerned look, he handed Fauston some sheets of rolled parchment. "I've had a clerk copy the latest pages of your chronicle," he told Fauston, "the part about the unfortunate destruction of the copper tower. We're sending them home. They're to be read in the pulpit of St. Stephen's Cathedral, so that people can learn what's going on here. I wanted you to look them over, to see if there's any errors."

This was something new. Fauston supposed the earl wanted to make certain he got no blame for the disaster of the Not-So-Invincible Tower. He glanced over the pages, which to him were a mass of squiggly lines. He let his eyes move back and forth across the lines, as he had seen men do when reading. "It all seems to be in order," he said and made to hand the pages back.

"Why don't you read it aloud?" Otho suggested. "Lord Geoffrey hasn't heard this passage yet."

Fauston kept the pages extended toward the priest, smiling modestly. "I've said before, Father, I don't like to read my own—"

"Please," Otho insisted. "Read."

Fauston glanced toward the earl. The squire was adjusting a white surcoat over the earl's armor, to ward off the sun. "Oh, humor the fellow," the earl told Fauston.

Fauston shrugged, took the pages and adjusted them. He'd taken to memorizing everything Roger wrote in case something like this happened again. Holding the parchment in one hand, he extended his right arm dramatically and declaimed:

"Joyfully did God's army make ready its attack. I have heard it told that every man in the camp was shriven and received the Holy Sacrament that day, but I cannot say if it is true or not. Listen to a strange thing. So eager were these men to enter the city, so desirous was each lord of securing the best house for himself, that their agents and servants and baggage fought with the soldiers for space in the lines (Fauston knew that Otho had been one of these). *There you would have seen stout chests and rich furnishings brought forward on carts and horses. There you would have heard bailiffs shout harsh commands.*

When all was ready, it was the bishop of Beauvais—no man was holier—who blessed the great tower and—"

Otho held up a hand. "I believe that will do," he said pleasantly.

Fauston stopped, looking bored, as if he had better things to do. Insouciantly, he handed the parchment back to Otho, who passed it to a clerk. Otho nodded to the clerk. "Read."

The young clerk, whose name was Bernard, tried to suppress a smile as he lifted the parchment and read:

"Inventory as of the Kalends of July, Anno Domini 1091: Horseshoes: three thousand.
Bacon rashers: five hundred, less thirty owed to his majesty the king as payment for—"

Otho held up his hand again. He turned to the earl and said, "This is an inventory, my lord. It is not the chronicle."

The pavilion fell silent. Fauston made a deprecatory gesture. "I knew that, of course, my lord. I was just having fun with—"

"You cannot read, can you?" Father Otho interrupted.

Fauston hesitated. It would do no good to deny it. They would only test him again. The earl was watching him closely.

"No," Fauston sighed.

Otho went on, enjoying himself. "From that admission, we may deduce that you cannot write, either. Is that correct?"

"Yes," Fauston agreed with an even longer sigh.

"Therefore, you cannot have written my lord Geoffrey's chronicle."

"No."

"I'm sorry, I can't hear you. Could you speak a bit louder?"

Fauston straightened. "I said no. I didn't write it."

There was a buzz round the tent. Otho turned to the earl with a bow and a look of grim satisfaction. "This fellow is a fraud, my lord. I've suspected it from the start." When they had taken down the tent belonging to the earl's whore, the servant Matthew had found a box containing writing materials. That meant that either the whore was writing the chronicle or Fauston was swyving her, too. The first alternative was impossible—no woman could write. The second was equally unlikely—even Fauston was not stupid enough to poach his master's game. That meant someone else was doing the writing, keeping his materials in the whore's tent.

The earl studied Fauston. The earl was angry, but there was interest in his look, as well. "You misrepresented yourself to me, Fauston."

"I did, my lord, and I apologize."

The earl raised his arms while the squire belted on his sword. "The obvious questions is, if you didn't write the chronicle, who did?" A look flitted across the earl's face as if he intuited the answer, then he shook his head as if to say, no, it couldn't be.

Fauston started to reply, then stopped. If he told the earl that Roger was the author, the earl—and Otho—would want to know how a common soldier could read and write. If they learned that Roger had been a monk at Huntley, Otho might put two and two together and recollect that a monk had been one of those who robbed him—not far from Huntley. More importantly, Alart of Vouzan might learn that his son's killer was in the English camp.

Giving up Roger's name could be a death sentence for both of them, but especially for Roger.

"I'd rather not say, my lord. The man in question is modest and does not wish his name bruited about."

"*Make* him tell," Father Otho said. He wanted to unmask the heretic who had written that play and have him punished.

The earl regarded Otho coldly. To Fauston he said, "I'd gladly offer the fellow your position as chronicler."

"He wouldn't accept it, my lord. He wishes to remain a—a knight. He only worked on the chronicle as a favor to me."

Again that look crossed the earl's face as if he might know who the chronicler was. Then he said, "It's of no matter. If the fellow doesn't want to be known, that is his privilege."

"I beg your pardon, my lord," said Otho, "but is it? This unknown man could only have learned to read and write if he was a cleric of some kind. He is obviously trying to conceal his real identity, and he can have no good reason for doing that."

"That's hardly my affair," the earl said. "Half the men in my command are here under false names." To Fauston, he said, "You disappoint me, Fauston—is Fauston your real name, by the way?"

"It is, my lord," Fauston said.

The earl said, "So, what shall we do with you?"

"Burn him," Otho demanded.

"Oh, for God's sake," said the earl. "On what charge?"

"Heresy," replied Otho as though the answer was obvious. "His lies were committed in the Holy land, which makes them crimes against Christ, which makes them heresy."

"I'll burn you an you don't keep quiet," the earl told Otho. He straightened his sword belt till the weapon felt comfortable on his hip. "I like you, Fauston. Lies aside, you've done me good service. I'm inclined to let you remain with my staff—I can always use good men."

Otho protested. "My lord—"

"Be quiet!" the earl thundered.

Otho backed off. The earl went on, speaking to Fauston. "But why lie? Why pretend to be a wandering scholar?"

"I had to, my lord. That bailiff's party back in England would have hung me else." He realized his mistake as soon as he said it, but it was too late to take it back.

"Mm," said the earl, "I see your point. Why did they think you were that fellow—I forget his name."

From the corner of his eye, Fauston cast an anxious look at Otho. He tried to shrug the question off, as though it were nothing. "I forget as well, my lord. We never heard of the fellow in Lincolnshire."

"Brock!" The earl snapped his finger, pleased with himself. "Brock something or other, wasn't it? He's famous, I believe."

Fauston made a face as though he had no idea.

"Brock the Badger," Otho intoned, and as he did his eyes came alight with recognition. He pointed a finger at Fauston. "I *knew* I had seen you before." He turned to the earl. "This man is Brock the Badger, my lord. He's not only famous, he's the most notorious outlaw in England. He robbed me on the Keslow Road."

At that revelation the tent first went silent, then exploded in noise. *Time to go*, Fauston thought. He wasn't going to talk his way out of this one. He turned and grabbed Eustace by the collar and belt. He picked Eustace up—thank God the brat was light—and hurled him bodily at Otho. The boy hit Otho and the steward Mainier, knocking them both to the floor in a heap. Fauston dodged the tangle of men on the ground, vaulted onto the head table, scattering cups and plates, and slid off the other side. Before anyone could stop him, he raced through the earl's private chamber and, dodging the guard, dove for the tent bottom where it rested between two pegs.

"After him!" Otho cried. "Stop him!'

Fauston half-slid, half-crawled under the tent. He freed himself from the heavy fabric, startling passersby, and sprinted away.

"Catch him, you fools!"

Guards followed him, but their armor and weapons got caught in the tent fabric. Other guards and servants ran from the tent's entrance and chased him.

Fauston raced across the crowded Toron. He took turn after turn in the warren of pavilions. After the last turn he slowed and mingled in the throng of men, boys, women and animals.

His heart was racing. He heard a distant hubbub behind him but he dare not look back. Just act as though he was out and about as usual.

How had Otho guessed he was Brock? Most likely he'd made it up so that the earl would be forced to hang him. The earl might let an ordinary highwayman go free; he'd be derelict in his duty if he didn't hang Brock the Badger.

Fauston made his way to the bridge across the ditch, trying to take his time, trying not to pay attention to the shouting behind him, expecting rough hands to be placed on his shoulders at any moment.

Then he was on the bridge.

Crossing.

Ahead, guards checked people coming onto the Toron. They paid no attention to those leaving. He was nearing the guards now—

"There he is! That's him!"

Fauston started to run.

"Guards—stop that man!"

A guard turned, raised his spear to block Fauston. Fauston lowered his shoulder and drove it into the guard's chest— Christ, this was like the old days—knocking the guard aside, Fauston stumbling but regaining his feet, and then he was across the bridge and running, running, running, until he had lost himself in the maze of shacks and warehouses behind the Concourse.

He bent over, hands on knees, breathing hard, safe for the moment. Someone shoved him aside. "If yer going to die, do it over there and stop blocking traffic."

Fauston hobbled to one side of the lane. Sweat poured out of his hair and down his body. What was he going to do now? He had thirty-five bezants, but that wouldn't see him far—it damned sure wouldn't see him back to England, assuming he even wanted to go back to England, where they were looking to hang him. Now they were looking to hang him here, as well. Maybe hanging was all he was good for.

He straightened, pulled out his pouch and juggled it, listening to the coins jingle. Then he grinned. If they wanted to hang him, they had to catch him first.

Chapter 93

Ailith spread a layer of ashes on the bucking cloth, which was stretched across the top of the soak tub. The washerwomen got their ashes from the camp fires. Ailith imagined ashes had been hard to come by during the winter, but now they were plentiful—wood was coming in by the shipload from Cyprus. She wondered if there would be a tree left standing on that island by the time the siege was over.

She poured a small bucket of hot water over the ashes and into the soak tub, where the dirty clothes were piled. The clothes had previously been soaked in a mixture of water and urine, the last of which which was never difficult to come by. Urine was good for getting out grease and oil; ashes were good for removing other types of dirt. The first mixture had been tipped into a little ditch that ran down into a cluster of rocks, around which bloomed scattered saltgrass and thorn bushes. The ash water would run through the clothes, then trickle out a pipe in the bottom of the tub and back into the hot water kettle, which was set over a small fire. There the water would be reheated and the process would start over again, until the water from the pipe ran clean. Between applications the clothes were stirred with a long stick so that the water could get to them evenly.

Fresh water was a precious commodity in the crusader camp. Some was caught during the infrequent storms, but most was still brought from the marshy River Belus. The Belus water was dirty, but the crusaders had discovered that, for some strange reason, if you boiled it before drinking, it seemed to cut down the incidence of disease. And though fresh water was one of the many items now being delivered to the army by ship (thank King Richard for that), only the higher nobles had access to it for washing. Everyone else was forced to make do with sea water. Sea water left a salt crust on the clothes that made them stiff and irritated some of the men's skin, but there was no help for it. On the positive side, the salt water seemed to do a better job of killing lice. There was also an unlimited supply of it, and each dawn saw a long line of women carrying yoked buckets from the beach to the camp.

Ailith's blonde hair was pinned back against the sun and the steamy heat from the tub. She wiped her forehead on her arm. Her skin had developed a deep tan. She didn't know what she thought about that, tan skin not being favored among well-born ladies, but there was nothing she could do about it. Besides, she wasn't pretending to be a lady any more. Her coarse wool dress clung wetly to her, and she fluffed the fabric away from her chest, fanning her skin, an action she performed a hundred times a day without thinking.

Around her the morning chatter of women and the beating of wooden battledores on rock or wood was punctuated by the squalling of Mary's babe. Mary was one of the lucky ones. Several hundred babies had been born during the siege, but only a few had survived. All of the earl's women felt protective toward the child. There had been a lot of sentiment for naming the boy "Miracle," but in the end Mary had called him "Richard," after England's king.

At the next station, Margaret had finishing soaking her load in the tub. She rinsed the load thoroughly in a tub of fresh seawater, then she pulled the first item—a much-darned shirt—from the tub and laid it on a smooth, angled rock. She dug at a flea bite on her neck and eased herself into a low box that was padded with straw and linen to protect her knees. She took a rectangular wooden battledore and began alternately beating and rubbing the wet shirt, to get out the remaining dirt. After the clothes had been beaten, they would get a final rinse, then be hung out to dry.

"Never ends, does it?" Margaret said as she whacked the wool shirt with the battledore. "You may not get rich doing wash, but you'll never lack for work. If men are anything, they're dirty."

Ailith laughed, wiping her forehead again. "God knows how they'd manage without us."

Margaret had lost weight since leaving the earl's retinue and rejoining the washerwomen; her skin hung loose on her big frame. "When the washing's done, there's sewing and mending to do."

Ailith watched the water running from her tub. One more soaking should do for this load. "I meant to tell you—Therese says there's new bolts of that material they call cotton on the Concourse. We should buy some and make shirts and hose for the men."

Margaret nodded sagely. "Aye, that'll bring us some good money. Be even better for you—you've an eye for the sewing."

Ailith shrugged, still watching the water. "Me dad made me practice. Said it would make me more 'attractive' to suitors."

"And did it?"

"Like a charm. I had this one old geezer, thatch of white hair growing out his ears like a bird's nest, thought it would be ever so grand could I cook and mend for him and his seven sons and daughters and God knows how many grandbrats."

Margaret laughed. "What did you say?"

"Told Dad I'd sew *him* in a shroud if he married me to that antiquity. Bugger was fifty if he was a day."

The washerwomen's camp was on the far side of the latrines from the men's camp. Ailith barely noticed the noise of battle at the city walls any more. The women were isolated here, detached, as if the battle didn't affect their lives, as if it didn't even exist except to provide them customers.

Some of the washerwomen were married to soldiers; a greater number were soldiers' widows. A few had tagged along with the army from a spirit of adventure or to escape their husbands or the drudgery of village life. When Ailith had been Geoffrey's mistress—God, how she *loathed* that word—many of the earl's nobles had assumed that washerwomen were whores, but they had been wrong. There were a few loose women among them, but not many—there wasn't time to service the men that way, and even if there had been, the women were usually too exhausted from the washing to think about sex. The men didn't hold that against them. There were occasional instances of rape or violence against the army's washerwomen, but on the whole, soldiers of all nations were surprisingly protective of those who rendered them such a valuable service.

Ailith poured another pot of hot water across the bucking cloth. Then she took a tin cup of drinking water from the communal barrel, using the cup to brush the surface of the water first, to chase away the myriad insects and break up the film on the top.

The rhythmic beating of Margaret's bat against wet cloth and rock faltered. "Look who's here," Margaret said, pointing with her chin.

Ailith followed Margaret's gaze and saw Roger carrying an armload of clothes across the open ground by the laundresses' tents. Ailith was certain he was coming toward her, and her heart stopped, because she didn't know how she would deal with that. Then—even though Ailith knew he saw her—Roger veered off to the left, where Delva—Delva the Bull, they called her—was spreading a load of freshly washed shirts and drawers and hose across some bushes to dry.

"Delva!" Ailith swore indignantly. "Of all the—"

Delva—or Godelva, for that was her real name—had been married to a spearman who had died during the famine ("Lucky for him," cracked Margaret.). When Ailith had first joined the washerwomen, there had been some resistance to her presence, even though she was a friend of Margaret's. Everyone knew she had been Geoffrey's mistress, and even though they themselves might have jumped at the opportunity to be kept by such a great man, it hadn't stopped them from resenting Ailith. It hadn't helped that Ailith was still wearing an expensive dress when she arrived. At Ailith's first evening meal in the washerwomen's camp, Delva, her dark hair cut short, had clomped up to where Ailith was sitting. Delva yanked the bowl of porridge from Ailith's hands.

Margaret started to rise, but Ailith restrained her.

Ailith stood. "Give that back," she told Delva.

Delva barked a loud laugh and turned, addressing the other women. "'Give it back.' 'Give it back,' she says. Listen to Miss High and Mighty." She turned to Ailith. "I'll give it back, all right." She hawked noisily and spat a great glob into the porridge bowl. She held the bowl out to Ailith. "Here, there's a bit of extra flavor for you."

She had just started to laugh when Ailith head butted her, breaking her nose. Ailith pushed Delva's shoulders backwards and swept the big woman's legs from under her, knocking her onto her back. Ailith drove a knee into Delva's midsection, forcing the air out of her, and stuck her knife into the bigger woman's ear.

"I'll dig the wax out of your ears and make candles from it. Would you like that?"

Blood gushed from Delva's broken nose; some of it ran into her mouth, making her splutter as she answered. "No."

Ailith pressed the knife tip deeper into Delva's ear. "You sure? I'm a fair hand at candle making."

"I'm sure," Delva whimpered, her feet scrabbling at the pain in her ear.

Ailith stood and stomped Delva in the stomach once for good measure, making her cry out. Most of Ailith's porridge had spilled on the ground when she attacked Delva, so Ailith crossed to the other side of the fire and took Delva's bowl. "You don't mind, do you, dear?" she asked Delva sweetly, using her best high-born accent.

There was no more trouble after that.

Now, Delva's nose was lopsided from where it had been broken, and Ailith felt bad about that. Delva hadn't been attractive to begin with; that sideways nose wasn't going to help her get a new husband. Ailith waited until Roger had finished his business with Delva. As he left, Ailith sidled up behind him. "What—you're too good to give me your laundry?"

Roger turned, and his face went red beneath its deep tan. He had filled out, despite the winter famine. He looked like a man now, not like the boy she had met so long ago. In fact, with his short hair and beard and his bright blue eyes, he looked rather dashing.

"I'm in the laundry business, too, you know," she went on. "I can use the money as much as Delva can."

Roger made a futile gesture with his hand and stammered, "I didn't . . . I didn't want you to . . . to see my—"

Ailith balled her fists on her hips. "Roger of—of wherever you're from! I'll have you know that at home I did laundry for six brothers, two sisters, and a grandad who fouled his breeches so often that we wouldn't let him sleep in the same bed with the rest of us. There's nothing I haven't seen before."

Before Roger could say anything, she added, "Not to mention taking care of *you* last winter when you were sick." She crossed her arms over her chest, stuck up her chin, and looked away from him. "You've hurt my feelings."

"I'm sorry," Roger said. "I guess—I guess I thought it would be better if we kept apart. After what happened when last we spoke."

She turned back to him and let down her arms, as though forgiving him some transgression. "We can still be friends, you know. I don't hate you."

He looked tentative, so she said, "And you needn't worry— I'm not trying to come between you and that Helvise."

Roger let out his breath as though relieved.

"She seems very nice," Ailith added.

Roger couldn't hold back a smile. "She is."

"I hope the two of you will be happy. I mean that."

"Thank you, that means a lot to me. She leaves for Germany on tomorrow morning's tide. I'm to join her when Jerusalem is taken."

"In Germany?" Ailith said, eyes widening.

Roger nodded. "Yes."

"I'm not even sure where Germany is."

Roger laughed. "Neither am I. It's a big place, though; I should be able to find it."

"I thought you were going to stay in the Holy Land until you died, to redeem yourself?"

Roger shrugged. "Things change."

"What about your father? If you go to Germany, you'll lose any chance of finding him."

Roger glanced at his ring involuntarily. "That was a dream. There was never any chance I'd find him. He's probably been dead for years. No one seems to live very long out here."

He looked like he wanted to change the subject. "How about you?" His ran his eye around the washerwomen's camp, as though taking it in for the first time. "How are you making out here?"

"Believe it or not, this is probably the happiest I've ever been in my life," Ailith said.

Roger frowned. "You're serious?"

"Yes."

"The earl's wife has gone, you know. I'm sure he'd take you back."

"He's already tried. More than once."

"And?"

"And I told him no."

Roger looked confused, and Ailith explained. "I'm not a whore, Roger. I realized that's what people thought of me. You can't believe how bad that made me feel. I was so humiliated—I had never thought of myself that way. I'd rather be an honest washerwoman than a lord's harlot." She cleared her throat, trying to make light of the situation. "'Course, my hands are a mess now."

She showed him her red, wrinkled hands, turning them over.

Roger said, "You don't miss the jewels, the fine clothes, the good food?"

"There's more to life than fine clothes and jewels." She

smiled. "All right, maybe I do miss the food, but it's not worth the loss of my self-respect. Geoffrey says he loves me, and maybe he does, but I won't put myself through that again. I won't lower myself."

"Do you love him?" Roger asked.

"I thought I did."

"And now?"

"Now I don't know. But even if I do love him, I'm not going back to him."

Roger looked down. Then he said, "I need to be going. I'm on duty soon. We're on duty most all the time now, with the siege nearly over."

Ailith nodded. "Hard to believe it's actually coming to an end. Sometimes it seems I've spent my whole life here."

Roger said, "Rumor has it that Meshtub—the Saracen commander—has been negotiating with King Richard, but I don't know if that's true. We always figured the Saracens would die rather than surrender." He paused, "Well, goodbye."

"Goodbye," Ailith replied casually.

Roger started away.

"Roger!"

Roger turned. Ailith came after him.

"There's something I need to tell you," she said. She paused, collecting herself. This wasn't going to be easy. "Remember when you told me you'd never forgotten that kiss we shared back in England?"

Roger nodded and she went on, slowly, her voice lowered. "The truth is, I never forgot it, either. It touched me in a way I can't explain. I'd never felt anything like that before. I never stopped thinking about you, but I never imagined I'd see you again. How could I? If I had . . . " Her voice trailed off.

After a moment, she continued. "When I did see you, I was already with Geoffrey." She stared into his eyes. "I chose security over love, and I ended up with neither."

They looked at each other a long moment, then Ailith said, "I'm glad we can be friends again."

"So am I," Roger said. "Will you be all right?"

She forced a smile. "I'll be fine, you know me." She waved an arm around the laundresses' camp. "This is luxury compared to sleeping with the pigs and keeping that old man with the carbuncled nose from trying to marry me. Always trying to lift my skirts and inspect the goods, he was."

Roger leaned over and kissed her forehead. "I have to go."

"I know."

He turned and started away.

"And I want your laundry!" she cried after him.

He raised a hand and waved in acknowledgement, not looking back.

Ailith watched him go, walking with his long, powerful stride, his big shoulders set square. She sniffed, brushed something from her cheek.

Margaret came up beside her. "You all right, dear?"

"Who me? Of course." Try as she would, Ailith couldn't keep her voice from cracking. "The heat from these tubs must be getting to me."

Margaret gave her a knowing look. "Aye, it'll do that."

"I better to get back to work," Ailith said. "I have a lot to do."

Chapter 94

Saladin read the message, squinting in the first faint light of dawn. A servant held a candle above his shoulder to make the task easier. Despite the early hour, the sultan was fully dressed, as he had not been sleeping well lately, while the men around him in his silk tent were in all manner of disarray, having just come from their beds.

The message had been inked in tiny letters on a strip of linen; it had come from Akko by pigeon, which was the only means the sultan had of communicating with the city's besieged garrison. The pigeons were sent out during the nighttime hours because the infidels had gotten too good at catching them with falcons when they flew by day.

Saladin finished reading and pursed his thin lips. He looked at his commanders. "Meshtub says he cannot hold out for more than a few days. After that, he must surrender."

There was silence. Saladin's counselors glanced at one another, their faces reflected by the torchlight. They had known it might come to this—the feringhee blockade had prevented them from sending supplies to the city for some months. Still, they had not imagined the crisis would come so soon. It seemed as if the city would hold out forever, as if this siege had a life of its own, almost as if it were not even real, so little progress had been made since its beginning.

Saladin went on. "If Akko falls, we are lost."

Qaymaz knew what this meant. "So we attack?"

Saladin nodded slowly, almost sadly.

Al-Afdal, "the Bull," Saladin's heavy-jowled oldest son, rubbed his hands together with anticipation. "We should have done this months ago. Years, even."

Saladin turned a hard eye on his son. "You question my

leadership?"

The Bull stammered. "No. No, of course not, Father." Though everyone knew that he did.

Saladin went on. "I had hoped starvation and disease would reduce the feringhees, but for every one of the infidels that dies, two more come from the west to take his place. They must have a limitless supply of men in those lands, so careless are they of their lives." He shook his head. "I cannot understand their thinking. Any sane commander would have abandoned this siege before the first winter, much less the second. Yet the infidels have persisted in their folly."

The Bull smiled grimly. "And now we will drive them into the sea."

"Allah willing," said his father.

Saladin was not as sanguine as his son. The Christians might be stupid, but they could be good fighters. Fourteen years before, the young Leper King had completely destroyed Saladin's army, and Saladin himself had only avoided capture by escaping on a racing camel. Given the right leadership, the Christians might beat him again. It was only by the will of Allah that the Leper King had died and the fool Guy of Lusignan had taken his place. If not for that stroke of fortune, Saladin might still be sitting on the far side of the Jordan river and Al-Quds would still be in the hands of the infidels. Saladin did not know what kind of leader Rik was, but it was probably best to fight him now, while Rik was still weak from illness.

Qaymaz interrupted his thoughts. "We will attack with our entire army this time?" It was more a statement than a question.

"Yes," Saladin said. His brother's Egyptian troops had finally arrived; Saladin at last had his full force. There would be no more diversionary attacks. "Come, let us look at the model we have built of the feringhee camp, so you know what you must do. There are many preparations to be made."

"When do we attack?" Qaymaz asked.

"Tomorrow."

Robert Broomall

Part IV

TO THE DEATH

Robert Broomall

Chapter 95

Betin shivered and pulled his cloak tighter around his shoulders. Fog had rolled off the sea after midnight and now covered the shore for some distance inland. Betin had been told he would be never be cold when he came to the Holy Land, but when you're a soldier, you learn not to believe anything you're told.

Betin was in charge of a five-man patrol of Burgundian spearmen, stationed in the no-man's-land between the camp ditch and the Saracen lines, watching for enemy movements. These patrols were dangerous and, by and large, hated by the men. When they blundered into similar Saracen patrols, there were nasty little skirmishes—hacking and stabbing in the dark. These skirmishes didn't receive the glory of battles, but the men killed in them were just as dead.

"Can't see a damned thing," Betin muttered to Etienne, beside him.

Etienne blew on his hands. "Waste o' time, us coming out here anymore. Goat Fuckers have been quiet lately."

Betin said, "Rumor has it they're pulling back because the city is about to fall."

Etienne, a lanky, scraggly bearded fellow who'd been a shepherd in an earlier life, went on. "One good thing about the fog—we don't have to take cover. We can stand up and move about without nobody seeing us."

"Don't move about too much," Betin cautioned. "Bad as this muck is, it would be easy to get turned around and go the wrong way when it's time to head back to camp."

"Wouldn't the Goat Fuckers like that," Etienne grunted.

Betin shivered again and stamped his feet to bring blood into them. "Knights don't pull this shit duty. No, they stay in their tents, snug and dry and warm, and leave the dirty work to men like us. It's men like us win the battles, the sieges, and the wars, but the knights and nobles get all the credit."

Etienne, a veteran of almost as many campaigns as Betin, nodded sagely. "The way of the world, *mon ami*."

Betin was 31 or so, he wasn't really sure. He'd been a soldier for fifteen or sixteen years—he wasn't sure about that either. He was of average height, well built, with dark hair that he kept short because girls liked it better that way. Not that he saw any girls at Acre, not even whores. Funny, since it was because of a girl that he'd become a soldier. Lysette, her name had been. She was a big, earthy wench, but she'd lifted her skirts to him, and when he was that age, he wasn't about to say no. Hell, he wouldn't say no if she lifted her skirts to him now. Inevitably, he had got her with child. She had wanted to get married, and she had four big, earthy brothers who were determined to see that wish become reality. Betin wasn't about to spend the rest of his life hitched to a plough horse like Lysette, though, so he'd ducked out of his village in the middle of the night and never looked back. Lucky for him there were always openings for young men who wanted to be soldiers. He'd seen a bit of the world since then, had a bit of fun. He'd come to the Holy Land with the duke of Burgundy. Before that he'd served with the count of Langlois. Before that—but what did it matter? Soldiering was soldiering, you just wore a different lord's badge. Sometimes you fought for one side; sometimes for the other. This job was different, of course. This was for more than money; this was for a cause. Sometimes Betin wondered what he'd do when he got too old to be a soldier. He had no money set aside, nowhere to call home. Maybe he'd make enough out of this job to buy a place somewhere and settle down.

Around them, the fog seemed to be lightening a bit. "Going on dawn," he told Etienne. "Let's go back."

"Past time," Etienne grumbled. "I'm freezing."

Then Betin heard a noise. He tapped Etienne's shoulder

and placed a finger to his lips.

He strained his ears. The damned fog made sounds play tricks. Maybe it was nothing.

He heard it again.

"Something out there," he whispered. He nodded for Etienne to pass the warning to the other men.

Betin strained his eyes into the mist. A prickly feeling ran up his spine. He motioned his patrol to begin backing up, toward the camp.

Etienne touched Betin's arm and pointed. Betin looked. Was it his imagination, or did the lower part of the fog seem thicker? He wiped his eyes, squinted.

The thickness became a line of men looming out of the mist. Coming forward. The line stretched right and left as far as Betin could see. Betin felt the ground move beneath his feet.

"Get out of here!" he said. "Now!"

He turned and started running for the camp along with Etienne and the other men, their footsteps muffled in the fog. Something punched Betin hard in the back and he stumbled. He looked down, saw the head of a spear protruding from his chest.

"Shit," he said.

He tried to keep running, but he couldn't make his legs work right. Everything was spinning. He found himself on the ground, without knowing how he'd gotten there. He tried to cry out, to sound an alarm, but all that came from his mouth was a hoarse gurgle. He gasped for breath; there were spots in front of his eyes, and he wondered why he felt no pain.

Then there was nothing.

Chapter 96

Roger escorted Helvise to the beach. The cool fog provided a welcome respite from the July heat. The ships drawn up on the sand were ghostly shapes in the murk; the ships anchored offshore could not be seen at all. The city walls were more of a gloomy foreshadowing than a reality. The muffled *thump*, *thump* of the mangonels was punctuated by an occasional *boom* as rocks from one of the trebuchets struck the walls. A pearly luminescence deep within the eastern greyness might have been the sun.

Tatwine and the ex-poacher Slowfoot had volunteered to carry Helvise's trunk and gear. It was a thoughtful gesture and saved hiring servants, though Roger suspected the two of them were just as interested in getting out of work detail. The beach and its access paths were crowded with laborers, merchants, soldiers and washerwomen, along with mules and donkeys and camels. Men and animals loomed out of the fog, went by, disappeared. The shouting of overseers and camel drivers reverberated dully, punctuated by the calling of sea gulls.

Roger and Helvise paused at the top of the low bluff, stepping aside to let others pass. They had made a passionate farewell earlier and were still lost in its afterglow. Helvise wore the green dress with a cloak against the chill. "It seems unreal," she said, looking down at the beach. "I knew this moment would come, but I never really thought it would *come*." She turned her head. "Does that make sense?"

"It does," Roger said. "I've felt exactly the same way."

She squeezed his hand. "I wish you were coming with me."

"So do I, but you'd think less of me if I deserted my men. Maybe not now, but in the future."

She sighed and nodded reluctantly.

Roger went on. "When you get the news that Jerusalem has fallen, you'll know I'm on my way." He grinned. "Who knows, I may even bring the news myself."

They made their way down the bluff to Helvise's ship, a one-masted cog called *Mary, Star of the Sea*. The ship was drawn up on the pebbly beach, strakes propped against her side to steady her until it was time to float her off. She had a Cypriot captain and was bound for Trieste. From that city, Helvise would make her way home overland, joining a company of pilgrims or merchants for safety.

They ascended the wooden plank that served as a ramp, Roger taking Helvise's hand. Roger stepped onto the ship's deck first and assisted Helvise down. Slowfoot and Tatwine followed. Slowfoot put down Helvise's trunk. Tatwine had Helvise's crossbow, her quiver full of bolts, and the scarred green pavise, which he carried on his back by its sling.

Roger picked up the crossbow and ran a finger across the ornate, dragon-head tiller. He gave Helvise a quizzical look. "Will you need these in Germany?"

"I'm going to hang them in our hall," she told him. "They'll remind us—and our guests, and our descendants—of what we went through out here." Her eyes twinkled. "You can add that helmet of yours with the painted skull on it."

"It might look good at that," Roger admitted.

There was a fog-muffled uproar in the distance, from the direction of the camp ditch.

Heads turned instinctively. It was probably a probing skirmish along the ditch, though there hadn't been one of those in a while. They expected the noise to fade, as it usually did after a few minutes. Instead it grew louder, spreading along what seemed like the entire camp perimeter.

Tatwine glanced over his shoulder at Roger. "Sounds like a big fight."

Slowfoot scratched the "B" branded on his cheek. "Real big."

The noise went on, growing louder and louder. "It sounds

like an all-out attack on the camp," said Roger, disbelieving. Was that possible? It had been so quiet . . .

Roger turned to Helvise. "We'd better get back."

He took her in his arms and kissed her, pressing his lips to hers, tasting the salty warmth of them, pressing her equally warm body against his as if trying to make the two of them one. Tatwine elbowed Slowfoot, who was staring, and the two of them turned discreetly away.

Tears brimmed Helvise's eyes; they spilled over and ran down her cheeks. "Goodbye," Roger whispered.

Helvise was so choked up she could barely speak. "I'll miss you."

Roger kissed her again, held her close and pressed his face against her wet cheek, hot from tears. "It won't be long, then we'll be together forever."

She clung to him as if she would never let him go. "What if something happens to you?"

He stepped back and wiped her cheek. "It won't. I'll make sure of it."

Above the distant roar of battle, they heard alarmed trumpets and drums from the Christian camp, along with cymbals and cheers from the city walls. There was no more time.

Roger took Helvise's hands in his. "I'll see you in Germany."

"Hurry," she said.

Roger forced himself to grin cheerfully and bowed. "I'll pass your request to King Richard, my lady."

He kissed her once more, then let go and motioned to Tatwine and Slowfoot. The ship's ramp was crammed with men bringing supplies on board, so Roger and his friends jumped off the side onto the sand, where they began running. Around them, the pace of activity had picked up noticeably.

Helvise watched the three Englishmen until they were lost in the fog and the mass of men and animals moving onto and off the beach. She turned toward the distant racket, whose volume was increasing by the minute. She crossed herself and prayed for Roger's safety.

Chapter 97

Because of the fog and the attendant lack of visibility, the Saracens were across the ditch and into the Christian camp before most of the Christians knew what was happening. The Saracens had scouted the places where the ditch was in disrepair, and they sent their columns across there. They captured two of the bridges and lowered them, letting their horsemen into the camp.

The Christians in the outer ring of camps tried to organize a defense, but the camps were spread apart, with gaps between them through which the Saracens poured. Before the Christians could cobble a battle line together, the Saracens were behind them, unseen in the fog. Men fought and died in little groups. Others were bypassed by the swift-moving enemy and left to wonder what was happening. Still others were taken prisoner, though most of them did not live long.

"Surely this fog is a gift from Allah," Saladin had told the generals who led the assault troops. "Drive as deep and as quickly into the feringhee camp as you can. Do not stop. The Egyptian infantry in your rear will eliminate any resistance behind you. Your goal is to reach the shore and cut the feringhee army into three pieces before they can regroup. While you do this, Qaymaz will attack the hill where the infidel commanders have pitched their tents. Allah willing, it will be like the Horns of Hattin again—when we take that hill, the rest of the infidels will give up and the day will be ours."

Roger, Tatwine and Slowfoot made their way off the beach

to the English camp. Ahead of them, the sound of battle grew louder. Roger took a last glance back at *Mary, Star of the Sea*, but the mist had rendered it invisible. He thanked God that Helvise was safely out of this.

They passed first a trickle, then a flood of men—both soldiers and noncombatants—along with a few women, running in the other direction. *"Sauve qui peut!"* they cried in French and a dozen other languages, and even those who didn't speak the language knew what they meant.

Some of the fleeing mob were laden with packs; others had bundled whatever valuables they possessed and carried them in their arms. Others had no more than the clothes on their backs. There were knights in hauberks, men in bed clothes, all running mindlessly.

Roger and his companions fought against the flood, twisting sideways, pushing. They burst out of the narrow street and onto the broad expanse of the Concourse, and there they stopped.

"Christ's blood," Tatwine said in amazement.

The Concourse was closed.

Never, not even in the darkest days of the famine, had the Concourse shut down. Now, the tents and shops were empty of customers. The owners who had not already fled were doing so now, taking as much of their money and jewels and wares as they could. Some of the fleeing soldiers stopped to loot the shops. Others broke into the wine tents and consumed the contents or already lay crazy drunk in the street, heedless of their fate.

Roger motioned Tatwine and Slowfoot on.

They passed the square where plays were performed, the stage empty, one of its supports knocked sideways by the mob. At last they came to the English camp and their own tents. The Death's Heads were drawn up in loose formation in the open space north of the tents, with Ralph the Red and the other centenars at their front.

There was a shout from the rear of the formation as Roger

and his companions were sighted. Ralph let out his breath in relief as Roger came up. "Thank Christ you're here."

The three men's equipment had been laid out on the ground, awaiting their return. "What's happened?" Roger said as he donned his stained leather jack.

"Goat Fuckers attacked," the centenar Wilbert said. "Looks like they broke through all along the line."

Roger buckled his helmet and put on his mailed gloves. He looked across Resurrection Road toward the knights' camp, what little he could see of it. The camp seemed to be empty, no sign even of servants. "Where are the knights?"

Ralph shrugged. "Where is anybody?"

"Can't see a bloody thing in this muck," said Hake, another of the centenars.

The fog was slowly burning off, but it had been replaced by a thick cloud of choking dust mixed with acrid smoke from burning tents and wagons. The crusaders had rehearsed for an attack like this. The infantry units were supposed to push forward into the empty space north of their camps and link up, while the mounted knights formed in the rear for a counterattack. Then the infantry would march forward through the camps north of theirs, join up with the men from those camps and form another line, with its hinge based on the Toron. Now that the day was come, nothing went as it was supposed to. Of the Scandinavians to their right, there was no sign, no sign of the native Christians to their left, either, or of the Irish behind them. And the men in the camps north of theirs appeared to have been overrun.

Roger saw a man running on the other side of their tents. The man wore a pointed helmet and carried a curved sword, and with a shock, Roger realized he was a Saracen. Before he could order someone after him, the man had vanished in the fog and dust.

More refugees from the fighting north of them pushed through the Deaths Heads' loose formation. "Get out of here while you can!" they cried. Some of Roger's men were nervous.

They edged backwards, ready to bolt.

Roger faced the men and raised his voice. "All right, you wanted those fancy helmets—it's time to earn them! Form up properly there—spearmen in front, axe men in the gaps and on the flanks—like you were trained. Straighten that line, look like soldiers. We'll hold the road here. Don't let anyone else through. If these cowards want to run from the Saracens, make them go around us."

"And if they won't?" someone cried.

Roger tried to think what a seasoned commander, a man like Henry the Lion, would say. "Run 'em through," he ordered grimly. "Front rank—lower spears. Second rank—make ready."

A bristling line of steel rippled as the front rank lowered their spears to a 45-degree angle, knelt, and braced the butts against the ground. The next batch of fleeing men and women halted, then ran around the Death's Heads, stumbling through the lines of English tents, knocking some of the tents over, like a stream flowing around an obstruction. Judging by the noise, the battle was not far away now.

"Shouldn't we fall back?" Hake said.

"What if the Goat Fuckers get behind us?" added Ralph the Red.

"They're already behind us," Roger said, remembering the Saracen he'd seen running through their camp. "There's no place to fall back to."

That caused a shuffle of fear among the men. Roger was as scared as any of them, but he pretended not to be. "We'll make a stand here. Better to die as men, facing forward, than as cowards, running away."

"What if it's just us against the whole Saracen army?" someone else shouted. "What if they've got us surrounded?"

Roger forced a big grin. "Then we've got the bastards right where we want them."

That drew a laugh. Then Roger remembered something. "The laundresses." He looked in the direction of the women's camp but couldn't see anything through the haze. He thought of Ailith, of the other women—men's wives and widows.

He turned. "Tatty!"

Tatwine stepped forward.

Roger said, "Go to the washerwomen's camp. Round up the women and see them safely to the beach. Get them onto a ship if the camp falls."

Tatwine scrunched up his eyes. "Can't you send somebody else? I want to stay here and—you know."

I want to die beside my comrades was what he meant. "I know you do," Roger said, "but I need a man I can trust."

Resignation crossed Tatwine's face.

Roger nodded his head toward the laundresses' camp. "Off with you now. And be careful."

Tatwine turned and jogged away, axe in hand. Behind him there were shouts, and the first Saracen arrows thudded into the Death's Heads' shields.

Chapter 98

The washerwomen were long awake when the sound of battle erupted. Some were building fires for the wash tubs and breakfast; others, like Ailith and Margaret, had just hiked back from the beach with buckets of sea water. Still others sorted piles of laundry, gathered ash, or added jugs of urine to their tubs, trying not to splash any on themselves.

When the noise broke out, some of the women stopped what they were doing; heads turned toward the camp ditch and the sound of fighting. Other women ignored the noise and kept to their work.

Ailith rubbed her shoulder, which was sore from the pressure of the wooden yoke with which she had carried the buckets. "A proper battle up there, sounds like."

Broken-nosed Delva the Bull squatted by one of the fires, turning a piece of salted camel meat on a stick. "Don't know how it was with you and your fancy friends up on the Toron," she sneered, "but down here we hear these dust-ups a dozen times a month. They never 'mount to nothing."

Minutes later, some soldiers—Hollanders, by their dress— ran through the washerwomen's camp, headed in the direction of the shore. They were followed by two women, screaming and babbling hysterically in an unknown tongue. Delva spat contemptuously as the women ran by. "Foreigners."

More soldiers appeared, some wounded. One, no more than a boy, staggered into the middle of the camp with his jerkin slashed open and blood pouring down the front of him. He stared at the women strangely, as though looking for someone he knew, then he staggered and fell dead. Smoke drifted over the camp; the smell of burning wood and tent fabric grew strong.

"This ain't no ordinary skirmish," Margaret told Delva.

Delva rose, cursing and jamming the last of the half-cooked camel meat into her mouth. "You're right."

As if by instinct, the washerwomen crowded together. "We need to be with our men," said a hard-faced young blonde named Estrild.

"That's the last place we need to be," Delva told her. "Let the men do their jobs. We'd just get in their way."

"Listen," Margaret said, angling her head. "The fighting's getting closer. Sounds like them damned pagans have broke through our lines."

That elicited murmurs of shock and disbelief. "We need to get to the beach," Delva told the women.

Estrild was adamant. "I ain't leavin' without my Tom."

"Stay here, then," Delva told her. "The rest of us are going."

Baby Richard wailed. Mary hugged the infant close, stroking his head and whispering to calm him. Ailith put an arm around Mary. "Whatever we do, we need to be sure Baby Richard is safe."

Delva's eyes met Ailith's, and there was grudging recognition in the bigger woman's gaze. " 'Bout time you said something that made sense. Here, then—you and Margaret get Mary started for the beach. Celia, you go with 'em." Celia was Mary's best friend. "The rest of us'll catch up as soon as we grab our things. I'll bring Mary's kit."

Ailith took Mary's arm. "Come on."

Mary said, "But—"

"Hurry," Ailith told her.

The four women started out the southeast side of the camp, making their way around the tubs and the drain. As they were leaving, a man entered the space in front of the washerwomen's tents, moving warily. The man was dirty and dark skinned and bearded. He wore strange armor, and his curved sword had blood on it. Another man came after him, breathing hard. They stopped and looked at the gathered women, and a strange light came into their eyes.

Delva took a deep breath. She reached down and picked up her laundry bat. In a low voice, she spoke to the other women. "Go on, get moving."

The two Saracens started forward. As they did, two more appeared behind them. Delva faced them with her heavy bat, resting easy, making no move. Behind Delva, the rest of the laundresses left the camp, even Estrild, who had to be dragged by one of her friends.

Chapter 99

Fauston lurched into the cleric—a Sicilian by the cut of his robe—bracing himself against the young man's shoulder as if to keep from falling.

The wine-breathed cleric pushed Fauston off, slurring his words even at this early hour of the morning. "Get away from me, you one-eyed cur."

"A thousand pardons, sir," Fauston replied, bowing and backing away.

The cleric made a dismissive gesture with his hand and moved on. Fauston kept walking, sliding the cleric's purse into his jack as he did. He turned down a side street off the Concourse before the bleary-eyed cleric realized what had happened.

The sound of a skirmish erupted from the direction of the camp ditch. The skirmish seemed to grow louder, and some of the men around Fauston began hurrying back to their camps, the confusion of their movements—combined with the thick fog—making it easy for Fauston to get away.

Fauston had exchanged the white robe he had worn in the earl's employ for shabbier garments. He had let his beard and tonsure start to grow and he wore a patch over one eye— sometimes one eye, sometimes the other, as it amused him.

He lived rough these days, sleeping behind the Concourse wrapped in a blanket, which was not so bad at this time of year save when it rained. On those nights he sometimes curled up in a corner of a wine tent, but that was the kind of place where men would look for him, and hiding had become his chief occupation.

Not only were the earl's men looking for him, but rumor had it that Otho had hired mercenaries to search for him, offering a rich reward for his capture. Fauston wasn't worried too much about the earl's men—the earl would be just as happy if he wasn't caught—but he knew that horse's ass Otho wouldn't rest until he was dangling from a gibbet. They should have hung the fat bastard instead of sending him off naked when they'd robbed him in Dunham Wood. Otho obviously had no sense of humor.

Fauston needed to leave Acre, but where to go? Constantinople was a possibility—there was always need for a good thief in a city that big. Fauston didn't speak the language, but he could pick it up. He wasn't that fond of cities, though; he preferred the open air. England? Mary was in England—if she was still alive—but it was wet and cold there, and there was a price on his head. Cyprus? Maybe. The weather was good, from what he knew of it.

Whatever his destination, he had to do something soon. Shipboard passage was expensive, and his money was running low despite his efforts to conserve. The purse he had just taken would help some, but it was lighter than he might have wished.

Fauston was jerked out of his thoughts as he realized that, a street away, the Concourse was emptying. To the north, the skirmish sounded like it had become a full-blown battle. Men and women were fleeing. What the Devil was going on? Was the fight going that bad? There was no way to tell from where he stood. The sound of battle was coming closer, though—and not slowly.

Curious, Fauston returned to the Concourse, eerie now in the damp sea fog. Shop after shop, tent after tent had been abandoned, and the rest of the owners were on their way, fleeing for the hoped-for safety of the ships. Good luck with that. There weren't anywhere near enough ships to evacuate the entire camp. Anyone seeking passage would need money, and lots of it.

He ducked into a merchant's tent, where he found a sack and began filling it with whatever looked like it might be worth something—rings and bracelets of gold and silver.

Second-rate booty—the expensive wares had gone with the merchants—but if you had enough of it, you might wangle your way onto one of the ships. Fauston wasn't the only looter, but there were enough empty tents for all. At one point Fauston could have sworn he saw Roger and two of his men going past on the Concourse, but before he could call to them they had disappeared in the fog.

When the sack was half full, Fauston stopped and put it down. *To Hell with it.* The beach would be mobbed by now. He wouldn't be able to get near one of those ships no matter how much money he had. He was stuck here.

Stepping over a passed-out Hungarian footman, he went into a wine shop. He examined the shelf, rubbed his beard thoughtfully and plucked out a jug of arrack half hidden in the back, the expensive kind that only the highest ranking nobles could afford, the kind Fauston never drank even when he'd been on the earl's staff. The kind reserved for the head table.

He found a clean wooden cup and sat at a table, placing his dagger on the table top with the blade facing him. He removed his eye patch and threw it away—that felt better. He uncorked the jug, sniffed the contents approvingly and filled his cup. He took a big drink. The warmth ran through him and relaxed him. It must be nice to be rich and be able to drink like this. He decided to spend the day here, till he ended up like the unconscious Hungarian in the doorway. Why not? He had no place better to go. He listened to the approaching sound of battle and shook his head. This crusade was a balls up. Always had been.

He drank again, deeply, leaning his elbows on the table and closing his eyes, bobbing his chin to an imaginary tune playing in his head. When he opened his eyes again, three men were standing in the wine shop's entrance, watching him.

The men were dark and greasy and bearded. They wore conical helmets and shirts of light mail. One had a gash across his cheek that was bleeding freely. Another's mail was rent so that part of it dangled across his chest. All were splashed with blood. All carried curved swords.

Fauston let out a long sigh of resignation. As the three men entered the shop, he smiled hopefully and said, "I don't suppose I could interest you gentlemen in a drink?"

Chapter 100

Tatwine ran down the company street, past the latrines toward the laundresses' camp. Dust and fog and drifting smoke made it difficult to see. The acrid smoke tickled his nose and lungs and made him cough so much that he had to slow down.

The laundresses' camp was up ahead. At the far end, he saw women leaving—some orderly, some running in panic past the drainage area. Near the cook fires, one of the women—Delva the Bull—faced four Saracens who were carrying drawn swords. Delva was motionless, her laundry bat at her side, even though the Saracens, circling warily, were almost upon her.

Tatwine yelled and raced forward to help, but he was too far away. Suddenly, with a speed belying her size, Delva leapt forward, swinging the bat. She struck one of the surprised Saracens flush in the face, felling him. She turned and swung the bat at a second man, catching him on the side of the head just below the ear. Before she could turn again, one of the other Saracens struck her across the back with his sword. Delva stumbled and tried to recover, roaring defiance, but the two remaining Saracens were on her, hacking at her, the thud of sharpened steel hitting flesh and bone.

Tatwine reached the melee and charged into it. Tatwine had learned to fight in the taverns and back alleys of Badford Town, where there were no rules and the object was to disable your opponent as quickly as possible, preferably by taking him unawares.

Preoccupied with Delva, the Saracens hadn't seen Tatwine coming. He crashed his axe into the skull of the middle one, splitting the man's helmet and spilling his brains. He jerked the axe free, pivoted and used two hands to ram the axe's pointed end into the face of the Saracen to his right. He pivoted again and hit the third Saracen—the one Delva had staggered with the blow to the side of the head—with a sweeping upward blow, catching him under the jaw and nearly cutting his head diagonally in two.

Tatwine dropped the axe and fell to his knees beside Delva. He'd never liked Delva much—in truth, she scared him—but she'd done a brave thing by covering the retreat of the other woman when she might have gotten away herself. He saw at once that there was no hope for her. Her head and body were gashed by deep wounds. Blood covered her body and pooled beneath her.

She was still alive, though. She tried to talk but no words came from her blood-filled mouth, only pinkish bubbles. Tatwine made the sign of the cross and said a prayer for her, then he plunged his dagger into her heart to help her go quickly. He got up and examined the Saracens. Two were dead. The man he'd hit with the pointed end of the axe was still alive, burbling blood through his destroyed face. Tatwine stuck his dagger in the man's eye, driving the point into his brain. The man's feet scrabbled, then he lay still. The Saracen that Delva had hit with the bat lay on his back, moaning, his nose crushed, some of his teeth missing, his eyes beginning to swell. Tatwine stabbed him in the eye, as well—efficiently, business like, the way he had done it on black nights in Badford, when he had been a sinner.

Tatwine rose, retrieved his axe, and hurried after the retreating washerwomen.

Chapter 101

Ailith, Margaret and Celia hurried Mary along, Mary holding the fractious baby close, vainly trying to shush him. They were nearing the seemingly deserted camp of the Irish when, out of the dust, a horseman appeared, leading a spare mount. The horseman wore a hauberk and a conical helmet with a nose piece; he had a blond beard, and his right hand was thickly wrapped as though it was injured.

The horseman reined in, blocking Ailith's path so that she had to stop.

Mary and Celia stopped as well. "Keep going!" Ailith told them. "Get to the beach. I'll catch up."

They hurried off, going around the horseman. Margaret hesitated, then waited with Ailith.

"You are the *ami*—the friend—of Lord Geoffrey?" the horseman asked Ailith in heavily accented English.

Ailith was stunned. Who was this man? How did he know her? She needed to get Mary and the baby to the beach, but she managed to say, "Yes."

"He has sent me for you," the horseman said, indicating the spare mount. "I am to take you to him."

Ailith turned to Margaret, who squinted at the horseman. "Do we know you?" Margaret said.

"I am Gervaise of St. Cloud, one of the earl's knights."

Margaret shrugged; the name meant nothing to her. The man looked familiar, Ailith thought, but it was hard to tell with the helmet and thick nosepiece. Ailith thought she had seen him among Geoffrey's troops, though not with the knights, but maybe he had been raised in station. "I can't. I have to get that woman and her babe to—"

"Roger will do it," Gervaise said. "He is coming for the

women. He is right behind me. My instructions are to take you to Lord Geoffrey. Hurry, there is not much time."

Why won't Geoffrey leave me alone? "No," Ailith said, "I won't leave—"

"Roger is coming for them, I tell you."

"Roger is your friend?"

"Yes, yes. Now hurry—I am in trouble if you don't come. Geoffrey has a ship waiting."

If the man was a friend of Roger's, Ailith assumed he was trustworthy, but Margaret squinted suspiciously. "All right," she told the knight, "but I'm coming, too. At least as far as the beach. Make sure there's no funny stuff."

"Yes, yes," Gervaise repeated. "Whatever you wish."

Behind them, more washerwomen were streaming from the camp, some running.

Ailith hesitated.

"Get on," the horseman urged.

Ailith helped Margaret heave herself onto the spare horse, then climbed on behind her. Ailith gave a last look back toward the washerwomen's camp as the armored horseman touched his spurs to his horse's flank and led them off. Ailith felt guilty for deserting Delva and Mary and the others. She didn't want special treatment. She thought about getting off the horse and going back, but Roger's friend Gervaise was going too fast and she didn't think he'd hear her if she called to him to stop. She clung tight to Margaret's ample waist, then with a start, she realized something. Margaret realized the same thing, because she turned and shouted, "We're going the wrong way!"

Chapter 102

"Prepare to pole off!" the bald-headed captain cried.

Helvise leaned against the packed rail of the cog's forecastle, smells of stale sweat and garlic overwhelming her as sailors positioned the long poles in the water. They would push *Mary, Star of the Sea* away from the beach into deeper water, then row her against the tide and out to sea. Ordinarily they would have waited for the tide to ebb, but the captain was in a haste to leave, lest the Saracens overrun the camp and capture his ship.

A pall of smoke rose over the huge camp, along with thick dust and remnants of the fog. There were shouting, screams of men and animals, the not-so-distant clash of weapons. The beach was jammed with people hoping to get on one of the hastily departing ships. Some waded into the water, holding silver plate or bags of money over their heads as bribes to be allowed on board. *Mary, Star of the Sea* had taken on so many of these fugitives that she was now overcrowded, the passengers pressed against each other like stacked cordwood but happy to be that way. The captain refused to take any more passengers because he was afraid his vessel would capsize from the extra weight. Still, men waded out to her, offering whatever treasures they possessed. When the captain wasn't looking, *Mary's* sailors beckoned to them. They took the proffered silver and gold, then laughed and pushed the would-be passengers back into the water as they tried to clamber on board. Some of the men wearing armor were dragged under water by its weight and drowned.

Mary popped free from the sand and floated. Before the waves could wash her back onto the beach, the sailors dropped the poles and rushed to their oars, a few remaining by the bulwarks, using their poles to fend off anyone else trying to climb on board. As the oars bit into the water and the vessel stabilized against the tide, Helvise made a decision.

She pressed her way into the crowded forecastle. Without caring who saw, she took off her dress and shift. A drunken clerk reached out to touch her bare breast. She jabbed her fingers into the clerk's eye and he fell against his fellow passengers, yelling with pain. Ignoring the commotion, Helvise donned her green leggings and jerkin. She grabbed her dragon-head crossbow and its quiver of bolts. She left the pavise behind—it was too heavy. Men were shouting at her but she paid them no heed.

"Where are you going?" cried the captain, coming forward. He had left the mate at the tiller.

"Ashore," Hevise said.

"We can't wait for you."

"I don't expect you to."

As she moved away from him, he said, "What about your trunk?"

"Sell it," she said. She sat on the rail, turned, and jumped off, landing chest deep in the water. Holding the crossbow and quiver high so they wouldn't get wet, she gained her balance and slogged her way to the beach.

Chapter 103

The three Saracens did not respond to Fauston's invitation. They gripped their weapons and advanced, grim looks on their faces.

Fauston sighed and shook his head in disappointment. Then with one smooth motion he grabbed his dagger by the blade and threw it, hitting the lead Saracen in the throat. Jumping to his feet, Fauston took his heavy stool and heaved it at the second man, clobbering him in the face and knocking him backward. Fauston leaped across the table and smashed the jug of arrack into the third man's face, shattering the jug. As the man reflexively put his hands to his face, Fauston snatched the man's sword from his hand and chopped it into his neck. The man dropped. The man Fauston had hit with the chair had partly recovered. He stumbled forward, but before he could do anything, Fauston used two hands and brought the sword down on his head, splitting his conical helmet and driving the blade deep into his skull. The man screamed, dropped to his knees and fell on his face, blood and brain matter spilling onto the wine tent's floor.

The man Fauston had struck with the dagger lay on his back, gurgling blood and feebly pawing at the blade in his throat. Fauston pulled the dagger free and finished the man off with it. He went to the Saracen with the neck wound and did the same. The third man was already dead.

Fauston wiped his dagger clean on the third man's shirt and put it back on the table, adjusting it in case he needed it again. The tent floor was awash in blood and expensive liquor from the broken jug, and Fauston shook his head again at the waste of good arrack. He selected another jug from the shelf, then resumed his seat, poured a cup and placed his feet on the table, resting his back against the bar.

"Rude buggers," he observed. "Wouldn't have hurt 'em to be polite."

Tatwine caught up with the washerwomen at the far end of the deserted Irish camp. "Agatha! Emma!" he cried. He knew those two best—they did his wash.

Ahead of him, the two women stopped. "Get the others!" Tatwine told them.

Agatha and Emma called to the others, most of whom stopped running and collected around Tatwine. A few kept on toward the beach, but Tatwine couldn't worry about them. Around them people were fleeing, horses ran loose. "Roger sent me to get you on ships in case the camp falls," Tatwine told the women.

Emma, a lumpy blonde, spit. "Hope you got money then."

Tatwine brandished his bloody axe. "There's other things besides money. Is everybody here?"

Somebody said, "Everybody but Celia, Margaret and Mary—they went ahead, to get Mary's baby to safety."

"And Ailith," somebody else added. "Ailith was with 'em too."

"No, she ain't," said Agatha. "I seen her and Meg—I'm pretty sure it was them—riding off with somebody."

"Riding off?" Tatwine said, frowning. "Riding off with who?"

"You'll say I'm crazy, but it looked like Dirk—you remember him."

"Dirk!" said Tatwine. "Dirk's long gone."

Agatha was sturdy and reliable; her husband was in Hake's company. "I know he is, but I'd swear that's who it were."

"But Dirk ran away and joined the . . ." Tatwine's voice tailed off and his stomach curdled. "Which way'd they go?"

Agatha pointed in the opposite direction from the beach, toward the Saracen camp.

"Christ save them," Tatwine murmured.

Chapter 104

King Richard had himself armed and tied to his horse's saddle. Alart of Vouzin supervised the squires as they attached the rope to Richard's pommel, wound it twice around his waist, through the cantle, once more around his waist, and back to the pommel again. His ankles were tied together beneath the horse's ribs. Alart tested the knots, then handed Richard his filigreed Danish axe and flat war cap. "You're still weak, Richard. Is this wise?"

Richard laced the steel cap to his mail coif, the axe dangling from his wrist by a lanyard. "I didn't come all this way to watch other people fight."

"But you can barely sit your horse."

"That will have to be good enough for now."

The fighting had not reached the Plantaganet force yet, but already the din was louder than anything Richard could remember hearing on a battlefield. In the open field before his camp, his footmen were arrayed in line, the last stragglers hurrying into position. His knights were formed behind them, the chivalry of Poitou and Acquitaine, their banners floating above the smoke and dust of battle. Richard thanked God for the camps to his west. Their sacrifice had given his own men time to rally; otherwise, they might have been taken by surprise and overrun.

Before them, Saracen footmen appeared in scattered groups. The Saracens saw the drawn-up Plantaganet host and halted, giving way to their mounted archers. Arrows began to fall around Richard as he rode out and walked his horse down the line in front of his cheering soldiers, a vast array of ten thousand men, the most powerful unit in the crusading army.

A head taller than most of the men in his force, with the

bulk to match, Richard was resplendent in polished mail and a red surcoat with the three gold lions of England embroidered upon it. He became the target for the wheeling, curveting horsemen ranged opposite him. Arrows bounced off his helm, they stuck in his shield and mail, but he paid them no more mind than he paid the waves that broke on the shore behind him. He raised his Danish axe—it was all his could do to lift it—and his men cheered until they were hoarse.

Richard cursed the luck that had rendered him ill at such a moment. His instinct was to counterattack, to smash through the Saracens before him, to drive them across the plain and back into Saladin's camp, to end this crusade here and now. He would have done it, too, but he lacked the physical strength, so he would have to stand on the defensive. He trusted his subordinates, but none of them—not Andrew of Chauvigny, not Alart—possessed the ferocity and skill in battle that it would take to make such a counterattack successful. Besides, he did not want to launch such an attack unless he himself could lead it. As he returned to his position behind the line, his nobles gathered around him—counts and viscounts and barons, great men in their own lands, of lesser importance here.

"We will defend the right flank," Richard told them. Inwardly he cursed the luck that had placed his camp on the right of the Christian line instead of in the center, where they would have been of better use, but there had been no other open ground upon which to situate his men, so he would have to make do with what he had been given. "The Saracens will try to break through us and relieve the city, to put a new garrison into it. We must prevent that—we will prevent it. When we have beaten the dogs here, we will aid the defenders of the Toron."

Alart, mounted now, stood in his stirrups and cast an anxious eye to the north, where the low summit of the Toron rose above the haze. The sound told him there was already hard fighting there. "Can they hold out that long?"

"They have no choice," Richard said. "Now let us see to these fellows in front of us."

Chapter 105

For the third time, the Saracen horsemen halted short of the bristling line of English spears and drew their bows.

For the third time, Roger cried, "Shields!"

They had practiced this drill a thousand times but never used it till today. The front row knelt, circular shields up. The second row moved close behind the first and slanted their shields to cover the heads of the men in front of them as well as themselves.

The Saracens loosed their bows. Arrows rattled on the Death's Heads' wooden shields, some sticking in, others bouncing off. Someone in the front rank yelped and rolled on the ground as a shaft drilled into his foot. The Saracens loosed another volley, then drew off, but this time a charge of footmen followed in their wake.

"Up!" Roger cried. "Up!" cried the company commanders and vintenars. "Up! Up!" And the spearmen rose to receive the charge.

The Saracens' tactic was to come in so quickly behind the horsemen that they would catch the spearmen before they had time to rise and set themselves, and it might have worked, so close behind their horsemen were the well-drilled Saracen infantry, but some of the Saracens became unnerved when they saw the Death's Heads' banner and painted helmets, and they had to be driven the last few yards by their officers, and that brief slowing of the attack gave the English just enough time to brace for it. There was a short, sharp fight along the Death's Heads' line, spears and swords and axes, but this was the kind of close quarters combat that favored the more heavily armed English, and the Saracens were soon beaten back. Their horsemen unleashed another volley of arrows at the Death's Heads, then faded into the dust.

Roger's men cheered. Their casualties were few—none dead.

"Teach the bastards to mess with us!" Wilbert cried, waving his short sword. Other men echoed him.

"Quiet!" Roger cried. "Quiet, there! You men act like you just won the war. This battle hasn't even started yet. See our wounded to the rear." He didn't have to say anything about the Saracen wounded. The Death's Heads were already dispatching them with daggers and spears.

Next to Roger, Ralph the Red shielded his eyes. The ground before them was clear. As suddenly as they had come, the Saracens were gone. "Looks like their main attack has passed us by," Ralph told Roger.

"Aye," Roger agreed, "though I've no idea why. We can't stay here, that's certain. We're too exposed." He tried to see what was happening in the Irish camp to their rear, but the dust and smoke and uneven ground prevented him from getting much of a view. "The Irish haven't come up to join us. Either they've retreated or they've been overrun. We're on our own."

"Where are our bloody knights?" swore Osric, the third centenar of spearmen. Osric was a seasoned veteran who had started life as a thatcher's mate.

"Wherever they are, they aren't here," Roger said, "so we can't worry about them. We have to assume they're not coming."

"Now do we fall back?" Hake said hopefully.

Roger thought. His heart, his instinct, told him to run for safety, told him so insistently that his feet seemed ready to move of their own accord. But his head told him there *was* no safety. That unless the Saracen attack could be blunted, the Christian army was doomed.

It seemed a miracle that the battle was passing them by, but that miracle was not likely to last long. There were Saracens behind them, Roger was sure of that, though he did not know how many. The Death's Heads were doing no good here, waiting to be slaughtered at the Saracens' leisure. They needed to move someplace they could be of use.

King Richard's men were somewhere to their right—going in that direction was a possibility. If anyone could save the situation, it was Richard. But Roger did not know exactly where Richard's force was, or if his men could cut their way through to join them. So he looked behind him and to his left, where the low rise of the Toron was obscured by dust, and from whence came yelling and the clash of weapons.

The Toron—where, with the exception of King Richard, the entire leadership of the crusade was gathered in one spot. Eliminate that leadership, and . . .

That was why the Death's Heads had been bypassed, Roger realized. The Saracen attack had been diverted to the Toron.

"We're not falling back," he said. "We're going to the Toron."

"We better talk this over," Hake warned.

"There's no time for talk," Roger said. He raised his voice, addressing the company commanders. "Fall your men in. Marching order. Reds—take your axe men and guard the right flank."

As Ralph and his men moved off, Wilbert said, "What about the wounded?"

Roger glanced at the wounded men resting on the ground. With a heavy heart, knowing he might be condemning those men to death, Roger said, "We'll have to leave them here. There's no time to take them with us."

"Wait!" Hake cried to the Death's Heads, stopping their movements. He planted himself before Roger, a hulking thug with a scarred face. "I been a soldier a lot longer than you have, boy, and I say we make for the beach—"

"We go to the Toron," Roger told him. The two men faced each other. Roger thought he would have to fight Hake, and to his surprise, he didn't care. He went on, looking Hake in the eye. "If you can't carry out that order, I'll find someone who will."

Roger tensed. His hand tightened on his axe, ready to bring it down on Hake's neck if the big man made so much as a move. Then Hake lowered his eyes. He growled a reluctant acceptance and went to join his company.

The spearmen fell in, with Ralph's axe men scattered along their right flank. Roger waved his hand and started them off. He hoped to God he knew what he was doing.

Chapter 106

Helvise pelted up from the beach, dragon-tillered crossbow in hand, struggling against the surge of men and women seeking the illusory safety of the ships. *Cowards*, she thought—that they should run now, after all the torment they had endured in this hellish place. What was wrong with them?

She reached the top of the bluff. Her first thought was to join Roger and his men—she felt more at home with them now than she did with her own Germans. She started toward the English camp, hoping that Roger had gotten there safely—there was no telling what had happened in all this confusion. Then she looked toward the city and stopped.

A large force of Saracens had sortied from Acre, crossing the city ditch on portable bridges and attacking King Richard's "bad neighbors," the two big trebuchets that were doing the city walls such harm. Through the dust and smoke, Helvise saw flashes of light, which meant that some of the Saracens carried torches—they intended to burn the trebuchets. That was a loss the army of God could ill afford.

Helvise changed direction and started toward the trebuchets. She could be more useful there than she could be with Roger and his men—assuming she could even find them. Besides, she felt comfortable under the city walls. That was where she had fought all those months before she met Roger.

"To me!" she cried as she ran, as though she could will the men around her to stop running away. "To me!"

The trebuchet's defenders were putting up a fight, but they looked disorganized and they were slowly being driven back. Like everyone else in camp, they had been caught unaware by the Saracen attack. People had been too confident of victory; they had no longer considered defeat a possibility.

*Pride goeth before destruction,
and a haughty spirit before a fall.*

"To me!"

Heads turned. "It's the Lady in Green!"

"She's back!"

Helvise's presence seemed to inspire the fleeing soldiers around her, men of all nations. They rallied and faced front. Helvise reached a small rise about thirty yards from the nearest trebuchet. As she did, a group of Saracens broke through the crumbling ring of defenders around the siege engines. The first Saracen carried a torch. The men around Helvise assembled for a counterattack, but they wouldn't be in time. Carefully, breathing hard from her run but taking her time because she had only one chance to get it right, Helvise put her foot in the crossbow's stirrup. She dropped the bow's cord into the hook on her belt and straightened, using the strength of her legs, tightening the cord and nocking it on the tiller. She placed a bolt on the tiller. She aimed at the first Saracen, who had stopped and was poised to throw his torch. She pulled the trigger; the crossbow thumped. The bolt hit the Saracen in the chest and he fell backward, the torch landing harmlessly behind him.

Men cheered, but there were more Saracens behind the first one, more torches. As more archers joined Helvise on the rise, she nocked another bolt and shot, bringing down another infidel.

It was like the old days. It was good to be back.

Chapter 107

The battle went much as the Sultan had foreseen. He had hoped that his left and right columns could push through to the sea and split the infidel army into three pieces, but he had always known that might not happen. The Christian camp was vast, and it was inevitable that the momentum of his attack would be dissipated. In the fog and dust and smoke, his units lost first their cohesion, then their forward progress. Men became disoriented and got turned around in the warren of tents and streets that made up the infidel camp. Other men stopped to loot the tents or to rape the feringhee women they found there. Still others, sad to say, forsook their faith and filled themselves with the alcohol with which the infidel camp abounded. Other men simply got tired, their initial burst of energy wearing off. In addition, the confines of the camp were unsuited for the Sultan's cavalry, who needed open space to loose their bows and wheel away from their opponents.

The Sultan's right wing had penetrated deep into the feringhee camp, hoping to capture the beach where the feringhee ships lay. For a while it appeared they would succeed, but they gradually seemed to have been absorbed into the camp, like water into a sponge, and had slowed to a halt. The left wing had done better, but they had failed to bring the relief garrison to the city, stopped by Malik Rik's armored horsemen. That was a failure the Sultan had not anticipated, but it was not fatal because it was in the center where the fight would be decided. There the Sultan had placed Qaymaz, his best general. From his vantage point in the hills, the Sultan could see Qaymaz's men pressing the Christians back up the hill on which their leaders camped. Soon the green banner of Islam would fly from the hill's top, and when that happened, this blasphemy that the infidels called a "crusade" would be ended...

❖   ❖   ❖

The Death's Heads made their way through the deserted camp of the English knights, the axe men guarding the right flank of the short column. They saw a few parties of Saracens, who paid them little mind as they hurried to the Toron. In the dust and smoke and confusion, the Saracens probably assumed the Death's Heads were co-religionists on their way to assault the Frankish lords.

"Furl that banner," Roger ordered. "We don't want to advertise ourselves."

Here, in the heart of a raging battle, they had found an improbable bubble of peace. It was incongruous, and Roger knew it wouldn't last, but it was a boon to him and his men. A few servants and sick men lingered about the knights' camp, hiding from the Saracens. The Death's Heads gave arms to those who were able to fight and made them join the column.

"What if we don't want to?" demanded a well-dressed servant who obviously thought himself better than these peasant soldiers.

"Then we'll slit your throat and save the Saracens the trouble," Roger snapped. As the man took a weapon and slunk away, Roger turned to the other handful of servants who had gathered around his men, "Where are the knights?"

"Gone to join King Richard," said a groom, gazing at the battle axe he had been handed as though it were an instrument from another world.

The centenar Osric spit contemptuously. "Bastards abandoned us," he told Roger.

"Doubt that matters to them," added Wilbert. "We're English and they're French. They feel more comfortable with their own kind. They don't care about us."

"It would matter if the earl was here," the groom argued loyally, "but he's stuck on the Toron, so the knights joined Canterbury's men—" they were still called that, though the archbishop was long dead—"and went to join the king."

Next the Death's Heads entered the camp of the Milanese, which was even more deserted than that of the English. "Hurry," Roger told his men. "Those of you with swords, leave your spears. Swords will be better in a close quarters fight."

A number of the Death's Heads dropped their spears or tossed them aside and drew the swords they had purchased from the effects of dead men, found on the battlefield or stolen. They were sweating in their heavy jacks and rounded helms. They crossed a dry creek bed and then the Toron was before them.

At the top were the colored pavilions and banners of the great lords of Christendom. The bottom and slopes roiled with seething dust, with yells and screams, with the racket of metal on metal and metal on wood. One thing was evident—the Christians were being pushed inexorably up the hill.

Roger waved the Death's Heads forward, trying to control the emotion building inside him, trying to act like what he and his men were doing was the most natural thing in the world. "Smartly, there. Heads up, not down. Act like good Saracens. *Allahu akbar!*"

"*Allahu akbar!*" a few men shouted back, laughing. In the confusion, Roger hoped that, despite their jacks and distinctive helmets, his men looked like the other columns that were converging on the Toron.

Hake grabbed Roger's sleeve. "This is madness, damn you. You'll get us all killed."

"Too late to do anything about it now," Roger told him.

Sweat ran down Roger's forehead; the inside of his mailed gloves was puddled with it. As they drew closer to the Toron, Ralph the Red's axe men rejoined the main column. Occasionally Saracens from one of the other formations glanced over. Some even peered suspiciously for a second, then shrugged and went on with what they were doing. There could not possibly be feringhee soldiers here.

The Death's Heads were approaching the rear of the Saracen forces now, so covered with dust they were hard to distinguish from their enemies. The Saracen horse were no good here, so they hung off to the rear while their footmen pressed forward with companies of archers behind them, sending flight after flight of arrows into the Christian line. The Saracen arrows were not as powerful as those of the Christians, but enough of them would bring a man down, sapping his strength bit by bit. The archers' backs were to Roger; no one paid him or his men any attention.

Roger halted the column and formed his men in line. "No tactics," he told them quietly, going down their front. "Kill a Saracen, then kill another one. No battle cry, either— don't let the bastards know we're here. We'll cut our way through to the Christian line. Do your best to stay together in case we have to form a shield wall." He nodded to the man who carried the flag. "Unfurl the banner."

The man did, and the red Death's Head on its white field came free, though few could see it in the swirling dust.

Roger waved his axe toward the Saracens. He tried to think of something stirring to say, but came up with nothing, so he simply said, "Let's go."

It was a steady advance. The men only broke into a run for the last few paces that separated themselves from their unwary enemies. With a two-handed swing, Roger sunk his axe into the back of an archer. He pulled the axe free and went on to the next man. The rest of the Death's Heads fell upon their enemy with axes and swords and spears. It was more of a slaughter or execution than a battle. So filled were the archers with their own blood lust that they didn't realize what was happening until it was too late for them. By the time they became aware of a threat to their rear and turned to face it, the axe and sword blades were already descending. The archers wore no armor, which made killing them all the easier.

The Death's Heads hacked their way through the Saracen archers like woodcutters hewing their way through a forest. Roger sensed a lessening of Saracen pressure on the Christians defending the Toron—the Saracen infantry had realized what was happening and turned to face this new danger from their rear. Resistance stiffened. Lightly armed archers were replaced by more heavily armed spearmen and sword men. The killing was not as easy now.

"Shields!" Roger cried. "Shield wall!"

The Death's Heads came together, the way they had practiced so many times, shields linked. "Keep moving forward!" Roger ordered. They had to cut their way through to the comparative safety of the Christian line. "Keep moving—not far to go now!"

The Saracen infantry bore down on them. Swords and spears and axes were thrust over the interlocked shields as the Saracens tried to get at their foes. The English fought back, stabbing and hacking, splashed with blood and unimaginable bits of gore. Their forward progress slowed as the number of enemies before them increased. They were forced to stop, then began giving ground reluctantly as their foes pressed down on them. Roger had a hard time fighting and commanding his men at the same time. He stepped back from the shield wall, another man wedging himself into his place. The wall was being bent into a semi-circle. An arrow stuck in Roger's armored jack, another struck his helmet brim, skewing the helmet sideways. He turned and saw Saracens moving into the open space behind them.

"Link up!" he cried, moving into the opening between the wings. He banged an onrushing Saracen with his shield, knocked him back, then hit him in the shoulder with his axe. "Form a circle! Quickly!"

The English frantically shuffled into a circle, enemies pressing from all sides, arrows falling like rain, the air filled with war cries and screams of pain. Along the shield wall, men fell. The circle grew smaller. There was no thought of reaching the Christian line now. They were all going to die here. They couldn't hold much longer.

Then the shield wall broke and the Saracens were pouring through. Roger was jerked back as though he had been on the end of a taut rope when it snapped. A huge Saracen leaped on Roger and bore him to the ground. The Saracen was helmetless, his long black hair hanging in stringy locks about his face. The man had lost his weapon, so he clamped his hands around Roger's throat and squeezed.

Roger tried to push the man off, but the man was too strong. Roger gagged and gasped, the man's contorted face inches from his as he tightened his grip around Roger's windpipe. Roger saw pock marks in the man's skin, saw his brown teeth, some of them missing, saw the individual hairs of his drooping mustache. His spit drooled on Roger's face; his breath smelled like a midden.

Roger flailed about until his hand found a rock. He swung the rock against the man's head—again and again, scraping the ropy hair and doing no damage. Roger was losing strength, his eyes seemed to be bursting out of his head and all he could see was red. He swung the rock one last time, with all the desperation he could muster. This time he struck home; the man's skull cracked like the shell of an egg. Roger swung the rock again and again and again, until the man loosened his grip and fell off of him. Roger's hand was covered with some kind of sticky mess.

Roger lay on his back, gasping, trying to breathe. He needed to get up and keep fighting, but he couldn't. The roar around him was like the roar of a great storm he had encountered at sea in the *Quail*, and for a minute he didn't know if he was on land or at sea again, and then the roar increased, turning into a frenzied cheer until all around him men were yelling. He heard the words "Richard!" "Richard is here!" And then he was aware that the Saracens were running.

❖ ❖ ❖

Just as the Toron's defenders were about to be overwhelmed, the pressure on them had eased, thanks to the Death's Heads. The defenders had taken advantage of the opportunity and mounted a counterattack—Philip of France, one-eyed Henry the Lion and Geoffrey of Trent, Balian of Ibelin, James of Avesnes, Conrad of Montferrat and Guy of Lusignan fighting side by side, along with other great men too numerous to mention—pushing their enemies back down the hill. Soon after, King Richard's knights had arrived. The two forces caught the Saracens between them, and before long the Saracens were streaming back through the Christian camp and across the plain to safety.

By his tent, Saladin watched. His face showed no emotion, but inside he was dismayed because he knew that all he had staked on this battle had been lost.

Chapter 108

Roger lay on his back; he couldn't get up. Around him the dull roar continued.

Men—he was so disoriented he couldn't tell who they were—helped him to his feet. He stood unsteadily. He couldn't talk, and he wondered if his throat had been crushed by the big Saracen. His helmet was ajar, and he wrestled it off and threw it to the ground. He was surrounded by bodies, by the stench of blood and voided bowels and bladders. Buzzing flies were already thick on the corpses. Sticky blood pooled under his feet.

He staggered and bumped into something. It was the Death's Heads' banner, planted where his men had expected to die. But they hadn't died. They had been saved, and now the dull roar resolved itself into shouts of triumph and laughter—the loud, exuberant relief of men who had expected to be killed but had lived.

Roger saw the lords coming down from the Toron, making their way across the Toron's body-filled ditch. Most hadn't had time to don mail before the Saracen attack; all were splashed with blood. They, too, were laughing and shouting and congratulating one another, celebrating their unexpected deliverance. There was Conrad of Montferrat, with his square, shaven head, walking alongside handsome Guy of Lusignan, laughing with him as if the two of them were best friends. There was the lordly young count of Champagne alongside the plainly dressed king of France.

Someone clapped Roger's shoulder. It was Henry the Lion, blood on his face and clothes, blood in his greying beard and on his eyepatch. He shook Roger's arm like a dog shaking a rat. "You came in the nick of time, boy. By God, I thought we were done for." Henry wore a dented conical helmet he'd found somewhere; for the rest, he was unarmored.

Roger found his voice. "Is the battle won?" he croaked.

"Won? I should say it's won. Damndest thing I ever saw, what you did. The bastards would have overwhelmed us else. Once you stopped them, we rallied and began driving them back. Then Richard's knights showed up and finished the job. Never seen the Goat Fuckers run so fast. It was close, far too close for my liking, but there's no denying it's a huge defeat for Old Sidesaddle." He shook Roger again, by the shoulder this time. "And you're one of the heroes."

"I'm no hero," Roger mumbled. The fingers of his right-hand glove were literally stuck together with blood and grey matter. He pulled off the mailed glove in disgust and threw it down. He took the glove from his left hand, too, then mussed his fingers through his sweaty hair. He saw Henry staring at him strangely, though he couldn't figure out why. Henry seemed to shake it off, but his demeanor suddenly chilled.

"I must find my men," he said. He nodded stiffly, then turned and made his way through the press of jubilant knights and soldiers.

❖ ❖ ❖

Geoffrey of Trent picked his way down the Toron. Lines of bodies and broken pavilions, like waves of wreckage on a seashore, marked the path up which the Saracen tide had flowed, crested, and then receded. Geoffrey stopped beside a corpse. It was young Eustace, his skull cleaved open. The boy had fallen in the retreat up the hill; Geoffrey had seen him go down. Geoffrey looked at the body and his eyes misted. He had just made Eustace a squire last week. Eustace had died bravely, sword in hand, facing the enemy and defending his God. Baron Shortwood would mourn him, but he would also be proud of him, as was Geoffrey.

Lower down the hill he found his chaplain, Otho, cut down in the early moments of the attack, with half a dozen wounds in his back because he had been running away. Geoffrey tried to feel something for the man, but couldn't.

Conrad of Montferrat clamped a beefy hand around Geoffrey's shoulder. Conrad had been the one they'd rallied around when the Saracens looked to overrun them. Conrad didn't say anything; he didn't have to.

Philip of France, stringy hair clotted with blood, shook Geoffrey's hand, then embraced him. Leopold of Austria shook his hand, as well—all the survivors were greeting each other as if they'd just met after a long journey. Big James of Avesnes, who had fought beside Geoffrey during much of the attack, laughed heartily, showing his toothless gums. "Got a good story for your chronicle this time—eh, Geoffrey?"

Geoffrey was too exhausted to reply. He had run the gamut of emotions that day—from certainty of death to the elation of victory—but now he had a sour taste in his mouth. He turned away from his bemused companions and went down the body-strewn hill to where his commander of footmen stood, propped with one hand on the Death's Head banner as if to keep himself from falling. The young man seemed strangely alone, distanced from the celebration around him. He was looking the other way as Geoffrey came up.

"Your saving the army is becoming a habit," Geoffrey said.

Roger started. He let go of the staff, turned and bowed. "Thank you, my lord, but I did my duty, nothing more."

"I'm not so sure about that," Geoffrey said, cocking his head to one side. "In fact, I intend to mention your actions to the king."

Roger's tired eyes widened. "King Richard?"

"He's the only king we have."

"Truly, my lord, there's no need for that. I did nothing special." Roger indicated his surviving men. "It was them. They—"

Geoffrey raised a hand. "That's for me to decide. I'll have a brace of oxen and some barrels of arrack sent over to your tents later, so you and your men can celebrate."

"Thank you, my lord. That's very kind."

The two men regarded each other for a moment, then Geoffrey returned to the nobles gathered at the base of the hill. Roger turned to his men, his head finally clearing. Those of the Death's Heads who were able were plundering the Saracen bodies—Christian bodies, too, when they thought no one was looking. Roger didn't approve of their robbing Christians, but he didn't try to stop them. They considered it their right, and who was to say it wasn't? There was Hake, bragging so much one might have thought the attack had been his idea. Roger had to laugh at that.

Casualties were not as bad as Roger had feared. The Death's Heads had lost about a third of their number, which was a lot, but Roger had expected more. Osric's company had suffered the most dead, and though every man in the unit seemed to have been wounded to some degree, most could return to duty.

"Roger!"

Roger turned to see Father Mayne kneeling beside Arcil, wrapping Arcil's right hand. The thick bandage was already turning red. Arcil held up the bandaged hand for Roger to see. The pain had not yet set in. "Lost four fingers. Blade went clean though them." His eyes suddenly brimmed with tears. "What am I going to do now, Roger? I can't guide a plow like this. I can't dig or cut wood. I can't do anything. I'll be a beggar, sitting on the church porch in Badford Town, holding a tin cup. What kind of a life is that?"

Roger patted the young man's shoulder. "It won't be that bad, you'll see." In truth, Arcil would be lucky if he didn't die—first his hand swollen and turned black, then his arm. "Keep your bandages clean. Go up the beach where the water's not fouled and wash your hand in sea water. No matter how much it hurts. I've seen it work."

Roger turned away. He had to see to the wounded and get

the dead buried. He had to collect the effects of the dead men. But before he could do anything, he saw Tatwine threading his way toward him through the milling throng of soldiers and knights.

Tatwine didn't seem to be sharing the general sense of celebration. "Best come with me," he told Roger grimly. "There's something you need to see."

Chapter 109

Roger picked up his helmet and gloves. He slid his axe into the loop on his belt and slung his battered shield over his shoulder. "Wilbert, you're in charge," he called out. "See to the wounded and have the dead buried. I'll be back as soon as I can."

"Aye, Roger," Wilbert replied, but Roger had already started after Tatwine, moving rapidly to keep up with the former cutpurse's rapid gait.

Men—soldiers, servants, merchants—and women were returning to their camps, streaming back from the beach where they had sought escape. Some of the soldiers and knights marched or rode in loose formation, pretending they had not been routed but had fallen back in an orderly fashion. Others moved singly or in small groups, some unabashed but many with sheepish, downturned looks on their faces.

"Where are we going?" Roger asked Tatwine.

Tatwine did not reply.

Roger went on, matching Tatwine's pace. "Did you get the women away?"

"Most of 'em," Tatwine said.

"*Most?*"

Tatwine stopped. "Delva's dead. Ailith and Margaret . . ." His voice tailed off.

Roger's heart sank. "Dead?"

"Captured."

"Captured? How?"

"Dirk," Tatwine said.

"Dirk!"

Tatwine nodded gloomily. "That's what I heard from the other women. They said that Dirk—they're sure it was him—

showed up in Christian armor, and Ailith and Margaret rode off with him. He was gone by the time I got there, the bastard."

Roger let out a long breath and wiped a hand across his mouth. Dirk. Isolated on the Toron, Ailith and Margaret wouldn't have known about Dirk deserting. They'd barely have known Dirk at all. The bastard must have come especially for Ailith. But why? Poor Margaret had probably gone along out of friendship for Ailith.

Oh, God.

Roger's gut felt like a millstone was grinding it. He remembered Dirk's smug look when Roger's ill-thrown knife had bounced harmlessly off his back. If only . . .

Roger turned his eyes toward the brown hills, flowered in bright colors by Saladin's tents. He could only imagine what lay in store for Ailith. Margaret's fate might be more merciful than Ailith's. If she was lucky, they would kill her outright.

Roger turned back to Tatwine. Suddenly he was very tired. "What is it you want to show me?" he asked.

"Come on," Tatwine told him.

Roger followed. Around them, parties were tending the wounded and the dead. The wounded Saracens were killed, their bodies gathered to be tossed in the city ditch. Wounded crusaders were carried back to their tents on litters. Roger saw Christian and Saracen bodies being lifted into the same carts, mixed together any old way, and he thought that must be a mistake. He stopped the nearest cart; blood dripped from its bottom boards.

"What's going on here?" Roger asked the carters. "Why are you placing our dead and the enemy in the same cart? Our dead are buried on the plain."

"King Richard's orders," said one of the men, a Picard by his accent. "We're going to fill in the ditch with bodies, throw a layer of quicklime and dirt over 'em, and get ready to cross for the big attack tomorrow. We'll give our boys a proper Mass later." The men nodded to Roger, and the cart creaked on.

Roger and Tatwine kept going. They were nearing

Richard's trebuchets. "Where the Devil are you taking me?" Roger demanded yet again.

Again Tatwine did not reply. Ahead of them was a hillock clustered with bodies. Tatwine stopped and stepped aside, motioning with his head toward the hillock.

Roger stared at him, not understanding.

Then he saw that one of the dust-covered bodies on the hillock wore green.

Roger was motionless for a moment, as though he had been turned to stone. Then he dropped his helmet and gloves and shield, and he started running. "No!" *It can't be!*

But it was.

Helvise lay sprawled on her face, blood pooled beneath her, her crossbow just beyond her outstretched hand.

Roger stared.

Tatwine came up behind him. "Found her on my way back from the beach," he said, his low voice almost apologetic. He moved away, to give Roger privacy.

Roger sank to his knees. Gently, he turned Helvise's body over and ran his fingers across her forehead and smooth cheek, trying not to look at her wounds. At least her face had not been touched. He drew her close to him and held her, his cheek pressed against hers, which was already cooling. There were dead Christians around her on the hillock along with a much larger number of Saracens. Helvise and the other Christians must have made a stand here and been overrun.

Why had she come back? She had been safely out of this.

Roger rocked back and forth with Helvise's body, crying freely. Helvise's short black hair was matted with the brown dirt of the Holy Land. Her green jerkin was soaked with blood, the dirt on it turning to reddish mud. All her wounds were to her front, so she had not been running away when she was killed.

Roger turned his head to the sky, squinting against the sun's glare and his tears.

Why, Lord? Why did You do this? How could *You do this?*

But God did everything for a reason, and it was not for Roger to question that reason.

Helvise had come back because there were things more important to her than her personal safety. She had come back because she believed in the cause, the crusade. She had come back because she had faith.

And, suddenly, Roger understood.

Staring at the sky, his head crooked, he understood why he had been spared when so many others had died. He had been spared because all those other men and women had gone to their graves secure in their faith, while Roger doubted his.

He had been spared so that he could learn to believe again.

He sank back on his haunches, Helvise's body held close to his. There was a faint smile on her lips, as though she were content, as though at any moment she might get up, laughing and talking about learning her letters, as though she was only taking a rest.

Roger raised his head to the sky again. He felt small; he felt petty. He felt disgusted with himself. What made him so special? Who was he to say this siege was senseless when uncounted thousands had believed otherwise and had willingly gone to their graves to prove it? Who was he to doubt their cause?

Who was he to doubt God?

He had sinned too much already in this life; did he wish to compound those transgressions with the greatest sin of all? Faith had gotten the army of God this far. Faith would enable them to prevail. Only the worst kind of sinner—an unbeliever like Roger—could have doubted that.

Roger felt tears running down his blood-and-dirt crusted face. He felt a sudden force welling within him. He had been given a second chance. God had spared him, and he must show that God had made the right decision. He must show that he was ready to do his part, that he was worthy to enter Heaven.

Tatwine moved closer and cleared his throat. The carters had begun clearing the hillock. "Want me to have her taken back to your tent?" Tatwine said.

Roger wiped his eyes. "No. I'll put her in the ditch with the rest of them. That's what she would have wanted."

He waved off the carters. Then he picked Helvise up. Cradling her limp body in his arms, he carried her toward the city.

Chapter 110

When Ailith realized they were headed the wrong way, she tried to reach around Margaret's bulk and halt the horse, but she couldn't get to the reins because Dirk had tied them to the pommel of his own saddle.

Ailith pressed against Margaret, who was holding on to the saddle pommel for dear life, and yelled in her ear. "Get off!"

Margaret hesitated, scared.

"Now!" Ailith yelled, giving the bigger woman a shove. Margaret awkwardly worked her feet from the stirrups and as soon as her feet were free, she lost her balance and more fell than threw herself from the galloping horse, knocking Ailith off the animal's back in the process.

The two women landed hard, the wind knocked out of them. Ailith rolled over and struggled to her feet, her head spinning. With difficulty, she focused herself and stumbled over to Margaret. "Get up!"

Margaret tried to stand, yelled in pain. "My ankle!" she cried. She waved Ailith on. "Run—get out of here."

Ailith assisted the bigger woman to her feet. "Get away," Margaret repeated, trying to push Ailith from her, "while you still can."

Ailith said nothing. She could have been off like a hare and lost herself in the confusion of battle, but she steadied Margaret and draped Margaret's heavy arm over her shoulder. They started off, Margaret hobbling because she couldn't put any weight on her right foot. "Leave me," Margaret said again, "Save yourself."

"No," Ailith said.

In the thick dust Ailith couldn't tell how far they'd gone from the washerwomen's camp or where they were now. The two women hobbled along, but within minutes Saracen foot soldiers caught up to them, surrounding them and menacing them with spears.

They were forced to stop, Margaret's arm still over Ailith's shoulder. "You should have gone without me," Margaret said, wincing.

Ailith grit her teeth, breathing hard. "I got you into this, I'll get you out."

Dirk rode up then and shouted at the Saracen soldiers in their own tongue. The Saracens seemed to know who he was—in fact, they seemed to have been expecting him.

Dirk walked his horse over and peered down at Ailith, who was still supporting Margaret. He looked Ailith over, taking in her plain dress and unkempt hair. "Well, well, well. 'Twould appear the earl's whore has fallen on hard times. The last time I saw you, you wore jewels and fine clothing."

He waited for a response, as if he expected Ailith to tell him what had caused her change in station. When none was forthcoming, he smiled. "It worked out well for me, as luck would have it. I doubt I could have gotten to you were you still on the Toron."

"So you're not Roger's friend," Ailith said. It was a statement, not a question.

"I'm as far from a friend to that prick as it's possible to be."

"I believed you to be one of Geoffrey's men."

Dirk's smile widened. "So I was—once." He touched his bandaged hand to his lips and forehead, then bowed. "I serve Allah now."

He motioned to the Saracen footmen. Ailith and Margaret were bound, thrown over the backs of horses and taken across the plain to Saladin's camp, where they were separated and Ailith was led—pushed, really—to a tent made of blue silk. The last she saw of Margaret, two Saracen footmen were making her hobble toward the other side of the camp, jabbing her with spears to make her go faster and laughing at the pain it caused her. Margaret cast a last look back at Ailith, then Margaret was shoved forward, stumbling and falling to the ground in pain. Ailith couldn't see any more because Dirk thrust her into the blue tent.

The tent was spacious. It smelled of cinnamon and cloves and some other spice that Ailith couldn't identify. Ailith stood with her hands bound in front of her. Dirk assumed a place behind her.

"What are we doing here?" Ailith said.

"Waiting," Dirk replied.

"Waiting for who?"

"You'll find out soon enough."

Time passed. Ailith listened to the distant sounds of battle from the Christian camp. It was impossible to tell what was happening from the noise, but the attitudes of the men she could see through the tent's opening indicated the Saracens were winning. When those attitudes gradually changed, and Muslim soldiers began streaming dejectedly back to the camp, Ailith turned to Dirk. "Your new friends seem to have lost," she observed.

Dirk appeared shaken, as if he had not thought such an outcome possible. "A temporary setback," he assured her. "The final outcome is not in doubt."

"Damned right, it's not. I want to be there when Roger takes off your head for treason."

A smile crossed Dirk's lips. "So it's Roger you long for, is it, and not Lord Geoffrey? Well, you little bitch, Allah willing, your friend Roger is dead by now, or better yet, bleeding his guts out on a pile of horse shit."

Ailith was about to reply when a dust-covered emir entered the tent, carrying a helmet around which was wound a long blue sash.

The emir was tall and handsome in a predatory way. The dust made his trim beard look like it had been powdered with flour. He had a large hooked nose and black hair matted with sweat from wearing the helmet all day. He set the helmet on a table and stood with his hands on his hips, examining Ailith with his dark eyes. Ailith met the emir's gaze unflinchingly, even though she was scared to death inside.

Dirk pinioned Ailith's arms, thrusting her forward so the emir could get a good look at her. "I told you she was beautiful, lord. You'll see better when she's cleaned up, but it's apparent even—"

"I will be my own judge," Qaymaz snapped. He was in a foul mood because the sultan's attack had failed, and the failure of his own part in that attack rankled even more. He had been given the most important role—the place of honor. His men had been so *close* to victory, then they had been attacked from behind by a small party of infidels and everything had fallen apart.

Qaymaz looked the yellow-haired woman up and down. He did not like the feringhee traitor Dirk, but he had to admit the fellow could be useful. And he was right—beneath her bedraggled appearance this woman was beautiful. She would provide some consolation for the day's failure. She would be a welcome addition to his *harim*. She would, perhaps, become the jewel of it.

With a curl of his mouth, the emir reached out and cupped the woman's breast with his hand.

Ailith twisted in Dirk's grip and aimed a savage kick at the emir's groin. The emir dodged it and her foot grazed his thigh instead.

The emir regarded her calmly for a moment. Then he punched her in the face so hard that she sagged in Dirk's arms and fell to her knees on the floor.

Ailith's brain was addled as Dirk lifted her to her feet. "Qaymaz is not a man to be trifled with," he whispered.

Ailith stood unsteadily in front of the emir. His dark eyes showed no emotion. He reached out to feel her breast again, and this time she drew back and spit in his face.

Slowly, deliberately, Qaymaz wiped the spit from his face with the sleeve of his blue robe. He sipped water from a cup on the table. Then he punched Ailith again, even harder if that was possible.

The force of the blow knocked Ailith out of Dirk's arms, and she lay on the floor of the tent, dazed. Blood ran from her nose and her teeth felt loose.

The emir spoke harshly and Dirk put his arms around Ailith's waist, hauling her to her feet once more. "He'll beat you to death if you don't give in to him," Dirk warned.

"Let him," Ailith said. Her voice was slurry from the blood in her mouth.

"Don't be stupid," Dirk pleaded, and there was a note of fear in his voice that told Ailith his fate might be tied to hers. It would be worth dying just for that, she thought.

The emir stared at her. Ailith glared back, bloody teeth bared, ready to resist again, daring another blow from his fist.

Before the emir could move forward, Ailith heard a new noise among the many outside the tent. It was someone speaking English—a familiar voice. Before Dirk could stop her, she yanked herself free of his arms, crossed the tent and looked out the open flap.

She saw a group of female prisoners, a few of them just children, roped together, huddled and looking terrified. In the middle of the group was Margaret, face lined with pain from her injured ankle. "Keep your heads up," Margaret urged the demoralized women. "There's always hope. Remember your God."

With her bound hands, Ailith gestured toward the prisoners. "What will happen to those women?" she asked Dirk.

"They'll be raped through the army," Dirk said, "those who are attractive enough. If they survive, they'll be sold as slaves." He snorted derisively. "As for your homely friend, I doubt any man will want her. She'll probably be used as target practice for the archers."

Ailith's chest rose and fell with rage. Keeping her eyes on Qaymaz, she said to Dirk, "Tell this piss-swilling Goat—" she caught herself, then smiled sweetly at Qaymaz, or as sweetly as she could with blood all over her face—"tell the *emir* that if he spares my friend and lets her stay with me, as my companion, I will do anything he desires."

Dirk translated. The hawk-faced emir took a few steps and peered outside at Margaret. His fingers tapped his thigh. Then he turned to Ailith and smiled. It was not a pleasant smile. He said something.

"The emir agrees," Dirk translated, the relief evident in his voice.

The emir added something else.

Dirk said, "Now I must get you cleaned up and bring you back for the emir's pleasure."

Chapter 111

Roger trudged back to the English lines, Tatwine beside him, neither man speaking. Roger's eyes were red; his cheeks, wet.

"Roger—where have you been?" It was Ralph the Red, running toward them. "The king is looking for you!"

Roger stopped, jolted out of his mourning for Helvise. "The king?"

"Yes," Ralph panted as he came alongside. There was a slash down the front of Ralph's jack from the battle; the brim of his painted helmet had been cracked, the cloth cover flapping loose.

Roger made a puzzled face. "Me?"

"Yes!"

"Why?"

"I don't know, but the earl sent enough men out looking for you, so it must be important." Ralph grabbed the sleeve of Roger's jack and hauled him forward. "Come on."

Ralph led Roger and Tatwine through the smashed-up camp, back to the foot of the Toron, where the Death's Heads were in loose formation, their banner planted in front of them, the surviving men smartening themselves up as best they could. Around them, servants and men from other units were busy collecting the dead and wounded.

Facing the Death's Heads was a group of high-ranking nobles—princes, dukes, counts. Some of them, like Conrad of Montferrat and the archduke of Austria, Roger recognized; most he did not. Archduke Leopold saw Roger, lifted his chin in greeting and smiled.

One man stood out above the others. He was huge and strikingly handsome, with a red-gold beard and eyes of the

559

deepest blue. His red surcoat bore three gold lions, and beneath it was a hauberk polished so thoroughly that it shone. On his head was a mail coif surmounted by a flat steel cap with a thin gold crown. Beside him was an attentive, dark-haired man with a ring in one ear, who from time to time cupped the big man's left elbow as though supporting him. From the plain beyond the camp came the sounds of battle, as mounted knights and men-at-arms pursued the fleeing Saracens.

Geoffrey of Trent saw Roger coming. "Here he is, sire," he told the big man with relief, adding, "His name is Roger." He beckoned Roger forward.

As Roger approached, King Richard smiled broadly. "Ah, Roger," he said in a booming voice. He indicated the Death's Heads. "You command these fellows, I understand."

Roger didn't know what to do when talking to a king—kneel, bow his head? In the end, he was so flustered, so overcome by Richard's sheer physical presence, that he did nothing. "Yes, my—" he corrected himself—"yes, sire."

"'Pon my soul, but I admire that flag," Richard went on, pointing to the Death's Heads' banner. "Wouldn't care to trade it for three worn-out lions, would you?"

Roger frowned. "Sire?"

"Just joking with you, boy, just joking." Richard held up a fat purse and called to the Death's Heads. "This is for you, men—for your work today."

The Death's Heads responded with cheers, beating spears and axes and swords against their shields. "Hurrah for Richard!" "God bless the king!" Judging by its size, the purse probably contained more money than they'd seen the whole time they'd been at Acre, Roger thought.

As the cheering died down, Richard handed the purse to Roger. "Where are you from, Roger?"

"Huntley, sire."

"Huntley?" Richard turned to the dark-haired man beside him. "One of your boys is at Huntley, isn't he, Alart?"

Roger's guts twisted.

Alart smiled. He had removed his helmet, revealing oiled hair brushed straight back. "He is, sire. Auberie."

"Well, there's a coincidence," Richard said. "Where *is* Huntley, anyway? My knowledge of England is rather limited."

"In southern Trentshire," Alart replied. "The abbey is quite famous—over a hundred books in the library, I'm told."

Richard harrumphed. "A lot of damned books." He turned back to Roger. "Are you from the abbey, Roger?"

Roger replied without thinking. "Yes, sire."

"What did you do there?"

Roger hesitated. *I killed your friend's son and ran away.* Then he had an inspiration. "I was a woodcutter, sire."

"Woodcutter, eh?" said the king. "Well, you've the build for it."

Alart spoke hopefully. "Have you by chance made the acquaintance of my son Auberie? I understand he's very well thought of."

He's the biggest shit I ever met. "No, my lord, I'm afraid I haven't. I didn't have much contact with the chapter."

"A pity. I'd like to know how he's doing. It's my hope that he'll be abbot one day."

"I'm sure he'd make a good one, my lord," Roger said. So the count of Vouzin didn't know his son was dead. That was not surprising. News traveled slow, when it traveled at all. A messenger would have been sent from Huntley to Vouzin, another from Vouzin to the Holy Land. There was every chance the messenger had been waylaid, or taken sick, or on a ship that was sunk or captured by pirates. The count might not learn of Auberie's death until he returned home. But what if he did learn of it here? Would he connect the "woodcutter" from Huntley with the monk who had stabbed his son and run away?

King Richard interrupted Roger's thoughts. "You did well today, young man. Better than well, I'd say."

"I was only doing my duty, sire," Roger said.

"Please God all my men did their duty as well as you."

Richard nodded to the earl of Trent. "All right."

The earl motioned with a finger. "Kneel, Roger."

Kneel? Roger thought. *Why?* Then—*One knee or two?* In the end, he opted for one. He was wondering what he was supposed to do next when Richard clouted him alongside the ear with his big mailed hand, almost knocking him over. "Accept this blow and no others," the king ordered in formal tones.

Roger's ear was ringing. Grinning, the count of Vouzin indicated that he should rise.

Roger stood. He had no idea why the king had hit him.

The earl of Trent explained, smiling. "The king has made you a knight."

Chapter 112

Roger was dumbfounded. "A knight?"

"Yes," King Richard said. " 'Roger of Huntley' you may style yourself until you've acquired property of your own. You should be proud of yourself, young man. You've come a long way from cutting wood."

A knight?

Richard seemed to have trouble with his balance, and Alart of Vouzin once again steadied him on his feet. Richard went on. "As custom dictates, upon elevation to knighthood, you may ask a boon of the one who confers the honor."

Roger realized that he could ask for money. Or land. Or both.

Then he thought of Will, of Egwulf, of young Cole and so many others.

He thought of Helvise.

"There *is* a favor I would ask, sire."

"Name it."

"I would be in the first group to attack the breach when the Accursed Tower falls."

Richard's blue eyes widened in surprise. Then he grinned and thumped Earl Geoffrey in the chest. "Damn me if I don't like this fellow of yours, Trent. By Heaven, that's the kind of thing I'd ask for myself were I in his place." To Roger he said, "You realize, of course, that half the army has requested that same privilege?"

Roger didn't know, but he could imagine they had.

"So why should I give it to you?" Richard said.

So I can be in Heaven with Helvise tomorrow night. "I—" Roger couldn't tell him the real reason, so he remained quiet.

Richard went on. "Do you ask this for yourself alone or for

your men as well?"

Roger glanced back at the Death's Heads, who were just as surprised by Roger's answer as the king had been. "For myself only," he told the king. "Enough of my men have died in front of this city. I wish to spare the others that fate."

Roger heard rustling behind him. He turned as Grandad Offa—of all people—threw his helmet to the ground and swore. "Oh, no, you don't! You're not going to hog all the glory."

"If you go, we go, too," Tatwine added.

"That's right!" shouted Wilbert. "We'll tear down that damned green flag and put our Death's Heads banner in its place!"

The fellows had lost their minds. They were all cheering and shouting, Short Peter and Slowfoot, boisterous Ralph the Red and quiet Hedde, pious Father Mayne—even Hake, though Hake looked less enthusiastic than some of the others.

King Richard regarded them with a smile. To Roger he said, "Your wish is granted. God be with you."

More cheers from the Death's Heads. Didn't the fools know they had just condemned themselves to death?

Richard gave Roger a conspiratorial wink. "Now I would request a favor of you, Roger. Lord Aubrey of Clement has taken a solemn vow to be first man into Acre. As Lord Aubrey is a vassal of mine, I'd be obliged if you did nothing to keep him from fulfilling that vow. You can be second if you like, just let him go first."

Laughter from the men. Roger said, "Certainly, sire."

"Good." Richard straightened and grinned again. "Of course, were I not so weak from illness, there's no question who would be first into the city, vow or no vow—" he cleared his throat loudly—"and it wouldn't be Aubrey."

More laughter from everyone.

Roger laughed with the rest, feeling the king's attraction. He would follow this man that some were calling Lionheart anywhere, do anything to remain in his good grace.

King Richard turned to Vouzin and the men around him. "Let us be off, gentlemen. We have much to do." He nodded to Roger. "I will see you on the morrow, sir knight." Then he mounted, Vouzin assisting, and, with his retinue and their banners, he clattered off.

The earl of Trent came over and shook Roger's hand. "Congratulations."

"Thank you, my lord."

The earl gestured at the fat purse in Roger's hand. "Make sure your men don't spend that all at once. They'll need to be clear headed for the attack tomorrow."

Roger was surprised. "I thought the attack might be moved back after—" he gestured at the battered camp around them— "after this."

"No. The Saracens are too close to discovering our mine— we dare not give them another day. We'll work through the night reorganizing the men and filling in the ditch."

"Will you be coming with us?"

The earl shook his head. "I and the rest of the English force are to assault St. Anthony's Tower. There's to be a general assault on the city walls to keep the Turbans from concentrating at the breach." The earl paused. "It's a rare privilege you've been given, Roger. My prayers will go with you and your men."

"Thank you, my lord, I appreciate that."

"Come to what's left of my tent after dark and I'll give you final instructions and tell you where and when to assemble."

"Aye, my lord."

As the earl turned to leave, Roger said, "My lord—there's something you should know. The Lady Ailith—" it seemed strange to call Ailith 'Lady'—"has been captured."

The earl's jaw fell. "My God."

"She was taken by a deserter from our ranks, a Brabanter named Dirk."

Geoffrey closed his eyes. "That poor child. God help me, if I hadn't . . ." His voice tailed off and his eyes opened again.

"You did right to tell me this, Roger. We lost a lot of good men today, but at least they're safe in Paradise. Poor Ailith . . ." He shook his head, and there was a hitch in his voice as he said, "Better see to your men."

"Aye, my lord."

The earl departed, leaving Roger to himself.

He was a knight. Becoming a knight had been his dream, his fantasy. But now that he had achieved it, it meant nothing. War was not glory, Roger had learned—it was shit and piss and blood and mangled men screaming for their mothers. It was Arcil with his fingers chopped off, Egwulf burned alive, it was Will so wasted away he seemed to have become part of his bedding, as though he had disappeared into it. It was Helvise, her body rent open by . . .

Roger felt sick to his stomach. He had been rewarded not because of anything he had done, but because he had somehow managed to stay alive through all this madness, nothing more.

Someone thumped his back.

Someone else pumped his hand. Another punched his shoulder. The Death's Heads had gathered around, pummeling him in congratulation. Roger noted that Hake was not one of them. "What do we call you now," Slowfoot said, " 'my lord?' 'your highness?' 'your supreme knightly-ness?' "

" 'Roger' will do," Roger said. He felt guilty because none of the rewards that had come to him would have been possible without these men. He handed the purse to Mayne, who had lost his gapped front teeth in the fight, blood all over his mouth and the front of his beard. "You're good at counting, Father. See this is handed out amongst the men. Usual distribution— centenars eight shares, vintenars four."

The men craned their heads, peering at the purse. Mayne pulled open the leather drawstring, revealing gold bezants. There were whistles and nods of approval. "How many shares for you?" Mayne said, his voice whistling because of the lost teeth. "Sixteen?"

"None," Roger told him.

"None! Why?"

"Because I don't want any." Roger changed the subject, trying to lighten the mood. "Why did you lunatics ask to join me at the breach? You could have stayed safe in camp."

"Ha!" said Ralph the Red. "And let you have all the fun? Not a chance."

"Bugger fun," said a grizzled spearman named Dick. "There'll be enough plunder in Acre to make us rich as bishops."

"Maybe we'll get knighted, too," Short Peter said, elbowing his neighbor playfully.

"You've got more chance of being buried," Roger retorted.

"That's all right," Offa said, "I always wondered what Heaven was like."

Tatwine nodded agreement. "Wasn't like none of us was getting out of this place alive anyway. Maybe in Heaven we can finally get a decent meal."

"And some ale?" Slowfoot said hopefully.

"And women," added Ralph the Red. "D'ye think there'll be women there?"

Roger realized how much he loved these men, and his eyes teared. He forced a grin and placed an arm around Ralph's big shoulder. "Of course there will be women there, ye great lump. Why do you think they call it 'Heaven?'"

Chapter 113

The torch was lit, bundled reeds daubed with pitch, its flames unnaturally bright in the pre-dawn darkness. In the trench before the mine entrance, Etienne, the grizzled master miner, went to one knee, holding the torch before him. He was stripped to his mud-caked braies, a length of cloth knotted around his thinning hair, wooden clogs on his feet. Wearing his hauberk and a helmet, and standing at what he hoped was a safe distance from the flames, the bishop of Beauvais—the same man who had blessed the ill-fated copper belfry—made the sign of the Cross over the torch. Chanting in Latin, he sprinkled Holy Water on it.

Don't put it out, you fool!—Etienne almost yelled his thoughts out loud.

The bishop finished, saying to Etienne, "Go with God, my son."

Holding the torch in his left hand, Etienne crossed himself—awkwardly, because of the heat of flames—and rose. He glanced toward the English king, who stood nearby, polished mail reflecting the torch's light so that it seemed like the king was on fire. Richard had already distributed the promised reward money to the miners. Etienne had received his five gold bezants plus one extra.

Now the king stepped forward and put his hand on Etienne's shoulder. "Good luck."

"Thank you, sire," Etienne gushed. Such a display of intimacy between a king and a commoner was unheard of. Nobles, even minor ones, usually communicated with men like Etienne only through their stewards.

❖ ❖ ❖

Richard watched Etienne and the torch disappear down the dark tunnel, the light growing fainter, then winking out. Richard wished he could go with Etienne and fire the mine himself—he wished he could have an *adventure*. He *would* have gone with Etienne—he had never been inside a mine and was curious to see what they looked like—but Alart and his other advisors refused to let him do it, threatened to physically restrain him, for his safety's sake. Lighting a mine was hardly the task for a king, they argued. What if it collapsed? What if it even *threatened* to collapse? Richard was too weak to run out. What if the Saracen counter miners broke through—they were said to be close. So here Richard stood, once again maddeningly helpless, yearning to *do* something.

"Come, sire," Alart said, taking his arm. "We must be in position when the tower falls."

❖ ❖ ❖

The mine shaft ran straight for about fifty yards, then began descending, the ceiling growing gradually lower so that Etienne, whose back was already bent from years in the mines, was forced to walk bent over, the flaming brand illumining his way far better than the tiny candles stuck in wall sockets did. Rats skittered across his path, but he ignored them. He passed the last workers leaving the mine, bare chested, grimy, rags wrapped around their heads to catch the sweat, some of them squeezing against the wall and crossing themselves as Etienne went by.

He had to hurry. The Saracen counter miners were near. Down, down, he went, then straight again, under the city walls, under the Accursed Tower—or so he hoped. The panicked thought came to him that he might have placed the mine incorrectly. He'd seen it happen before, seen an empty section of ground collapse in front of a castle to laughter and jeers from its defenders—even worse, seen fools tunnel up right into a besieged castle's courtyard.

He reached the tunnel's end. It was strangely quiet now with the diggers and shorers gone. The timber supports had been soaked with oil and slabbed with pitch so that they would burn quickly. Around the supports were piles of hay and more wood, arranged so that they would burn free and not suck up all the air and go out. That was something else Etienne had seen happen before. The smells of the combustibles mingled with those of wet earth and urine and feces where miners had relieved themselves.

Etienne moved cautiously. A misplaced movement with the torch in these cramped quarters could set the mass alight and him with it.

Suddenly, breaking the silence so abruptly it made him jump, he heard a noise.

Digging.

Frantic digging.

The Saracens had found the mine and they were racing to stop it being fired.

The digging was very close. Etienne thought he could hear voices, though he told himself that was his imagination.

Etienne forced himself to remain calm, even though the enemy might burst through the dirt wall at any moment. He placed his torch at the foot of the left-hand bonfire. It smoked, then caught, fingers of flame running through the hay, leaping up the sides of the timber supports. He did the same to the bonfire on his right, ignoring the ever louder scrapings of the Saracens.

Etienne took a last look at the burning timber. He had done as much as he could. The rest was up to God. He threw the torch onto the flames, turned and made a hasty exit, bent double and racing against the spreading fire, the flames hot at his back.

DEATH'S HEAD

❖ ❖ ❖

Yazid sat next to the earthen wall at the end of the gallery, one end of a conical glass tube pressed to the wall, the other to his ear. Behind him, some of his men waited, while others propped up the low gallery with wooden supports. Still others carried buckets of earth to the surface, emptying them between the walls behind the tower.

With his scraggly blond hair and blue eyes, Yazid could have been mistaken for a feringhee. He was naked to the waist and barefoot, and in his belt was a dagger with a saw-toothed edge, ideal for shredding muscle and tissue in the narrow confines of a mine shaft.

Yazid was in charge of the counter miners, succeeding the previous commander, Timurhan, who had been killed in the underground battle last spring. Yazid and his men had suspected the infidels were digging a new mine and they had been digging counter shafts to find it. After months of frustration, Yazid had felt vibrations in the earth. He and his men had tunneled toward the vibrations, until, using the hearing glass, they had at last detected the unmistakable sounds of digging. They had worked toward the sounds, trying to muffle their own digging, hoping to surprise the infidels as they had done last spring.

Finding another mine shaft underground was an inexact science. You could easily pass above or beneath it. If you did break through, it was best to come in from the side, especially if you could get behind the diggers and cut them off. But you had to be lucky for that to happen. Last spring they had literally fallen through the roof of the shaft on top of the infidel miners, but that had worked out well enough. The heads of the infidels had been displayed from the city walls for months, until birds and weather had turned them to skulls and they had been cast down.

Yazid came from a family of gold miners in eastern

Anatolia. There had been good years and bad years finding gold, but more bad than good, which was what had prompted Yazid to leave his wife and children and join the sultan's army. He had trained as a spearman, had fought against both the so-called Crusaders and the sultan's Arab enemies, and had been posted to Akko with the relief force last winter. He had volunteered for the counter-mining job. It was important work, and Meshtub, the garrison commander, paid the miners well. It was exciting work, too. The constant threat of death from tunnel collapse terrified Yazid yet made him feel alive as he never had before. But the real excitement was breaking into an infidel tunnel, coming to grips with the devils he had seen only at a distance. Such had been the case last spring when, *Inshallah*, they had come upon the enemy tunnel. There had been a desperate struggle in the shaft's narrow confines, lit only by flickering candles, men grunting and heaving and clawing at one another, and the saw-toothed knife had done its grim work well. Meshtub had rewarded Yazid and his men handsomely for that. If they stopped this new shaft, Yazid reckoned he would have enough money to buy a small farm where he and his family might live in something approaching comfort.

So now Yazid sat with his ear to the gallery wall. For days, the digging sounds had grown increasingly louder, then last night they had stopped. That puzzled Yazid. There was no evidence the Christian tunnel had collapsed—he and his men would have heard. Perhaps the feringhees had struck rock and been forced to stop digging, or perhaps yesterday's battle for the camp had forced them to withdraw. Perhaps they had heard Yazid's men and were preparing an ambush for them. Or perhaps . . .

Perhaps their shaft was finished and they were preparing to fire the mine.

Yazid threw down the glass tube and began digging. "Quickly!" he cried. "Muharren!" He motioned to his second in command to join him. Muharren, a swarthy goat herder from near Lake Van, had joined the army at the same time as Yazid. They had served together their whole time as soldiers, Muharren volunteering for the miners only because Yazid had done so.

"What is it?" said a man behind them. "Do you hear them?"

"They're going to fire the mine. We must stop it." To Muharren he cried, "Dig!"

"How do we know we're going the right way?" Muharren said.

"We must trust in Allah. We have no other choice."

The two men knelt side by side, hurling dirt, moving forward foot by foot. Behind them, others cleared the thrown dirt away.

It was growing warmer in the tunnel; it was not Yazid's imagination. Sweat poured off him. He touched the blade of his shovel. "The metal is hot," he told Muharren. "I was right, the pigs have fired their mine."

"We need to get out!" cried a man named Ayet behind him.

"No!" Yazid commanded. "We still have time to put out the fire." He needed the reward, he needed that farm.

He dug furiously, Muharren matching him shovel for shovel, almost laughing with the intensity of it, as though it were a contest.

"Bring dirt!" Yazid ordered the men behind him. "All the buckets you can. We'll use it to put out the fire."

Ayet said, "But—"

"Do it!"

Beside him, Muharren's bearded face was blackened by dirt and sweat. "We're close," he said. "I can feel the fire beneath my knees."

Yazid thought, *We're going through the roof again.* Then, without warning, the floor of the tunnel collapsed beneath them. Yazid had a vision of billowing smoke interspersed with stabs of red and yellow and orange, and then he and Muharren and the rest of his men tumbled into the flames.

Chapter 114

In the first light of dawn, Acre looked so destroyed, it scarcely seemed worthwhile capturing it. The once-proud circuit of its walls now resembled a rat-eaten cheese, pocked and nibbled all over. Here and there the cheese had been tastier and larger bites had been taken, with a rubble of crumbs trickling from them. The battlements in the vicinity of the Accursed Tower were no longer recognizable, though Meshtub's green flag still flew defiantly.

The plain between the city and the Christian camp was covered with two years of war's refuse. There were bones of animals and men, burnt-out belfries, rotted and broken mangonels. There were wagons, barrels, articles of clothing and equipment. There was a belt of stones that had been flung from the walls and not reused by the Franks. The ground had been churned by attack and counterattack in the mud and subsequently baked rock hard by the Mediterranean sun.

In the crusader camp, palls of smoke still hung over the lines from the previous day's attack. Eastward, Christian graveyards carpeted the edge of the broad plain, which was littered with bones and the wreckage of forgotten battles and skirmishes.

Now, all was quiet save for the gentle wash of the surf and the occasional cry of a gull, but the previous evening and night had been chaos. Dead and wounded were everywhere. So many valuable horses ran ownerless that men stopped what they were doing to catch them for the rewards. Soldiers had looted some of the wine tents on the Concourse, and they ran in drunken packs, singing and pawing any women who had the misfortune to come near them.

Once order was restored to the camp, the men worked

through the night to make ready for the morrow's battle. Clothing and armor were hastily repaired. Weapons were sharpened. Roger had his bleary eyed spearmen cut the hafts of their spears three feet short, then wrap them with rope, twine or cloth to keep them from getting slippery from sweat and blood. "Short spears will be better for fighting in close quarters," Roger told his men as they practiced thrusting one handed with their re-worked weapons, adjusting their grips to account for the change in balance. Roger carried one of the shortened spears himself; his axe was in his belt.

Those who were able had eaten what remained of the two bullocks the earl had sent them—many were too hung over or could not bear the thought of food before a fight—then they had been shriven and heard Mass, all but a few taking Communion. After that, they had armed themselves and marched to their assembly point just across the camp ditch, opposite the Accursed Tower. All around the city, other men were moving into position for the attack.

The Death's Heads were the only footmen assigned to assault the tower breach. This was a great honor—King Richard could easily have chosen some of his own Poitevins for the task. The rest of the assault party consisted of knights and men at arms, clad in burnished mail, carrying painted shields and a variety of weapons. One or two of the knights carried the new bucket helmets—so called because they resembled a bucket placed over the head with slits to see out of—though Roger did not fathom how men wearing them could function in this heat.

"Death's Head!"

It was Leopold of Austria. He waved a greeting to Roger, then took a deep breath and thumped his chest. "Good morning for it, eh?"

"It is, my lord," Roger called back.

One-eyed Henry the Lion was there, too. He gave Roger a queer look but did not greet him. A beautifully armored young man who must be Aubrey of Clement shouldered his way to the front of the force. Not to be outdone, Tatwine moved forward and waved the Death's Heads' red skull banner in the slack dawn air, so that the Saracens on the battlements would know who was coming for them.

Once in position, the men waited for the mine to be fired. Those who were able lay down and caught some much-needed sleep. Others rolled dice or joked, their laughter a bit too loud, a bit too forced, as they pretended to be unconcerned by what was to come. Still others took this last chance to relieve themselves. Not far from Roger, Grandad Offa fumbled under his metal-scaled jack, swearing mightily.

"What's wrong?" Slowfoot asked him.

"I can't find my dick!"

The men around him groaned. "Not again!"

Ralph the Red did his best to be helpful. "Where was it the last time you saw it?"

"In your girlfriend's mouth," Offa snapped, still flailing with his hand under the cumbersome jack.

"That explains it, then," Ralph said brightly. "A right termagant, my girl is. Like as not, she got that little stub of yours, chomped it off and spit it out. No use looking for it now—it's gone."

Offa was about to retort when there came the sound of approaching horses. Everyone turned as the kings of England and France rode up with their retinues, broad banners flying behind them—the three lions of England, the red oriflamme of France. The kings greeted archduke Leopold, Henry the Lion, Aubrey of Clement and the other knights, many of whom they knew by name.

King Richard walked his horse over to where Roger and the footmen stood, while King Philip remained with the nobles.

"Good morrow, men!" Richard cried.

The men were on their feet now, because their king was here. "Good morrow, sire!" they shouted back.

To Roger, Richard said, "Good morrow, Roger of Huntley.

It appears your men are ready."

"They are, sire," Roger replied.

In the grey light, Richard eyed the city. "Shouldn't be long now." He looked down from his horse—Roger saw that he was tied to the saddle—and grinned. "Sure you don't want to trade that flag?"

Roger grinned back. "I'm sure, sire."

"Look!" someone cried.

"Smoke!" cried another.

Roger stared. Indeed—faint wisps of smoke were rising from the ground around the Accursed Tower. The mine had been fired. The men around him began to cheer, and then the cheering spread up and down the mass of soldiers surrounding Acre until it seemed that the very force of it must bring down the city walls. Roger was one of the few who didn't join the cheering; somehow he was beyond that.

The smoke became more dense; the men could see panicked movement on what was left of the tower's battlements.

The smoke billowed for a bit, then gradually died, until the last wisps were borne away on the breeze.

Nothing happened.

The cheering died away, and a glum silence enveloped the Christian lines. Roger was vaguely aware of the science of mine firing. The thing had to burn, but not so quickly that it sucked all the air from the mine. Consequently, after an initial burst of flame, it might be some while for the mine to show its effects. Still, this one seemed to be going for an especially long time.

The king's parties dismounted, to stretch their legs. Richard was helped from his saddle to a camp chair. The sun grew hot. The men waited and waited. Had the mine failed?

Suddenly, from the Accursed Tower came a grating, squealing sound, tormented, like a rusted flywheel in Hell. Every man came instantly alert, watching eagerly.

The tower wavered and shifted slightly, but it did not fall.

The army let out its collective breath in disappointment.

"A breach!" shouted Tatwine, pointing.

He was right. A small breach had formed where the tower joined the city wall, rubble tumbling out of it in a cloud of dust.

Assisted by Alart, King Richard got to his feet. "It's not as big as we had hoped, but it will do," Richard said in a commanding voice. "Up and at them, men! Good luck, and I'll see you in the city!"

There was a loud cheer from the assault force. The knights donned their helms and, led by Leopold and Henry the Lion, they fell into line. Roger turned and cried, "Death's Heads, form up!"

The men formed into a column. Roger held his arms outstretched to keep them from advancing. He looked them over, and for a moment he saw all of them—Will and Cole, Black Jack and Bald Matthew, Tom the beekeeper, Watford Wat, Uwen and Unforth and James of Claire. They were all looking back at him, grinning.

He blinked the vison away and cried, "Band!" He had arranged to have the earl's band present.

The band's leader stepped forward. " 'Girls of Falaise,'" Roger told him.

Roger turned and dropped his arms, and as the band struck up the familiar tune, there was a wild burst of cheering, and to the keening of the pipes and the *boom-boom-booming* of the bass drum, the Death's Heads advanced.

Chapter 115

The Death's Heads crossed the broken ground toward the city, the skirling of bagpipes and booming of drums urging them on, their hearts racing to "Girls of Falaise." They were behind the knights in a loose column ten men across and twenty deep, the axe men in the front rank.

Boom-boom, boom-boom. In addition to axes and spears, a number of the men carried swords—straight-bladed Christian swords and curved Moslem weapons much prized because of the temper of their blades and their sharpness. The centenar Osric had a mace he'd taken from a dead Saracen the day before; Slowfoot carried a war hammer, a shaft with a long spike at the end that could penetrate any armor. Roger didn't have to urge the men on, nothing was going to hold them back, though Roger noted that Hake had managed to slide his company to the column's rear.

Ahead, some of the younger knights could contain their eagerness no longer. They broke ranks and began running forward, yelling their family battle cries. Other knights and the footmen shouted invective at them, as though what they had done was a breach of etiquette. "Let them go," Roger told his men. "We don't want to get tired out before we get there."

Boom-boom, boom-boom. The breach drew closer. Helmeted figures clambered through the opening, splashing buckets of liquid on the rubble field leading up to it.

Tatwine said, "What the—?"

"Oil!" cried Henry the Lion. "They're making it slippery. Watch your step, boys!"

Boom-boom, boom-boom, boom-boom. Closer, closer. From the city walls, the first arrows fell among the attackers. The men raised their shields. A shaft grazed Roger's helmet. A knight fell screaming with an arrow in his eye. King Richard had detailed the poacher Rob and his gang of longbowmen to cover the assault, though, and their deadly arrows kept the Saracen archers largely behind the cover of the parapets.

Boom-boom, boom-boom. Closer, the men moving faster now. The breach was far too small to accommodate knights and footmen side by side. There was going to be a jam.

Closer. They passed some of the young knights who had been running; the knights were bent over, catching their breaths, one of them vomiting in the heat. Ahead of them, the oil-slicked blocks of rubble loomed large. It would be a hard scramble to the top of the breach. Another man fell from an arrow.

Almost there. They picked up their pace, yelling, cheering. Aubrey of Clement sprinted ahead, armor gleaming in the sun, waving his sword to those behind. "I am first! *Apres moi, messieurs!*" He bounded up the slick rubble as nimbly as a mountain goat—an incredible feat of athleticism—and disappeared over the top.

With a roar, the men followed.

They hit the rubble in a jumble and began making their way up the low incline to the top of the breach. Men slipped and fell on the oily rocks. Ankles and wrists were broken, knees were twisted. The press behind them drove the men forward or caused them to fall. Men trod on those who went down. A few laughed at the insanity of it all.

They heard a terrible cry from behind the wall and stopped. A moment later, Aubrey of Clement's head came flying over the breach and bounced among the rocks. There was a silent pause, then the Saracens boiled over the top and rushed down to meet their attackers, yelling "*Allahu akbar! Allahu akbar!*"

The two sides clashed, both forces eager to get to grips with the enemies who had tormented them for two long years. Attacking downslope, the Saracens had the advantage, and they sliced through the crusaders, breaking the jam of men. All cohesion on both sides was lost. There was no shield wall, no lines of any sort. It was a brawl. The Saracens wanted to defend the rubble that had not been doused with oil, where they would have better footing than their adversaries, but their momentum and eagerness carried them further than they had intended, and they were soon sliding and falling on the oil-slicked rocks along with the Christians.

The knights ahead of Roger were fully engaged, and then it was Roger's turn to lead his men into the fight, yelling, his blood lust up, the battle madness upon him. Thrusting with his shield, he crashed into an oncoming, out-of-control Saracen on the slippery rubble, using the man's momentum to knock him sideways and off balance. The man fell. A jab of the cut-off spear pierced the man's chest; Roger felt the man's sternum break. He withdrew the spear and shouldered forward.

It was hard to keep his footing on the oil-slick rocks with the press of men around him, friend and enemy jumbled together, sweating and grunting and pushing and trying to punch steel through each other's bodies. He couldn't watch where he was going or look around to rally his men because if he took his eyes off the fight, someone was likely to kill him.

Tucked behind his round shield, Roger jabbed with the cut down spear. He drove the spear head into an enemy's face, shattering bone and flesh; he rammed it through another man's chest. He bent low when someone battered his shield with an axe and stabbed the spear deep into the man's thigh. The man stopped hitting Roger's shield, and someone else must have killed him because he dropped from sight.

Roger moved forward. Beside him, Offa was brained by a man with a spiked club. Roger reached across his shield and drove his spear at the man's neck, but the man moved at the last second and the spear went through his ear and into his brain. Roger left his right side open when he did this, and there was a stinging sensation in his right cheek, as though he had been bitten by a large insect.

All around Roger, men grappled, stabbed, ripped at each

other's faces with bared teeth, like maddened dogs. Roger was splashed with blood. He was hot; sweat flowed over him. He wiped the sweat from the right side of his face and found that it was blood. His cheek had been laid open. He started moving again, pushing and sliding to get to the front of the fighting. He saw a dark-faced man with his teeth bared, and he jabbed his short spear into the space just under the man's throat. The spear got stuck, and when the man fell Roger put his foot on the man's neck to pull it out. As he did that, a Saracen jumped on him. Roger fell backward, and his helmet hit the edge of a rock. He was stunned, unable to move. The Saracen above him raised an axe with both hands. As the Saracen brought the axe down, there was a flash of steel and the Saracen's hands and the axe went spinning away while the Saracen completed his downward motion with arms that now ended in stumps.

The Saracen stood staring stupidly at his wrists, which were white for a heartbeat, then began gouting blood. Roger looked to his left. Fauston was there, wearing a hauberk and conical helmet and holding a sword.

The handless Saracen fell to his knees. Fauston pushed him over with his foot. Long, kite-shaped shield raised with one hand for cover, Fauston pulled Roger to his feet with the other hand.

Roger stood unsteadily, still woozy from hitting his head. Fauston covered Roger while Roger looked for his spear. He couldn't find it and drew his axe. "Thanks," he told Fauston, mumbling the word because his head was spinning.

"My pleasure," Fauston replied.

"How did you get here?" Roger went on.

Fauston said, "I'll tell you about it tonight, when we're in Heaven."

"Heaven?" Roger said.

"Hell, then. I was trying to be optimistic."

Roger gripped the axe, took a couple deep breaths to steady himself and moved forward, back into the fighting. Almost immediately he lost sight of Fauston. One moment they were shoulder to shoulder; the next moment, Fauston was gone, lost in the madness. Roger had a glimpse of Slowfoot, who had lost his war hammer and was pounding a man's head with a block of stone. Then Slowfoot was lost to sight, as well.

The fighting had attained a sort of equilibrium about halfway up the slope of the breach. The crusaders could advance no further in the narrow gap, but the Saracens could not drive them back. More or less solid lines had formed. The narrow breach filled with the bodies of dead and wounded, and men climbed onto the backs of the fallen in order to fight.

On both sides, as men tired out they fell back and were replaced by others eager to join the fray. All the drills and running in full gear paid off for the Death's Heads. They were in better condition and able to keep their place in line longer than the knights, who were unused to fighting dismounted. As more and more knights reeled back from fatigue, the Death's Heads replaced them, until a large portion of the narrow front was manned by Roger's men. Henry the Lion was in the forefront, bellowing defiance, with Archduke Leopold beside him, slashing away at his enemies with a grim, almost detached determination, like a man intent on solving a problem in mathematics.

Roger took advantage of a break in the fighting to take a long drink from his water bottle, but the water bottle fell out of his slippery hands onto the ground. Then the men in front of him fell back, and Roger was once more in the front of the line. A grandly mustachioed Saracen loomed before Roger, who buried his axe at the base of the man's neck, nearly severing his head. Men pressed around him, it was difficult to move.

Roger was sweating profusely. Despite the drink, he was burning with thirst. Ralph the Red stumbled past him, his chest opened up like a gutted fish, covered with blood.

A Saracen raised his shield in front of Roger, as though hiding from him. Roger hooked his axe blade over the top of the shield and pulled the shield down, but before he could strike, he realized the trap he'd fallen into as he saw a bloodied spear point coming right at his face. He threw himself backwards, felt a *whoosh* of air as the spear point missed him by the merest fraction of an inch. He slipped and fell.

He was on his back, being trampled into the rocks. He didn't know where the man with the spear had gone. He raised what was left of his shield to protect himself, and something bashed it, sending pain up and down his forearm. He looked for an opening to get to his knees and rise. Next to him he saw the kind of soft leather boot that could never belong to a Christian. Awkwardly, because of his position, he raised his axe and chopped it down on the foot. The boot's owner howled and what was left of the foot was pushed backward and the boot's owner fell beside Roger with his face hacked open.

Roger took advantage of a break in the crush of men around him and pushed to his feet. The rocks were slippery with oil and blood and every imaginable kind of gore. No sooner had he regained his feet than something slammed into the top of his helmet. He dropped his axe and fell to his knees. Blood gushed from his nose. He dropped and rolled desperately, covering up with his shield for protection.

He flailed around on the ground, saw another axe— beautifully crafted, it must have belonged to a knight. Before he could grab the axe, a spear was thrust at his head, missed and stuck in the ground. Roger grabbed his assailant's legs, twisted them and dragged the man to the ground. He jumped on the man and smashed the man's bearded face with his mailed glove. The man jammed a thumb into Roger's eye, trying to gouge the eye out, but Roger hit the man again and again and again until the pressure on his eye lessened and the man's face looked like pulped fruit, aware even as he did that a slash with some kind of weapon had opened the back of his armored jack.

He picked up the axe and got to his feet again, his eye pounding with pain, blood and hair on his glove. He could barely breathe now because his throat was so sore from thirst. He kept moving forward, borne along by the tide of fighting.

He saw a Saracen attempting to make a stand and brought his new axe down on the man's shoulder blade, but he was so tired that his stroke had no force behind it, and the axe blade, which was supposed to go into the man's neck, bounced off the man's shoulder instead. As the man turned, Roger hit him weakly in the face with the metal boss of his shield. He lost track of the man as the press of fighting drove him on. On and up, because, slowly, the Christians had begun driving the Saracens up the breach. The pace quickened, the Saracens were definitely falling back. Quicker still—the fight was becoming a rout.

Roger couldn't go any further. He stopped, bent over and heaving for breath, nearly blinded by the swelling in one eye and sweat in the other. Somebody shoved him aside, almost knocking him down as he joined the rush forward. It was Hake. Now that victory seemed certain, Hake wanted to be one of the first to reap its spoils.

From ahead came a great roar—the Christians were over the top of the breach and down the other side. They were in the city. Roger cursed because he wasn't among them. A last burst of energy carried him to the top of the breach. Below him, crusaders were battling the enemy on the ground, the crusader front widening like spilled water. Then Saracen engineers counterattacked with pots of naptha, hurling them at the Christians pouring down the far side of the breach, setting them afire, driving the others back in disorder. The smell of roasting flesh mingled with agonized screams. Roger saw Hake alight, dancing grotesquely, but there was no way to help him.

Exhausted, both sides drew back. Neither had the energy for more fighting. The survivors of the assault force made their way slowly back from the breach. Of Roger's shield little remained save the boss, and he threw it away. He saw Fauston and fell in beside him, neither man speaking as they picked their way through the bodies jumbled in the rocks, the bodies—Christian and Saracen—so covered with blood and dirt it was impossible to tell them apart. Tatwine joined them. Other Death's Heads coalesced around them, as well, but not many, and Roger's stomach turned as he realized that most of his men lay behind him in the rubble of the breach. The archduke of Austria stumbled down from the breach, coughing from the dust in his throat. He was followed by one-eyed Henry the Lion, the last Christian out. Henry's conical helmet was gone, his surcoat was in tatters, his shield little more than splinters.

The assault on the city had failed, but despite their failure, the Christians were exultant because they knew that the Saracens had given their last effort. They had nothing left.

The long wait was over. Tomorrow the crusaders would take the city.

Chapter 116

What was left of the assault force retired to a spot just beyond reach of the Saracen archers on the walls—the Saracen catapults on the Accursed Tower had been smashed, so they were no longer a threat. The men muddled around half dazed, seeking what was left of their original groupings. In the west, the sun lowered peacefully toward the sparkling sea. From the Concourse, music could be heard, as though for the merchants this day had been no different than any other.

Roger didn't think he had ever felt so tired. All he wanted was to lie down and sleep, but he commanded men so sleep was not an option. Tatwine had retrieved the Death's Heads' banner from where he had left it when the assault started. Now he planted it in the ground, and he and Fauston sank wearily beside it while Roger remained standing, watching his men trickle in and gather around the flag. The wound on Roger's face had more or less stopped bleeding, but it stung like the Devil. He should get it sewn, or at least put a bandage on it, but what was the use? He would be dead by this time tomorrow. In a voice cracked with thirst, he cried into the lowering sun. "Death's Heads! Death's Heads, over here!"

The number of men who responded to his call was dismayingly small. Roger doubted there were thirty left. He was afraid to count them, as if not knowing the exact number would somehow make that number larger, as if it would make Roger feel less guilty about leading them to their deaths. Most were wounded; all were covered with blood, their own and other men's. Helmets and jacks and shields were battered shapeless. None of the centenars was there. "Where is Wilbert?" Roger asked.

A wounded spearman inclined his head in the direction of the breach.

"Osric?"

No one knew.

Three axe men remained, one of whom was Slowfoot. Of Hedde and Mayne there was no sign. Roger had seen Ralph the Red and doubted he could survive that wound. Poor Offa, of course, was dead.

King Richard had water and food sent up to the survivors—bread and orange jam and roasted oxen. Roger used the men who had brought the food and drink to improvise stretchers and carry his most seriously wounded back to camp—over their protests, most of them.

Everyone drank and drank deeply because they were parched with thirst, but eating was more difficult. A few of the men picked at their food. Most just stared numbly into space. One of the spearmen was crying. Here and there, more by rote than from necessity, men began building fires, using the ample supplies of discarded wood around them for fuel.

From the direction of the camp came the squealing of wooden wheels. Two of King Richard's massive trebuchets were slowly being repositioned to attack the breach, the men tailing on the pull ropes urged on by cursing vintenars. The trebuchets were followed by mule-driven wagons laden with huge rocks. Spotters with torches jogged past Roger and placed the torches at either end of the breach, so the artillerists would know where to aim when it got dark.

"Don't waste no time, does he?" Tatwine observed while he constructed a fire.

"By morning, that breach will be beaten so wide, you could march an army through it," said a guttural voice. Roger turned, and it took a moment to recognize the blood-covered apparition before him as the archduke of Austria. Leopold's squire stood behind him, blood dripping from a bandaged hand.

"Hello, Death's Head." Leopold unlaced his helmet and

took it off, his blond hair a sharp contrast to his blood-spattered face and beard. "Would you mind if we shared your fire? You're the only person I know here who's not dead."

Roger stammered. "Of course not, my lord. It would be an honor."

Leopold nodded thanks and gestured at Roger's face. "You are wounded."

"It's nothing," Roger said.

Leopold let his helmet and shield fall to the ground. "Congratulations on your knighthood, by the way."

"Thank you, my lord."

Awkwardly, because of his bandaged hand, Leopold's squire handed the archduke a cup of watered wine. After making sure that the squire had refreshment, as well, Leopold drank. "How fares the Margravina Helvise?" he asked Roger. "On her way home by now, I trust?"

"She's dead," Roger said. "Killed in the attack on the camp yesterday. She came back off the ship to fight."

Leopold paused a long moment, eyes downcast, his thick lips pursed. "I am sorry to hear that," he said. "She was a great lady."

Roger nodded.

"I am sorry for you, as well. I know how much she meant to you."

"Thank you, my lord."

Leopold drank more wine, then unbuckled his sword belt. "My God," the squire gasped. When Leopold turned to see what had elicited this response, the squire pointed at him. "Look, my lord."

Leopold's wool surcoat was completely red with blood—as red as if it had been dyed—save for a band of pure white where his sword belt had covered it. The white band was so straight, it looked like it had been sewn onto the red surcoat.

The squire, a tall, athletic teenager with a wispy beard, shook his head in amazement. "It looks like . . . like . . ." He couldn't think of a comparison.

Tatwine twisted his head sideways. "Looks kind of like a flag."

"You know, it does at that," Leopold said. He frowned and his jaw hardened. "If Almighty God sees fit that I should survive this fight, I will make this the new banner of my house—two bands of red separated by one of white."

"Do you think that's possible, my lord?" Tatwine said. "Us surviving, that is."

Leopold spread his hands. He had taken his hands out of the mailed mittens attached to his hauberk, and the mittens dangled from his wrists. "One never knows. I hear rumors that Richard is negotiating with Saladin for the city's surrender."

A number of nearby knights straightened at those words. "By himself?" said a battered Frenchman. "Without consent of the council?"

"He wouldn't dare," said a man wearing the black surcoat and white cross of the Hospitallers.

"He doesn't have the right," said one-eyed Henry of Deraa, who had wandered up. Henry had grown strangely cool toward Roger and he ignored Roger now, speaking directly to the archduke.

"Richard has a habit of abrogating rights to himself," Leopold told them.

As he said this, there was a deep thunk from the trebuchets, followed by the sound of something heavy flying overhead, then a crash as the rock hit the city wall near the breach. A few fire arrows flew from the walls in retaliation—halfheartedly, it seemed—but they fell well short of the trebuchets.

As eyes strained into the gathering gloom to see where the rock had struck, Leopold's squire pointed his bandaged hand toward the Christian camp. "My lord."

They turned. Knights and footmen were filing across the camp ditch, taking places near the spot where Roger and his men had waited for the attack the previous evening. Alart of Vouzin rode at their head. Alart walked his horse toward the survivors of the assault force, and the men—those who were able—gathered to hear what he had to say.

Firelight glinted off the ring in Alart's ear. "King Richard sends you greetings," he told the men. "Your deeds today will live for all time." He let that sink in, then he said, "The king asks that you retire to your tents and let the men behind you assault the breach on the morrow."

There was shocked quiet. The men looked at one another.

"Go on," Alart prodded, not unkindly. "The king has wine tuns waiting for you across the ditch."

"No!" a voice cried, and Roger realized it was his own voice. He moved forward, suddenly tired no longer.

Alart gazed at Roger, frowning in recognition. "You're that fellow the king knighted yesterday, aren't you? The woodcutter?" Alart tried to keep the condescension from his voice, but it was there, and Roger couldn't blame him. Who was Roger to question the king of England's order?

But question it he did. "Yes, my lord. Roger of Huntley." He indicated the survivors of the morning's battle. "These men fought for that breach. They have earned the right to be first into it tomorrow."

From the assault's survivors came weary growls of approval. The fight had become personal beyond all reasoning. These men had unfinished business in that breach, even though it meant their lives.

"It is your *king's* order that you refuse, sir knight," Alart said, and beneath his polite manner was a hard undertone.

"I agree with Roger," said the archduke of Austria, stepping from the shadows.

Alart's eyes widened at the archduke's appearance, then he recovered. "The king of England commands here, and he wants fresh troops to lead the attack, my lord archduke. Your men —
"

"The king of England is co-commander," Leopold corrected, "along with the king of France. And these are not my men. Save for my squire, none owes me fealty. We have become equals here. We have become brothers, if you will, and we wish to go first." Then his tone mellowed, and there was a twinkle in his eye. "After all, we are not so many. No doubt we shall die quickly and Richard's men can take our place."

Alart cleared his throat to give himself time to think. Was Leopold serious? Did he truly intend to die here, or was this some kind of trick? And what was this "we have become brothers" nonsense? Richard had regretted agreeing to Leopold's joining the assault party almost as soon as Leopold had proposed it. If the negotiations with Saladin broke down, Richard was afraid Leopold would get credit for taking the city, not him. He wanted Leopold away from the breach. Alart had no choice in the matter, though. Richard had not been named sole commander of the army, so he could not issue orders to a member of the grand council without the consent of Philip of France, and Philip would never give that consent, if only to spite Richard. Richard would be angry with Alart, but there was nothing Alart could do about it.

"Very well, my lord," he said reluctantly. "You may lead your 'brothers.' But my men shall be directly behind yours."

"Of course, of course," Leopold agreed with bluff good humor.

As Alart rode away, Leopold smiled and gestured to the assault survivors. "Now, gentlemen, let us eat and get some rest. We have a busy day ahead of us."

In the purplish light of dusk, the men retreated to their fires. Some ate and drank, others fell dead asleep. On one side of Roger's fire, Leopold removed his mail. His squire, with the bandaged hand, had difficulty helping him, so two of Roger's spearmen assisted them, then helped the squire remove his own hauberk. Leopold thanked them and gave them each a gold coin. "To spend in Heaven tomorrow," he joked. Then Leopold and his squire lay down and slept.

With difficulty, Roger removed his blood-stiffened jack, which was sliced open down the back, and took a place on the other side of the fire, beside Fauston and Tatwine and Slowfoot. Fauston had elected to leave his hauberk on, as had many of the surviving knights, uncomfortable and cumbersome though it was, because he was too tired to remove it.

It was dark now. Around them was the crash of rocks against the city walls, the rumble of loosened and falling stones, the moans and cries of Christian and Saracen wounded in the breach, the chanting of the priests with Alart's men, the distant shouts of the city's defenders as they prepared for what was coming on the morrow. The Saracens attempted to fill the ever-widening breach—piling rocks, tree trunks, even furniture into a makeshift wall. Every once and a while, one of the trebuchets' rocks would smash this barricade to pieces, almost contemptuously, and the Saracens would be forced to start anew.

Roger noticed Tatwine staring at Fauston, the newcomer. "This is Fauston," he told Tatwine. "He was the earl's—"

Tatwine wagged a finger at Fauston. "I know you," he said. "Brocky—Brock the Badger! I was there when they hung you in Badford Town."

"Which time?" Fauston said.

Tatwine considered. "Let's see. Must be going on four years now. St. Thecla's Day it was."

Fauston nodded. "Ah, yes. Interesting day."

Roger gave Fauston a look. "How many times *have* they hung you?"

"Successfully, none," Fauston said. "Unsuccessfully, twice."

"Don't forget that time in Lower Ealton," Slowfoot put in. On learning who Fauston was, the other Death's Heads had gathered closer.

Fauston made a face, "Very well, three, if you must count that."

Slowfoot got up and shook Fauston's hand. "Brock the Badger. Right here. I can't believe it."

"I *was* Brock the Badger," Fauston corrected. "I'm an honest man now."

There was knowing laughter around the fires, and Roger

could imagine the men telling Brock the Badger stories all night and being dead tired in the morning.

"You men get some sleep," he ordered. "You're going to need it."

There was some grumbling at that and more shaking of Fauston's hand—Roger noted Archduke Leopold's bemused reaction to Fauston's celebrity—then the men settled in, weariness overcoming them once more. Tatwine was soon snoring loudly; Slowfoot lay curled by the fire.

Roger was on his back, head pillowed on his jack, which he had folded inside out to keep the blood out of his hair. His wounded cheek throbbed. "What made you come today?" he asked Fauston.

"Guess I decided it was time to do my bit," Fauston said.

"I thought you didn't believe in what we're doing here?"

"Beliefs change."

Roger nodded agreement. "Where'd you get the armor?"

"Nicked it." He paused and added, "All right, maybe I'm not completely honest. Pain in the arse to get it on, had to pay somebody to help me with it."

Roger stared at the innumerable twinkling stars overhead. If the stars truly were the souls of the dead, as the priests claimed, would he soon be one of them? "I've enjoyed this earthly life, for all its faults."

Fauston grunted agreement.

"I wonder what Heaven will be like?"

Fauston said, "I just hope it's not all angels and clouds and playing on harps, like the priests say. Bloody awful, that would be."

"Despite the Pope's indulgence, we may have to go to Purgatory first," Roger warned, "to atone for our sins. We could spend years there—centuries. Some say you have to stay there till the Second Coming."

Fauston shook his head. "No, I think *this* was Purgatory. Whatever our sins were, we've paid for them here."

DEATH'S HEAD

❖ ❖ ❖

Dawn found the attacking force on its feet. Last drinks of watered wine were taken, last scraps of bread or meat stuffed in mouths. The men were clad in blood-caked armor and jacks—Roger's torn jack was so stiff he had a hard time getting into it. His mailed gloves were even worse, and he flexed his hands repeatedly to loosen them. Around him, men adjusted helmets, those who still had them. They buckled on blunted swords, picked up chipped axes and spears. To their front, the once-narrow breach in the city walls had been battered wide by King Richard's trebuchets. Behind the survivors of yesterday's assault were Alart of Vouzin and his column of Poitevins, with another column massing behind that one. The Christians were going to smash their way into the city today and nothing could stop them.

All along the circuit of the city walls this routine was repeated, and soon trumpets sounded the advance. Rob and his Yorkshire longbowmen trotted ahead to cover the parapets. As senior noble present, Archduke Leopold, the red on his surcoat crusted brown as the blood dried, stepped before the men and raised his hand. He held his hand in the air for a moment, then, when the men were formed up, their eyes on him, he lowered it.

The men started forward, shoulder to shoulder in two grim lines. Fauston and Roger, Tatwine and Slowfoot, Leopold and one-eyed Henry the Lion were among those in the first line—all rank forgotten, Tatwine next to Roger carrying the Death's Head banner, which even the knights seemed to have adopted as their own. There was no music this time, just the tramp of feet on sun-baked ground.

The widened breach drew nearer and nearer. With its promise of the unknown beyond, the breach looked like the Gates of Heaven, and for Roger and his companions, that's what it was going to be. They were under no illusions—they were going to die here. The city would fall, but they would not live to see it.

Roger gripped his new axe in both hands; he didn't have a shield. The beautifully crafted axe would never do for chopping wood but it was well suited for this kind of work, and he was anxious to put it to use. His eyes were fixed on the breach and on the Saracens waiting there. He saw nothing else. His breathing was heavy. Inside him, the pressure for action built and built until he thought he might explode. Someone was shouting at him but he had no idea what they were saying.

Closer. Roger's breathing was like a waterfall roaring inside his head now.

"Roger!" he heard a cry nearby but he ignored it. Nothing could stop him.

"Roger!" Someone grabbed his arm.

He whirled, and his eyes were so wild that Fauston stepped back, afraid Roger would strike him with his axe.

"Look!" Fauston shouted, pointing upwards.

Roger's eyes followed.

Atop the Accursed Tower, Meshtub's green flag had been replaced by a white one.

Acre had surrendered.

Epilogue

The small church just inside the city walls had been turned into a stable by the Saracens, but Roger didn't care. It was still a church, even though he had no idea to whom it had once been consecrated.

Roger still wore his blood-crusted jack. The wound on his cheek needed to be attended to, but that was for later. Outside were music and shouting and prayers of joy. Inside it was quiet, peaceful. Roger stood in the cool shade of the nave, facing what was left of the altar after the Saracens had desecrated it. The floor was littered with moldy straw. There were faint smells of the mules and donkeys the Saracens had stabled here, though those animals had long ago been eaten by the city's defenders.

Once again Roger had been spared. Once again he lived while others died, and once again he struggled to understand why. He struggled to understand God's plan. He was about to fall on his knees in prayer when he heard a footstep behind him.

Before he could turn, he was slammed face first into the stone wall. A dagger was held to his throat and a familiar voice said, "Before I kill you, tell me how you came by that ring."

Historical Note

If the siege of Acre is remembered at all today it is as some vague preamble to the adventures of Richard the Lionheart in the Holy Land, yet it is arguably one of the pivotal events of both European and Middle Eastern history. Had it not occurred, or had it occurred differently, the history of the Third Crusade—and all that came after—might have been vastly different.

History is largely the study of people and "what if's." And by those lights one of the most influential men in medieval history is someone few have ever heard of. *If* Guy of Lusignan had not launched his army on its ill-fated march to Hattin, the kingdom of Jerusalem would not have fallen to Saladin and there would have been no Third Crusade. *If* Guy had not taken his meager force and in a fit of pique planted it before Acre, the crusade would likely not have turned out as it did.

The initial plan was for the crusading armies to rendezvous at Tyre and proceed to Jerusalem from there. Would the crusaders have sailed down the coast to Jaffa and bypassed Acre? Would they have marched down the coast and left a blocking force to watch the city? Or would they have laid siege to it? We'll never know, but a siege would have been different with the entire army committed at once instead of piecemeal. And even though he got to the Holy Land late, it is hard to picture a mercurial personality and astute soldier like Richard I wasting two years on a strategically meaningless siege. And though there are always those pesky "what if's," it is difficult to imagine that the vast force sent to the Holy Land would not have recovered Jerusalem had it not been squandered at Acre.

In her book *The Crusades*, the French novelist and historian Zoe Oldenbourg called the Third Crusade "the medieval equivalent of putting a man on the moon." That the primitive European societies of the 12th century, in which most men had never been more than a few miles from their homes, could raise and equip vast armies, send them a thousand miles overseas, and keep them supplied was as much of a technological and organizational miracle as was sending Neil Armstrong and Buzz Aldrin to the lunar surface in our time. There would be other crusades, but none would approach the Third in size and expense and religious fervor. This was the last time Christendom was united in its desire to free the Holy Land, probably the last time Christendom has been united in anything. This was its ultimate effort.

Ms Oldenbourg compared the siege of Acre to the battle of Verdun, a crucible through which an entire generation of Europe's manhood passed. The siege left a deep scar across European society; there was scarcely a noble house that was not affected by it. How many Christians were involved? A rough rule of thumb when dealing with numbers quoted by medieval chroniclers is to divide by ten. Some of the chroniclers estimated a million to a million and a half men at Acre, which leaves us with a hundred to a hundred and fifty thousand, and even if we split those figures in half, we still have an astounding number, especially considering that medieval armies of this period typically mustered two to five thousand men, and the populations of London and Paris were approximately 30,000 and 50,000, respectively. How many of these men died? There is no way of telling, but we know from the chronicles that an unusually large amount of high-ranking nobles perished from battle, disease or starvation, and if that is the case the amount of common soldiers and others who lost their lives must have been enormous. The force that Richard led south after the fall of the city consisted largely of the men he and King Philip had brought with them. The old army—that huge force with such potential—lay in its grave at Acre.

Of the events surrounding the siege itself, details are scarce, few of them first hand, and many of them confusing or contradictory. I have followed the general course of events as they are known, but have not hesitated to change things for the sake of the story. I have not mentioned most of the prominent nobles and churchmen who were present at the siege, because there were so many that to do so might needlessly confuse the reader. Any historical mistakes are mine and for them I apologize to the memory of the brave men—and women—on both sides who fought at Acre.

So now the main actors are on stage. Richard the Lionheart and Saladin. The titans of the age. Champions of West and East, at the height of their powers. Prepared for the contest which will bring them immortality, the results of which shall be seen in a future volume.

About the Author

Robert Broomall is the author of a number of published novels. Besides writing, his chief interests are travel and history, especially military history, the Old West, and the Middle Ages. He also likes to cook, much to the dismay of those who have to eat what he prepares.

Amazon author page: https://www.amazon.com/author/robertbroomall

Facebook:
https://www.facebook.com/RobertBroomall.author

Connect with Bob: robertbroomall@gmail.com

Printed in Great Britain
by Amazon

56181673R10353